FICTION
Roy-Bh
Roy-Bhattacharya, Joydeep

The Storyteller of Marrakesh

The
STORYTELLER
of
MARRAKESH

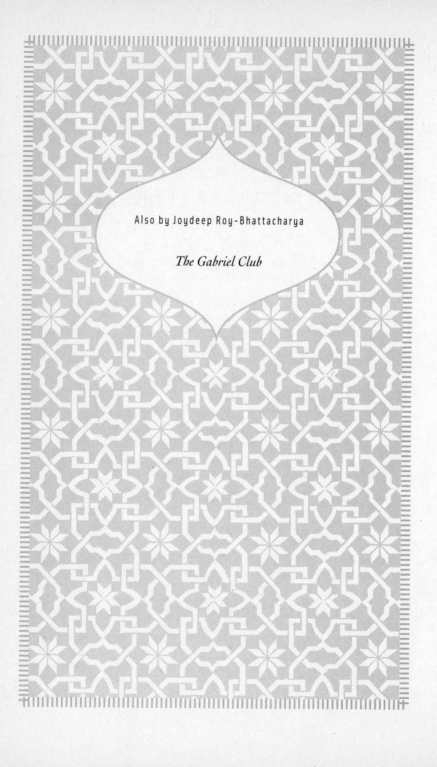

Also by Joydeep Roy-Bhattacharya

The Gabriel Club

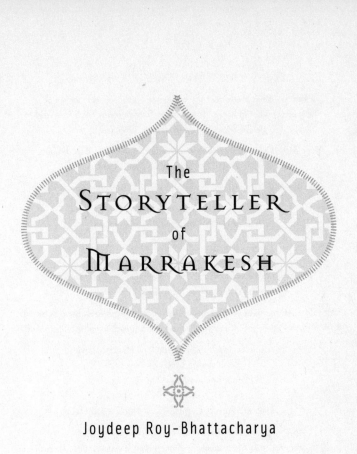

The
STORYTELLER
of
MARRAKESH

Joydeep Roy-Bhattacharya

W. W. NORTON & COMPANY

New York • *London*

Page 3: "What matters in the end is the truth" is a reworking of
"The truth is what matters," from Tahar Ben Jelloun, *The Sacred Night*
(New York: Harcourt Brace, 1989, p. 1).

Page 319: "Ce qui importe c'est la vérité," from Tahar Ben Jelloun,
La nuit sacrée (Paris: Éditions du Seuil, 1987, p. 5).

Calligraphy cover stamp and illustration © Behzad Baba-Rabi'

For information about permission to reproduce selections from this book,
write to Permissions, W. W. Norton & Company, Inc.,
500 Fifth Avenue, New York, NY 10110

For information about special discounts for bulk purchases, please contact
W. W. Norton Special Sales at specialsales@wwnorton.com or 800-233-4830

Manufacturing by RR Donnelley, Harrisonburg
Book design by Chris Welch
Production manager: Devon Zahn

Library of Congress Cataloging-in-Publication Data

Roy-Bhattacharya, Joydeep.
The storyteller of Marrakesh / Joydeep Roy-Bhattachrya. —1st ed.
p. cm.
ISBN 978-0-393-07058-3
1. Storytelling—Fiction. 2. Missing persons—Fiction.
3. Marrakech (Morocco)—Fiction. I. Title.
PR9499.3.R596S76 2011
823'.914—dc22

W. W. Norton & Company, Inc.
500 Fifth Avenue, New York, N.Y. 10110
www.wwnorton.com

W. W. Norton & Company Ltd.
Castle House, 75/76 Wells Street, London W1T 3QT

1 2 3 4 5 6 7 8 9 0

For Nicole Aragi and Alane Salierno Mason

in gratitude

Marrakesh

Place Jemaa el Fna

Evening

Wh_at matters in the end is the truth.

And yet, when I think about the event that marked the end of my youth, I can come to only one conclusion: that there is no truth.

Perhaps there is reason to believe the philosopher who realized, to his dismay, that the truth is precisely that which is transformed the instant it is revealed, becoming thereby only one of many possible opinions, open to debate, disagreement, controversy, but also, inevitably, to mystification.

In other words, there is no truth.

Put differently, truth is that which inevitably contradicts itself. Perhaps that is what is borne out by my story in the end. That might explain why, instead of the truth, I offer you a greater consolation: a dream.

Msa l'khir. Good evening. Permit me to introduce myself. My name is Hassan. I am a storyteller, monarch of a realm vaster than any you can envisage, that of the imagination. My memory is not what it used to be, but if we can settle on a democratic price, I will tell you a tale the like of which I promise you have never heard before. It is a love story, like all the best stories, but it is also a mystery, for it concerns the disappearance of one of the lovers or the other or perhaps both of them or neither. It happened two years ago, or it might have been five or ten or twenty-five. These details are unimportant. The pink dust hung suspended in the air that evening just as it does tonight, the light from the spice and fruit stalls cast bright plumes like desert wraiths, the restless throbbing of drums rose and fell like bodies in the sand, and, in the end, the events surrounding the lovers brought an entire fabled city to a standstill and transformed forever the character of its renowned meeting place, the Jemaa el Fna, perhaps the most mysterious, most storied city square in the world.

Let me repeat: the truth of my story is immaterial, as is whether or not a woman vanished or a man or both of them or neither. What matters in the end is life, the breathing of air, the breasting of waves, the movement of sand on dunes and surf, each grain of sand a mirror of conflicting perceptions and testimonies.

What language do you speak, stranger? English? All right, I will try my best, though my French is better, and, of course, Arabic would be the easiest. Tell me where you are from. From far away? I see. It doesn't matter. Here in the Jemaa everyone is an outsider. I don't mean to pry, but these are preliminary introductions, necessary to set the tone. Sit down, please, and join my circle of listeners. The ground may seem hard in the beginning but I will weave a magic carpet of words that will soon take you away from this place. Permit me to pour you some mint tea to accompany my narration. We have our traditions of hospitality. There are ways in which things must be done. If I don't make you comfortable, how can I expect you listen to what I have to say? A story is like a dance. It takes at least two people to make it come to life, the one who does the telling and the one who does the listening. Sometimes the roles are reversed, and the giver becomes the taker. We both do the talking, we both listen, and even the silences become loaded. From a small number of perfectly ordinary words a tapestry takes shape, suggestive of a dream, but close enough to a reality which, more often than not, remains elusive. It is a feat of mutual trust, of mutual imagining. What matters is whether or not we can believe each other's voices, and the test of that will lie in the story we make together. It will lie in the pieces of the past that swim into the present. Maybe it is precisely what we don't remember that will form the kernel of our tale, imparting to it its grain of truth and transforming memories into mythology.

But these are ruminations that travel in circles without beginning or end, like smoke in the air. They are good for passing long, introspective evenings with friends in the green valley of Ourika, in the High Atlas Mountains, where I am from, though I might also be from white-walled Essaouira, on the Atlantic coast, or from sand-coloured Zagora, where the last rock-ribbed mountain roots give way to the Sahara's golden desolation. These are all very beautiful places, and I come from them according to the needs of the particular tale I am engaged in telling, its flavour, atmosphere, and circumstance. It's the way we set our mark, you see, with one eye on reality and the other firmly fixed in fantasy. It helps to broaden the compass of the narrative, especially since I haven't travelled much, certainly not as much as you, nor, for that matter, my brother, Mustafa. But I have been to Rabat and to Casablanca, and one day I intend to visit more distant places like Meknès and Fès and Tangier. Fabled names, fabled cities: they have long and illustrious histories, and their attractions beckon. Meanwhile, I make this trip to Marrakesh every winter to escape the bitter cold of the highlands, the desert, or the sea— depending on where I might be that year—but also because I am driven to come to terms with what happened that night, here on the Jemaa, when there was a scent of something amiss in the air, and this even before the two strangers made their first and, as it turned out, final appearance.

For I am haunted by them.

JEMAA

Dusk came early that evening. The sun congealed on the horizon in a thick red clot, and dark, low clouds added to its intensity. Spirals of woodsmoke rose from the clustered roofs of the souks, and the calls of the muezzins rang across the square. It was the hour of prayer, of ablutions, when shopkeepers shutter their stores in the souks and head homeward. So it was on that evening two or perhaps five or ten years ago, just as it is tonight.

I had set up on the southeastern side of the square, near where the Rue Moulay Ismail leads into the Jemaa, past the pink stone steps of the post office, past where the Chleuh boy dancers perform their sexual routines and offer themselves up to clients, their movements leaving nothing to the imagination. I say this neither as a moralist nor as a prude, for I am not easily shocked, but I must admit that sometimes I have to look away, even as I benefit from the crowds that gather around the boys.

Since the events of the night of which I am about to speak, however, I no longer sit in my old location. It may be that I am superstitious, but the memories associated with the place are too painful. So nowadays I lay down my kilim on the other side of the square, next to the brightly lit citrus stalls and adjacent to the police station. It allows me to relate my stories in peace even as I keep a cautious eye on the goings-on around me. There are times when the sight of a young female tourist, often the merest glimpse of a shoulder, or a glint of dark eyes mirroring the sulphur lamps, is enough to bring back that dreadful evening and throw off my concentration. Then I have to scramble to retrieve the threads of my lines and remember what it was that I was engaged in telling. But this happens only rarely. I am well known among the storytellers of the Jemaa for the ease of my narration, the strength of my lines, the versatility of my imagination, and for pausing only for queries from children. Or, at least, that is the way it used to be before those two unfortunates vanished into thin air, irretrievably changing the course of many lives, not least my own, and leading to the disgrace of my headstrong brother Mustafa's arrest and imprisonment. But I'm getting ahead of myself, and perhaps I ought to defer for a moment to the fortuitous appearance of my friend Aziz, who was among

the first to sight the strangers that evening before they ventured
into the chaotic darkness of the square.

RIAD

Aziz had brought a pot of mint tea and a few glasses. As he
passed them around, a flock of pigeons swept over our heads to
the far end of the square, where a group of brightly clad tourists
was emerging from the souks. The birds advanced in a frenzy of
wings, and Aziz stood watching them for a moment. The twilight
air was rose-tinted and clear, and you could still see through the
gathering darkness. The pigeons moved in a funnel across the
square and one of the tourists, a young woman with long blonde
hair, ran after them, laughing. Aziz followed her with smiling
eyes; then he took a seat in the middle of my circle of listeners
and I suddenly noticed that he had on the same olive-green jellaba he'd been wearing on the evening of the disappearance.
It induced in me an unexpectedly physical sensation of being
transported back in time. I recoiled a little, which Aziz must
have noticed because an uneasy look crossed his face. He was
silent for a moment longer than manners merited, and when he
began speaking, it was in an undertone of distress, even regret.

Thank you for inviting me to speak, Hassan, he said, and
paused, his dark eyes glittering. What do you want me to tell
your listeners? Perhaps I should begin with a word about
myself? All right? Very well. My name is Aziz. I come from a
small village near Laaoyoune, in the Western Sahara. I am a

waiter in the restaurant of the Riad Dar Timtam, in the heart of the medina, and on the night that Hassan speaks of, I was nearing the end of my workday.

He paused again, searching for words, his gaze remote with the effort of remembering. I did not intervene but let him take his time, recognizing the importance of accuracy. His words softer than before, he went on: It was around seven in the evening. I was nursing a headache occasioned by the strange dream I'd had the previous night, of walls of sand advancing on the Jemaa and swamping everything in their path. It was terrifying, and I recall sharing it with you, Hassan, in an attempt to understand its meaning.

He did not look at me as he spoke, his eyes half closed in concentration. Sipping his tea slowly, he continued: I was still thinking about that dream when they came in from the street—the two outsiders—from the direction of the Souk Zrabia, where, in the old days, the slave auctions were held in the hours before sunset. As they hesitated on the threshold, casting long shadows, I hurried forward to greet them. At once I sensed something different about them. The girl was a gazelle, slender, small-boned, with large, dark eyes, and considerably shorter than her companion. She did all the speaking, accompanying her words with graceful gestures and appearing to perfectly anticipate his wishes. The boy was darker, his skin the colour of shadows cast on sand. He reminded me of an Arab nobleman, tall, with thin limbs and black hair, with something in his erect carriage that suggested otherworldliness. They seldom looked at each other, but when they did, their eyes seemed transfixed by the other's presence.

Aziz took another sip of tea and I glanced at our rapidly growing audience. They sat quiet and attentive, their faces thoughtful in repose. The moon had just come out, the air was soft and luminescent, and Aziz threw off his blanket and straightened his back, obviously growing in confidence as he recalled concrete details.

They asked for a quiet setting, he continued, and since it was crowded inside the restaurant, I escorted them to the courtyard, where there was a scattering of tables amid citrus trees and flowering shrubs. They chose an especially dark spot in the corner—they seemed to gravitate towards darkness. I brought them water, and when they looked at me, their eyes shone like candles. That disconcerted me, and when the slender youth asked me a question, I couldn't meet his gaze. His companion's eyes had the equally unnerving quality of seeming to rest on me and on something else at the same time. That was when it occurred to me, with a kind of guarded premonition, that Death had entered the Riad in the guise of that beautiful youth and maiden.

Unsettled, I pleaded a sudden bout of fatigue and asked my friend Abdelkrim to attend to them instead. He agreed that there was something exceptional about them. He told me later that even as they ate, he recalled, abruptly and without reason, the flowering trees that had greeted him many years ago when he'd first come to Marrakesh. It was the strangers' gentleness that most moved him, he said, unlike the effect they'd had on me. I found his equanimity reassuring, and when the couple had finished eating, I returned to serving them myself. They asked for mint tea, which the youth drank thirstily, without looking up from his glass, while the maiden gazed at him with a tenderness that set my own heart racing. The winter night fanned a cool breeze. There were no other guests. I went back to my station and let them be with their thoughts amidst the courtyard's lanterned silence.

Aziz had spoken in a level, restrained tone and now he glanced at me as if to seek my approval before continuing. I nodded, and he resumed speaking, but in a higher voice that betrayed a note of anxiety:

These were my thoughts as I watched them leave that evening. They went out as quietly as they'd come in. She held his hand while he walked erect like a sentinel. The streets breathed darkness; they were swallowed up by it. I recall glancing up at the sky: the clouds had formed a double ring around the moon, which was a peculiar shade of red.

When I returned to the courtyard to clean their table, I saw that their glasses were ice cold, with condensation forming around the rims, even though I had served the tea steaming hot. I brought it to Abdelkrim's attention and his eyes grew wide in disbelief. Then he pointed to the ice inexplicably encrusting the mint leaves at the bottom of the teapot.

Aziz shook his head slowly, his gaze fixed on the ground.

I went out into the street to smoke a cigarette and calm myself. The night had turned hazy and cold. Most of the shops in the souks had shuttered their doors. Only a few shafts of light from lanterns pierced the shadows. I sat on a stoop, nursing my cigarette and attempting to convince myself that there is simply no explaining some things.

Truth and Method

Aziz sighed and looked about the square as if trying to find some escape from the memory. He moved his shoulders uneasily, glancing at me in the hope that I would offer some explanation. But I said nothing. What could I have said? His experience had been of the same order as everything else that evening.

Aziz sighed again. Without trying to convey the association of the ideas behind the words, he said: I suppose there is always the expectation that telling others will help in understanding.

Understanding what? I asked, and he flushed as if I had poised a particularly obtuse query. Why, what happened to them, of course, he said.

I felt the need to reassure him. I hadn't realized the memory of his encounter was so fraught with misgivings. Rising to my feet, I walked over and embraced him. In a reassuring tone of voice, I said: Those two young unfortunates weren't visitors from the netherworld, my dear Aziz, they were human in every sense. To contend otherwise would be to give way to errant superstition, and there's been enough of that already concerning the events of that evening.

Aziz shook his head and said mournfully: What you fail to see, and what I have probably failed to communicate adequately, is the great distraction those two strangers have been for me. Unlike you, I'm no teacher of life; I'm a humble man, a waiter in a café, and a modest devotion to duty is all I can offer to complement your storytelling expertise. When something happens for which there is no explanation, it unmoors me.

I understand, I said.

He cast a despondent glance at me. Do you, really? Perhaps you do. After all, you're a master of memory. More than most, you know about these things. All the same, can anyone truly know what it means to be human in this day and age? Is it possible to know what darkness resides in the heart of man? I ask these questions because it seems to me that there are times when the truth hardly matters anymore, though of course one cannot dispense with it. It's what makes sense—what really makes sense to oneself—that counts for me.

I'd been standing next to him; now I moved away and addressed my circle of listeners. I didn't speak to any particular member of the group, but my gaze fell on each in turn as they sat cloaked in their blankets and hanbels, rapt absorption in every line of their faces. Speaking slowly, in an even, unhesitating tone, I said:

Certainly it is possible to know what elements constitute a man. Consider me, for instance. You know me as Hassan, the storyteller, for that is how I've chosen to introduce myself. I come from the highlands, and I am here to entertain you, because that is my calling, as it was my father's and his ancestors' before him. All around me the city spreads out its wares—its many narratives—and I survey them as if from a high place and determine which are worth the telling and which must remain untold, consigned, perhaps with good reason, to the darkness of oblivion. You have gathered around me in the expectation that my imagination is what it used to be, that you can rely on it and on my powers of narration. Tonight, however, I have set up things differently. Tonight I invite you to marry your memories with mine and trace an event altogether unlike any other in our experience. What will that entail? More than anything else, our trusting one another, because it is this element of trust that will give our investigation its freedom, its boldness and tenacity. But who can be the guarantor of its truth? And who among you will stand up and testify that there was indeed a story such as the one that we are now engaged in telling? For each of us carries deep within ourselves a chamber filled with secret memories, and it is a place we would rather not reveal.

The Crow Tree

I paused for a moment to catch my breath, and as I did, the moon crested the ramparts of the medina, its light bringing the houses surrounding the Jemaa into relief. A chill came with its ascent. I put on my cloak, and some of my listeners, loosening the blankets tied around their jellabas, drew them over their heads. One of them, a heavily bearded cleric, now raised his hand and spoke quickly and with an intensity that commanded attention. He was a swarthy man of middle age. Although he wore rustic clothing, his voice was remarkably sophisticated, and I felt in him a keen and discriminating intelligence.

Of course what you say sounds reasonable, he said quizzically, but there's a plan behind it. It's patterned to a particular end, and that is the absolution of your brother from the crime he freely admitted to committing.

I gazed calmly at him.

If a pattern does exist, I replied, it is aimed at one thing only:

the investigation of the truth—the simple, vital truth at the bottom of all experience. As for my brother, I will not conceal my hope that if each of us can be true to our memories of that evening, if we spare no pains and recount everything thoroughly, we will end by lighting on what now lies concealed. And we'll do much better work if we return to the same starting point, if we dig deeper every time and go a bit further in understanding.

My interlocutor remarked politely and noncommittally that he found my faith in imagination touching.

It isn't as much imagination as memory, I answered.

Which is nothing but imagination, he countered, isn't it? Our imagination spins dreams; memory hides in them. Memory releases rivers of longing; the imagination waters the rivers with rain. They feed each other.

I refused to be provoked.

I am driven by the need for truth, I replied firmly. My brother is in prison for a crime he did not commit. I want to find out what put him there. It is a difficult task, I agree, but it isn't impossible.

His smile was skeptical.

You don't seem to realize that your truth is a paradox, because memories can be imagined, he said. Armed with your arsenal of intentions, you are setting out to explore the events of that evening—but as fiction, not as remembered fact. Where is the centre, the point of orientation, in this game of shadows?

The centre is where the heart is, I replied determinedly.

His mouth turned down. He drew his blanket around himself.

You're weaving a mythology around a crime. I'm sorry to be so blunt, but that is how it seems to me. Faced with the terrible fact of your brother's guilt, you are attempting to spin a web between yourself and reality. When the memory is indistinct, the imagination becomes infinite—and the beautiful illusion is always preferable to the truth, especially if it is ugly.

I am not weaving anything, I responded. If it is a spider's web, it isn't one of my making. My endeavor is different. I want to unravel it.

For a moment he stared at me with a disconcerting intensity. The rest of my audience might not have existed for all the sign he gave of acknowledging their presence. Abruptly he bent his body in a stiff bow and a faint smile of irony seemed to crease his lips. When he straightened up, he waved his hand and said coolly: You have great faith in language and its ability to communicate.

One must believe in something, I said quietly.

But what if the narrator is flawed and his motives unreliable?

I hesitated for an instant, aware of the danger of alienating my audience before the evening had even begun. Deciding to qualify myself, I said conciliatorily: I'm sorry. Perhaps I haven't explained myself well. Surely the evening's narrative will assuage your suspicions?

He did not acknowledge the apology but said instead, all the while maintaining a standoffish tone: Inshallah, we shall see.

I returned his courtesy, my head held high.

After a short pause, I resumed speaking:

Allow me, then, to take you back to that evening. Although it seems unlikely that we should lose our way on this journey, rest assured that, given the nature of the event, we will. Our varying recollections will erase every familiar landmark: the mosques and the minarets, the souks and the qaysarias, the square speckled with pigeon droppings, and the maze of alleyways leading into it. Beneath our feet, the very ground will crumble to dust, while overhead, the red sky of Marrakesh will undergo so many metamorphoses that we will consider ourselves fortunate in the end to have any sense of orientation left.

But all that is in the future. For the moment, our point of departure is the needle of the Koutoubia Mosque as it casts its shadow in the direction of the Jemaa. We commence tentatively as in a dream, following the needle as it inches across the Avenue Mohammed V and past the row of calèches that wait patiently for customers through the heat of the day and the coolness of the evening. Between the seventh and eighth carriages, in the shadowy darkness of the Place Foucauld, a noble cypress dwarfs its neighbours, mirroring, as it were, the mosque's towering minaret. I call that cypress the Crow Tree, owing to the multitude of desert crows that nest in its branches. It was the latter that alerted me to the unusual nature of events that were to follow that evening, their agitation a sure sign that something was amiss.

There were other signs. The city smelled of ashes. The rose-carnelian moon was full, with a ring of light around it. An unnaturally damp wind blew down from the mountains, soaking the head in chill. Later, a red fork of lightning dried up the air, its splatter of light flaying the streets.

Despite all these omens on the evening of the strangers' disappearance, I set up in my usual place, with an obtuseness that still surprises me, and prepared to begin my session of storytelling.

THE ACROBAT

Who was it that first drew my attention to the streak of lightning? Or to the disconnected clap of thunder at twilight which preceded the lightning rather than the other way around? Was it Tahar, the trapeze artist? Let me think; this imperfect memory will be my failing.

I remember now. It wasn't Tahar, who appeared on the scene much later on, and in ambiguous guise. It was the acrobat, Saïd, who lives in the small room with the sky-blue door that adjoins the Bab ed-Debbagh, perhaps the oldest of the gates piercing the ramparts around the city.

Saïd is unusual in more ways than one. It is rumoured that a dog ran away with his afterbirth before it could be buried, which might explain his preference for dwelling in the air rather than on the ground. More: he is an acrobat who wears glasses. You might have seen him performing around the square, his glasses fastened precariously with a string tied around his head. He is a dancer of the air, someone who has liberated himself from everyday constraints to give full rein to his imagination. When I watch him perform, I am always amazed by the ease with which he moves around his palace of dreams. My friend Driss says that Saïd, in the veracity and magnitude of his leaps, is the closest amongst us to God. He doesn't hesitate; he doesn't falter. He is a natural, gifted with grace. None of us who knows him have ever seen him angry or despondent. He is one of those whose elemental joy in living is manifested by an ever-present smile and, more often, laughter.

So when I tell you that it was this same Saïd who came to me with a look of great concern, speaking in distress about the unusual fork of lightning—shaped like a sand snake, he said, with a head at both ends—it caught my attention. He said that he had already folded away his trampoline and his ropes and poles, and, for the first time since his arrival in the Jemaa twelve years ago, had decided to stop performing before his usual hour of nine in the evening. There was something about that fork of fire, he said, that was worthy of fear; it signified pain and destruction.

And look at that orange moon with that perfect ring around it! he went on excitedly. It's like a visitation from Saturn, that baleful entity. You can almost taste its burn on your tongue. In its ochre light we've stopped casting shadows, or haven't you noticed? There's something wrong here! These are auguries that must not be ignored. That moon has robbed us of our traces! It has made us empty.

I tried to reassure him. I tried telling him that the Jemaa is like a field of smoke; it transforms everything, even the moon. As for the red fork of lightning, it signified fire, and the element of fire, even as it destroys, holds the key to purification. So he should linger and listen to the story that I was about to tell, for I would banish his fears with the cooling stream of my imagination.

If you delve into fear, I said soothingly, you can turn it around so that the predator becomes the prey. Have faith in yourself. Trust in my ability to transform what terrifies you.

But Saïd would have none of it. He said that, in the middle of a leap, he had glimpsed the ground where the lightning had struck. In the smoke and ashes he had read warnings that we were all in grave danger. He said that it was imperative that we leave immediately.

I watched him go. Then I waited as usual for my audience to gather, but my heart was uneasy.

EL AMARA

Marrakesh, El Amara, imperial capital, red-walled oasis between the desert and the mountains. Here the ochre expanse of the sky is mirrored in the tabia bricks and façades, and, especially at dawn, when silence cloaks everything, there is no more satisfying way to greet the new day than to stroll along the ramparts and watch the camel trains arrive from the south and the east. In the distance lie the dark fringes of the Palmeraie. Beyond, hues of cinnabar, rust, crimson, vermilion settle on the snowcapped peaks of the High Atlas Mountains.

It is a landscape filled with allegories, where the imagination is law, and storytellers can spend entire days resuscitating mysteries. We sit cross-legged on our kilims and craft chronicles from the air in our sonorous voices. The kilim is our castle for the evening. It is our luminous heart, the crucible for our imagined histories. It is our winter in the Jemaa, our summer in the mountains, our perennially fruitful season that we carry everywhere we visit. It is our home, our kasbah, our makhzen, our sanctuary. The door is always open; we wait inside and also outside it, fitting all possible tales into chronicles of our making.

VOYAGE

On the evening of the strangers' disappearance, I'd decided to use the colour red as the theme for my storytelling, for red was the shade of the ringed moon, as it is of fire, and, of course, of blood and of sacrifice. Turning my face towards the Jemaa el Fna—which, in our tongue, has two meanings, "Assembly of the Dead" and "Mosque of Nothingness"—I spread out my kilim and prepared to begin. Surrounding me were the usual implements of my trade: the battered leather trunk that held my parchments, the mirror with which to reflect my listeners' faces, the knotted piece of thuya wood from which I derived inspiration, the dream symbols in the form of sheaves of wheat and carved wooden rattles and glossy black pebbles shaped like snake heads and porcupine quills. The kilim was a gift from my father. It had been in our family for generations, its faded red weave patterned with stars and bordered by black clouds of precisely configured geometry. I customarily sat in the centre and arranged my collection of story sticks in a half circle in front of me. Each stick was carved out of ebony and notched with ivory rings. The sticks represented particular story lines and the rings stood for themes. I waited for dusk to see which stick the setting sun would light upon first and thereby determine the story I would be telling.

The Jemaa was especially crowded that evening. Busloads of villagers had arrived from the interior, from the mountains as well as from the desert as far south as Tan Tan and Tafraoute. Pilgrims are good for my line of business: they prefer the magic of make-believe to their own dreary reality. They go for epic tales, with plenty of digressions to postpone the return to the quotidian.

I usually wait until I have at least eight listeners. As a rule of thumb, the larger the audience, the greater their credulity. Then I begin to speak very softly so that my words, as if melting into the air, promise an unimaginably intoxicating voyage. To travel thus is to live a dream. My story forms the vortex, which, for the space of the evening, delivers the peasant, the sharecropper, and the drover from their dull and cheerless existences. Gradually my voice rises to offset the noise of the Jemaa. I find my rhythm and settle into a steady cadence. By nightfall, my audience is mesmerized for the rest of the journey.

That evening, to my right, a father and his four sons had begun to pluck subtle Andalusian melodies on their ouds and violins. Farther away, a group of Gnaoua musicians had set up with their long-stemmed guitars and iron clanging hammers. They were accustomed to performing for hours on end, inducing in their listeners a trancelike state akin to ecstasy. Tonight they were accompanied by three fiery youths who danced in white-stockinged feet, gyrating their heads in time to fixed rhythms. After a brief interval, however, the Gnaoua moved to a better spot near the centre of the square, leaving me with the more appropriate stringed Andalusian accompaniment with which to launch my tales and sustain their mystery. The Andalus were from the north, near Tangier, and they played with superb finesse, their mournfully introspective tunes dissolving into the air, leaving no trace save the barest intimations of longing.

Inspired, I took out the customary piece of ambergris from my jellaba, filling the air with its fragrance. I slid off the hood of my cloak, tilted my head to one side, and strained to hear the voices that I knew would soon resound through me. My listeners gathered. I placed my collection box on the ground, the bejewelled hand of Fatima on its lid glinting its blessings. Studying my audience, I noted their faces—their eyes and gestures and expressions—to determine the level at which to pitch my story. Then I took a deep breath and commenced speaking.

THE STRANGERS

My tale, I began, is entirely true, like life itself, and, therefore, entirely invented. Everything in it is imagined; nothing in it is imagined. Like all the best stories, it is not about conventions, plot, or plausibility, but about the simple threads that bind us together as human beings . . .

With that relatively brief and straightforward prologue, I went on to talk about El Amara, the crimson city, crucible of so many dreams. I was just getting into my stride, my voice taking on the lilting stridency of the practiced storyteller, when I noticed a restlessness on the part of my audience, many of whom were craning their necks to make out what was going on behind them on the northern edge of the square.

I followed their gazes.

That was the first time I saw them.

That was the first time I saw the two foreigners.

They had emerged into the open space of the Jemaa from the direction of the Rue Derb Dabachi, from within the souks, and their entrance instantly caused a lull in the commotion of the square. All eyes, including mine, swivelled in their direction. The more modest amongst us immediately cast down our glances, as if abashed. Others, more bold, continued to stare and to follow them hungrily with brazen eyes. There was something about the intrusiveness of our collective response that left me ashamed. It was as if we were already implicated in their story, as if it were part of our own biographies, and hardly in the most complimentary of ways.

Perhaps it had to do with the woman's beauty, which was the first thing that everyone noticed. It was unnatural, and it made us uneasy. It seemed to cast a glow as they made their way across the square, and, as if in homage, the crowds fell silent and parted before them. As my brother Mustafa later recalled, it was a beauty possessing the purest intimation of grace. My own sense was that such beauty was worthy of respect, but from a guarded distance. One had to have courage when faced with it. But one also had to have probity. Mustafa did not agree with me, and this discord would come to weigh heavily on my mind in judging his future actions.

MUSTAFA

Mustafa was not an inhabitant of Marrakesh. He lived in the small fishing port of Essaouira on the Atlantic coast. He owned a shop in the medina where he sold lanterns he'd made. Every month, on the fifteenth, he would supplement his earnings by taking the bus to Marrakesh to sell his wares and, flush with cash, visit the whores who waited for him. He was young and handsome—and incorrigibly hot-blooded. A stranger to despair, incapable of being a spectator in the game of life, he usually enacted his desires in the most impulsive and yet perfectly natural ways. His vision was energy, his poetry was genuine, and true poetry is all-consuming.

When he was young, I once saw him rising naked from the lake near our village, the water streaming off his back as he paraded before the girls who had gathered to admire him. He let them touch him one by one. I caught up with him on the outskirts of the village and gave him a hiding. It wasn't as if I was a puritan, but his vanity astounded me.

I didn't speak of the incident to our father, nor did either one of us refer to it again. But deep in my heart I knew that Mustafa would always hold it against me. I had injured his pride, and I think that he attributed my actions to jealousy. From that day onwards a wall descended between us, a mutual reserve. Until his departure from our village at the age of eighteen, I was determined to keep my peace and look the other way if such a thing should recur, but he was careful never to let me catch him in a compromising situation again.

When we first heard that he, a child of the mountains, had decided to settle in seaside Essaouira, far from his native environs, I took the initiative to reassure my parents about him. Let him be, I said with equanimity. The salt air will calm him. Meanwhile, you have two other sons who will look after you in your old age and tend to your needs.

A year later, Mustafa and I met in Marrakesh, and he informed me, with an air of defiance, that he was living with a woman but had decided not to marry. I didn't think it my place to comment but merely wished him happiness. At our next meeting, a few months later, he said with a smile, as if as an aside, that he'd left his companion whose importunate demands on his time and affection had begun to annoy him. Instead, he was living on his own in the heart of the medina, where his bronzed skin, curly hair, and easygoing ways had made him popular with the tourists. He'd taken up a sport called windsurfing. Some Frenchwoman named Sondrine had taught him. She lived on the beach; she was a free spirit like him. Once again, I refrained from commenting.

That's why, when I saw Mustafa rising to his feet from the edge of our circle that evening in the Jemaa, it attracted my attention. His face was a conversation without words: it betrayed the ardent and disconsolate thoughts that permeated it. His eyes glittered; they told a story where the strangers were already distillations of the desire barely contained within. It was as if, in a matter of seconds, my brother's lust had mastered him.

Mustafa! I cautioned, don't act in haste. Our religion is gentle. It does not permit transgressions and vice. It has strong conventions of hospitality. It emphasizes modesty.

He glanced at me with scorn. Scared of losing your tourist trade, Hassan? When I declined to dignify his accusation, he burst out: What is the point of my freedom if I hesitate to use it? There's nothing sordid about passion!

I must disagree, I said with gravity. Unbridled passion breeds anarchy.

Well then, he said heatedly, I must tell you that in your presence this wide-open square feels like a prison cell to me! But my

heart is racing, and I must follow its call. What you see as surrender, I see as victory.

You are my brother, I said calmly, and your rashness will be
your undoing.

You are my brother, he replied, and I find your timidity
womanish. The first mark of a man is boldness, and I intend to
exhibit it.

You reprobate! I retorted, finally losing patience. There is no
more luminous pleasure than that which is muted. Animals rut.
I expected more of you than this head rush that is clouding your
judgement.

He laughed in response and left without answering.

FIRST LOVE

Mustafa had not always been so impetuous when it came to
women. Or perhaps he had. As his brother I suppose I'm too
close to him and it's difficult for me to tell. Perhaps I should simply relate a story about him and leave it up to you to judge.

This happened many years ago. Mustafa was five years old at
the time, I was ten, and my middle brother, Ahmed, was eight.
Our village was visited by a medical team from Rabat as part
of a nationwide flu prevention campaign. They arrived in our
house the first thing in the morning, even before the sun had
come out. Initially, when we heard noises in the courtyard, we
thought it was the mailman bringing a letter from Mother's older
brother, Uncle Mounés, who worked in a factory in Salé, and

periodically wrote to us. But then we heard a woman's clearly educated voice asking if anyone was home, and we scrambled out of bed, all agog with curiosity. I was the first out, which was appropriate, since I was the oldest son; then Mustafa; followed by circumspect Ahmed bringing up the rear. Wiping the sleep from our eyes, we emerged into the dawn light to behold a young lady doctor in a pink silk headscarf and smart white medical coat. She was beautiful, tall, with full lips and high cheekbones, and her fair complexion was in striking contrast to the brown, weather-beaten women we were used to seeing. Confronted with this unexpected apparition, we halted uncertainly and gawked at her. Now that I think back on it, I realize we must have looked like a trio of village yokels with our sleep-tousled hair and our sooty woodsmoke-stained faces.

When Father emerged on our heels, tall and stern, with his gandoura hitched up to his knees, the doctor apologized for intruding at this early hour, before going on to explain that since ours was the most outlying house in the village, we were the first on her round of calls. In a pleasant but brisk and no-nonsense manner, she proceeded to introduce herself and her companions. The man on her right, unshaven and hard-faced, but also in a white medical coat, was her assistant, while the uniformed soldier with the raw shaven head was the driver of their medical van which was parked right in front of the rickety wooden gate that gave entrance to our courtyard.

Father didn't say anything at first, but I could tell that he was ill at ease at the prospect of dealing with a woman in a position of authority.

The doctor must have sensed his discomfort, because she immediately explained why they were there, on account of the

flu raging through the region, and why it was necessary to inoc-
ulate us. She demonstrated the procedure on her arm and said
that we'd all be done in a few minutes.

While she'd been speaking, her assistant had brought out a
folding chair and a metal table from the van, on which he now
arranged a medical kit bag, an instrument case, a siphon box, a
metal pan, a metal tray with cotton wool and swabs, and a few
bottles.

Catching a glimpse of the row of shiny needles in their sealed
plastic packets, Ahmed began to edge towards the house, but
Mustafa overtook him and re-emerged moments later with a
cushion which he plumped onto the doctor's chair.

This glissa is for you to sit on, he informed her.

Thank you, little one, she said, taken aback, her businesslike
demeanor relaxing perceptibly.

It's my pleasure, he piped up, and extended his arm. May I
go first?

Of course!

As the oldest son, I should have intervened at that point
and asked to take precedence, but, for once, I was glad to hold
back.

As she swabbed Mustafa's arm with alcohol, Father cleared
his throat. In a tone of dignified rectitude, he asked if she were
proposing to carry out the inoculations herself.

But of course, she said matter-of-factly. I'm the doctor here.

Yes, but still . . . Father began, before she cut him off. Don't
worry, I've done this more times than I can remember.

Somewhat irresolutely, Father fell silent, but I could tell that
he was confused by the situation. I also noticed that my usually loquacious little brother was uncharacteristically quiet, his

eyes fixed on the doctor as he hung on her every word. When she instructed him to make his hand into a fist and slipped the needle into his arm, he didn't grimace a bit. She withdrew the needle and taped his arm with a sticky bandage and some cotton wool, and he made way for me, since both Father and Ahmed appeared reluctant to come forward. Fevered with uncertainty, I stood before her and extended my arm in imitation of Mustafa. The alcohol swab felt like ice on the skin, and the needle stung, but it was over sooner than I'd expected, just as she'd said it would be.

That left Father and Ahmed. Father stepped forward, reluctantly, but Mustafa cut in before him. Can I go again? he asked the doctor.

She smiled and ruffled his air. You're a brave little boy, but you only get one chance, I'm afraid.

I stood beside the wooden bench that held Mother's clumps of mint in whitewashed tin cans and watched Father take his shot. Then Ahmed—who'd attempted to unsuccessfully conceal himself in the shadows where the red and white oleanders overhung the patio—was persuaded to come forward. He let out a bloodcurdling yell when the needle slid in. As he backed away, biting his lips and holding his arm, Mustafa shot forward again like a jack-in-the-box.

Ana moajaba bik, he said adoringly, quite obviously unable to stay away from the doctor: I love you.

She gasped, her eyes widening as she gazed at his fine brown hair, almond-shaped eyes, and chubby cheeks. Semehli, she said, I'm sorry, little one, but what did you say?

Mustafa repeated himself, louder this time, and with his hand clamped over his heart.

Oh, you dear baby! she exclaimed in delight. I love you too, habibi.

Glancing at Father, she said: You've a charming little child.

Father didn't respond.

She smiled warmly at the rest of us. Is there anyone else in the household? she asked.

Mustafa hurried forward with Chakib, our orange tabby, squirming in his arms. The soldier laughed. The doctor smiled and said: It's all right, my dear, you can let him go. He doesn't need this vaccine.

Promptly dropping Chakib, Mustafa rushed back into the house and returned with the canary in its wicker cage. The lady doctor shook her head. No, not the bird either.

She turned to Father. Anyone else?

Father looked wan in the grey light. His small, deep-set eyes flicked over us, warning us to hold our tongues. There's no one else, he said stolidly.

Are there no women in the household?

There are none.

Both Ahmed and I kept silent at this blatant untruth, but Mustafa couldn't control himself. Suddenly darting forward and clutching the doctor's hand, he said in a clear and high-pitched voice: That's not true! There is someone else. Mother's inside, making helba, and that's the truth.

In the silence that followed, a brisk gust of wind swept through the courtyard, stirring the straw litter strewn across the earthen floor. Our donkey, Huda, flicked her tail.

Please go in and get your wife, the doctor said. Everyone must be inoculated against the flu.

Father refused to budge.

It's against our taqlid, our tradition, he said firmly. Women must be excepted from your rules.

Nobody can be excepted in this case, I'm afraid, the doctor replied. I'm here on orders from the ministry in Rabat.

It doesn't matter, Father said. In the mountains we Berbers follow our own rules.

At that point, the soldier addressed Father, quite rudely, I thought.

What is your name? he rapped out.

Now the soldier's going to get it, I thought, expecting an explosion of Father's famous temper. Instead, to my surprise, Father shuffled his feet and said: Hamou.

Well then, Hamou, didn't you hear the doctor? In the name of His Majesty the King, go and fetch your wife.

Father paused uncertainly as Ahmed and I exchanged amazed glances. In the name of His Majesty? Father asked.

Indeed.

To my astonishment, Father nodded wordlessly and went into the house.

He emerged moments later. She won't come, he said, his eyes fixed on the ground.

If she won't come on her own, the soldier said, then we'll have to go in and get her.

Father started. His voice changed, falling to a pitch I'd never heard before. There's no need for that, he said, sounding utterly vanquished, while Ahmed rolled his eyes, as embarrassed as I was at witnessing our formidable parent cut down to size. Looking like an old man with his greying beard and sunburnt face, Father went into the house again and we heard his voice rising in anger as he took out his frustration on Mother. It was then that

I realized that gauging who has sulta, authority, in a particular situation, is the first step towards maturity.

Shortly after, Mother emerged behind Father in her best jellaba, brown with white and red stripes, with heavy silver bracelets on both wrists, and with the lower part of her face veiled with a black scarf which she held in place with the corner of her mouth. Her eyes were terrified, and when I rushed over to reassure her, she clutched my hand tightly.

I looked around for Father, but he'd retreated into the background, mortified and silent.

Mabrouk, the doctor's assistant said to him with heavy irony. Congratulations on your ability to quickly understand the rules.

The doctor took Mother under her wing.

It'll only take a moment, she said gently.

That's right, Mmi, I said, you'll hardly feel it and it'll be over before you know it. It's just like a mosquito bite.

It isn't like a mosquito bite, Ahmed said dourly. It hurts like hell, and you know it.

It doesn't hurt, Mustafa cut in. You're a sissy, Ahmed!

I'm not! Hold your tongue, midget.

Distracted by her sons, Mother was about to admonish us when the doctor told her that she'd already injected her and that she could go.

Amazed, Mother simply stood there in disbelief before breaking into a girlish giggle of relief.

See, I told you, I said to her.

So did I, Mustafa chimed in. Don't forget me!

May God grant you grace, Mother said to the doctor, before adding shyly, I've made sfinge. Will you have some, madame?

Yes, she will, Mustafa said, answering for the doctor. Her doughnuts are the best in the valley, madame. You must try them.

The doctor laughed. You have beautiful sons, she said to Mother.

No, *you* are beautiful, Mustafa interjected.

Hush, Mustafa, Mother said, scandalized. What's come over you? Please excuse him, she said to the doctor. He's so mischievous; constantly getting into trouble. He doesn't know what he's saying.

But it's the truth, isn't it? Mustafa asserted. You always tell me to speak the truth.

That's enough, Mustafa, Mother scolded. You talk too much.

To me, she said: Bring our visitors some water to drink, Hassan.

I returned with water kept cold in goatskin bags.

Shukraan, the doctor said. Thank you.

Mother brought out the sfinge on our best terracotta platter.

She glanced shyly at Father. Will you try one and tell me if they're all right?

Instead of answering, Father abruptly turned on his heels and disappeared into the house. To spare Mother further embarrassment, the doctor tasted a sfinge and answered in his stead.

Wonderful! she pronounced. What accounts for their delicate scent?

I flavour them with eucalyptus honey from Kenitra.

Your little boy was right. They're the best I've ever tasted.

As Mother blushed deeply, the doctor asked Mustafa if he'd like to accompany them on their rounds for the rest of the morning. Struck speechless with delight, he could only look at Mother for permission. When she nodded fondly, her innate good nature getting the better of her annoyance with him, he let out a whoop and danced a frenzied jig around the perimeter of the courtyard, while Ahmed and I tried to conceal our envy with disdainful indifference.

With a smile, the doctor gave him her instrument case to hold. He gaped in awe at the privilege. This—this is for me to carry?

He could barely encircle it with his arms.

I'll bring him back by noon, the doctor assured Mother.

We watched them leave in their medical van, with Mustafa sitting in the front seat between the soldier and the doctor's assistant.

They dropped him off a little before noon, as promised.

Ahmed and I were playing chess in the shaded patio. The air was hot and thick; sheets of sunlight pierced through the slatted roof of the patio. We tried to ignore Mustafa as he bounded in through the gate.

Look! he yelled. I got two medals!

He pointed to the badges on his chest, one with a red cross against a white background, and the other with a star inside a crescent.

I nodded without interest, while Ahmed yawned.

Mustafa walked over to us. You're jealous, he taunted.

Khain! Ahmed replied with scorn. Traitor! You made Father lose face and now he won't speak to us.

Unfazed, Mustafa proceeded to tell us about his day, and, despite ourselves, we found ourselves listening. He said that even the fqih in the Qur'an school, who'd cited the authority of the hadiths in order to avoid being inoculated, had eventually been dragged out of the village mosque by the soldier and suffered the indignity of the needle in his arm.

He squirmed and squealed like a girl! Mustafa said with glee, and both Ahmed and I shared in his mirth, because the fqih was a tyrant who bullied us unmercifully.

At that moment, Father emerged from the house, and our laughter dried up. Unable to stomach the loss of his authority, he'd spent the entire morning lying in bed with his face turned to the wall. Now he glared at Mustafa, the muscles of his face tight and drawn. There could be no mistaking his intentions as he headed purposefully towards his youngest son.

Mustafa stood his ground. He tapped the two badges on his chest.

Madame gave me these as a reward for being a good boy, he announced with pride.

When Father continued to close in, Mustafa faltered and began to retreat in his turn. He tapped the badges again, this time with an element of panic, in case Father hadn't noticed the first time around. I am now a servant of His Majesty the King, he said, his voice indignant and shrill. The soldier, Shouash, told me that. You can't hit me, Bba!

Father hesitated for the merest fraction of a second before resuming his advance. We'll see about that, he said grimly.

Ahmed had tipped off Mother by this time, and she ran pell-mell into the courtyard and pleaded with Father to desist.

Be quiet, Mabruka! This boy made a fool of me in front of strangers.

Mustafa now had his back to a wall. Trapped, he went down in a crouch as Father towered over him. It was of no use. With a deranged blow that reverberated through the air, Father sent him hurtling across practically the entire length of the courtyard.

I stepped forward inadvertently but Father stopped me with a glare.

Mustafa tottered to his feet, the imprint of Father's hand like a brand on his face. He coughed once or twice and shook his head in a daze. Blood welled out of his mouth. Mother let out a wail, but Father stepped in between. Trembling uncontrollably, my little brother made for the wooden gate and let himself out of the courtyard. When Mother attempted to follow him, Father stopped her with a curt command.

Let him be, he said. It will serve as a useful lesson.

We watched helplessly as Mustafa disappeared behind the line of boulders that ridged the nearest hill. Mother collapsed on her haunches and began to moan. My baby! Oh, my poor little baby!

As Father re-entered the house, Ahmed doubled over and threw up.

I held Mother by the shoulders, finding it difficult to breathe myself.

Mustafa didn't return until late in the evening, and even then, he refused to speak to us for days. The red bruise on his face darkened to purple, and then to a mottled black.

MALICE

That night in the Jemaa, as I watched Mustafa's rapidly disappearing back, I was reminded of that episode from a long time ago. Mustafa vanished into the shadows before I could stop him, and the manner of his departure weighed as heavily on me then as it had on that very different occasion when he was a little boy. I was afraid for him, and didn't feel up to the task of going on with my evening's worth of storytelling.

I surveyed the Jemaa and recalled the acrobat Saïd's warning. Left to myself, I would rather have pleaded inclement health, asked forgiveness from my circle of listeners, and abandoned the square. I might even have gone searching for my errant brother, determined to bring him to his senses.

But I did none of this. Heeding my obligation to my listeners, I willed myself instead to return to my storytelling. I ignored my conscience, which counselled attending to my brother, and became captive to my duties.

And so it was that I found myself talking about the Jemaa in unusually dark terms, portraying her as a woman of great charm, old beyond imagining, but with a young girl's voice and face, a fickle creature, sometimes given to nurturing her children—the inhabitants and itinerants who frequented her open spaces—and sometimes to bringing them great harm and grief.

She is dangerous, I said, but some women are like that: their dark mythology overwhelms them, vanquishing their beauty Treat them with circumspection, for they are not to be trifled with.

One of my listeners asked me, with some indignation, what mythology I could be referring to. He said: I have come to the Jemaa from my village many times, and each time I've felt enthralled, uplifted. There is something in the air here that is like a tonic. It braces me and leaves me wanting more. So what lies behind this malignant portrait that you choose to paint of her?

I reminded him that until recently the square had been a place for public executions and hangings. Both the guilty and the innocent met their end here, some dying with cries of despair, others with a defiance born of hopelessness. If you listen closely enough, I said, you can still hear their cries echoing across the pavements.

That was a long time ago, he said dismissively. You talk like the government officials who wanted to build a car park here and for a while stopped all meetings and festivities. Go back to your village if you don't like it here. But if you're going to make your money off the Jemaa, at least have the decency to praise it.

I acknowledged his point.

I love the Jemaa as much as anyone else, I said quietly. And as a storyteller, I am more conscious than most of her beauty. Every evening at sunset I observe her as she turns her young girl's face to the setting sun and bathes in its radiance. But I am also aware of her dark side, her failings.

At that moment, I heard a chuckle from the circle of onlookers and beheld my plump friend Mohamed, who owns a fabric shop in the Souk Smarine.

My word, Hassan! he exclaimed. What is the matter with you tonight? You are uncharacteristically morbid. And tonight, especially, I can tell you that your mood is not fitting. For I have witnessed something truly exceptional.

What have you seen? I asked, when he offered no further explanation.

I have seen the two foreigners who have become the talk of the souks, he answered. I have seen them with my own eyes, and they are like angels, gentle and beguiling. So enough of this grim talk. It is time to praise our good fortune this evening.

With that, he stepped out of the crowd and, with a nod at my listeners, asked me if he could relate what he had seen.

Aᴎɢᴇʟ

Mohamed spoke simply, with a mixture of spontaneity, candour, and a disarming naïveté that compelled our attention.

What I have to tell you, he began, took place earlier this evening. It was during the quiet hour, when the shops in the souks shutter their stalls and the evening crowds have yet to congregate in the Jemaa. Silence was everywhere. The dust of the day had had time to settle. The last embers of the sun burned quietly.

I had shuttered my stall and was about to set out for the Qessabin Mosque. The neighbouring shops had already closed for the day. The alley was deserted. I put my keys in the pocket of my jellaba and turned to leave.

I had barely taken a step when I froze. There, like an incandescent spark, in a pool of light cast by an opening in the reed-mat roof of the gallery, stood the most wondrous woman I had ever seen. She was like a houri of legend, an angel, a peri. I drank in her luminous eyes, her black mane, her flowing limbs, her smile as fluid as a ripple of wind. My head swam as if under the influence of some intoxicant. I found it difficult to breathe. Stunned by her beauty, I drew back into the shadows and stood quite still.

I have no idea how long the moment lasted. She lingered in that shaft of sunlight like a butterfly, and from somewhere deep within me a voice began singing. I did not call out. I did not attempt to engage her in conversation. I did nothing.

I don't know when it was that a miserable old donkey limped into the alley. It had been savagely beaten: bloody wounds ran down its flanks, and its tethers were swollen. Even I, who am not ordinarily possessed of patience for these dumb beasts, was moved to pity. It swung its head from side to side, spittle flaking its lips, and, before I could react, lurched suddenly towards the peri.

I silently cursed its intrusion and was about to step out of my place of concealment to chase it away when, once again, a surprise arrested me. This child, more beautiful than a bird of paradise, with large, dark eyes and the gentlest of smiles, reached forward and stroked the animal on its wounds and, instead of rearing away, it turned its head towards her and nuzzled her hand.

I watched, lost in contemplation. Her touch was steeped in a tenderness as light as water. Its infinite solicitude moved me. I realized that I had just witnessed an act of compassion, unpremeditated and direct. It was an expression of love, and I saw no evidence of anything other than the impulse to heal. Surely there was nothing enigmatic in this behaviour. It was worthy of emulation. There was nothing there to foster superstition or mystery.

Presently, comforted by the girl's attentions, the animal moved on. She watched it leave, her eyes glistening with tears, then turned to her companion, whom I noticed for the first time. He was well-built, his arms strong and muscular, his face thoughtful and genteel. He reached for her hand. I shared in their silence, which had the evanescent quality of a smile. Oblivious to my presence, they stood there for a while before walking away. I bade them a wordless farewell. A cat passed noiselessly across my line of sight. I emerged from the encounter as if from a dream.

Mohamed paused, his voice still full of the sweetness of his experience. He gazed at us one by one and said quietly, his lips scarcely moving: I carried their spell here. When I heard you speak, Hassan, I felt saddened, so I asked your leave to tell my story.

His grey eyes sparkled, and he went on in a louder voice:

Ah, you who are speechless now! Those two strangers are not of our kind, my friends. They are brighter beings. There's a rare innocence to them, a purity. It is through such encounters that the soul drinks its fill. Each of us carries a universe within us, but we must look outward to understand the world and our place in it.

Mohamed lifted his shoulders and looked past us into the square. After a moment's thought, he said: That is all I have to say to you this evening.

THE SCARLET İBİS

I remember how we were all silent that ill-omened evening after Mohamed's impassioned plea.

This memory illuminates the night, I'd acknowledged. It is beyond curiosity or desire. We perceive a stranger as someone different from us, and this woman is profoundly different—that much is clear.

Now I paused for a moment and turned to Mohamed, who was also present in my audience on this occasion, attentively listening to my recapitulation of his role from long ago.

Have I described your intervention that night as it happened? I asked.

He smiled and inclined his head in assent. Indeed you have, Hassan, he said. I couldn't have related it better myself. I was moved by their innocence, and it left me feeling immensely reassured and sanguine.

Very well then, I said, and was about to carry on when another graver, deeper voice interrupted me: It seems to me that you are quilting a story of contradictory instincts.

I turned towards the speaker. He was a Tuareg, one of the "blue men" from the south, his hands and face dyed from years of wearing the indigo weave. Aloof and serene, his demeanor showed that discipline of life which the Sahara requires of all who inhabit it.

With a natural elegance, he removed his tagilmoust, the black strip of cloth that, in the manner of his people, veiled his face.

Spreading his hands, he addressed Mohamed, his voice echoing with the sonority of vast desert spaces.

I am sorry to have to say this, my brother, but lovers always exert a strange fascination, and your account concealed as much as it revealed.

Mohamed bristled. What do you mean?

The man looked troubled.

Simply this, he answered. Sometimes our perceptions are twisted by encounters that are beyond our understanding. In listening to you, I must conclude that, moved as you were by their foreignness, you failed to realize the true implications of their presence. I too encountered the two strangers of whom you've spoken so eloquently. I'm afraid the woman made little impression on me, but the beautiful youth accompanying her wore the face of tragedy. Together, they reminded me of the abyss that is existence, and the only way that I can explain what I mean is through an analogy from my own experience.

I will use as my point of departure your comparison of the woman you encountered to a bird of paradise. To illustrate my point, I will speak of a different bird, though one equally resplendent, I think.

You are no doubt familiar with the bald ibis? It is a large bird, black, rather short-legged, with massive wings and a bright red down-curved bill. It is clumsy in flight, almost ungainly, and it is only when it is on the ground that its black plumage takes on a metallic purple sheen and gives it a strange kind of beauty. Perhaps that is why our marabout consider it sacred, and we are accustomed to the presence of these frequenters of barren terrain, which, though increasingly rare, are still easy to spot on the cliffsides lining wadis and creeks.

Last summer, a colony of these birds built their nests, as usual, on the sheer cliffs. It was during the time of the annual archery festival for which our village is well known. It is a moussem dedicated to the memory of a holy man who died long ago and was fabled for his gift of curing epilepsy. Since the creeks shelter the ibises during the daytime, the archery contests are held only after dark, when the birds return to their nesting grounds high up on the cliffs. Targets of smouldering wood are set up at regular intervals along the banks of the main creek. At a signal, bowmen from all over the Sahel try their skill with burning arrows, an innovation for which our moussem is famous.

As far as I am aware, there is no record of an ibis ever falling to a stray arrow. But last summer, things transpired differently. Archers from all over—from the far north, from Tetouan and Chefchaouan and the Rif, and also from the south, from Timbuktu and Oulata and Agadez—had already gathered for the contest when the presence of two dramatically different birds was reported in the ibis colony. They were also ibises— the family resemblance was clear—but much more slender than our resident birds, with longer necks and wings. Most exceptionally, they were bright scarlet from beak to tail, with glossy black wing tips. They left an indelible impression, and even the most hardened skeptics—the veterans of wars and so on—were moved to concede that our humble lives had been elevated by their beauty.

At first, no one knew where they had come from, but one of us, more lettered than the rest, investigated their provenance and declared that they were scarlet ibises, from a distant land across the ocean. Immediately we sensed that they posed a dangerous temptation for the visiting archers. To prevent mishap, we formed a squadron from the ranks of our youth to guard the cliffsides and keep an eye on the scarlet voyagers.

The first three days of the weeklong festival passed without incident. Everyone monitored the birds. Even the toddlers rushed to their parents with hourly reports. On the fourth day, however, calamity struck. Only one of the two red birds could be seen. Horrified, we redoubled the contingent of guards and, after hours of deliberation, ordered a search of the contestants' tents. Outraged by what they saw as a flagrant breach of traditional hospitality, the entire contingent from Gourma-Rharous packed up and left. We didn't care. We were determined to protect the remaining scarlet ibis. Our squadron of youthful guards invented new ways to keep it under observation night and day. They patrolled both sides of the wadi, a considerable stream at that time of the year, and some of them even set up a nightlong watch on the sand dunes that banked up against the yellow-grey cliffs.

By the penultimate day of the week, we began to relax our guard, for the bird had survived, even though the atmosphere of the archery festival felt compromised. The visiting bowmen were surly and contentious; they clearly resented the surveillance under which we'd placed them.

But it was all to no avail. Despite our precautions, and perhaps with a grim inevitability, the final day of the festival proved catastrophic. It dawned with a sandstorm the likes of which we had seldom experienced. It raged with fury the entire day, driving everyone, including the guards, indoors. One or two brave young souls attempted to venture out, but the lacerating sand defeated their vigilance. Resigned, but also filled with misgivings, we realized that we had no option but to wait out the storm.

Alas, when it died down in the evening to reveal a yellow sliver of moon, the precious bird had vanished. We scoured the rocky cliffsides and the banks of the creeks, but we couldn't find any traces of it. Not a single feather remained to offer a clue to its fate. The bird was gone as ineffably as if it had never existed.

We had no heart for the contest that final night, and the next morning the visiting archers abandoned our village with loud oaths and imprecations, vowing never to return. We watched listlessly as they left. None of us exhorted them to come back the next year. Our age-old festival would never regain its spirit.

MEDINA

Now the Tuareg addressed me directly. He said:

Nine mediaeval gates pierce the ramparts encircling this city, and there is something to the warren of narrow streets within that lends itself to storytelling. I think of this whenever I let my imagination soar like a bird in order to contemplate the shadowy expanse of houses and streets unfolding towards the mountains. At my feet, on all sides of my airborne kilim, lie the low rooftops and perfumed gardens of the medina. In the far distance, barely visible in the mist, snowcapped peaks. The sun rises in the east from behind those peaks. It sets in the west amid foam-crested waves. In between, the music of Marrakesh, the Baghdad of the

West, a city unthinkable without its square, the Jemaa, as integral to it as the crown of snow is to the mountain peak.

He paused and looked at me intently. His face was alert and contemplative.

Throughout his soliloquy, I had been content to remain silent, but when he paused, I said: You are yourself, quite obviously, an inaden, a weaver of stories.

Yes, I am, he said, and smiled.

What is your name, homme bleu? I asked him.

I'm called Jaouad.

I thanked him for his contribution and he smiled again.

Dust rises from the plains, he said. The heat of the day dissipates. And we both stand in the shadow of the Crow Tree, weaving.

In our shifting circle of onlookers were the usual impatient souls, eager to proceed with the story, and one of these now exclaimed: But what of the two strangers? What happened to them?

In reply, it was Jaouad who turned to one corner of the square, near the booths piled high with mounds of oranges, and gestured.

There they are now, still haunting the square, he said, although we saw nothing.

He shrugged, and there was mischief in his eyes.

They are as slippery as fish underwater, he added. Now you see them, now you don't.

There was uneasy laughter on all sides, but my friend Mohamed, who had been brooding in silence, refused to participate in the merriment. Instead, he walked up to the Tuareg. Folding his arms, he addressed him coldly: You used the words "the abyss of existence," if I recall correctly. Please explain your meaning.

ABYSS

A lull followed Mohamed's question. The Tuareg pursed his lips. The laughter disappeared from his eyes. Instead, his gaze conveyed a melancholic solemnity.

After an expectant silence, he said: It's about possibilities. Things change when you care enough to give everything to what you love. Then you enter the abyss—dreamlike, certainly, but also a reality that, more often than not, is excruciating.

He paused and wrapped his indigo cloak around himself. His eyes weighed upon us. He cut a sombre figure in that convivial setting.

With a sideways glance at Mohamed, his speech precise and full of images, he continued:

Since it is the one human quality that is, strictly speaking, purely subjective, beauty usually triumphs over wisdom and rationality. The beholder, the privileged witness, lives the beautiful dream. He escapes reality through passionate identification with this dream. It is a mystic marriage, a union that embraces joy and light as much as despair and darkness. The one who has encountered such beauty is forever transformed. His experience of the world will never be the same again. Rather, it will be sadly reduced. Such is the abyss, a state of existence without satisfaction or happiness.

He paused again to shape his thoughts. Somewhere the wheels of a cart squealed in the darkness. I now expected him to talk some more about the beautiful stranger who had captivated Mustafa. Instead, he introduced a different analogy.

Consider, he said, the gentle red glow of the ramparts of Marrakesh, the seductive shelter of their shade in the heat of the day, the temptation to rest in the shadows such that perhaps, with time, one may soak up their cooling impress and become formless oneself, without substance. That is the abyss.

Avoiding Mohamed's eyes, he turned to me and said:

So our nature overcomes us. Its sand comes pouring through our doors. From deep inside us, desire rises like a storm. Faced with its might, all else—logic, virtue, circumspection—is useless.

No one spoke when he'd finished. As we contemplated his words, long threads of gossamer drifted across the square. I wondered where they had come from. Someone in the crowd, evidently a farmer, said: It will be a beautiful harvest.

Perhaps taken with the unintentional irony of the remark, the Tuareg smiled. He joined me in gazing at the two black pillars of the Crow Tree and the Koutoubia minaret. The full moon shone high in the sky. Holding up his middle finger so that it made a straight line with the minaret and the tree, he said quietly:

You and I have a cruel talent.

I knew what he meant. We storytellers regard the middle finger as the indicator of death.

I wish it could be different, he added. It is a heavy burden. It makes us less human.

Now he turned to Mohamed.

Farewell, he said, and raised his hand to his heart.

Mohamed did not acknowledge the gesture.

With a quick glance around, the Tuareg left the ring of onlookers. I watched him go with regret.

FRACTURE

But something about his discourse on beauty stayed with me and brought back memories of a conversation I'd once had with my brothers when we were in the prime of our youth and, each of us, in our own very different ways, incorrigibly idealistic.

We'd been perched on a ridge overlooking our valley, with the village at the very bottom, and our house at an elevation above it. There were rain clouds massing in the distance, and, in a while, we watched them break over the High Atlas peaks. The sky turned black, then an uncanny shade of purple, against which the snow-white mountains stood out like a jagged streak of lightning.

That's beautiful! I exclaimed, with a low whistle of admiration.

I don't know if I'd use that particular word, Mustafa cautioned. I usually reserve the term "beautiful" for members of the fairer sex.

You would, scoffed Ahmed. You're obsessed with girls.

What's wrong with that? I've a healthy curiosity. After all, I'm no spring chicken, I'm already fourteen.

I still maintain that the storm is beautiful, I said with equanimity. I lit a cigarette and offered another to Ahmed but not to Mustafa, who protested: Hello? What about me?

You have to earn the right to smoke, Ahmed said. It isn't an automatic privilege when you come of age.

Fine, Mustafa said. How does one earn the right to smoke?

Ahmed chortled. By losing your virginity.

Oho, Mustafa replied, by that measure I ought to be the only one here with a cigarette.

We stared at him. Then Ahmed asked him if he was joking.

Why don't you believe me?

Without a convincing counter, Ahmed could do no better than to fall silent.

Feeling the need to come to his rescue, I cleared my throat.

What're you talking about, Mustafa? I asked.

What do you think?

We don't believe you, Ahmed said. Then: Who've you done?

All of them, Mustafa said with a grin.

What? In the village?

Where else?

Ahmed! Mustafa! I reprimanded them. Behave yourselves.

Ahmed pressed on regardless. Names, please.

Mustafa began counting on his fingers. Let's see, there's Salima, Zubeida, Douja, Huda . . .

I interrupted him. What a load of rubbish!

So that's what he does when he goes swanning about the village pond, Ahmed said with contempt.

Mustafa drew himself up with an air of injured dignity.

On the contrary, I don't go "swanning" about the pond, I'll have you know; I merely prefer the water temperature there as compared to our own frigid spring.

The waters of the pond warmed, no doubt, by your many admirers' wildly beating hearts, I said with irony.

It could be, Mustafa said, lowering his eyes modestly.

You're shameless, Ahmed said, and spat on the ground. I suppose you've also slept with Hayat, Shama, and Zina, he added recklessly, naming some of the girls who were his own age.

Please! Mustafa said. Give me some credit for taste. Hayat is fat, Shama has a squint, while Zina's growing a beard from her chin.

You fool, Ahmed said, get your priorities straight. Hayat's father has money, Shama's father is the village moneylender, while Zina's brothers own a taxi company in the Tafilalt. And that's what matters in the end: money.

You can't sleep with money, Mustafa said crudely.

But you can lie on it, Ahmed retorted, undeterred. He paused for a moment, then asked, with less assurance, naming a girl we knew he was attracted to: What about Mallika?

Don't worry, Mustafa said. She's all yours for when you're ready.

Anyway, Ahmed said, returning to the attack, I don't care for your taste in women, quite frankly. All the girls you named, especially Salima and Zubeida, wear bright red lipstick that makes them look like whores; and I've nothing but scorn for girls who attempt to enhance their sex appeal by using such fripperies. But then again, I suppose that's what attracted you to them in the first place.

As a matter of fact, no, my dear Ahmed, I was attracted by their beauty, but what would you know of that? You haven't seen what I've seen.

Shut up. You're such a braggart.

And this from the boy who confessed he slept without trousers the day he first saw his precious Mallika so that he could have better dreams?

At least I didn't wear serwal, harem pants, as you once did!

All right, you two, I said sharply, cut it out.

They carried on as if they hadn't heard me.

What's wrong with wearing serwal to bed now and then? Mustafa said, before adding provocatively: They add to your dreams, and you know how much I love to fantasize, to conjure up moments of bare skin and silk. What's better still, one can add to the erotic element the next day by setting fire to the serwal and watching it go up in smoke before starting all over again.

You'd better plan on opening a serwal shop, Ahmed said.

I'm suspicious of illusions myself when it comes to love, I observed, making my first substantive contribution to the discussion at hand.

That's because you're such a hopeless bore, Mustafa said. At fourteen you don't think about reality, you live on dreams.

I'm eighteen, may I remind you, I said haughtily. I've more weighty matters to think of than a chabab's puerile fantasies.

Oh yes? Ahmed said, jumping in. You can tell us that when you get married and start earning real money, like I do already, at the village gambling pool. Unlike the two of you, I've no wish to be old and poor in my dotage, like Lalla Nizam in the village.

Lalla Nizam may be poor, I said, but she has dignity and tenderness. Only those with the very best of consciences have what's most important. Tenderness, and the other priceless gift that God has given us: reason.

I'm not yet ready for that kind of narrow rationality, Mustafa said. I want to dive into life and get on with it. Life is all about testing limits and shrugging off the bruises after each stumble. I've no use for your reason, Hassan, or Ahmed's money. For me it's the pursuit of beauty and the freedom that comes with it.

And I happen to think that both beauty and wealth are ephemeral, I said calmly. Love should be based on more permanent things. It should lead to marriage, for one, and married life should be like an island to which one returns from an always unpredictable sea.

Should, should, should . . . Mustafa said in a jaded voice.

Yes, should, I said, nettled, because the most beautiful object of all is that which is real, even if it doesn't meet some abstract standard set by your fantasies.

No! Mustafa expostulated. What is the point of beauty if you can't dream it?

I disagree with you completely.

Disgruntled in his turn, Mustafa picked up the lute he'd brought along and began to strum on it.

Oh Lord, Ahmed protested without effect, must we now be subjected to the whine of your guenbri?

You've no ear for music, Ahmed, Mustafa said. You can leave if you don't like it.

Returning to an earlier thread, I said: According to Uncle Mohand in Marrakesh, what's hardest is not making someone fall for you, but sustaining that love over time.

What does he know? Mustafa scoffed. With that harridan he has for a wife he's in a state of permanent misery.

And you know better? I challenged him. You talk as if you possess some kind of magic over women.

With his typically insolent self-confidence, Mustafa said: Oh, I do have magic. He grinned, then blew a kiss at his crotch. I owe it to Sidi, my Lord. Sometimes a lamb, more often a lion, he knows how to bewitch them.

You're drunk on desire, I said. And that's disgusting.

Desire is disgusting?

Runaway desire is disgusting—and dangerous.

What's wrong with danger?

You wouldn't know, Mustafa. You're still a boy.

But I'm not a virgin, he said tellingly. And unlike you, when I finally fall in love, it'll be with a beauty who won't drag around her stove and charcoal everywhere she goes, tending to practical reality, as your beloved probably will.

So all these girls you've been boasting about—what do they mean to you? If you're not in love with any of them, what are you doing?

I'm playing around, Hassan, isn't it clear? I'm gaining experience.

So what exactly is love according to you?

True love?

Yes.

Mustafa paused, for once contemplative. To our amazement, he produced his own hidden cache of cigarettes and lit one musingly.

Finally, he said: Do you know how the full moon is called qamar, which also means an extraordinarily beautiful woman, because it is then that the moon is at its peak? And when you look up, it's as if your eyes are climbing a ladder from shadows to light? Well, I'll know it when I find my full moon.

How will you know it? Ahmed challenged him.

I'll be blinded by her luminosity. Her burning gaze will embrace me. Our meeting will be unexpected, dreamlike, and reflected in her eyes I will see my destiny.

Oh, come on! Ahmed said.

No, I'm absolutely serious, Mustafa said, and something in his voice made us attend to him. It's a matter of intuition, I think. Intuition, recognition, and affirmation. And when that happens . . . he said, pausing with a catch in his voice . . . When I feel my heart rising to my throat, I will beg that grace, beauty, to redeem me.

These are merely pretty words, Ahmed said, unmoved.

And in any case, I added, what you've described isn't love, it's infatuation.

Mustafa slowly put down his lute and rose to his feet.

Then all I can tell you is that I think of the moment of falling in love as akin to being struck by the shaft of lightning that just cleaved that distant peak. Or like falling from a height and feeling myself smash against the rocks below and knowing that life will never be the same again.

Obviously, genius, Ahmed said, you'd be dead.

Mustafa ignored him. With an air of great solemnity, he said: In the game of love you're playing for very high stakes and you have to be willing to risk everything. Everything.

Once again, Ahmed scoffed and said: Words.

Mustafa gazed at him with a smile and extended both arms like an airplane. Crouching low, he began to run along the ridgeline, quickly picking up speed.

Slow down, you young fool! Ahmed called out in warning.

Mustafa ran on heedlessly, heading straight for the edge of the ridge where it ended abruptly.

Both Ahmed and I stood up in alarm.

What the hell? Ahmed growled.

The words had scarcely left his lips when Mustafa hurtled over the edge and out of our sight. Scarcely able to breathe, we ran helter-skelter and peered down the sheer cliff.

Mustafa lay spread-eagled on a rocky ledge several dozen feet below us. He smiled weakly when we climbed down to him.

I think I've broken my leg, he said. It hurts like hell, but I wouldn't have missed that moment of launching myself into the air for anything in the world. I think that's what true love is going to be like for me. Do you believe me now?

Ahmed and I looked at each other in disbelief, before speaking in one voice: You're mad!

ZAHRA

It took us two hours to haul Mustafa up the cliff. The storm caught up with us as we carried him home. Soaked to the skin, we lied at home about what had happened, of course.

A couple of days later, on a bright, sunny morning, I was giving Mustafa company as he sat glumly on the patio with his plastered leg propped up, when Ahmed tore in through the courtyard gate on his bicycle and skidded up to us.

Hassan, he said, get off your ass! The girl that Father's arranged for you to be married to is walking down the northern road leading away from the village, and if you're quick enough, you can catch up with her and get a good look. Here: take my bicycle.

Are you sure it's her?

Yes, yes, it's Zahra, for God's sake. I'm one hundred percent certain.

But she isn't from around here. What is she doing in our valley?

How do I know? Maybe she was visiting someone in the village. My friend Dehili tipped me off. He knows her brothers and recognized her as she was leaving the village. Do get a move on, won't you?

I shifted uneasily. Ahmed, I began, I don't know if I want to. After all, I trust Father's good judgement, and there's a certain order to the way these things proceed . . .

Mustafa gave me a shove. Hassan, don't be such a stick-in-the-mud! he said exasperatedly. Ahmed's right. Hurry up and go, and then come back and tell me what she's like.

I glanced at both of them. All of a sudden, to my own considerable surprise, I leapt with alacrity onto Ahmed's bicycle and took off, furiously pedalling down the uneven piste to the village.

She's wearing a bright green boubous, Ahmed yelled after me. You can't miss it.

He was right: I didn't, especially given that she was the only person on the road going north. I felt my mouth turn dry and my heart begin to pound.

Slowing down about twenty metres behind her, I sailed past before turning my head swiftly to take her in. By God, she was beautiful, like Scheherazade, with a triangular face, huge brown eyes, and an exquisite green tattoo on her chin. She smiled when she saw me looking back, and, at that very instant, I lost control of the bicycle, going careening off the road and ending up on my backside with a resounding thump.

We were married four months later. Zahra had just turned sixteen. She was Ahmed's age, two years younger than me.

The Healing Garden

So that's the way it was with my brothers, I said, interrupting my narrative to look at my audience. Ahmed's still the same; he hasn't changed a bit. He still holds on to the tangible things in life, his belief implicit in the capacity of the world to satisfy his needs. As for Mustafa and his absolute faith in beauty, well, we'll just have to wait and see where our story leads us, won't we?

Glancing at my listeners again, I added after a lengthy pause:

But this much is certain. If one were to contemplate Mustafa's fate following his meeting with the two strangers in the square, then the Tuareg was uncannily perceptive in apprehending the hazard that beauty poses for those who encounter it—for my brother's life was indeed forever transformed into a state of existence with neither satisfaction nor bliss.

A new voice now spoke up, slightly mocking and droll:

Oh, I don't know about that, Hassan. I didn't agree with that denizen of the desert when he spoke, and I can't say that I agree with you now. All this strikes me as rank pessimism.

Turning to locate the source of the voice, I recognized the slight figure of Youssef, the middle son of one of the orange merchants of the Jemaa. He was small and sallow and rumoured to be something of a skirt-chaser. He passed around a basket of sweet and bitter oranges.

I'm celebrating the birth of my third child, a boy, he announced with pride.

He gestured rather disdainfully in the direction in which the Tuareg had disappeared.

As a philosopher, he said, that man might have a lot to talk about, but that's not enough for me. He told me almost nothing about life that I didn't know already. Yes, things can sometimes be grim, but where's the surprise in that? Real life, on the other hand, rewards me constantly. It's always revealing something unique, something I've never seen before. That's why we're given eyes, and the faculties of sense and reason, so that we may use them to learn from our experiences, however negative. And love? That's the most rewarding thing of all. So there it is, my friends. Say "No" to pessimism! If there are auguries, they must be respected, but why tarnish happiness with the darkness of shadows and storms? Rather, tell yourselves: I am the board on which I play my life!

Turning to Mohamed, the shopkeeper, he said with sparkling eyes: In the name of my newborn son, I salute your good fortune in witnessing the foreigner's kindness to that humblest of beasts, the donkey. It was an act of genuine compassion. And I am envious of your eyes, for I too saw her, perhaps shortly after your own encounter, and though I was rather less impressed, your account has ennobled my own experience.

You had seen the strangers as well? someone asked, and Youssef laughed and said: Yes, yes, I saw them, these two persons around whom Hassan is spinning a tale such as only he can tell.

Pausing like a seasoned storyteller to gauge the effect of his words, he selected a particularly delectable orange and peeled it with ease. He spit out the seeds as he chewed so that there was soon a scattering of them about him.

My own encounter with them took place late in the afternoon, he said, but lacking Hassan's facility with words, all I can say is that to me they merely seemed like two young, naïve, and extremely tired foreigners, exhausted perhaps by aimless meanderings around the medina. They had strayed into the courtyard of a house near the Qessabin Mosque. The house belongs to a friend of mine who was visiting his in-laws in Meknés, and, as is his custom whenever he goes away, he'd given me the keys so that I could keep an eye on things.

So it was that I was taking a siesta in the patio facing the courtyard when I overheard voices and, opening my eyes, was surprised to discover a young man and woman half hidden in a corner of the garden amidst some flowering trees and bushes. Their dress, though modest, revealed them as foreigners. She was wearing faded blue jeans, flip-flops, and a white T-shirt with "I ♥ NY" printed on the front. He carried a water bottle slung around his hip and a crumpled map of the medina to which he referred repeatedly. They were both grimy and sweat-stained, as is often the case with these Nasranis when they've been walking around in the sun for a while. As for their appearance, which has already been the subject of considerable discussion here, I would say that he was skinny and looked constipated, to be quite frank, while she was pretty in a cheap, fraudulent way, with the kind of makeup that can turn even unattractive women into mysterious, desirable creatures. In other words, there was nothing about either one of them that was remotely out of the ordinary, and my first instinct was to chase them away, but something about their haplessness arrested my intent. I noticed that she was crying soundlessly and that he was attempting, rather ineffectually but with obvious tenderness, to stem her tears with his hands. They seemed oblivious to the fact that they were trespassing. Indeed, it was as if the shrubbery within which they had taken shelter had been planted there just to offer them sanctuary.

Chewing on an orange, its juice dribbling down his chin, he continued: At length, the woman's tears ceased, and her companion, with evident relief, turned his attention to a worn leather wallet which he'd taken out of his pocket and now emptied of its contents, mostly coins and a few bills. He counted the money before turning to her and saying something which reduced her to tears again.

I was about to offer my help when I recalled my responsibilities as caretaker and realized I ought to be telling them to clear out instead. Believe me when I tell you that I wasn't looking forward to ordering them to leave. I detest confrontations, a shortcoming for which my father has often taken me to task. But fortune was in my favour because, even before I could venture forth from the patio, they rose of their own volition and slipped out into the street.

Laughing softly, Youssef went on with a casual dismissiveness:

So there it is, my friends. A perfectly ordinary encounter, albeit pregnant with possibilities. They were tourists, plain and simple, obviously down on their luck, but to all purposes innocents abroad, and hardly justifying the dire attitude of our Tuareg friend.

A Weight Lifted

Youssef's account seemed to have displeased Mohamed, the shopkeeper, even more than the Tuareg inaden's because he stood up and left the circle sullenly and without a word. Meanwhile, Youssef seemed planted there, placidly chewing on his inexhaustible supply of oranges while darting quick glances here and there to gauge the effect of his contribution.

I gathered my wits about me. Preparing to return my story to its intended course, I found myself interrupted once again as someone directed a terse question at Youssef.

What did they look like?

I thought I'd already described them, Youssef said, partly with irritation and partly with surprise.

Give us details. Hair colour, eyes, height, and so on.

The interjections came from a short, swarthy, powerfully built young man, his hands jammed into his pockets. He had the appearance of a professional bodybuilder, his face shiny with sweat as if he'd just been engaged in some strenuous exertion.

He planted himself in front of Youssef, who drew back a little.

Why do you want to know? Youssef asked in a reed-thin voice.

Because you only gave us the most general descriptions, the man answered.

The woman was tall and slightly overweight, Youssef said, somewhat defensively. He ran his tongue over his lips before continuing: She was taller than the man. She had scraggly brown hair, grimy feet. He had on a frayed brown jacket. He wore rimless glasses. He was fair and clean-shaven.

The bodybuilder grimaced and jammed his chin forward.

Well, I think that's nonsense, he spat out.

What do you mean? the orange merchant's son gasped.

Your depiction contradicts all of the others we've heard so far. I think you're making things up. You're a liar.

He pronounced the word *liarrr*, drawing it out as if to lend it additional emphasis.

Youssef flinched and rose to his feet. Beside the hefty youth, he seemed like a sprig of straw. His face drained of blood, his lips pale, he looked terrible.

You've got nerve questioning my veracity! he exclaimed. He glanced at me for reinforcement, but I was enjoying the show too much.

And I'm telling you that you're a piece of rubbish.

Well then, so is everyone else! Nobody remembers them clearly. My description is as good as any of the others!

I'm talking about you, not anyone else.

They glared at each other, Youssef seemingly impregnable, despite the odds. Then the bodybuilder leaned forward. Planting a beefy fist against the orange vendor's chest, he exclaimed: Who wants to hear about your siestas and your well-off friend's in-laws? We're not here to listen to you prattle, you self-satisfied piece of nothing!

Tilting a pugnacious chin in my direction, he went on:

Let that man tell his story, won't you? I like his version better.

Youssef took a step back, his pallid face clearly betraying fear as much as indignation.

I'm not going anywhere, he said stubbornly. I won't have my reputation sullied.

At that, the bodybuilder lost patience.

Oh really? he yelled. Clear off now, or else I'll . . .

The unspoken threat had its desired effect, for Youssef backed away hastily from the ring of listeners, his retreating form shrinking to a black dot across the vast expanse of the square.

Well then, that's that, the bodybuilder announced with characteristic eloquence. He turned to me with a grin. I don't like my stories ruined. You can depend on me the next time you have killjoys. I'm Hocine, from Zagora, in the far south. I'm new here. I'm a weightlifter. I can do a hundred bench presses with one hand. I've set up my stall on the western edge of the square, in front of the Café de France.

I smiled, grateful for his swift and effective intervention. He had recognized the danger posed by Youssef and restored to my story its necessary mystery.

All of a sudden a young boy in a tattered smock came running up to Hocine and whispered something in his ear. He reacted as if struck by a whip.

Someone's made off with my barbells! he exclaimed, swivelling to scan the four corners of the Jemaa. I'm off!

He turned and followed on the heels of the young boy with all of the determination of a hound chasing hares. We watched him leave and I'm certain that I wasn't the only one in our circle to wonder if the culprit was the recently departed Youssef.

THE MOORS INVADING SPAIN

Hocine's rough-and-ready intrusion had acted like a tonic on my spirit. He'd spoken excitedly, artlessly, but straight from the heart, and his confidence in me gave me hope for the evening. I prepared to resume speaking, taking up the thread of the narrative from where Youssef had left off, but with a very different energy. I stroked my beard and surveyed my audience, my gaze lingering on their faces—now alert and intent, now dormant and secretive—and it was as if I could not feast my eyes enough on their countenances.

Their thoughts crowded the air. I could hear them, and I closed my eyes to listen so that I could decipher their meaning. That is the storyteller's way, and it has taken me a long time to train myself accordingly. It was easier in the village, where the silent quilt of air made listening simpler. All you had to do was to distinguish words from the surrounding sounds—the chirping of insects, the burbling of the streams, the whisper of the wind—and the rest came naturally. The stories formed themselves out of slow, slumbering daydreams.

It was different in the city. The sounds were louder, shriller, and the effort it took to separate the words from the surrounding cacophony made my head spin.

My first visit to Marrakesh was with my father. I was six, and he'd decided that I should accompany him from our village so that I could get my first taste of our trade by watching him tell his stories. We'd set up on the Jemaa in the late afternoon and remain there till well after midnight, when we'd leave to sleep in my uncle Mohand's shack in the Berrima quarter, outside the walls of the medina. I was allowed to sleep in most mornings while he left for the souks. On other days we'd take shelter from the blazing sun by visiting the cool and shadowy palaces in the medina. He seemed to know all the attendants, who respected him as a learned man, and we were often—though not always—allowed to enter without having to pay the usual fees.

The palaces contained many historical paintings and my father explained them to me with his usual patience. My favourites were the battle scenes, especially the spectacular painting in the Bahia Palace entitled *The Moors Invading Spain*. It depicted the Battle of Bajadoz in which our Almoravid king, Youssef ben Tachfine, the founder of Marrakesh, routed the Christian forces. The painting, done in the European style, depicted the battle from the Spanish point of view. A brass plate at the bottom of the frame, translated into Arabic, explained that the painter had been influenced by someone called El Greco.

I was fascinated by that painting because the Spaniards, who occupied the foreground, had peculiarly elongated bodies and heads. They looked like weaklings—decidedly effeminate—and it didn't surprise me that they hadn't been able to stand up to our tough Moorish troops, who formed a disappointingly amorphous black mass on the horizon.

A few years later, when I was nine, I came across a tattered Spanish novel lying on the pavement in the Jemaa and the picture on the cover once again depicted a scandalously skinny Spanish knight charging some windmills. From that point on, for the rest of my childhood, I possessed a healthy contempt for Spaniards.

My father was a traditional storyteller, well versed in folk-lore, but he was also unusually erudite for someone raised in a mountain village without any formal education. He knew several Berber dialects, he spoke classical Arabic fluently, and he even used a few words from French and other foreign languages in his stories when it suited his purpose. He had a keen eye for physical detail and peopled his tales with unforgettable characters. His best stories were composed of a series of episodes where the promised closure stretched out for weeks before the hair-raising ending.

He was a tall man with close-cropped hair, courteous and reserved, but there was a dark energy about him. Every spring, with the melting of the snows, he would give in to black moods that would last for days during which we all kept away from him. It was rumoured that in his youth he had killed a woman who'd been unfaithful and that her spirit returned year after year to haunt him. One had only to be near him to sense the taut quality beneath his reticence, the knife-edge of bitterness arising from that old betrayal. Looking back now, I realize that it was no wonder that his favourite theme was "longing."

Outside of his storytelling sessions, he wasn't given to speaking much. Life's vicissitudes had carved a permanent ridge between his eyes so that he always looked troubled and aggrieved. Sometimes I wondered if his bitterness was exaggerated—an outlet for some other, unknown, malady—but I did not hold it against him. It gave him character, and I respected him for it. He was kind to me and exercised great patience when we came down to Marrakesh from the mountains.

Bajadoz

My uncle Mohand, who put us up in Marrakesh, was a day labourer, and the black sheep of the family, but he worshipped my father, who could do no wrong in his eyes. Although his ramshackle home comprised only two rooms, he would insist on sleeping outside and giving one of the rooms to his elder brother and nephew, a point of some considerable contention with his wife, who was a regular harridan. She resented the fact that her husband refused to take money from his brother for the duration of our stay, and berated him bitterly when Father was not around. But my uncle remained unmoved and would not hear of any change in the arrangements.

For the first two years, my father kept me at his side while he told his stories, training me to listen and to keep my eyes and ears open. He knew that the Jemaa was a whetstone for the imagination, its shifting cast of characters a veritable library for an apprentice to browse in while developing the subtle tools of the trade. But I was a restless child, and my mind often wandered from my father's complex narratives. Even though I usually caught myself with a guilty start, once I lost the thread binding the tales it was all over for me for the day. Father often caught me daydreaming, but he never chastised me. Rather, he encouraged me to keep myself busy with my own narratives.

So it was that after that first exposure to *The Moors Invading Spain*, I spent hours at his side replaying the battle, imagining numerous gruesome encounters in which the Muslim army inevitably triumphed. I would sit behind him, taking over a corner of his kilim and using its geometric patterns to demarcate the positions of the two armies. Shaping the contours of the kilim into valleys and hills, I spent hours painstakingly carving hundreds of soldiers from wood chips and organizing them into regiments. The brave Muslim squadrons I named after the elements: Smoke, Fire, Water, Earth, Air. The skinny Spaniards were more crudely carved and constituted nothing more than a black mass that took to its heels every time I unleashed the invincible force of the elements. It was my revenge on the painter of the canvas, and I gained tremendous satisfaction in thus restoring fidelity to facts.

I kept busy for two seasons with my reenactment of Bajadoz, and then one day a German tourist, portly and good-natured, offered me what seemed like a princely sum of money to part with my elaborately crafted Almoravids. I turned him down outright the first time, but when he returned the next day, I accepted the loose change in a moment of folly and betrayed my obligation as custodian of history.

I broke down that night and remained despondent for days. My uncle encouraged me to re-create my armies, but the spirit had gone out of me. Appalled by my greed, I could no longer trust myself to safeguard the Muslim cause.

My father laughed at my retrospective disappointment.

He ruffled my hair as we lay down to sleep one night.

Never sell your dreams, he said.

The Disembodied Eye

During my third season on the Jemaa, I worked in one of its many food booths to supplement our income. The owner of the booth was Abdeslam, a native of Marrakesh. He was short, skinny, and pale, he came from a poor family and had worked very hard to save the money to buy the permit for his stall. All his energies were devoted to the stall: he worked from dawn to dusk like a dog and expected his helpers to do likewise. Sometimes he chased after them with a stick when he felt they weren't doing their share, but he left me alone because he was afraid of my father. I think he believed him to be possessed of necromantic powers.

Abdeslam liked to recite verses from the Qur'an, which he alternated with Raï songs from Algeria and the Rif. He had an active clientele and made good money, but my own work was tedious and boring. I was an odd-job boy, helping out in a medley of tasks that ranged from slicing vegetables to hosing down the long wooden tables and benches that fronted the stall. We sold brochettes, olive salads, fish sandwiches, kefta, habra, mechoui, b'stilla, fekkas, dellahs, almond milk, and a tart ginseng drink called khendenjal reputed to be an aphrodisiac. Our most popular item was the blood-red merguez sausage, which my employer spiced with a piquant harissa sauce of his own making. He was immensely proud of his harissa. His favourite saying was: The mark of a real man is his ability to handle my harissa!

I worked there from nine in the morning to four in the afternoon before joining my father at the other end of the square. The hours between meals were the most wearisome, especially in the late afternoon, and I whiled the time away by imagining myself to be a disembodied eye that travelled the square. It was a trick Father had taught me to improve my imagination and memory. Off I'd send my roving eye, making detailed inventories of the things I saw so that I could reproduce them in ever-longer lists to him. He set me a target of a hundred different objects and the day I was able to list them was my proudest moment.

To me these lists were like trails of smoke that I could conjure out of thin air. Trapped in my cycle of menial tasks, they provided a necessary escape and also gave me a growing sense of confidence. At first, the lists were random: a caged nightingale, handwoven baskets, Berber jewellery, brightly coloured Rahalia—large decorative plates from Fez—in shades of glossy blue and green and yellow, delicately ornamented terracotta oil lamps, copper water jugs and silver teapots, a brass hand of Fatima to ward off the evil eye, wrought-iron chairs, ill-tempered geese and hens, silk tassels, leather slippers, jellabas and burnooses, mounds of dried mint leaves, plastic spice jars filled with jujuba, caba caba, indigo, rose sable, fenugreek, ambergris. Later, I set my memory more challenging tasks, confining myself to lists of particular things, like sweetmeats, or hand-painted boxes, or camel saddles. One day, I found myself sated with lists and set my roving eye more challenging tasks. I sought to see through doors and walls, or I peeled away the pavement of the Jemaa to reveal tens of dozens of pickled heads of desperadoes from centuries past, their bleary-eyed visages impaled on spikes. In another spot beneath the pavement I uncovered acre after acre of plucked jasmine flowers.

I began to call myself the Master of the Disembodied Eye.

No one, and nothing, was safe from my probing gaze. I put the fear of God into the most hardened criminals. When I told my father, he warned me against arrogance.

ZOUAQ

Deep inside the medina, on the second floor of the Dar Si Said palace, there is a wedding chamber covered from floor to ceiling with zouaqs, floral and geometric motifs painted on Atlas cedar wood. In a corner of that chamber, on a small panel different from the ones surrounding it, a stylized engraving depicts a storyteller in the Jemaa, with his small son sitting next to him. Although the engraving, unique in being figurative, is more than a hundred years old, I like to think it portrays my father and me. It makes me smile: this immortalization in painted wood that somehow escaped the Islamic prohibition on images.

In the past, when I sat in the shadow of my father on his kilim, I would think about that engraving and try to remain perfectly still, feigning its immobility. Impressed by my ability to remain motionless, a woman in a veil once gave me five dirhams and a piece of sticky candy. My father frowned at the coin, clearly bothered by its unorthodox provenance.

He said: I believe in the immortality of wordcraft. I do not believe in subterfuge. Reality must never be confused with the purity of the imagination.

Perhaps providentially, in that same room in the Dar Si Said palace, a candlestand made of beads also took my fancy. It was handcrafted of the finest wire mesh, through which the beads were laced, as if trapped in amber. I fell in love with that candlestand the very first time I saw it. It was evening, the setting sun had cast a crimson wash across the distant mountain peaks, and through a stained glass window the dying light entered and sparked the candle. Every night thereafter I went to sleep dreaming about it. It was a calming empathy, a connective vibration that made me shiver every time I visualized it. I lay in bed with a smile of secret happiness.

One night my uncle Mohand asked me what I'd been dreaming about and burst out laughing when I told him.

Well, at least it's a harmless obsession, he said, unlike many others. He blew his breath out of his mouth. Inanimate objects don't bite back, he said, they don't harass you without cease. He glanced tiredly over his shoulders in the direction of my aunt, who was in the kitchen.

Give me your daydream, he said. I can use it.

Then he said: Beware of women. They are dangerous.

THE HÔTEL ALİ

But this woman was beautiful, Abdellah said with a sad smile, and I believed him. He glanced at me and I caught the gleam of wonder in his eyes.

Abdellah was a regular in my circle of listeners. He was a Berber from the Dadès Valley on the eastern slope of the Atlas Mountains. It was rumoured that he was the son of a qa'id, a tribal chief, who had fallen on hard times. Ever since I'd known him, he'd been working as a waiter at the popular Hôtel Ali, on the Rue Moulay Ismail, just off the Jemaa el Fna. My circle of listeners somehow never seemed complete until he joined it, his tall, stooped figure bestowing benediction on the proceedings.

Who're you talking about, Abdellah? a voice called out rudely.

Gentle Abdellah shut his eyes as if in recollection.

The two strangers on the square, he said in a soft voice. The two outsiders. She had blue eyes, golden hair. I dream of her still.

The same voice interjected quite irascibly:

I thought she had dark eyes, dark hair.

You were mistaken, Abdellah replied, with a candour that made the sincerity of his remarks believable. Her image is imprinted in my mind's eye. She was utterly and completely unforgettable.

He hesitated for an instant, his ears turning a bright shade of red, and then he went on: There is no reason for me to lie. I've just been diagnosed with cancer. I do not have much longer to live. But I will carry her memory with me to the grave.

There's no need to be such a fatalist, I said gently.

Abdellah smiled. Actually, he replied, I'm being quite realistic.

He coughed softly and, in that muffled sound, we could already sense the disease working its poisonous way through him. As if aware of our scrutiny, he lowered his head.

I am not the subject of the conversation here, he said awkwardly. Listen to my story. It is not without surprises.

With a quick gesture he pushed back the lock of hair that

dangled over his forehead. He stared past us at the square and his eyes widened as though he were plunging headlong into some dark vortex of memory. With his eyes still fixed on the square, he described to us his night in the Jemaa, adding detail to detail with the attention to minutiae that was characteristic of him.

I was working the night shift. It was exactly nine o'clock because the antique clock in the restaurant chimed the hours and I counted them off as always. Like the clock, most of the objects in the restaurant were from another era. The divans and the sofas were from the time of the Sultan Moulay Abdel Aziz, the saltshakers were rumoured to have belonged to the Pasha El Glaoui, the tiled floors and walls dated from the turn of the century, while the tajines and the teapots were from a mediaeval caravanserai in Mali.

It was warm inside. I had hung up my jacket on the clothes rack in the corridor and was waitering in my shirtsleeves. In his glass cubicle, my friend the accountant Idris was tallying the day's earnings. The cooks played cards in the kitchen while tending to the tajines. At some point in the evening, a chair tilted over and fell, making the sound of a bird quarrelling. And over everything there rose the usual sounds of a busy restaurant: the clatter of crockery, of cutlery, the muted conversation in many languages, the sidelong glances. The special for the night was fig soup. I ladled its warm, limpid essence into bowls over and over again for tourists.

The two strangers materialized as if from thin air. I'd looked away from the tables one moment and in the next they had made their appearance. The sounds of the restaurant died down instantly. Glances riveted. Shadows filled the room. Then the young woman moved towards me with a gliding movement.

We're exhausted, she murmured. May we have a quiet table?

From those very first words I knew that they were foreigners. Her voice was strangely accented, while his clothing and manners betrayed a more cosmopolitan background than ours.

I escorted them to the back room, dimmed the light, and moved the chairs without touching the floor. He sat down on the couch and closed his eyes. His features were refined and more than a bit weary, his beard neatly trimmed. I brought them water perfumed with orange flowers. She dissolved a white capsule in his glass and made him drink it. I watched attentively. It was as if the three of us were complicit in each other's movements.

Uncharacteristically bold, I asked them where they were from.

From far away, he said without interest.

He's from India, she said. I am half French, half American. This is our first time in the Jemaa.

What about Marrakesh?

Our first time here as well.

And Morocco?

The first, she said, and smiled. We've been walking around the medina the entire day. It's a good place to lose yourself.

I indicated his beard and asked him if he was Muslim.

He raised a hand to his heart but didn't say anything.

I'm a fan of Indian films, I volunteered, especially from the fifties and sixties. I love the actors and the singers. Geeta Dutt, Kishore Kumar, Lata Mangeshkar, Mohammed Rafi. There's a rare gentleness and innocence to them.

He nodded noncommittally but remained silent.

I hope you like it here, I said with feeling.

Making my way back to the main room, I searched among the cassette tapes until I found an old collection of songs by

Mohammed Rafi. Soon the words of a love song, a mournful tune full of longing and hope, filled the air.

When I went back to serve them, they were still sitting as I'd left them, lost in silence. He didn't seem interested in anything. All of a sudden he groaned and began kneading his forehead. She reached forward with concern and held his head in her hands. His right hand clutched her wrist. Gazing at him protectively, she whispered endearments and caressed his cheeks. It was a private moment, so I left them.

When I returned with their bill, she asked me when the drum circles would begin playing on the square. I cautioned her against going there this late at night.

But we must hear the drums, she replied. Her bright blue eyes were eager. We've heard all about the drummers who come here from distant places.

Oh yes, they come here from all over, from Niger, from Mali, from the Rif and the Atlas, the Sahara and the Sahel. They play gimbris, ghaitahs, ouds. Their drums ring through the night with a primal beat. But it isn't safe for you. There are pickpockets there and thieves and all manner of criminals. The men smoke kif and are often drunk, even though they are Muslim. They lose control. Things happen. I've heard stories.

I turned to him. Do not go there.

Don't take her there, I repeated.

I couldn't tell if he heard me. He seemed very distant. He got up from the table while she turned and looked at him for a long time and with a surprising intensity. We'll be careful, he said in a low voice, finally acknowledging my advice with a shrug.

She thanked me. I loved the food here, she said, especially the fig soup.

Come back in the daytime for our tanjia, I urged. Everyone in Marrakesh knows of our tanjia. It is world-famous.

She turned her face to the square.

I'm looking forward to hearing the tambourines, she said. It will be like a step back in time. I've waited a long time for this.

I had said enough. I made a resigned gesture of acceptance. He left me a ten-dirham tip.

She smiled and said farewell in Arabic.

Bessalama, she said, rendering her smile into another tongue.

I watched them leave with trepidation.

Treq salama, I thought to myself.

The oil lamp on their table had died down. There were a few lees at the bottom. One of the house cats jumped up on the table-top and began chasing a moth. I pushed her off, but she purred and rubbed herself against me. For some reason, that reminded me of my house: its solid wooden door, the security of its walls. Within such a house, one lives outside of time. Then I thought of the Jemaa and its wide-open tracts where, at any given moment, anything could happen.

That night I dreamt that the Jemaa was covered with snow. A layer of dazzling ice coated the surrounding rooftops and the entire landscape was crystalline. Stalactites hung down from the reed-mat roofs of the qaysarias; stalagmites climbed up from the zellij-tiled floors of the palaces. There was a glistening sheet of ice all the way from where the Palmeraie used to be to the slopes of the Atlas Mountains.

In a different dream, a wall of water swept across the Jemaa and devoured it.

JAMUR

They were married, a voice spoke up with authority. I can attest to that. She wore a wedding ring, though she lacked the assurance that comes to most women with marriage. The oddly trusting manner with which she followed her husband's every word was not the sign of an experienced woman. She was shy, as shy as the fire in a hollow in the sand. As to her appearance, I must disagree with Abdellah, whose integrity I otherwise respect: she was slender and of medium height, she had dark hair and dark eyes, though when the light caught her pupils they appeared a vivid green.

The speaker was Samir, a Berber merchant who was something of a celebrity in the Jemaa because his name, or rather, the name of his village, near Tinzouline, was in *The Guinness Book of World Records*. The story is a miracle of fate—and determination. It happened like this. A few years ago, in an attempt to draw attention to the plight of their centuries-old kasbahs, subject to relentless erosion by wind and sand, the villagers banded together and sculpted a record number of sand angels. Everyone in the community took part, from infants who could barely walk to ninety-year-old matriarchs. The reward was a mention in the world-famous book, a television documentary, and funds from the United Nations to restore the kasbahs and designate the village a World Heritage Site.

Samir claimed credit for the entire affair. He did not boast about it but simply stated it as an established fact. There being no one else from his village to dispute his claim, he was widely respected and admired in the Jemaa. Since then he had accomplished little but had nevertheless come to be regarded as a paragon of respectability, his deed inscribed in our people's ledger of achievements.

Against the word of such a venerated man, even Abdellah, the son of a qa'id, fell silent. Perhaps you are right, he muttered with downcast eyes. Perhaps she did have dark hair and dark eyes.

Memory can be deceptive, my friend, Samir said benevolently. His voice was full and suave, with something bland about it.

Memory is certainly a fickle mistress, I assented. The most honourable men have been known to be taken in sometimes. But tell us your story, Samir. Where did you encounter them?

Where else but in my jewellery store off the Souk El Kebir.

He paused for effect and surveyed us. On his face was the intense look that comes with trying to recall an event from a long time ago.

It was midafternoon, he said, around three o'clock, on what had been a slow day. I had hardly made any sales, and, resigned to fate, was just beginning to doze off.

So it was well before their appearance at the Hôtel Ali? I interrupted.

He spread the fingers of his right hand to indicate the rays of the sun.

Oh yes, it was in broad daylight. That's why I remember her clearly. There was a quality to her that was touched with light.

He turned to Abdellah with a magnanimous smile.

Perhaps that is what deceived you into believing that she had golden hair.

But I saw her in the darkness, not in daylight, Abdellah demurred.

A mere detail, Si Abdellah, Samir said with a laugh.

She entered my shop first, he went on, her face aglow with vitality, and it was as if my eyes distrusted my own sight. Come in, come in, I managed to say to them. Bonjour, ça va? There's no need to buy, you can just look around. What good fortune to have such a peri grace my humble portals. What will you accept for her? I joked with him. Ça coûte combien? I own a kasbah in El-Kelaa M'Gouna, on the eastern side of the mountains, with fine rooms, a stable, and baths. Or if that isn't good enough, I can take you to Imilchil, in the Middle Atlas Mountains, to the fabled marriage fair, where she will fetch you at least fifty camels. We can stay in my tent in the great valley between the two emerald lakes—Isli, "the fiancé," and Tisli, "the fiancée"—and celebrate her betrothal to some rich Berber qa'id in the grand style, with dances and feasts such as you have never experienced.

The young man merely smiled dryly and raised his companion's left hand so that I could see her wedding ring, which was rather plain, in my opinion, and unworthy of her beauty, but I kept my thoughts to myself because I sensed some defensiveness on his part.

Well then, I said, appropriately businesslike, what are you interested in, my friends? Everything is for sale here. I have amulets from Egypt, gold jewellery from Timbuktu, silver bracelets from Nubia, even this ancient and dazzling necklace from Sudan. Or you might consider these delicate earrings made by our very own artisans in the old Jewish quarter, or these Berber anklets with bells and chimes, good to wear both at home or outdoors, at all times.

She was less distant than him. She smiled at me and slowly walked the length of the shop, studying everything with an avid gaze. She held herself very straight. They did not look at each other. I lit a cigarette and let them take their time.

When she finally spoke, her voice was like soft laughter.

How much is this? she asked.

I followed her gesture. She was pointing to an amber amulet with a fragile gold scarab embedded inside.

You have exquisite taste, madame, I answered. That is from the Sahara, and it isn't too expensive. In fact, I will give it to you below cost because you have astonished my eyes. For you, and only for you, I will part with it for a mere seven hundred dirhams.

She turned to him. He smiled thinly and said: Seventy dirhams.

I bowed my head and knew the game was on. We went back and forth in the accepted manner. I cited my reputation as a Berber of the Aït Morghad tribe, whose honesty was legend; he feigned interest in a silver jebana, a long-necked coffee vessel, and examined a basket filled with trinkets.

You will bankrupt me, m'sieur, I said with dignity, and offered him a final price, which seemed to set him thinking.

Why spend such a long time pondering? I urged. It's barely a trifle for your beautiful bride. Even her smile is worth much more.

But he was already looking at something else, and with great attentiveness. After a while, he turned to her with an abrupt movement and spoke in a low voice. She raised her eyebrows, nodded, and glanced at me.

What is that object? she asked in French.

It is a jamur, madame, from a kasbah in a ksar—a fortified village—in the Drâa Valley, near Tinzouline, where I come from. It is an old piece and very precious. Jamurs are roof spikes, usually made of polished brass, like this one, and they consist of up to five globes of increasing size. They are sometimes surmounted, unlike this specimen, by our national emblem, the star inside the crescent. The most famous jamurs in Marrakesh are the ones atop the Koutoubia minaret.

They gazed at it for a long time, and then he said:

You could kill a man with it.

For once, I didn't know how to respond.

To my surprise, he took out his wallet, counted out a number of notes, and gave me the last price I had asked for the amber amulet.

What about the jamur? I asked, but he waved my query aside. It belongs to someone with a house, he replied, and not a rootless wanderer.

I said: In the Maghreb, we believe that the first thing one should own is a house, and it is the last thing one should sell, for it is our tomb this side of paradise.

And how is your house? he asked, echoing the traditional Maghrebi greeting.

I smiled in acknowledgement of his courtesy.

It is a good one, I replied. It is near here, behind the Mouassine Mosque.

She interrupted us and began to thank him for the amulet,

but he took her aside and said something in a quiet voice, which I couldn't catch.

You've overtired yourself today, she said with concern.

He addressed me directly: Can you suggest a good place to view the night sky?

Any of the rooftops of the medina should serve that purpose, I replied, once again taken aback.

He nodded gravely, as if I had imparted some necessary piece of information.

If you want to see the stars, I volunteered, I would recommend the terraces of one of the riads outside the medina, where there is less light from the souks and the streets, and you can observe the progress of the moon through the palm fronds.

You are a poet, he said, and smiled.

Encouraged, I went on: I have a friend who has such a riad, the Villa Quieta, near the Palmeraie. He is a good host and would be glad to put you up for the night.

But what of the Jemaa el Fna? he persisted.

I laughed. You can certainly see the sky from the Jemaa, but there will be much else to distract you there at night.

Then we will go to the Jemaa, he remarked.

Puzzled, I stared at him. Then I shrugged and said: I will think of you when I watch the moon tonight.

He went down on his knees to examine the jamur one last time, and then he stood up and shook my hand.

Do you think I may need this in the Jemaa tonight? he asked.

Only if you are attacked, I answered, and the chances of that are very slim. There's a police station right next to the square. They keep an eye on things.

They took their leave after that enigmatic exchange, and I found myself thinking, much like Abdellah, about my house, glad that I would be returning there that evening. I thought of the winter moon glistening on the asbestos rooftop, its bluish-white evanescence entering the rooms one by one, and I sensed that I would see the night in a new way as a result of this encounter.

Samir paused and drew the plume of his jellaba contemplatively through his stubby fingers.

Of course, he said, the moon wasn't bluish-white that night. There was nothing calming about it. It was crimson, bloodshot like an eye, and it filled me with disquiet.

THE ROYAL TRUTH

He sighed and looked at the sky, where the moon hung low over the horizon, solitary and majestic. His face was both pensive and shadowed with regret; the remembrance seemed to have cast a pall over his features.

He turned and gazed at me questioningly for some moments.

I straightened up. It is certainly safe inside a house, I agreed, but safer inside a story where everything connects, which is more than can be said of our story, where we cannot even seem to agree upon the most basic elements, such as what the two wanderers looked like. Perhaps it is because in retelling our various encounters, each one of us is intent on honesty, as well as the absolute commitment to memory that inspires what we storytellers, with our voracious appetite for physical detail, call the imagination. And so it transpires that even as we free ourselves from the bondage of time, we deliver ourselves into ever more subtle bonds of our own making. But then again, to rephrase a question I asked earlier, what is the truth? Do we speak the truth, or do various, often incompatible versions of the truth speak us? Especially here, in the Jemaa, where what matters at any given moment is only that which is most significant. That which holds the attention. That which convinces. Now, and for the next several hours or years. That which is beautiful, above all, and forged of love, because truth is beauty's sister. Like the luminous young woman and her dark and taciturn companion, truth and beauty redeem each other.

DATURA

Now a new voice made itself heard:

I have always wondered what the Angel of Death would look like if he were to show himself, if he were to manifest an earthly form. Would he, for instance, resemble that Indian, with his cold, hard profile, his wheat complexion, impossibly straight nose, and cloaked eyes? Would he, by some whim of character, reveal himself one day in the heart of an old Muslim medina, accompanying a young woman he had doomed to early extinction? How many of us can verify that he indeed existed, that she was not alone, that the person we saw beside her was nothing but our own fear of mortality when faced with beauty the like of which we had never seen? Indeed, how many of us would have the courage to confess that, driven by the small-mindedness and avarice intrinsic to man, we desired to possess her and, knowing that we could not, conjured up a dark companion who was forbiddingly silent, like the blind walls that surround our houses and render them more tomb than shelter?

These are my questions to you, because I too was unfortunate enough to witness her beauty, albeit fleetingly, and surprised myself with feelings I had not known existed in me, feelings that shaded into sadness once the moment was over, for much in the manner of the Tuareg youth in the tale of the scarlet ibis, I knew that my age of innocence was over.

My one-legged nephew Brahim, who spoke these grave and melancholic words, was a custodian at the Ali ben Youssef Medersa, which lay adjacent to the souks. Brahim was something of a prodigy. He was renowned in our family for his calligraphy, on which he spent many hours each day, a feat made remarkable by the fact that he was afflicted by a disease that made his hands tremble ceaselessly. He was a familiar figure in my afternoon circle, his quavery, bookish contributions lending credibility to my stories. In the sound of his voice I heard the polyphonous music of the medersa, its many melodies, and it reassured me, for it was as if my humble calling had divine blessings.

Brahim's most precious possession was the camelskin journal in which he recorded, in the most minute script, the gradual perfection of his calligraphy. Once I asked him what he would do when he reached the end of the journal. He answered that he intended that moment to coincide with the zenith of his art.

And then? I'd persisted. What would follow thereafter?

His eyes had taken on a dreamlike aspect.

I would like to commence building my house, he'd answered. I would cover its walls with writing. It would be a house of poetry, with the finest inscriptions at the highest levels, so that the eye would perforce have to raise itself as if to contemplate the sky.

And when this house was completed and the walls entirely covered with inscriptions?

His laughing eyes had regarded me indulgently.

Why, Uncle, then my life would have come to its natural end. I would have met my fate, and with gladness welcomed the termination of this mortal coil.

So it was that I asked Brahim now:

Tell us about your encounter with the two strangers. Tell us how your loss of innocence came to transpire.

Brahim did not take long to respond to my query. But he did not answer it directly, which was contrary to his usual manner. Instead, he heaved a sigh, shrugged his shoulders as if to rid himself of a burden, and said:

Some would contend that beauty contains a poison seed, that it contaminates everything with which it comes into contact. I do not believe that to be the case because beauty, as you have pointed out, Hassan, is akin to truth, and truth is energy, and energy is always in motion. So even as I rue the day I glimpsed her, I feel that beauty is neither completely good nor evil; rather, as beholders, we respond to it in different ways because we are each in different stages of life.

He paused, and his face took on an indefinable cast of sadness.

As some of you may know, apart from my religious studies

and my calligraphy, I tend to the narrow strip of garden between our mosque and the medersa. There is something common to flowers and calligraphy: they speak the same language. To seek inspiration, I study the rose and jasmine bushes, the oranges, the bamboos, and the figs. But my favourites are the datura. The luminosity of these nightshades have always astonished me. They look translucent, as if shaped out of moonlight. Every moment that I spend with them is a moment spent meditating upon my art, and I like to think of that garden as bearing the charm of the eternal paradise depicted in the Qur'an. It is there that I find the most peace.

A space of silence followed. His hands resting on his lap, his face turned away from us, Brahim gazed pensively at the square. Then, speaking in a level, restrained tone, he said: And so it was that on the morning of the day that concerns us, I was tending a datura sapling when I looked up and found myself gazing at a slender young woman drinking from the fountain at the edge of the garden. She was dressed in traditional garb: black headscarf, ochre jellaba, brown seroual. Had it not been for her red-bearded companion, I would not have known that they were foreigners.

He had a red beard? I interjected, for this was a significant detail.

Brahim looked at me at length. His eyes were thoughtful.

There are some things which, by their tone or their tint, leave a lasting impress, he said. The man was wheat-complexioned, or, one might say, his skin was the colour of sand—but his beard was the hue of saffron.

The hue of saffron, I said with a smile. That's easy enough to remember.

With a familiar gesture, Brahim passed his hand over his head. I waited for him to continue. Staring straight ahead, he said: It was many years ago, Hassan. The details are unimportant as long as I remember the essence.

Of course, I hastened to agree with him, for I wanted to hear everything that he had to say. Please continue, I prompted.

He moistened his lips. Gazing into space and speaking softly, his brow furrowed yet strangely serene, he recaptured the moment for us.

At first, I could only see her profile, he said, as she bent over to drink from the fountain. Facing downward, she was an image of serenity suitable for meditating upon. I gazed at her as I would at an inverted waterfall, I savoured the aromas of the garden that surrounded me, and I felt suffused with happiness. It was a joyful paralysis, like a siren's song, to which the flowers themselves seemed to respond, rising out of the dark soil with shining heads of light. I don't know how long the moment lasted, but I basked in its radiance.

He shook his head and coughed, and when he spoke again, his voice had changed perceptibly. It was thicker and choked with darkness.

Sometimes the world transforms in an instant, he said.

Listen to this, he said. We are still at the fountain. The woman is drinking like a gazelle, her lips are moist with water, the folds of her headscarf flecked with beads of spray.

He stood up and bent over to show us what he meant. We watched, intent. Suddenly he swung round. Stifling a sigh, he said: When she had drunk her fill, she straightened and turned in my direction, and I was dumbstruck by what I saw. For an instant, all sights and sounds disappeared. I felt myself plunge into an abyss, and when I emerged from my daze, I was appalled, for I realized that her beauty had, quite simply, turned my world upside down. It eclipsed anything I had ever seen or done, and the very essence of my soul, the source of my being, my lifelong love for my art—those countless hours spent contemplating the abstract perfection of calligraphy—would forever be overshadowed by this contact with the world. I felt broken.

Drawn to her as if by some outward force, I left the garden. My wooden leg knocked on the cobblestones of the street, but my shoulders had grown wings. My heart raced, my breath quickened. I flew towards her. But as I did, I saw her bend towards her bearded companion and I heard him say: I love you. Then he smiled and walked away, leaving her alone in my presence.

Overcome with tenderness and despair, I shouted: My dear! What jinn has brought you here? You have ruined me forever!

Startled, she swivelled her neck, exactly like a gazelle, and gazed in my direction. Her headscarf slid off, her brown hair glinted with gold. Trembling wildly, I raised my hands. I wanted to caress her face. What have you done? I yelled. That man is not worthy of you. Anyone who places the "I" before the "you" in speaking of love is misbegotten and cancels the intent of his words. Ah, you who are mesmerized! The self can never precede the object of its affections! That isn't love, it is self-love. Do you understand? I would say to you instead: You I love! You I love! You I love! But not "I love you." Never "I love you." My angel!

Mistaking my intent, she backed away with a look of alarm. Her eyes widened, her cheeks drained of colour. With a terrified cry, she broke into a run. I tried to chase after her, but, of course, she was faster than I was, with my single leg, and, even as I reached the fountain, she had turned the corner and disappeared from my sight. I rushed past the fountain and looked down the long expanse of the mosque, but she was nowhere to be seen. She must have run into one of the many narrow alleyways that riddle the medina.

I was crestfallen. I felt abandoned by fate. A burning sun coursed through my veins and, parched, I drank from the same fountain from which, moments earlier, she had refreshed herself. But the water did nothing to cool the burning inside me. It was a weak palliative, nothing more. Overcome by despair, I slumped beside the fountain.

When I looked up again, Red Beard was standing there. He was magnificent in his indifference: implacable and cold. He gazed down at me, but in his closed mouth I read neither empathy nor kindness. We stared at each other, his heavy-lidded eyes almost drowsy, until, intimidated by his immobility, I cast my glance down. I sensed him make a move and raised my hands to protect my face. A coin clattered beside me. I watched it roll into the gutter of the fountain. His footsteps receded.

Such is the overwhelming power of love that, despite my humiliation at being mistaken for a beggar, I decided to follow him, hoping he would lead me to her.

He crossed a storefront with a mirror leaning against a chair. I glanced at the mirror just as he walked past it. He was not reflected in it. It was a large mirror; I had ample time to check.

Astonished, I glanced back at him, but he had vanished. One moment he was there, the next moment there was only the semblance of a shadow, and then even that disappeared. I felt as if I had nothing to hold on to, as if reality meant nothing.

Brahim smiled sadly and turned his face away.

Sometimes when I sit in my cramped room and reflect back

on that day, fear overtakes me. I try to put it out with good thoughts. I do aimless things. I avoid the garden. I ask for forgetfulness. I call it resistance to death.

But that fear—it is red, like fire. It burns like pitch.

I can't put it out.

He said this very loudly. He stomped the ground with his peg leg. His fear was real. We looked away.

He smiled again, his despair palpable.

All of this is in my journal, he said, addressing me. How unfair is it that that which took days to write is recounted in a few seconds? And even then, it feels so incomplete, such an approximation of the real thing.

Before I could respond, he added:

But then again, isn't that true of life itself?

Isn't it? he repeated, staring pleadingly in my direction as if seeking reassurance. Then, abruptly, his gaze turned inward. His voice dropped until we could barely hear him. For a while there was nothing but a secretive whispering. Once or twice he appeared about to speak, but nothing came of it. Finally, just as I was about to intervene, he opened his mouth wide as if to suck in air. We stared at that yawning mouth, fascinated. It was as if the entirety of the Jemaa was contained in its chasm.

He wiped his lips with the back of his hand.

With a slightly defiant smile, he said:

That night, when I heard about her disappearance, I was glad. It was as if the equilibrium of my life had been restored. I threw the windows of my room wide open and let in the fresh air. I heard the sound of many drums. I heard the clamour of police cars from the square. I decided to go down to my sanctuary, the garden. I watched a pack of stray dogs fight over a bone near the fountain. I fell asleep under a datura bush. What else is there to say? I could return to my art with relief again.

That is my confession.

Khadija

The child must have come to me shortly after your encounter with her. She was pale and shaking like a leaf, the poor thing. You must have terrified her with your attentions. How can you know what it means to be a woman and to have to deal with the likes of you? You ought to be ashamed of yourself!

For the first time that evening, we heard a female voice, and it was stentorian. It belonged to the formidable Khadija, one of the oldest of the Jemaa's immense and enigmatic clan of fortune-tellers. She spoke bitingly, and it was clear that she viewed my nephew's rather provocative "confession" with grave disapprobation. To his credit, Brahim made no reply, but, subjected to her withering stare, he shrivelled.

Khadija was a Sanhaja Berber from the Western Sahara, from the region known as Saquiat Al-Hamra, the Red Canal, on account of the waterway that traverses it, even though it is dry for much of the year. It is also known as the Land of the Saints, a nomadic place of pilgrimage long reputed for its piety and learning. Khadija herself claimed direct descent from the Almoravid warrior monks of Audaghost, now a bleak ruin in the Chinguetti hinterlands, but once the fortress city from where they'd poured out and conquered the known world and founded Marrakesh. She was widely respected, even feared, and it was rumoured that she could alter a person's future with her predictions.

No one knew how she had come to be in the Jemaa. As far as we could tell, she had always been there. Some claimed that she was ageless, that she had been around during the time of the notoriously decadent Pasha of Marrakesh, T'hami El Glaoui, or perhaps even further back in time, more than a hundred years ago, when the profligate Sultans Moulay Hassan and Moulay Abdel Aziz had presided over the declining empire. What was without question was that no one doubted her great age. One sensed under the folds of her cloak the resilience of an ancient tree bole.

In the daytime, she could be found in the cramped square of the Rahba Kedima, in the shadow of the apothecaries' stalls, where she did a brisk trade selling herbal and animal potions for black magic and reading the callused palms of itinerant wool and sheep merchants.

At night, she relocated to the Jemaa el Fna, where she was known for taking out her glass eye before she commenced each session of fortune-telling. Some said it was the right eye that was made of glass; others insisted that it was the left and sought to prove their point by discoursing upon its steely glitter which they maintained was the hallmark of the finest flint glass. Perhaps both of her eyes were glass, perhaps neither. Either way, it lent her an allure that was part of the mythology of the Jemaa. Like everyone else, I was in awe of her mantic abilities, and I think she looked upon my storytelling endeavors with indulgence, having known both my father and my grandfather in their prime.

Now, having summarily vanquished poor Brahim, she surveyed my predominantly male audience with a jaundiced eye.
We glanced away, blushed, and faithfully intimated contrition.

The poor child was terrified, she repeated with emphasis. She
was shaking like a leaf, and I made her sit down. I drew her into
the shade of my tent, offered her water infused with the essence
of rose, and spoke to her in soothing tones. When I sensed that
she felt more composed, I offered to read her palm, more as a
distraction than anything else. She agreed and asked me where
I was from.

I am from the desert, I replied. From the land known as
Saquiat El-Hamra, where the dunes are fathomless, like the
depths of the ocean. There the sands wash over caravans as
water over a raft.

And you? Where are you from? I asked.

I am a child of the plains, she answered modestly. I have never
had my palm read before. This is my first time in Marrakesh.

Then welcome. Everyone is welcome here. People come to
Marrakesh from all over the world, they are happy, and they
never want to leave. Many buy houses in the medina. Or they
wander into the desert and disappear. By the grace of God, I
myself have read the palms of the citizens of one hundred and
fifty-six countries. When I reach the magic figure, I will retire.

What is the magic figure? she asked.

I laughed. It is the total number of countries in the United
Nations. Both democracies and dictatorships. Both infidels and
believers. When I reach that magic number, which is one hundred and ninety-two, I will fold my tent and return to my desert
home. But until that time, there are many palms waiting to be

read, many fortunes to be made and unmade, much happiness and unhappiness to be deciphered and, perhaps, resolved.

She looked concerned. But there are one hundred and ninety-four countries in the world, she said. Why discriminate against the two that are not members of the United Nations?

I was aghast. Are you sure, my child? I asked.

Yes, I am quite certain. If you stick to your magic number, then you will have omitted both Taiwan and the Vatican.

Bismillah ir-Rahman ir-Rahim! I exclaimed. In the name of God most Gracious, most Compassionate, you have added to my burden, my child. Two more nations! Inshallah, God willing, it shall be so.

I am sorry, she said, but I did not want the omissions to burden your conscience.

Her concern moved me. I reached forward and patted her hand. I said: There is no need for contrition. Please excuse the ignorance of an old Sahrawi woman. I was measuring my days against a false benchmark. Now, thanks to you, my mind is at rest. True knowledge adds to certainty, and certainty brings peace. You are a messenger of light, and for this I will not accept money from you to read your fortune.

Blushing a little, she demurely held out her hand.

I took out my glass eye. I made her palm flat. As always, that gently undulating plain at first seemed impossibly vast. I stroked her wrist with my fingertips. Her pulse began to quicken. The noise of the world died down.

Between her lifeline and her heartline, I noticed a fig tree, a lodestone, and an armed galleon with many sails. Also a winged shadow flying over a desert filled with prickly pears.

These were difficult signs, so I decided to put her hand aside and interpret her zodiac first. I asked her for the usual details: her date of birth, her birthplace, and the hour of her birth. She was born under the sign of the crab. I noted the rest of her responses. Then I listed her attributes one by one.

Your ascendant is in Sagittarius, I began. This means that you are outgoing, brave, you like to travel, and have an aptitude for poetry.

Your Jupiter is in the fifth house. This means that, like the desert lizard that lives under the sand, you are fond of children, family-oriented, and faithful to your tribe.

Your Jupiter is in Taurus. This means that, like the purest Arabian thoroughbred mare, grace is manifest in your life, you attract wealth, you are accustomed to comfort, and you thrive in prosperous company.

Your Sun, Mercury, and Venus are in the seventh house, all signs that, like the heavenly birds that reside in paradise, life is not complete for you without a partner.

Your Sun and Venus reside in Cancer, which indicates that, like the stork that nests atop the minaret, domestic life is key to your happiness, and you need its welfare and security.

Your Mercury is in Gemini, which means that, like the arrow of pollen that travels great distances, you are intelligent, curious, and communicate with an ease that is lighter than air.

Your Moon is in the eighth house and in Leo, a sign that, like the fire that surges forth and fills the hearth, you are a creature of intense emotions. Impulsive, proud, and dramatic, you love being admired and place yourself in situations where you are the centre of attention.

I concluded by telling her that she was energetic, possessed great willpower and creativity, and that she was a confident and ardent lover who easily captured men's hearts. At the same time, she was very sensitive about how she appeared to others. She was frank, disliked dissembling, and preferred to be transparent in her behaviour, but she often tended to discount the environment and came across as being indiscreet. Stubborn, willful, and independent, she appreciated living life simply and in a straightforward manner, she demanded the freedom to do as she chose, and considered social niceties to be hindrances to communication.

With that, I put away my notes, indicating that I was finished. But she smiled shyly and extended her hand to me, palm upward, as a reminder that I had avoided telling her fortune.

I was reluctant, but a promise made is a promise that must be kept. I spread out her palm again and, ignoring the other signs, decided to single out the winged shadow because it was this, more than anything else, that troubled me.

This is the sign of Saturn, I said, and you must beware of it. Darkness has fallen on you. For the next few days, avoid the night. Try not to walk on black earth or dark sand. Stay away from surfaces that reflect the light of the moon. Avoid mirrors bleached by the sun. Do not trust anyone, prefer safe roads, and keep a watchful eye on your surroundings.

With that admittedly terse dispatch, I let go of her hand.

She blanched, and her eyes grew wide with distress.

I sought to reassure her, without making light of my warnings.

You have just had a frightening encounter, I said gravely, but you were able to escape it. I don't know why, but you've been

chosen to walk through fire—the signs are here, and here—and
if your foot slips again, there is a danger that you will lose your
life.

With that sombre pronouncement, Khadija made a sign in
the air to indicate that she had finished speaking. We recalled
her omens with wonder and speculated upon the meaning of the
ones that remained unexplained: the fig tree, the lodestone, and
the galleon. But we knew better than to ask.

Azziza

A black motorcycle pulled up just then at the edge of our circle. It was driven by a tall man clad entirely in black, his leather
jacket held together by knotted strands of camel hair. There was
an air of authority to him but also an unmistakable sense of
menace. He parked his machine and seemed content to look on
in silence.

In the meantime, encouraged by Khadija's bold intercession,
a beggar woman now stepped out of the circle. She wore a veil
so that only her eyes showed. She thrust her young daughter
forward. Have pity on my child, she pleaded. She has leprosy.
Her father cast us into the streets, and now we have no succour
but to trust in your beneficence. Have mercy on us, please, my
brothers and my sisters. I am a respectable woman forced from
my house into the night.

I stood up and walked over to her side.

Don't worry, I said quietly. Your needs will be met here.

I addressed my listeners: Give her your money instead of giving it to me. Tonight the rules are different. Tonight I will not accept any money for this story.

The man on the motorcycle grimaced and gunned his engine.

Sentimentalist, he said.

You are not welcome here, I replied.

He smiled without humour, but he did not leave.

I passed the collection plate around. When it came back to me, I handed the proceeds to the beggar woman without a word.

She began to thank me brokenly when Khadija interrupted her.

Tell them about your dream, she commanded.

The beggar woman started and gazed at Khadija in fear.

How do you know about my dream? she asked faintly.

Because I am Khadija, and I know everything, the redoubtable fortune-teller answered.

But I don't think it is pertinent! I don't even remember it clearly.

It does not matter what you think. That dream was not addressed to you. You are not in a position to judge its pertinence.

The beggar woman turned to me for help.

Although this same night that surrounds us is the sky over my dream, she said, it has no place here. It has nothing to do with the disappearance that is the basis for your story. It is not even meaningful.

In reply, I asked her what her name was.

I am Azziza, and my daughter is called Aisha. My father, Abolaziz Belkassem, is a respectable potter in Safi.

I smiled at her reassuringly.

Then you may speak, Azziza, and tell us about your dream. Perhaps it will come into my story. Perhaps my story will go on without it. It does not matter. We will not look to your dream for illumination. Nor will we scour its darkness for meaning.

Now speak, Khadija said.

THE TEN THOUSAND HORSEMEN

Azziza leaned on her daughter's shoulder for support. She closed her eyes and composed herself. Throughout her narration, she would keep her eyes closed, as if to better recall the dream.

It was a night when the moon was very bright, she began nervously. Nights like that are easy to remember. They hold the darkness at bay. We had taken refuge deep in the heart of the souks, under the shadow of a storefront awning. Aisha was fast asleep beside me. The moon cast its beams through the slatted rooftop trellises. It reflected the passage of clouds on our blankets. The awning shone like white stone. It was quiet in the galleries.

Azziza paused for breath, and when she spoke again, her voice had gained in strength.

That day Aisha had adopted a puppy. At first I tried to prevent her from keeping it. Then I realized how much it meant to her. It was only a few weeks old. It was helpless, a wisp of a thing. Aisha slept with it pressed to her breast.

She made a gesture with her hands to show us how her daughter slept. She was about to go on when she was interrupted. Enough of this nonsense about puppies! a man called out brusquely. What about your dream?

Azziza flinched, her fragile confidence shattered.

My dream was simple, my master, she said falteringly. Biting her lips, she turned to me. Do you want me to continue?

Don't mind the hecklers, I said, just carry on speaking.

Where was I? I'm sorry, but I've forgotten . . .

You were in the souk with Aisha, I said encouragingly.

Perhaps I should go directly to the dream? she ventured, and paused, waiting for my assent. Then she said: What can I tell you, my masters? It was as if I had just woken from sleep. I was no longer in the souk, but in the middle of the Jemaa. I was alone; Aisha was no longer with me. I saw the Jemaa as a moonlit field. A vast silence cloaked everything. Never before had the medina appeared so empty. It was as if all life had drained out of it.

Filled with unease, I began to cross the square slowly. I sought the familiar shelter of the souks, but when I was less than a hundred paces away, a line of gravediggers walked out into the open. Clods of dirt fell from their shovels. One or two of them kicked at the clods and spat, but no sound escaped their lips and no one acknowledged my presence. Terrified, I watched as they filed past towards the tombs of the Saadi kings, my fear rendering me incapable of movement.

An eternity later, ten thousand horsemen entered the Jemaa. They came from the direction of the palace of Ahmed the Victorious. They were fearsome and magnificent, their flags filled with shadows, their armour shining like scales. I watched as they

began to circle the Jemaa, at first trotting with great deliberation, then whipping their steeds to a frenzied pace until all that
could be seen was a moving, glinting wall of black and steel.

One by one, they began to shoot arrows into the air. The
arrows caught fire, they arched through the night like torches,
and one of them pierced my chest. My eyesight blurred, and
the Jemaa seemed to bend and curl out from beneath me in the
shape of a woman. She was beautiful and imperious, with large
black eyes that were lined with kohl, and a crown of desert
winds. She rose into the air and walked away, and when I called
out to her for help, she turned and put her fingers through my
eyes and blinded me. I knew then that she was a jinn, an evil
spirit. I woke from my dream with my fear choking me like a
noose.

Azziza took a deep breath and adjusted the folds of her burnous with a shaky hand. She ran her eyes up and down the
square before speaking again, her voice almost inaudible under
the burden of her recollections.

Oh, my masters, only a couple of days later, I dreamt about
those horsemen again! I dreamt that I was back in the Jemaa
seeing those terrifying soldiers rise into the air, the strangest
of sights! From the darkness of the square my eyes followed
them as they rode through the sky, their standards streaming
behind them. They straddled the horizon like mountains. I kept
up with them until they came to a bridge between two banks
of clouds, and that was when I knew I would have to lower my
eyes and leave them to their crossing. I was glad for them, for
who amongst us would not have liked to be in their place, on the
threshold of paradise?

Azziza paused again, and I could not tell if she had finished or there was more to come. With her eyes closed and her head slightly raised, she stood alone in the centre of the circle and we had the impression that she had become one with her dream.

Finally, she opened her eyes.

That is all I have to tell you, she said, her voice trembling with emotion. I hope I have not disappointed you, my masters and mistresses.

It was Khadija who broke the silence.

On the contrary, child, she said in her deep and sonorous voice, you were able to convey the shape of your dream, its texture, its scenes, and its manifold branches quite perfectly.

Azziza lowered her head and I sensed her smile sadly beneath her veil. I gazed at her demure form, covered from head to toe, and was moved to rise to my feet and greet her as an equal.

You narrated your dream beautifully, I said. You led us through that most difficult night, that most difficult dream, with grace and dignity. You did well.

She should take your place, Hassan, someone quipped.

Indeed, she should, I replied with a smile.

Azziza raised her hand to her head in a gesture of remorse.

But I wasn't there the night the foreigners disappeared, she said.

I was not there that night, she repeated. I still had a life, a house, a husband, a small garden. I was not forced to seek shelter from the night. That night I was not in the square.

But I was, a man's voice said.

HENDRIX

I was there that night. I was on the square.

We turned to the speaker. He was a Gnaoua musician, his bright white finery stark against the night, his drum slung across his shoulder and resting against his waist. Sitting very still, he cut a flamboyant figure in that setting, pride in every line of his bearing. His drum seemed an intrinsic part of him: he caressed its head as if to glean from it secret meanings only he could sense.

He raised his dark visage so that it merged with the night.

My name is Bilal, he said. I was one of those drumming that evening, but I did not see her, and I did not see him, and yet I dreamt about her a few days after her disappearance. I do not know why I was visited with that dream. It has left me with all sorts of questions.

He laughed, showing brilliant teeth.

I am a simple man, he said. I like the simple things in life. I am not like you. I do not like difficult questions. I play music for a living because it makes me happy. I like to be happy, so the music plays me. My group comes here every year from Amizmiz. There we practice all year round in a large orchard attached to a fondouk. It is the only green space in our arid township. We play and we play, we play our hearts out, we play ourselves into a sweat, and we are happy. We believe that there is no meaning in life other than this happiness. It banishes the heat, makes the hours quiver, and sets everyone's feet dancing.

He raised his callused hands.

One day I would like to play with that man Hendrix, who

was here many years ago, and I have heard still visits occasionally. I would like to greet him as my brother and accompany his
guitar with my deff. We will have a good time. There will be no
secrets between us. He will go away filled with joy. Of this I am
convinced.

He laughed again and regarded me wistfully.

But that is an altogether different matter from my dream. And
it is the dream that is like a bird in my head. I cannot get it out,
and I would like to get it out. I would like that very much indeed
because, until I do, it is getting in the way of my music.

He drummed out a quick tattoo on his deff.

But what do you want from me? I said.

He rested the drum on his knees and reflected for a moment.
His head was bowed, his eyes on the ground. Suddenly, with
a gentle, boyish smile, he spread his hands wide. Only this, he
said, an answer to a question. How is it possible to feel nostalgia
for a woman I never met?

I gazed bemusedly at him. There was something appealing in
the naïveté with which he'd asked his question.

What we think in life echoes in our dreams, I said.

But I didn't even know her!

You knew of her. Men talked about her, and incessantly. The
entire city was abuzz with the news of her disappearance. The
legend was enough to send your mind spinning. So one night
you dreamt about her. It's as simple as that.

Is that why dreams are the last things to die in a body?

They are roads only, I answered. Signposts to be deciphered.

Then where did my dream take me? Where did that road
lead? Tell me, because I understand nothing.

I cannot tell you unless I know what you dreamt.

He did not answer. Instead, he turned to two of his fellow musicians who had joined our circle and said: Brothers, we should start a fire because the night is turning cold.

They had wood with them. We started a fire.

Bilal opened his shoulders to receive its warmth.

Beyond him, all over the square, companion fires were springing up. Their winking luminescence mirrored the stars. Only the lightest veil of woodsmoke separated the Jemaa from the sky.

With a weary sigh, Bilal propped his head in his hands and gazed at the fire. Where I'm from the spirit of the desert is everywhere, he said. It is our father and our mother. It permeates everything. It laps at our feet like the ocean. Its dust colours our breath.

He took off his sandals and held them to the fire. They were warped by the desert sun, creased by its sands.

In my dream I was travelling from Tetouan to the camel souk in Goulimine, he said. I do not know why I was bound for Goulimine; I have no interest in camels. And I have never been to Tetouan. But such is the logic of dreams. I was part of a slave caravan. We were traversing endless dunes, following timeworn trails, journeying from oasis to oasis. I had no music with me; a chain bound me by my neck to my companions. If I felt the frequent lashes on my back, I said nothing. The hunger and the thirst that filled my being made all other feelings redundant. Above the closed sack of days only the hope of a quick death sustained me in that hell.

One night our caravan stopped beside a red wadi; the horses and camels were browsing in its shadowy depths. The wind blew across the sand and I knew, from its damp fragrance, that we were not too distant from the ocean. When the first drops of rain struck my back, I didn't know what was happening. I had never known rain. I curled up like a terrified animal. I thought the raindrops were whiplashes. But as my hair and clothes began to get drenched, I felt a strange and delirious happiness. I burst into laughter. It was as if I had died and ascended to heaven.

Moments later—how many moments?—I felt her hands drumming on my back. I tensed and tried to get up, but her weight rested on my hips and made movement impossible. One, two, three—One, two, three, four—I began to breathe in time to her rhythms. She was good, her hands lightly leaping from shoulder to shoulder as she played with practiced ease, using the heels of her hands and her fingertips. And, all the while, she planted shapes on my back—large, wet bouquets of geraniums, showers of lilies, moist almond blossoms such as those that grace the most exquisite gardens. In the depths of that wintry desert, spring rain!

Soon I was running with that rain on my back. She urged me on with small, sharp cries. My happiness lent me wings. I covered great distances. Behind me, time had stopped; before me, I glimpsed the ocean of eternity. The desert sped by in clouds of dust, then fell away. I shouted out in triumph. Her drumming hands had released me from my enslavement.

He lowered his dark eyes. We waited in suspense.

And then I woke up, he said.

An audible sigh of disappointment went up from our circle.

He shrugged, disconcerted by our reaction.

What can I say? I felt as you did. My heart felt lighter than my head. My back was still vibrating. I sprang out from my bed. There was an owl hooting outside my window. It described frantic circles in the air. I watched it for a while, and then I turned away. The sudden end of my dream was painful. I would have liked to have at least said farewell.

From the edge of the circle, my nephew Brahim spoke up, with more than a trace of jealousy in his voice.

Did she say anything to you at all? he asked.

Only this. Right at the end. She said: Enviably, this is the way.

I asked, very gently: How did you know her identity?

Oh, I knew who she was, he said. Dreams are like that.

Then I must disappoint you, I said. I don't know what your dream signifies. At the most elemental level, I could tell you that women represent the forces of life. But apart from that, your dream is beyond my capacity to interpret.

He took off his cap and fanned himself. He gazed at us one by one and pursed his lips when no one offered to help.

Is that it? he asked, and his tone was heavy.

That is it, I said.

Then why did I dream about her? he asked insistently. Why did she visit me even though I wasn't one of those she'd met? I was there that night, he repeated, performing on the square. I remember the crimson moon, the long black limousine, the evening's haze. The police were out in force. There were rumours of a visiting Arab sheikh. But I did not know who she was. And I did not see her on the square.

But I did, a man's voice interjected.

I was on the square that night, and I met her there.

CASABLANCA

The speaker was a slim young man in a threadbare suit. He wore a red rose in his buttonhole and a cheap wool scarf around his neck. His tone was cool and fastidious.

I saw them both, he said. In fact, I spent some time with them.

He surveyed us with an air of triumph, pausing to let us digest his words. We did not know how to react, so we maintained an impassive silence. I wondered where he'd come from. I could not recall ever having seen him on the square.

Have you seen the movie *Casablanca*? he asked. They were like the stars of that movie, Humphrey Bogart and Ingrid Bergman, only younger. He was smart, in a brown suit and fedora; she wore a lightweight plaid coat over a knee-length red dress. I wouldn't call her beautiful, but she was certainly arresting. Her features were delicate but vigorous. She had long arms and legs. She let him do all the talking. She seemed withdrawn, but contented.

How do you know so much about them? someone asked.

It's quite simple, really. I had the pleasure of painting her portrait. He commissioned me. And paid what I asked for. It was a privilege.

I took him in at a glance.

Where are you from, I asked. And what is your name?

He was silent for a moment; he flicked off a fly that had alighted on his forehead, then answered: My name is Taoufiq. I am an art student from Tangier. I come here from time to time because it amuses me to set up on the square. I'm not in it for the money. I only paint portraits.

Someone behind me muttered mockingly in Tashilhait, our local Berber tongue: Pretentious bastard. *Casablanca* wasn't even filmed in Morocco but in a Hollywood back lot.

That raised a laugh, but I was curious to hear the art student's story, so I gestured to him to get on with it.

He lit a cigarette, adjusted his scarf, examined his fingernails. With a quick, rather contemptuous smile, he flicked a glance across our circle. Oh, I don't know if I should bother with this lot, he said. I should probably just leave.

Barakalaufik, the same voice behind me whispered in Tashilhait. Thank you kindly, and good riddance.

I suppressed a smile. Instead, in a preceptorial tone, I said: Either tell us what's on your mind, or leave. The choice is up to you. But don't take all night thinking about it.

So that's how things are, he said. I should have known better than to open my mouth. Your rules are ridiculous. I'm not going to stay and be insulted.

Indeed? I said. Very well then. Have it your way.

He took out a large handkerchief and blew his nose. To my surprise, I saw his eyes filling with tears. He fussed with his cigarette, but made no move to leave, just as I'd anticipated.

I spread my hands in a conciliatory gesture.

I have no desire to humiliate you, I said. That is not the way we do things here. If you have something to tell us, please go ahead.

Clearing his throat, he remarked brusquely: All right, I'll tell you, if only to honour their memory, given that everything else that I've heard here has been nothing more than abject fantasy and wish-fulfilment. You want the truth, don't you? I'll give it to you, despite the fact that, quite frankly, you don't deserve it.

He paused to draw deeply on his cigarette. Blowing a ring of smoke into the air, he gazed around the square as if seeing it for the first time.

It's strange to think that this is where she disappeared, he said. Right in the middle of a crowded square. And I was probably one of the last to see her.

So you'd like to believe, someone piped up derisively from the back.

Giving him time to compose himself, I interjected: Do not take offence at our rough-and-ready ways. You are an artist, and we do not mean to offend your sensibilities, the likes of which we don't often encounter on the square. What draws us here tonight is a common endeavor, the sharing of a unique experience. In remembering that singular encounter, with all its drama and disorientations, each one of us reveals how rarely the sublime appears in this life. For beauty, like faith, is food for the soul. It ennobles us and we want to hold on to it because it arrests us in our depredatory course through life. Beauty transforms our desire—it doesn't do away with desire but exalts it. After all, if we cannot imagine ourselves as different from what we are, wherein lies the promise of existence? Beauty gives us the capacity to reimagine our lives, and in so doing, to dignify ourselves.

THE PROFESSOR

I had barely finished speaking when a mild-looking man raised his hand as if he were in a classroom. He was bespectacled and balding, with a round face and belly. Forgive me, he said apologetically, I probably don't have any business speaking here, but my name is Larbi and I am a lecturer in rhetoric at Al Qarawiyin University. I'm studying traditional modes of storytelling, and your little discourse on beauty reminded me of an incident a few years ago involving a famous professor at our university. This professor, while addressing a large audience on the subject of beauty, asked that a piece of ambergris be passed from hand to hand until, by the time it reached the last person at the back of the massive hall, it had crumbled away to nothing. But the entire hall smelled of ambergris, and every person there had been touched by its essence. The professor concluded his lecture at that point, stating that he had nothing more to say on the nature of beauty.

And that, said the bashful rhetorician, sweating profusely, is all I have to say. I hope you will excuse my interruption.

I acknowledged his contribution with the dignity befitting such an illustrious person, from the oldest university in the world no less, and thanked him for his story.

The Portraitist

The art student, who had been listening in silence, now bowed his head. When he looked up again, it was to address us collectively. In a sombre voice, he said:

Forgive me, my brothers, if I came across as opinionated. I was clumsy. In reality, I am quite shy, and I try to make up for it by acting arrogant. I would like to ask your leave to introduce myself again. My name is Taoufiq Bouabid. I am from Tangier. I am a bona fide artist, and I specialize in miniature portrait painting in the Persian style, for which there is very little demand today. My colleagues mint money by catering to rich Westerners with a taste for large canvases in fake ethnic styles; I come to Marrakesh because it feels shameful to busk in the streets of Tangier after four years of training. I visit here once a month; I stay for a fortnight and work every day, though not always in the Jemaa. Sometimes I set up in front of the Saadian tombs, or you will find me in the narrow alleyway leading to the Jardin Majorelle, or next to the Dar Si Said or the Royal Palace. At night, I stay with a friend, a guide attached to the La Mamounia Hotel. He alerts me to where the tourist traffic is likely to be concentrated on any particular day, and that's where I set off with my easel. Yes, I am a tourist whore, I suppose you could call me that, but they are the only ones who will pay for my art, alas, and that is the one thing in life that I will not compromise. I would rather starve—for the last two years I've often lived on one meal a day—because even a whore has his principles, and my art is my salvation.

Are you a good painter? someone called out.

The portraitist hesitated. He scanned the ring of onlookers to see who had spoken; then, with the shadow of a smile, he said: I am the best.

That raised a laugh, and the man who'd asked the question said: Then you will paint a portrait of my oldest daughter, who is engaged to be married in three months. And if you are really as good as you say, then I will spread the word among my friends, and you will be assured of customers in Marrakesh.

The art student raised a hand to his heart.

I will try not to disappoint you, he said.

What will you charge me for your services?

For you, nothing. The honour will suffice.

Perhaps you can offer him the hand of your middle daughter in exchange, Fouad, someone suggested to the man who'd made the offer, to a renewed outbreak of laughter.

How large will the painting be? the elderly Fouad said suspiciously, his native Marrakchi guile getting somewhat the better of his generosity.

Two inches by two inches, which is the standard size, the art student replied, before adding that he would also include a cedarwood frame, three inches wide on all sides, on which he would paint a traditional touriq design composed of interlacing floral, palmiate, and foliage patterns.

Your offer is generous, Taoufiq, I said with a smile. I am sure that Fouad will be more than satisfied. Now repay our hospitality by telling us what happened that night on the square.

The art student blushed deeply, nonplussed, it seemed, by both my curiosity and my forthrightness. All the same, as if

in acknowledgement of his obligations, he launched immediately into his account with a quick, awkward declaration that
it was the first time he had ever spoken about the encounter.
He sat very straight as he took us through the events of that
evening, speaking slowly and with frequent pauses, scrupu-
lously careful of every word that passed his lips. It was clear
that fidelity to the past was important to him; quite often he
peered into the distance as if to glean from it half-remembered
details, and, when he succeeded, his large, dark eyes widened
in astonishment.

THE MINIATURE

It was a winter evening, he began, much like this one. From a
distance, everything looked hazy. A thick fog of woodsmoke
had clogged up the square. From the food stalls came the scent
of burning shavings. Out of the open windows of the Café de
France floated green clouds of smoke from many cigarettes.
The faces within gazed out at the vast darkness of the square
as at a jungle, from a safe distance. There was an unmistakable
excitement in the air, a sense of danger, of the sudden and the
unexpected. It was night in the Jemaa el Fna, where anything
is possible. From the numerous drum circles that punctuated
the space, there emanated a deep and unsettling thunder, like a
steadily reverberating roar. It was the signal that the Assembly
of the Dead had sprung to life, its predators on the prowl. And I

was sitting there in the midst of it all with my paintbrushes and my paints, well past the hour I normally frequented the place. I don't know why I dallied that night. Sometimes things happen for reasons we don't understand.

I've no idea where the two strangers came from. I saw him first: he was standing about ten paces away. He was impossibly elegant and, to my eyes, looked completely out of place. He reminded me of a younger, darker, Cary Grant, who should have starred in *Casablanca* opposite Ingrid Bergman, in my opinion, instead of Bogart. He even wore an ascot, as if he were in the lobby of the luxurious La Mamounia Hotel rather than the most hazardous place after dark in Marrakesh. When he noticed me staring at him, he walked straight up to me with a smile.

But he surprised me by addressing someone else who was apparently standing behind me. I turned my head, and that's when I saw her. She was looking over my shoulder at the samples of paintings arranged on my easel. She was slender and lithe, with long brown hair and a waist so slim that I could almost span it with my hands. Since she seemed interested, I ventured to explain my art to her. I told her that I painted miniatures in the Persian style. I showed her examples of the different schools, such as Shiraz, Tabriz, and Herat, and pointed out that most of my miniatures were in the Safavid manner, after well-known painters of the fifteenth, sixteenth, and seventeenth centuries such as Kamal ud-Din Behzad Herawi, Reza Abbasi, Mirak Nakkash, and Shah Muzaffar. She listened attentively as I spoke and I noticed that one of my portraits, especially, seemed to catch her eye. It was a copy of a painting of a young princess admiring a rose, done by Mirza Ali in Tabriz around 1540. It was painted in shades of orange, blue, and black, with a pale blue frame on which lines of poetry were inscribed.

She picked it up and studied it for a while before turning to her companion and exchanging a few words which I couldn't catch. Then he turned to me and asked, rapidly, in English, whether I would mind painting her in the manner of the portrait of the Persian princess. Since I didn't know the language, I couldn't follow him and had to ask for her help in translating. Of course, when she'd explained his request to me, I readily agreed. We negotiated a price—they proved surprisingly amenable—and she placed herself at my disposal.

I invited her to sit on a folding chair and positioned her hands and feet. I asked her to look me in the eye and, when she did, I was startled and nearly turned away because her gaze was so penetrating. I felt a little intimidated, my heart beating faster than usual. At the same time, recalling my obligation to capture her likeness, I forced myself to study her objectively. Avoiding her gaze, I took in her broad forehead, slightly elongated nose, delicately proportioned chin, full lips. She had a small scar above her right eye, a beauty mark on her right cheek. And yet, for all of that, she remained enigmatic. At length, with my eyes half shut, I visualized her as the Persian princess. Observing her closely, I drew a trial sketch on a piece of paper, my drawing board resting on my knees. I took my time, suggesting changes to her pose as I worked. When I had finished, she asked to see the sketch and seemed pleased with it.

A moth had wandered into one of my paint jars. We spent some time freeing it, which established a connection between us. I gave her some mint tea. My teapot had an Arabic seal which she admired, and I told her where she could find one just like it. Then I selected a suitable piece of wood on which to paint, picked up my easel, and asked her to hold a pose for as long as it felt comfortable.

I painted swiftly, my eyes switching between my subject and the canvas. As I worked, a storyteller's resonant voice—it could have been yours—echoed marvellously through the air. She asked me to interpret as I painted, and I did my best. The storyteller was telling the story of Layla and Majnun, the ill-fated Arabian lovers, and, even in my very rough rendering, it brought tears to her eyes.

Don't move, I instructed her. Stay as motionless as you can.

She sat loose-limbed in the chair with her profile to me, her eyes slightly unfocused as she gazed down at the half-empty glass of mint tea that substituted for the rose in the painting. She made a superb subject, and I painted with quick strokes, filling in the details to capture the semblance to the Persian princess.

Meanwhile, her companion walked over to stand beside me and asked if I always worked as rapidly. Always, I replied, though as I grow older I find myself slowing down because I think I am gaining in understanding.

And that affects your technique?

It makes me attend more to matters of expression and personality. And that takes time.

He seemed satisfied with my response and did not ask any more questions, which was a relief, because I always find it difficult to talk while painting.

At last, after a few final touches, I put aside my paintbrush and easel. She thanked me and stretched her arms and back. The entire session had lasted a little more than forty minutes. I complimented her and told her that she made an excellent model. She smiled when she saw the painting.

Am I really so pretty? she asked.

Prettier, her companion offered gallantly.

I would let it dry overnight, I cautioned.

We'll take it back to our hotel room right now, he assured me.

We'll send you a photograph after we hang it, she said.

I smiled and didn't reply. Over the years, many of my subjects have given me similar assurances, but I have yet to receive a single photograph. It is in the nature of things, I suppose, and I do not begrudge them for it: the gesture is well intended.

Perhaps we'll return tomorrow for a companion portrait of my husband, she said in a playful tone of voice.

I am your servant, madame, I said gravely.

Wouldn't you like one? she asked him.

He merely stroked his beard and refrained from answering.

We dealt with practical matters; then they shook hands with me and took their leave. I felt sad as I watched them go, but then again, I am usually overcome by melancholia when I have to part with my work. It is in the nature of things. I followed them with my eyes as they walked towards the Avenue Mohammed V, and even took a couple of steps in that direction. But I came to my senses soon enough and returned to my place of work. As I put away my easel and box of paints, I contemplated the rough sketch that I'd made and felt pleased.

I tell you all this without shame, the portraitist said, and fail to understand how it could be otherwise. I liked them enormously and received the news of their disappearance with disbelief the next morning. The thought of them clung to me and kept me from working. My head was cluttered with their faces; they got between my work and my eyes. At times I was seized by the mad desire to drop everything and run away, but I reminded myself of the necessity that kept me here. I couldn't let any distractions get in the way. So I stayed; I painted.

With that, he lowered his eyes and fell silent.

Khadija beckoned to me and drew me close. Lowering her smoky voice to an undertone, she said: There is someone here with an unclean conscience.

I cast a quick glance around.

I know, I replied.

She turned suddenly and addressed the portraitist.

Tell me something, young man, she asked. Is there anyone here whom you recognize from that evening?

The portraitist looked around, hesitated, and pointed to the man on the motorcycle. I saw him on the square that night, he said in a resolute voice.

The man on the motorcycle made his feelings clear:

Your words are as bogus as your stupid story.

The portraitist began moving towards him when Khadija held up her hand. Let him be, she said, if you know what's good for you.

Who is he? the portraitist asked, coming to a standstill.

He is an undercover policeman, came the reply. The Jemaa is his beat.

The man on the motorcycle smiled humourlessly. He addressed the artist: Tomorrow you will show up at the police station next door at nine o'clock on the dot. We will talk about the minor matter of your permit, Mr. Artist from Tangier.

Khadija intervened immediately.

There's no need to be so drastic, Sergeant Mokhtari, she said. The boy was merely responding to a question I'd asked him. Perhaps he could reach some sort of an agreement?

The policeman smiled again, unpleasantly.

I don't want his bloody paintings, he said. Turning to address me, he said: I'm leaving now. Break this up at midnight. Is that clear?

He gunned his motorcycle. We watched him go in silence. When he was safely out of sight, the portraitist sighed and said in a crestfallen voice: That's it, I'm done for.

No you're not, came Khadija's surprising reply. She gazed in the direction in which the policeman had made his exit from the square.

That poor man, she said.

We stared at her, but she didn't elaborate. I began to ask her directly but she brushed my query aside and, instead, turned to Azziza, the beggar woman.

What is the name of your dog? she said, somewhat peremptorily.

Azziza started, uneasy at being the centre of attention again. Lucia, she replied falteringly. Lucia, which means light.

Who named her that? Khadija persisted.

Azziza's daughter, Aisha, preempted her mother's reply. A foreigner suggested it, she answered brightly. He was young. Dark-skinned. Handsome.

Bearded?

He had a curly, reddish-black beard, the child said. It encircled his face like a lion's mane.

Was he alone, or with someone?

He was with a very beautiful lady. Her voice was warm and

soft. He didn't speak our language, so she interpreted for him. They listened to our story with sympathy.

Khadija turned to me. She said: You see?

A fat man sitting near me raised an objection:

But how do you know the child is talking about the same persons who concern us? There must be dozens of bearded foreigners with attractive companions passing through the Jemaa on a daily basis. How do you know it wasn't someone else altogether?

I *know*, Khadija said, speaking with conviction.

She addressed me again. Her voice was quietly triumphant.

What was the name of the girl who disappeared?

I smiled. Lucia, I answered.

And how do you know that? someone else called out.

My answer was simple.

Because I asked her, I said.

El Maghreb Al Aqsa

Khadija said: There are so many ways to tell a story, so few to do it well. There was no need for Azziza to be here. No need for her dream or her daughter. But the dog? That dog is another matter altogether. Her name provides a link to our story, and that is important.

But what is going to happen to me now? the art student said plaintively. I'm in danger of losing my livelihood, and all because I sought to answer your question.

Instead of responding to him directly, Khadija took out a handful of earth from a worn leather pouch and scattered it on the ground before her. As she studied the patterns, Bilal, the Gnaoua musician, murmured superstitiously. The rest of us, aware that she was practicing geomancy, the art of divining the future from randomly thrown traces of earth, watched her in silence.

At length, she looked up from her endeavors and contemplated the portraitist. It was a while before she spoke, but when she did, it was to assure him that nothing was going to happen to him.

Go home and rest, she said. You can put your mind at ease.

But I don't understand how you can say that, he persisted, bewildered.

Take Khadija at her word, I observed, and don't dwell any more on the matter. She will take care of everything.

In the meantime, Khadija said, addressing the artist, I do have a bone to pick with you, and it is this. I did not care for the manner in which you characterized our Jemaa.

Oh God! he exclaimed, distraught. Now what have I said?

She smiled to show that he did not have anything to fear from her.

You earn your livelihood here, she said, but from your description it's clear that you don't know the first thing about your place of work. Now listen to my words carefully. The Jemaa is our sister and our mother; she attends to our needs and looks after us; she is the source of our sustenance and to depict her otherwise is to belittle her. You have to get used to her many faces. Sometimes she is young, sometimes old; sometimes she is full of energy, sometimes she is tired. At her worst, she isn't dangerous; she is capricious, and her caprices reflect the conditions of our society. But at her best, she is filled with joy and celebration, and people flock here because they seek to share in her happiness. Her fevered atmosphere—a fusion of many elements—is a creation of our own desires. We all have a share in shaping her magic, and it is this magic that is her life. It seizes you and doesn't let go, and its vitality and emotions are mesmerizing. Everything evolves, harmonizes, and falls into patterns here, and beauty is born. That is how the Jemaa changes you, reshaping you in her own image. You have to look at her with the eyes of a child, and you will find yourself transformed. It is a matter of the soul—do you understand?—as much as it is of the senses. The Jemaa is a symbol, a meeting point of all the peoples who have passed through and continue to come through this part of the world. She is Maghrebin, Sahrawi, Mediterranean, Arab, Berber. Her winds encompass the ruagh, the khamsin, the simoom, the leveche, the zephyr. The music that results carries within it all of these melodies. Listen to that music: it is a mosaic that dovetails African, Middle Eastern, Jehudi, Andalusian, contemporary and mediaeval motifs. Dance to that music: you will learn much about yourself. When you are here, the centuries swim together, and you are beyond time. When you are here, the cultures meld their weaves, and you are elevated beyond your origins.

That is the magic of the Jemaa, Khadija said. She is a microcosm of our Maghreb. But she is also more than a mere meeting place, and, if you were to encounter her in the early hours of the morning, when the first rays of the sun alight upon her skin, you would find that she can impart a sense of tranquillity difficult to find anywhere else in the universe. Bliss tinged with melancholy, the rarest of all pleasures: therein lies her mystique.

So you do see the Jemaa as a woman? someone called out.

I see her as a very beautiful woman, Khadija assented.

Perhaps even as beautiful as the woman who disappeared, I added, somewhat provocatively.

Then why don't you tell us about your meeting with her? the same voice said.

I laughed, finding my interrogator's zeal amusing. Very well, I answered, I will. Even though you are impatient, I will indulge you, because that is my role here.

THE MIRROR

I was about to continue when I found myself interrupted.

I have something to say, a feminine voice blurted out. May I have permission to speak? It might be important.

The matronly peasant who spoke these words flushed fiercely when she saw our faces turn towards her. She was dressed in a voluminous and somewhat faded fouta, the traditional scarlet-and-white-striped garment native to the women of the Rif mountains. She seemed out of place in the Jemaa, and I wondered what she could be doing here, especially this late at night.

My dear sister, I said, you are certainly very far from home. What brings you to the south?

A child's hot tears, she said. My son and daughter-in-law live in Marrakesh and they both work during the daytime. So I am here to take care of their firstborn, my grandson. But that is not why I spoke up. I have something to share with you about that ill-fated night on the Jemaa.

You were there? I asked, taken aback.

Yes, yes, she affirmed, at the time I was employed in the hotel where they'd put up, across from the Koutoubia Mosque.

She spoke Tarifit, the language of the Rif region, rapidly, with a thick rural accent and in staccato bursts, as if her speech couldn't keep up with her memory and she was anxious to communicate all the details before she forgot them.

I was the night maid, she said. They were staying in Room 14, on the second floor, which overlooks the boulevard. The faucet in their bathroom wasn't working, and the manager had sent me up with a bucket of water. I knocked on the door and they asked me to enter. The young lady was lying facedown on the bed. She seemed out of sorts. I think she might have been crying. I tried to be as unobtrusive as possible, slipping into the bathroom with my bucket. That is the way it is with hotel work: you try to be invisible to the guests so that they are not disturbed by your presence. But even though the two of them spoke in low voices, I caught the gist of their conversation. They had had a disagreement and I gathered that it had to do with her wanting to return to the Jemaa that night and his being against it. They were both holding firm, neither one of them willing to compromise.

When I re-entered their room, preparing to leave, she was standing before the mirror and wiping off her mascara which had smeared. She looked unhappy but determined, and I had the sense that she wasn't used to having her wishes contradicted.

Well, you know, she was saying, what's the use of fear? Can't you hear the drums? They are calling out to us, and if we don't respond, it will be as a kiss that isn't returned. So I am going, and it's up to you whether you want to come with me. If you refuse, you're not a gentleman.

I must say that he was a true gentleman. He tipped me ten dirhams for my efforts, which was much more than I could have expected, and held the door open for me as I stepped out into the corridor.

As I walked away from their room, I reflected on how strange it had been to encounter them like that: two young, vibrant people caught between love and despair. And that is what I told the police when they came around looking for clues the next morning. They searched the room but, as one of them confessed to me, they themselves did not know what they should be looking for. By that time Room 14 had already stood vacant for many hours, like the plume of dust that remains on the desert horizon long after the caravan has vanished.

Gathering from her words that she had finished, I thanked her for having taken the initiative and asked if, by any chance, she had seen our friend Taoufiq's portrait of the woman in the room.

She nodded her head vigorously.

I was just about to tell you about it. I noticed it leaning against the mirror as I left the room. That's why I thought it important to speak up and establish the proper chronology of events.

The proper chronology of events? I repeated after her, bemused. That sounds quite technical. Did the police talk about that when they visited the hotel?

Oh no, they had nothing to do with it, she said, laughing. But I'm an avid watcher of the crime programs on television, especially the Egyptian one featuring the middle-aged female detective. Every time it is like a window into human wickedness.

I regarded her simple Berber face, shining with enthusiasm, and had to admit to myself that, for once, I was at a loss for words.

A commotion from a distant corner of the square saved me from the need to respond. It came from the direction of the boulevard, past the Place Foucauld, where the Rue Moulay Ismail intersects with the Avenue el-Mouahidine. As we tried to make out what was going on, someone approached rapidly from that direction. We stopped him and asked what had happened.

There was an accident, he explained, a collision between a tour bus and a motorcycle. The driver of the motorcycle, a policeman, was killed instantly.

Did you catch his name? I asked.

Mokhtari, the man answered. He was a sergeant on the Jemaa beat. A real bastard, if you don't mind my slandering the dead, but I'm a trader in the souk and he made our lives miserable.

His revelation burned a hole in the night. We turned as one in Khadija's direction, but it was as we should have expected. She had left only moments before, her place was empty.

Aisha's Question

At this juncture, little Aisha, Azziza's daughter, interrupted the uneasy silence by asking the erstwhile hotel maid if she knew what had happened to Taoufiq's painting.

The old woman answered the question with her usual rushed enthusiasm.

Oh, the police took it with them, child. They wrapped it up with an air of triumph as if they had found the one who had disappeared instead of her mere image. After they'd left,

I flung open the shutters and let in the light. In the street outside, life was going on as usual. I remember everything as if
it were yesterday. A truck filled with fresh loaves had pulled
up in front of the neighbouring bakery. A man was nearly
run over crossing the street. And a little further down, the
muezzin of the Koutoubia Mosque began calling the faithful
to prayer.

She paused and regarded Aisha with humour.

Have I answered your question? she asked.

Aisha nodded vigorously, with an effervescent, toothy smile,
while I stepped forward, ruffled her hair, and addressed my
audience.

Zellij

My middle brother, Ahmed, I said, is a maalem, a master
craftsman of zellij, those inimitable mosaics made of handmade
enamel tiles. There is a discipline to his craft that is akin, in
many ways, to storytelling. Perhaps that is why I am always
reminded of him when I tell my stories. Watching him work, I
have marvelled at the fact that all his designs are based around
the same three patterns—geometric, epigraphic, and floral—
with the sole variation coming in the placement of the tiles.
Rectangles fit together to constitute chequerboards; circles and
semicircles interlace into rosettes and arabesques. It is a craft
dedicated to symmetry and repetition, the aim being to preserve
the mathematical integrity of the motif. Ahmed likens it to the

harmony of body and spirit achieved through certain forms of
Sufic meditation. Settling into a deep, rhythmic breathing pattern, he cuts the tiles with a steel hammer, often making the
incision with a single sharp blow of uncanny accuracy.

Ahmed is the pragmatic one in the family, cautious but determined. Early on in life, he decided not to follow in Father's footsteps. The first time he told me, I refused to believe him. I was
fourteen years old at the time, he was twelve. It was a bright,
sunny day, filled with the sounds of birds and rushing mountain
streams. The spring snows were melting. We had set out to visit
our friend Jalal, who was tending sheep in the valley's upper
reaches. By the time we reached the place, we were both winded.
We paused to admire a laurel grove exuberant with pink blossoms. Carried away, Ahmed lay down on the damp ground, his
face to the sky. Gazing at the sun with narrowed eyes, he told me
he didn't want to be a storyteller, he wanted to be something else
altogether.

What do you have in mind? I asked.

Oh, I don't know! he said impatiently. I just don't want to tell
stories. You know how much I hate talking. I'd be miserable in
that line of work.

You're too young to be thinking that far ahead, I said dismissively. Perhaps we ought to have this conversation in another
year's time, but not right now.

He turned on his side and gazed at the pink and green che-
querboard around him.

It's beautiful, isn't it? he said. So orderly, so restful to the eye.
Doesn't it remind you of zellij tilework?

It's very pretty, I agreed.

Do you think there's money to be made in zellij?

Do you mean as a maalem?

Yes.

Oh, I'm sure there is. It's a respectable trade.

He seemed to forget my presence for a moment, then sat up excitedly. That's it then! he exclaimed. I know what I want to do with my life. I'll teach myself how to make zellijes.

It takes years of training, I pointed out.

He examined his hands through half-closed eyes.

Do you think I can carry it off, Hassan? Do you think I can master the craft? In Marrakesh, I've heard the maalems talk about it. They have their own names for the patterns: inverted tears, hen's feet, heifer's eyes. It's like poetry, isn't it?—only better.

Gazing at the polychromatic mosaic of petals, he said, almost wistfully: No matter what, I want to work with my hands.

I stared at him, moved by his enthusiasm but not knowing what to say in reply.

We had a similar exchange six years later when, faced with his stubborn determination, my father and I found ourselves constrained to remind him that we were Berber tribesmen from the Atlas Mountains, and, where we lived, there was no native tradition of zellij tile-making. It was an aristocratic craft, a feature of the great northern palaces. Personally, I didn't care for it: I found it too busy, too ornate. And, as I tried to stress, it wasn't part of our culture. Even in our biggest city, Marrakesh, the emphasis was on much more spartan lime-based surfaces, whether of the rougher, pounded kind, or dess, or of the smoother sort, or tadelakt, used in wealthier residences. In other words, if he was serious about his ambition, he would have to leave us and go north, to Fès, the centre of zellij craftsmanship.

He listened to me with his bare feet sticking out of his trouser legs. All around him the heat of the sun reflected off whitewashed lime floors and walls. I praised the virtues of that kind of simplicity but he merely heard me out with indifference.

I suppose I'll just go to Fès then, he said, and that was that.

Father was apoplectic. You want to go and live among those gentrified Arabs! They're all about money; they have no culture!

Ahmed laughed. They have more culture than you could dream of, Father, and you know it.

He returned to his room, rolled up his belongings in a bundle, said goodbye to us, and walked out into the sunlight. A few steps behind him followed his dark, skinny dog.

Mother cried bitterly that night, bereft at losing her second son. My father went around stony-faced for days. In the evenings he'd turn up the volume on the wood-panelled radio but between bouts of reports on army exercises it spat only static. I placed a pot of mountain daisies in Ahmed's room, but they died soon after of inadequate light.

When Ahmed visited us a few months later, I asked him about his dog. I'd been fond of that little creature, sad to see her go.

The dog? he said ruefully. She ran away somewhere on the way to Fès. But I'll get another one soon enough, a purebred this time.

Years later, when we were older and both well settled, we would still carry on the discussion about our respective trades. By that time, Ahmed had not only worked his way through the various stages of apprenticeship, he'd made a name for himself as a reputable maalem, going so far as to receive an award for his expertise in laying the tilework for the fountains in the giant mosque in Casablanca named after His Majesty the King. We were all proud of him, but I didn't know what to make of his need to praise his craft at the expense of mine.

In one of his letters to me, he wrote:

Storytelling is a cruel talent, haunted by ghosts and spirits. I would like to do something else with my life, something more realistic and meaningful.

I wrote back:

I reject your criticism because only love can grasp and fairly judge any form of art. You can be fair in your assessments only if you are committed to understanding without judging.

He replied immediately, in a lengthy telegram:

I would at least like to leave a mark that is permanent. People visit the places where I have laid zellij and admire my handiwork. I know that it will give pleasure for ages to come. I could never tell stories day after day and watch my words dissipate into thin air. Where is the satisfaction in that? Where is the necessary smell of fire and kiln and clay? Where is the glory of a victorious struggle over matter? Empty air is not an adequate substitute. Nor, for that matter, are echoes. It's the difference between reality and artifice. Your work is a mirage. That is the impossible truth. When a man lives out his entire life telling stories, reality disappears and something else appears in its place: a random collection of details reworked by the imagination.

I resisted the temptation to reply in a telegram. I couldn't afford the gesture, for one. But in the letter I sent him, I wrote: Even your work is a fiction, my dear brother, if only you would have the humility to admit it.

His response:

Where is the fiction in my work?

My answer:

Your belief in its permanence. The next time you are in Marrakesh, visit the rubble of the El Badi Palace, considered incomparable in its time, and recall the remark made by the court jester to his emperor that it would make a great ruin.

I waited for his reply, but it was several months before he retrieved the thread of our correspondence. During the interval, he'd moved from Fès to Meknès and set up his own business there. He became the first member of my family to live in a brick house. My parents visited him and, on his return, my father said, with more than a trace of irony: Prosperity has conquered my son.

In his next letter to me, in which he enclosed a photograph of his house, Ahmed wrote:

Do you remember what I said about zellij a long time ago? I compared it to poetry, but deemed it even better. Well, Hassan, that assessment still stands.

My reply:

Why compare, my brother? Poetry is everything that you find sublime. The sublime is what gives you pleasure. The rest is nothing but fleeting emotions. Be happy with your art, as I am with mine, and let us share in each other's happiness.

I agree wholeheartedly, he wrote in response, but then he felt the need to add: I've just added a third story to my house. Naturally, the floors and the walls are covered in zellij up to shoulder height. I ought not to be writing this, but it is some of my best work. There are places where the geometry of the panels gives rise to uncanny optical illusions. A friend of mine who teaches mathematics compares it to fractal patterns, even though I have no idea what that means. Amina, my wife, says it gives her headaches, but shows it off to her friends nevertheless. It feels as if we are living in a palace, Hassan. You should visit us sometime.

In a postscript, he added: Please give my regards to our brother Mustafa. Do you know what he plans to do with himself? Father has written to me complaining about his lack of direction. Tell Mustafa there will always be a place for him in my business if he would care to join me here.

THE LION OF THE ATLAS

It is written in books that the great tribes of Atlas lions died out in Roman times, reduced to half-starved captives in gladiatorial circuses. Ahmed once told me that the Roman ruins of Volubilis, near Meknès, are rumoured to still resound at night to the roars of the captured beasts as they fall victim to some power-mad proconsul's bloodlust. He said the locals avoid the place like plague after dark. Other books record the death in 1922 of the last Atlas lion, a magnificent beast with a reddish-black mane encircling its face like a beard. Yet both Abdulkhalek and Fathallah, shepherds in our village, insist that they have heard the roars of lions prowling the higher mountain slopes at night. They are reliable men, so there is no cause to doubt their word. And they are not the only ones. In the neighbouring villages, as well as in the pastures of the Jbel Sahrho region, we have heard of livestock carried away at night by marauding lions.

Sparked by these rumours, a team of zoologists from Rabat spent several months in our valley, interviewing shepherds and tracking alleged sightings. The government backed up their efforts, offering a sizable reward. What they wanted was proof: body parts, skulls, bones, earthen casts of pug marks, photographs. It caused considerable excitement in the villages. Numerous objects were brought in as evidence. A trader in the Dadès Valley produced a perfectly preserved pelt, but it turned out that he had stolen it from a qa'id who had purchased it in a caravenserai in Mauritania. Someone else in the Todra Valley presented a set of canine teeth, but they were found to be more than a hundred years old. The zoologists from Rabat eventually ended their search without reaching any definite conclusions, but the government's offer for a reward in exchange for evidence still stands.

My eleven-year-old brother Mustafa heard about the reward when a group of government officials passed through our village. One of them spoke of the matter to my father. It was a lot of money, and Mustafa was immediately entranced.

What is the Atlas lion? he asked.

Father laughed. It is the only large wild animal left in our mountains, he said. The rest have all been hunted out.

But what about the Atlas bear and the Atlas leopard? I asked.

They were killed off a long time ago, even longer back than the lion, Father replied.

How does one recognize this Atlas lion? Mustafa asked.

Father showed us the illustration in the booklet the officials had left behind.

Look at the heavy mane, he instructed. It is dark brown in colour, almost black, with a blond fringe around the face which creeps down the belly to the hind legs. It is the largest of the lions in Africa, he added with pride. Its closest living relations are the lions of India, but ours are bigger at the shoulder, with larger skulls and more luxuriant manes. They are truly magnificent beasts. The Romans had hundreds of them in captivity. They used them to kill the Nazarenes.

Mustafa fell silent, lost in thought. My father and I chatted for a while longer about the lions, then turned our attention to the more pressing matter of our forthcoming sojourn in Marrakesh. But Mustafa did not join in our conversation. My father winked at me and stroked his white moustache. We left Mustafa there, his chin propped in his hand, staring first at the picture of the Atlas lion and then into the distance where the mountains creased the horizon.

That night he confessed to me that the lions had fastened on his soul. I am intoxicated, Hassan, he said in a whisper so as to not wake our parents. I had a vision this afternoon while you and Father were talking. I saw a lion with a mane of flames instead of fur, and, as I gazed, that lion was transformed into a man.

Did you recognize him? I asked with interest.

No, but I am convinced that the lions exist. I must find them, or at least their traces.

They are woodland creatures, I warned. They remain in the shadows and reveal their presence only after dark. Don't you think many others have tried and failed? They will not be easy to track down.

I will find them, Mustafa declared. And when I do, I will kill the biggest male and claim the reward. Give me your hand, Hassan, and wish me success. I'm off tomorrow to find the lion of the Atlas.

All right, I answered drowsily, not believing him for a moment. Now go to sleep.

He set out the next morning, at dawn, before the rest of the household had stirred. His absence was first noticed by my mother, and it took me all of my composure to tell my parents where I thought my brother had gone.

The entire village set off in search of him. It was the week after the spring harvest, and I think everyone needed an excuse to release their pent-up energies. It was like a picnic, really, and no one minded that it took us two days to catch up with my errant brother. And even when we did, on the high ridges near the tizi that led out of our valley, it was difficult to censure him because he was so crestfallen. Instead, we smiled at the motley collection of objects he'd gathered in the course of his lion hunt: a dented copper canteen; a folded red banner bleached by the sun; a dessicated elephant shrew, that peculiar mouselike crea- ture with a nose that extends into an oversized proboscis; an oak branch sculpted into a spear by the wind; an old dynamite fuse; a large, flat stone with vivid white scars that Mustafa insisted had been caused by a lion sharpening its claws.

I fastened on this last object as possible proof of the existence of lions in our valley in order to salvage my brother's dignity, but it wasn't enough. On the procession back to the village, some wag nicknamed Mustafa "the Lion of the Atlas," and all of us, including my father, burst out laughing.

Later on, Mustafa would tell us about the small grey bird that had dropped out of the sky and died at his feet as he'd set out on his odyssey.

It was a bad omen, he said darkly. I should have known that nothing was going to come out of my search.

In an attempt to mollify him, Father said: What is important is the dream, not the trophy.

But Mustafa remained inconsolable.

My father was convinced that it was that signal humiliation that lay behind my brother's subsequent decision to leave the valley and his resolve never to return. But I knew better, because Mustafa himself told me the real reason. It was due to something else altogether, something that transpired a few years later and irredeemably altered the course of all our lives, for much the worse. I knew that my brother's departure had to do with his sense of helplessness when faced with the death of my beautiful young wife—whom he'd adored, like everyone else in my family—in childbirth.

Πasib

Zahra had been named after the morning star, Venus. There was always a scent of lavender about her. She had the most infectious laugh. She was my chosen one, the heart of my hearts, the love of my life . . .

These were my scattered thoughts the evening we buried her with my stillborn son on the slope of the hill behind our house. The memory of that evening will never escape me: of the dust rising from the twin graves; of the hopelessness on the faces of those all around; of my own suffocating sense of desolation; of the night heedlessly lighting up with stars, and the one bright star suddenly snuffing out as if extinguished by a hidden hand.

Sleep was evanescent that night. Zahra's slippers stood by the bed as they always had. I arranged the blanket as I'd always in the past. I breathed her lavender scent on the pillows. I continued saying her name over and over again in my head as if that would bring her back.

Early the next morning I told Father I was going for a walk.

I left the house and, turning my back to the valley, headed for the mountains. Far below lay the cricket-sized houses of our village.

The day passed. Night came, then went. Then day again; night once more. I lost track of time. Meaningless days; sleepless nights. The stars shone, some white, some blue. Clouds trailed like smoke along the ground. The sun spiked fingers through wooded slopes. I watched an eagle soar into the air in spirals. The east wind, that messenger of love, stirred fallen leaves and dust.

A young girl herded sheep, life going on as usual.

In the village in the next valley they were celebrating the greengrocer's second marriage. The ululations of the women rose in joyous song. The slate-roofed dwellings vibrated with the pulse of drums. Past the village, the stone-strewn path shone white in the sun. All the land was covered with pastures, thick and endless, stopping short of the highest peaks in cliffs of rock. Tangled trees interrupted the pastures. A cooling breeze blew up in quick gusts. There was autumn in the air. Half the meadows were already golden.

I ascended a steep slope. The grassy meadows gave way to a broken landscape, half trees, half shrub. Rows of stunted pines stood about in aisles. I emerged from a bank of cedars onto a narrow ledge overhanging a ravine. Around me only bare cliffs gleamed sheer and stark. A stream was visible below, and in the distance, the snowy crown of Jbel Toubkal, remote and white.

The sun was in my face as I sat down. I leaned my back against a boulder, resting in its shadow. I remained quite still and the embers of my life began to draw near. Only then did I become conscious of the silence of what was missing now that Zahra was gone.

When evening came, a fog crept over the rim of the mountains. A film of moisture covered my rocky perch. Rigid with cold, I watched a lavender pallor suffuse the sky and wash over the dark ramparts of the mountains. For an instant, it penetrated right through them and coloured the entire world. Moments later, with a rush of shadows, night descended.

Stars lit the sky; a crescent moon rose over the earth. From behind a high ridge, there floated a thick grey cloud which proceeded to envelop the ledge I was on, wholly obscuring my surroundings from view. The stars went dark, the sky black. And so I was left in the night, literally alone.

I took out Zahra's slippers from my pocket and flung them over the edge. I followed them down with my eyes, imagining what it would be like when my own body slammed into the rocks. I held on to the thought, conscious only of feeling entirely unlike myself, at a great remove from the world.

The sound of hastily indrawn breath encroached upon my stillness.

Turning my head, I saw Mustafa crouching in the haze, his eyes riveted on me. He looked grey, haggard, more desolate than I'd ever seen him. I felt an uncanny calm overtake me at that instant. I motioned him to sit down beside me and pulled myself back from the edge.

How did you find me here? I asked.

I've been following you ever since you left the house, he said huskily.

Then: Hassan, you've been gone three days!

Has it been that long? I asked.

He flung his arms around my shoulders and burst into tears.

Maniyya

I found my parents aged almost beyond recognition on my return.

Mother held on to me and trembled without cease. Father's thin, dark face was tense with insomnia. He said he could no longer carry on with the storytelling: his heart was not in it.

He said: Zahra is now beyond our world, but her spirit will always remain with us.

I said: Yes, Father.

But what about you, my son? We watch you, as from a distance, helpless. This sorrow is like a shadow in our hearts.

I said: Don't worry about me.

Everything is up to fate, Hassan, and death is nothing but the end that fate prescribes.

I said: I know, Father.

Mother said: Zahra is now in a much better place than this. She was too good for this world.

I said: I know, Mother.

She said: We grieve for you. We don't know what to do.

I said: Give it a little time, Mother.

We must leave it up to God, Father said. It is His will. Everything has a reason and a purpose.

What about my stillborn son, Father?

He lowered his head and remained silent.

The Storyteller of Marrakesh

Ten days after Zahra's death, I asked Father if I could take up his storyteller's mantle, since he was resolved to give it up. It took me a long time to convince him that I felt strong enough, but when I finally said that I needed to do it in order to lose myself in another world, he understood immediately and no longer resisted.

Come with me, he said, gathering up his story sticks in their bag.

We walked to the cave where he practiced his craft every morning without fail. On our way there, he paused and said: I have never felt more tired than I do now, Hassan. I suppose old age is when you begin to feel the motion of time as a dead weight.

You're hardly that old, Father. This will pass.

I don't know, Hassan, but I hope that you are right.

We entered the cave and sat down on its cool grey stones. He didn't speak for a while, but merely looked around as if he were seeing the place for the first time. Finally, he drew a deep breath and said: This has been like a second home to me.

This, and not the Jemaa?

He smiled. When I'm in the Jemaa, I imagine that I am here. It suits me. I feel safe.

He turned to look at me; he had a strange expression, a mixture of joy and regret. My father brought me here as a child, he said. I was three or four, I don't remember. It hasn't changed a bit.

His eyes were bright.

Generations of our family honed their craft in this humble cave. These living stones have absorbed hundreds of stories. Countless flights of fancy. Countless. When I was young, I liked to press my ears to the walls and listen to what they had to tell.

I'll remember that when I'm in the Jemaa, I said gently.

He nodded. Don't worry. I'm not going to reminisce endlessly. I know we're here for a purpose. He wrapped his arms around his body as if he were cold.

I'm not worried, Father. I have plenty of time.

But we should begin, or else I'll do all the talking. It's time.

Opening his arms, he made a wide gesture embracing the cave.

Imagine that we are no longer here, but in the Jemaa, in Marrakesh, he said. He held out one hand horizontally before him and angled the other at a perpendicular to it. This is the Jemaa, he said, indicating the horizontal plane, and this other hand represents the minaret of the Koutoubia. Now: tell me what you see.

For an instant, I saw myself as I appeared in my father's eyes and realized that I couldn't imagine playing a more challenging role. I gazed at his hands; I didn't want to disappoint him, but I wasn't sure what to say. Nevertheless, I found myself speaking:

I see the sun. I see the sun on bright awnings, and open stalls steaming with scents, and the hazy blue smoke from many stoves rising into the air. The sky is filled with vendors' voices. The oranges are especially fragrant today: I feel their juicy succulence on my tongue. It is a clear day, so you can see the mountains in the distance. On the other side of the mountains, in a lush green valley watered by cooling streams, there is a father testing his son on the art of storytelling inside a cave. The son's footsteps are still visible in the air as he travels between the Jemaa el Fna and the cave, but there's a brisk breeze blowing, and only the very faintest of imprints linger on the horizon. Inside the cave, a mirror reaches to the floor, and before it the father stands revealed as no other than the Storyteller of Marrakesh. Through the space of the mirror he views the familiar concourse of the Jemaa, but instead of seeing himself holding forth before his circle of listeners, he sees his son, Hassan, inventing this story, naming, describing, doubling the world just as if he himself were standing there.

Father smiled. Almost confidentially, as between peers, he said: Fine, we'll simply move on to the storytelling then. I'll select a theme, you pick the setting, and we'll proceed in the usual way.

He took out his story sticks from their bag and was about to choose one when I interrupted him. Father, I said gently, is this really necessary?

He stared at me. What do you mean?

I mean that I have just lost my wife.

Then how will I know that you are adequately prepared?

Believe in me. I've accompanied you to Marrakesh for the better part of fourteen years. I know what to do. By the time I get to the Jemaa I'll be in a different frame of mind. I won't let you down.

He bent his head. I could tell that he wasn't satisfied, and with good reason, but took it as a measure of his love for me when he gave his assent, however reluctantly.

There is something I would like from you, however, I added.

What is it?

Advice. Suggestions on how I can smooth the way.

He gave a wan smile. You want tips on how to grease a story?

I do, I said.

Very well.

He thought for a moment. Then:

First, always remember that either a story carries love and mystery, or it carries nothing. Second, outside of the broad themes determined by the story sticks, the trick is to make up everything out of whole cloth. Third, a story must not have a clean resolution. That way you will keep your audience coming back for more. Finally—and this is the most important thing— our craft demands discipline and hard work; a fertile imagination is not enough.

With a dignified expression, he added: You are about to enter a privileged profession, Hassan. Always remember that the fraternity of storytellers is a closely knit one, and the ties that hold us together exceed even those of family. If a fellow storyteller is ever in need of your assistance, offer it without reservations or regard for consequences. Is that clear?

Yes, Father.

In that case . . .

He stopped suddenly. He looked tired and out of breath.

What else can I tell you? he said. What else? Oh yes, there is one other thing. Never forget that the bond between the storyteller and his audience is based on good taste, mutual respect, and on manners. Never compromise on etiquette, Hassan. I mention this because the Jemaa can be an unsettling place. If hooligans intrude, be firm, stand your ground, don't get intimidated.

Rest your fears, Father. I have learned from your example.

He nodded and sat up straight. Then that is all I have to say now. Perhaps some other things will come to me later.

Thank you, Father.

He made as if to rise to his feet, and I was about to follow him when he gave a wordless exclamation and sat down again as if he'd just remembered something. With a sideways glance at me that was strangely diffident, he sighed and said: What I have to say next concerns you personally—or perhaps it would be more accurate to say that it concerns your personal affairs—and although it might not strike you as appropriate just yet, our time together is short, and I have no option but to bring it up. And your mother agrees with me, by the way, he added.

What is it, Father?

It is this. Once we've all recovered from this tragedy, I'll take up the search for a wife for you. He paused, then qualified delicately: A second wife.

I didn't reply, but turned and looked fixedly out of the mouth of the cave. The sky outside was a clear, bright blue, without a trace of clouds.

After a few moments, I felt his hand on my arm.

Is something the matter? he said.

I have decided not to marry again, Father.

But who will give us grandchildren? Who will continue our line?

I looked calmly at him. I felt neither hurt nor anger at his questions but only a deep sadness.

Why worry about that now? You have two other sons.

That is not the issue here. Your mother and I seek your happiness.

Then rest assured that, with time, I will be content.

He leaned forward and stared at me without blinking.

Perhaps I didn't explain myself clearly. We desire your marriage, Hassan. It is part of our tradition, our faith. You honour God by obeying your parents. Even when they are mistaken, a Muslim obeys them, for the trees must not be allowed to fall if the forest must stand.

I had so much respect for him that I found it difficult to answer; and yet I felt obliged. I placed a hand on his wrist. You know how much I honour you, Father, but in this case I cannot obey, I said.

Even before I'd finished speaking, I saw his shocked expression and felt ashamed. I looked away at once. He removed my hand from his wrist. I waited a moment before looking at him again.

Hassan, he said.

I gazed at him intently. His voice was not displeased, or disappointed, but apprehensive.

You are caging yourself in a prison of your own making, he said.

That is one way to look at it. The other is to believe that I am honouring my marriage vows to my wife.

Life is not so stark, my son. You're only nineteen. You have your whole existence ahead of you. Don't condemn your future with a decision dictated by your present circumstances. A life-time of nurturing pain is not a sound exchange for vitality.

I gazed at his wrinkled features as he spoke, but my mind was elsewhere. I made an effort to reply: Father, must we talk about this now?

He shivered slightly and closed his eyes. His hands rested on his thin knees. It's cold here, he said. I'm an old man now and feel the cold.

I watched him with tenderness and sympathy.

He opened his eyes and rose slowly to his feet. He looked exhausted, and I felt the dull pain of regret. I stood up as well.

I don't want to disappoint you, Father, I said.

He glanced at me; he seemed resigned and sad.

I am sure you don't, Hassan. You are a good son, and I've always felt a deep understanding between us even when we've had our disagreements. You could even say, especially during those times.

He smiled, but it was a smile that wrung my heart. I could think of nothing to say. After an interval, he went on: But I worry about Mustafa. Not about Ahmed, but Mustafa. Ahmed will be fine, he knows the ways of the world. But Mustafa is a source of constant anxiety for your mother and me. He is far too impetuous and overconfident.

Overconfident, yes, I said kindly, and he is rather emotional, but always with a lyrical note. I wouldn't worry if I were you, Father. Mustafa knows how to take care of himself.

I hope you are right. He is more intelligent than Ahmed, and his character is more attractive. But he eludes me. At times he is as imprudent as a child.

He hesitated for a moment, then:

When do you intend to leave for Marrakesh?

Perhaps two or three days from now, I said, before adding quickly, for I realized I had given him no room to answer: Or whenever you deem it best.

May God in His wisdom be with you, Hassan.

And the spirit of our ancestors, Father, I said with a smile.

If you are ever in danger, take recourse to Allah, for He is mindful of those who believe in Him, and is filled with compassion and forgiveness whenever we stray from the straight path.

I will, Father.

And if it doesn't work out for you in the city, come straight back here. Don't hesitate. You know your home is here.

I know, Father.

BLACK SUN

And so it was that I left for the red-walled city many years ago and grew into my father's robes. And Ahmed departed for Fés soon after and was able to provide for himself over time, just as I'd predicted. But Mustafa went in the opposite direction, as it were, and confirmed my father's worst fears. Something about him changed fundamentally after the death of my wife and child, and his irrepressible good humour gave way to long and frequent spells of anger, a trait quite alien to our family and one he seemed to relish stoking until it had hardened into a set feature of his personality. Ahmed, who had the misfortune of being at the receiving end of that temper on more than one occasion, once mourned to me the presence in our family of that stranger, our brother.

Once, when we were meeting at my uncle Mohand's house in Marrakesh, Mustafa made a remark to Ahmed of such unusual harshness that Father said gravely: I will not let you turn this meeting into a battleground. Ahmed is older than you and deserves your respect. Either apologize to him, or leave this instant.

Why must I respect him? Mustafa demanded.

Father turned pale with anger. Barely able to control himself, he said in measured tones: Because he is worthy of your respect. Because it is your obligation. Because he is doing something valuable with his life. Because I am telling you to.

I will not apologize to him, Mustafa said obdurately, rising to his feet.

At this stage, my uncle intervened. Speaking rapidly and in a voice pitched high with displeasure, he said: Does nothing matter to you, boy? Obey your father and let's be done with it.

Mustafa stalked out without a backward glance.

Father gazed at the open door through which his son had left and said, disconsolately: That boy was born under a black sun.

We learned subsequently that Mustafa had walked all the way to the Supratours bus station in a rage, bought himself a ticket for Essaouira, and departed without a second thought. We next heard from him after four months, but only after my father had written to a mutual friend asking him if he knew anything about Mustafa's whereabouts.

İɱDYAZɳ

Now I surveyed my listeners with a look of sadness sparked by my recollections of my brother. I wanted to spare no details in the effort to help them understand the roots of Mustafa's disaffection. But I checked myself because I didn't want to depress them. More importantly, perhaps, I didn't want to depress myself. So I began speaking about the Jemaa instead, returning my story to its nucleus.

I drew their attention to the juice stalls that cradle the northern end of the square. For me, those stalls are the essence of the Jemaa because of the shower of fresh fruit smells with which they inaugurate each day. The progression of the smells leaves an indelible mark on the hours that follow such that every hour has its own distinguishing fragrance, from the stimulating poetry of early morning to the sickly-sweet musk of night. In between lie many shades of happiness. Mustafa, on his first visit to the Jemaa at the age of four, counted six distinct fragrances and attributed colours to each. With his eyes closed, nose held to the air, he recited, in a singsong voice: Bright golden—freshly peeled oranges at five in the morning; golden-orange—the first jugs of juice at seven; yellow—flies dizzy with heat drowning in the juice at noon; brownish-yellow—the pulp beginning to turn rancid in bins at two; brackish brown—the juice beginning to ferment at five; seaweed and salt—the spoilt juice thrown away at seven.

During the daytime, the Jemaa is a cross between a festive ground, a meeting place, and a marketplace. In the past, any

articles that could not be sold in the souks were traded here in
the morning. Set areas of the square were apportioned off for
livestock, produce, camels. Nowadays, it's a free-for-all, and, as
the saying goes, what cannot be found in the Jemaa is not worth
having.

By midday, the first bands begin to strike up music. In the
whistling, droning, ever-changing sounds of the nai, lotar, rabab,
and nakous, the great ear of eternity manifests itself, and yet, in
the shimmering heat of the sun, the silence is what seems most
audible. Although the music forms a constant backdrop, I hear
it as nothing more than a cacophony because, curiously enough
for a Berber, the melodies that most appeal to me are the muted,
plucked-string meditations of the Andalus. But I am the rare
exception. For everyone else, it is the drums that constitute the
essence of the Jemaa. In their presence, everything—the small
mirrors glinting in the sunlight, the sky trembling at the sound,
the white clouds descending as paper streamers on tables, the
vendors' booths dancing along the pavements, the horse-drawn
calèches on the perimeters of the square—longs to join in.

In the afternoon, the entertainers arrive. Sluggish snakes and
sad-faced monkeys strive to hold the attention of a fickle crowd.
Many animals perish in their captors' attempts to impress. They
are casually discarded. There is no room for sentimentality in
the Jemaa. Even as the earth is red and the sky blue, between
the monkey and the snake squats death. It is a rule that does not,
however, appear to extend to humans. Mule carts and motor
scooters alike weave recklessly between the crowds, daring
catastrophe. But the Jemaa has its own rhythms, and disaster
is—nearly always—averted.

After sundown, the square alters character. Musicians, acro-

bats, trapeze artists, faith healers, water sellers, henna artists, juice
vendors, snake charmers, belly dancers, glass eaters, lantern car-
riers, storytellers—all assume the quality of apparitions that are
both dramatic and ageless. Unchanged in their essence for hundreds of years, they are the Jemaa's enduring symbols, images of
stability amid the ceaseless turmoil of the world. The moon comes
out too: between the various stalls, iridescent white branches of
light leap from table to table, illuminating faces, leaving traces. In
the midst of the excitement, noiseless dancers swirl.

For the outsider, to come face to face with the knowledge that
the impenetrable really exists and that it manifests itself in a
form of life that has continued for centuries—this sentiment is
at the heart of the Jemaa. After the initial moment of contact,
which many describe as akin to a spiritual encounter, there is
only one thing that matters: the relation between the individual and the Jemaa. As my father used to say, one experiences
the Jemaa with a love analogous to that which one reads in a
beloved's smile. In this realm of passions and unleashed tempta-
tions, where sensuality is the highest form of expression, there is
a peculiar harmony between nature and conscience. It is an order
of things founded on spontaneity and confidence. One does not
seek the truth from the Jemaa but one's own nourishment.

DRUMS IN THE NIGHT

The ascent of drums signals the advent of the night. It is a
sound that can be heard for miles around the Jemaa, a black

sound, throbbing like restless wings, sinuous, the darkness gathering around its edges. Invisible doors seem to open all over the Jemaa, signalling a new beginning. Inhibitions surrender in a speechless rite of passage, belts unbuckle, buttons unfasten, smiles appear and disappear, the innocence of laughter dies down, cut off as if by a knife, unprepared and bewildered in the face of this sudden coup. The moon descends onto the middle of the square. Woodsmoke drenches the pavements; it weaves, gleams, congeals into a fog. On any given night, the bendir, the guedra, and the deff combine to create a seamless, shadowy mosaic that sets the heart racing and pierces straight to the soul. There is no other sound quite like it, and there is no resisting its seduction.

In the not-so-distant desert, the wind roars. It roars on the Atlas mountaintops and sweeps across the rocky islands off the Atlantic coast. But on the Jemaa el Fna, even the wind surrenders to the drums in the night.

COFFEE TO DIE

On the Avenue Mohammed V, next to the Hotel Islane and across from the Koutoubia Mosque, where there is now the large and airy bookstore selling Qur'ans, there used to be a glass-walled Western-style ice-cream parlour. Some of you may remember it. It was one of those regrettable innovations aimed at making a quick profit from the tourist traffic around the Jemaa. It was called Labes—"Hello"—and was open all night.

Mahi, the youngest son of my friend Mahmoud, worked there. Mahmoud was originally from my village but settled in Marrakesh many years ago. Mahi was born and brought up here. A street-smart young Marrakchi, I doubt that he has ever been to his father's birthplace.

On the night that my brother Mustafa went looking for the two foreigners, Mahi was working the night shift at Labes. His coworker had accidentally injured his hand and gone home early, so Mahi had the place to himself. Mahi told me about his meeting with my brother when, having finally given up all thought of carrying on with my storytelling and gone in search of Mustafa, I encountered him on the square. It was in the early hours of the morning, and Mahi was on his way back home from work.

He said that the two foreigners had come to the ice-cream parlour at around ten o'clock that night. They were speaking to each other in low voices and appeared to be having an argument. The man looked tired and distracted, and didn't once look at Mahi, but the woman seemed determined to take her time making her selection and eventually ordered two scoops of the Coffee to Die flavour, which she ate with obvious enjoyment.

Did you manage to overhear any of their conversation? I asked.

Only some of her remarks, Mahi said, and only when she spoke French. Once, I heard her say: I have very deep reserves and I am drawing on them. Another time, she said: Despair is a luxury I cannot afford.

Despair? I asked, surprised. Not fear? Are you certain?

Absolutely certain, Mahi said.

It was the man who paid me, he added, and she made him

give me a tip even though I hadn't served them. They'd been standing next to the counter the entire time they were there.

And then they left? I asked, disappointed.

No, she was still eating when your brother walked in.

My brother Mustafa?

Yes, Mahi said.

And then what happened?

Your brother glanced at the woman and stopped in mid-stride, as if he'd been shot. His hands dropped by his sides and he grew so pale that I thought he was about to lose consciousness. Instead he made it to the counter somehow and asked me for water.

Mahi, he said in a voice that was at once thick and faint, give me some water, and make it quick.

When I handed him a glass, he drank half of it in a single gulp and threw the rest on his face. If the gesture was designed to draw attention it could not have succeeded better, for the two strangers immediately glanced at him, startled. Without missing a move, Mustafa wiped the water from his face and stepped forward. He addressed the woman directly, asking her her name, where she came from, how long she planned to be in Marrakesh—all in one breath. He seemed entirely oblivious to the presence of her husband, who looked on with a faint, ironic smile as if he'd had long experience in dealing with men instantly enamoured of his wife.

After exchanging a few polite words, the woman was about to turn away when Mustafa reached out suddenly and grasped her hand, gazing at her widening eyes with a smile of rapture.

Labes? he asked her breathlessly. Are you happy?

Not entirely understanding his question, she removed her hand and said uncertainly: Alhamdullilah, by the grace of God, I am happy.

You speak Arabic?

I am studying to be an interpreter at the United Nations.

Perfect! Absolutely perfect! Mustafa exclaimed. He turned to her husband for the first time and said in a low and fervent voice: Ssalamu 'lekum. Your companion is beautiful. As beautiful as a rare gazelle. Those liquid eyes! They remind me of an oasis in which to parch my thirst.

At this point, Mahi made a sweeping gesture in imitation of my brother. With barely concealed excitement, he repeated Mustafa's next words. How much will you accept for her? my brother asked.

It was evident to me, Mahi said, that he was dead serious, but the woman, who was the only one who had understood the proposition, which he'd made in Arabic, just laughed as if conscious of nothing but its absurdity.

Still laughing, she translated for her husband's benefit while Mustafa listened with dilated eyes, drinking in every note of her voice. When she had finished speaking, her husband laughed in his turn. Though every bit as polite as his wife, his reply seemed fraught with condescension, as if Mustafa were no more than a minor irritant, and one barely tolerated at that.

Thank you, he said politely, but I must decline.

Mustafa turned red and his eyes glowed like embers.

I have a lamp shop in Essaouira, he said insistently. I have shares in a beachfront hotel. I will give you both in exchange for her. You won't regret it—they will bring you excellent profits.

The woman blushed as she translated, and her husband put

a protective arm around her. This is preposterous! he said in clipped tones. We are flattered but must decline. Please leave us alone. Good night.

Later on, in his prison cell, Mustafa would tell me that he had watched that man with envy, wondering how he had acquired his air of casual superiority, and wondering too if he himself could ever attain the same elegance of manner, he to whom every word, every gesture and handshake, seemed fraught with the potential to incite and insult.

When I sought to correct him by pointing out that he had no cause for envy given that he came from old Berber stock, he brushed aside my reminder with contempt. Instead, he said: If only you could have seen his impeccable behaviour and air of refinement, you would have realized that it instantly put to shame my own ill-bred shabbiness.

Why must you always run after Westerners? I asked, greatly pained. Why is your own heritage never good enough for you? We are Berbers, Imazighen, noble men and freeborn, we bow to no one. You have no cause for your sense of inferiority.

Mustafa's expression showed only that he was controlling himself with effort. We are Berbers, he repeated mockingly, and all that means is that our world is so small that it makes me want to laugh. Open your eyes, Hassan. Have you ever left the Maghreb? The limits of your existence are defined by the length and breadth of the Jemaa, and that leaves me speechless.

Speechless? I asked.

Yes, deprived of speech and gasping for air. On the Jemaa one always sees the same faces, the same dull and provincial countenances, and what inspires you leaves me feeling oppressed.

I replied with dignity that I begged to disagree. The Jemaa

was a crucible of people and ideas. One only had to look at it with open eyes to see that it was a microcosm of the world and encapsulated all that was best in it.

You are welcome to your illusions, he said tersely. Now go away and leave me alone, please.

I complied, sadly, but as I left the prison I thought back on that long-distant midnight conversation with Mahi. He'd told me how, when the woman's husband had first asked Mustafa to leave, my brother had refused, as if blind and deaf to anything but the spell the woman had cast on him.

It was an awkward moment, Mahi said, and I was afraid that Mustafa would do something hasty. But the husband placed himself before his wife, and even though Mustafa tried to evade him, he stood his ground and dealt with the situation calmly.

I felt mortified by this account of my brother's behaviour and sympathized with the husband's predicament. Admiring his presence of mind, I asked Mahi what exactly the foreigner had said to make Mustafa leave.

Mahi thought for a moment, his eyebrows furrowing. Then he assumed the role of the husband, drawing back a little and straightening his back. Making his voice deep, he said firmly:

Please don't stand there and stare at my wife. It makes her uncomfortable. Seer fhalek, go away and leave us alone. Bessalama, goodbye.

Stung by the dismissal, Mahi went on, my brother had stalked out of the ice-cream parlour, but not before he'd cast a last, longing look at the woman he had so admiringly compared to a gazelle.

I thanked Mahi for his account and resumed the search for my brother with a bitter taste in my mouth. I felt ashamed for Mustafa—ashamed, more than anything else, at his inability to respect boundaries.

Many months later, when I had the chance to bring up the matter in the course of another prison visit, Mustafa responded with indignation and surprise. In every inflection of his voice I could detect that sense of aggrieved pride and denial of reality that was so much a part of his character.

She was made to be loved, Hassan, he insisted. And I could tell that she was unhappy with him . . . clearly dissatisfied. It was in the look in her eyes. The merest hint. It wasn't much, but it was all I had to go by, and it was enough.

She was married, I reminded him.

That's what I found out later, he replied, but I didn't see any signs on that first encounter. Believe me, Hassan, I'm not lying when I tell you that. She wasn't wearing a ring, and I should know, because I held her hand.

Listening to him, I had rested my elbow on the arm of the chair. I'd felt drained, exhausted by his obduracy. Now, embarrassed for him, I lowered my head. I wanted to tell him—clearly and categorically, so that there could be no mistaking my meaning—that I'd seen her wedding ring. It was made of gold and formed of intertwined snakes. But I realized that I didn't have the heart to contradict my poor brother when he was rotting away in prison with only his illusions to keep him company. So I kept my thoughts to myself and said nothing at all.

Spleen

I paused in the midst of telling my story and ran my hand over my beard, marking the moment with the gesture. With my mind still on Mustafa, I gazed at my listeners one by one, taking my time to register their faces. Some of them held my gaze; others, clearly uncomfortable, looked away. Some had distinctive features; some others, less memorable, merged with the shadows and I had difficulty remembering them. Quite appropriately, it was the latter that I found more interesting, for they challenged my abilities as a storyteller, holding my attention until I could fix on some quirk or other before moving on to the next face. And yet, in the end, all that emerged from this prolonged exercise in close observation was a simple conclusion, and it was this. There was nothing in any of them that I could draw on to remind me of Mustafa or highlight as a point of comparison. He was unique in every sense, an entity unto himself.

Mistaking my interminable silence for distractedness, someone in my audience interrupted my ruminations. This is not the time to fall asleep, Hassan! he cried. Go on, keep talking, the night is too cold for lengthy pauses.

Acknowledging his point with a smile, I resumed my story by giving voice to my thoughts. I made my memories visible—but I also went a little further. I articulated the astonishment that I felt every time I contemplated the extent of my brother's incomprehensibleness.

My brother Mustafa, I said, is the most handsome man I've ever met. Unusually fair-skinned for a Berber, tall, wide-shouldered, tousle-haired, with light-coloured eyes and a penetrating gaze, he was the envy of all the men in our village. Even as a child, his looks were legendary. The moment he appeared in public, he became the cynosure of all eyes. Once, when he was six years old or thereabouts, my father discovered him dressed as a pagan god being pulled along atop a narrow cart drawn by eight girls swathed in white sheets. At other times he would pose as a statue in the village square, the object of universal admiration on the part of the women and derision of the men.

By the time he reached puberty, Mustafa was spending so much time attending to his words, his expressions, his gestures, that it became a matter of jest in our family. But one day, when I caught him admiring himself in the mirror while smoking his first cigarette, Father decided that something had to be done. He asked me to accompany the two of them to Marrakesh, to the Jemaa, where he knew of a man from the Sahel, an itinerant Mauri healer, who could cure my brother of his vanity.

This man, whose name was Bassou, was immense, heavyset, and entirely bald. He sat on his kilim like an impassive monument, smoking a hookah. After he had exchanged the usual greetings with Father, he summed up Mustafa at a glance. As much to him as to my father, he said: There are vapours in the air which contain impurities, and our bodies are like flypaper which attract and soak up these toxins. In past ages, my ancestors used to address these vapours as jinns and deal with them accordingly. But I am more scientific and believe in keeping up with the latest methods of diagnosis. At a single glance, I can tell you that your son is riddled with a number of complexes which have resulted in his attempting to mask an overriding sense of insecurity with excessive vanity. With your permission, I would like to prescribe a foot bath for him that will provide a thorough and painless purging of his—shall we say—malady. The foot bath will clean his organs, glands, arteries, nerves, muscles, tissues, and joints, and remove, in the process, the body's toxins. It will do this by generating a war between good and evil spirits in which the forces of light will vanquish those of darkness by attaching themselves to the impurities and purging them through pores in the feet. I call the process osmosis. It is a scientific term, and you will find it in use in the best hospitals and clinics. Following my treatment, your son will experience a heightened sense of well-being, whose most obvious manifestation will be a healthier attitude towards life and also more energy.

After this impressive peroration, Bassou unrolled a scroll of paper on which were pasted numerous testimonials attesting to the benefits of his technique. They were from grateful patients from all over the Maghreb, and I read out some of them for my father, who was unlettered:

—The eczema on my neck and chest is gone after four baths.
—After years of riding camels, the pain in my scrotum was so bad that I cried every night. Now, after ten treatments, I am able to be a man again.
—My ninety-six-year-old mother had arthritis in both legs which crippled her. Now, after eleven foot baths under your tender care, she is back cooking in the kitchen and doing housework.
—My ten-year-old son is handling his work much better since he started his osmosis treatments. He is less sullen, smiles more often, and no longer complains when he has to wake up at dawn to help me around the farm.

—After two sessions, my wife no longer talks about running away. We are a happy family now and I will return to you when I want to get her pregnant.

Satisfied? Bassou asked Father with a smile.

Satisfied, said my father, highly impressed.

Then it will be twenty dirhams for half an hour's worth of treatment. The usual rate is forty, but for your son, my old friend, it is half price.

Father handed him the money, and we settled down to wait while the healer went to work on my brother. First, he ordered Mustafa to go and wash his feet in a nearby fountain.

Scrub them well, he instructed. I want them spotlessly clean.

Somewhat sulkily, my brother complied and, when he returned, Bassou immersed his feet in a white enamel basin filled with water.

This water has special cleansing properties, he said. It is from the purest mountain springs near Jbel Toubkal peak. I collect it myself when the winter snows melt. There is nothing else like it.

He watched carefully until my brother's feet were flecked with silvery bubbles. Apparently satisfied, he covered the basin with an impervious black tar-cloth and turned his attention to some other patients who'd been waiting.

Exactly half an hour later, he returned to my brother and removed the tar-cloth with a flourish. He directed our glances to the water in the basin. Father and I craned our necks to see. To our surprise, the water had turned a dirty green.

Your son, said Bassou to my father, has an excess of spleen. Green is the colour of bile, and it is floating around freely in the boy's system instead of being stored. It explains his attitude, and, if it isn't treated now, will lead to his becoming a poseur and an exhibitionist. It's an unusual problem, but I see it more and more in our youth. It must have something to do with the general corruption in the air: television, Western-style cinema, and the like. I will give you some minerals in a bag. Use them in four foot baths and he will be cured.

To my brother, he said: After the session you will experience thirst, light-headedness, a slight headache, hunger, and the need to rest. You may also experience loose motion for a couple of days. There's no need to worry: these are all normal responses to detoxification. Just make sure to relax, eat fresh food, drink plenty of water, and be respectful to your parents. Do you understand?

He paused and gazed at my brother with a benevolent smile.

As if in response, Mustafa, who had been staring fixedly at the green water swilling around his feet, suddenly leaned over his knees and vomited directly into the basin.

Merde! the healer cried out in French, all dignity forgotten as he sprang to his feet with an alacrity I wouldn't have believed possible in a man of his bulk.

I fffeel wweak, Mustafa managed faintly.

GUEDRA

A few years later, when I visited my brother in Essaouira, we recalled the incident and burst into laughter. At the time, Mustafa was living in a rented room in the working-class Chbanat

district, near the Bab Doukkala entrance to the medina. It was
a small room without windows, and with a door opening into
the well of a gloomy courtyard. The furniture was spartan. The
bed sagged in the middle, the sheets were patched and worn,
and, as far as I could tell, Mustafa possessed only two things of
his own: his leathercraft tools—he was just beginning to make
the lanterns and lamps that would form the basis of his future
shop—and his handmade bendir drum. An inverted wooden
crate next to the bed served as his worktable.

One evening, Mustafa invited me to meet his friends who
played in his drum circle. Their sessions were held in a tiny
drum shop located below the battlements of the Sqala de la
Ville, a cannon-lined sea bastion overlooking the Atlantic. It
was already late in the evening when we arrived, and Mustafa introduced me to his friends one by one: Saad, Abdou,
Farid, Mbarek, Khalid, Lahcen, Bouchaib, Abdeljalil. They
were mostly young men his age, barring Omar, the owner of
the shop, who was also the leader of the drum circle. The room,
which was barely eight feet square, was lined with an impressive array of percussion instruments behind which the boys had
taken up stations. There were jembes and tam-tams, bendirs
and talking drums, doumbecs and darbukas, tars and taarijas,
guedras from Goulimine and handheld Gnaoua deffs. Musical
names, musical sounds. From hooks on the damp-stained walls
hung an assortment of metal castanets, karkabats, and various
kinds of cymbals played with rods. I sat cross-legged on the
floor in what appeared to be the only free corner of the room
while my brother, to my surprise, placed a massive, deep-voiced
jembe between his thighs and, at a signal from his leader, led
the plunge into the first song.

Moments later, a foreigner arrived and, slipping back the hood of her jellaba, revealed herself to be a woman. I stared at her, scandalized, but it was in the middle of the song, and I didn't think it polite to interrupt, even when she seated herself next to me, forcing me to edge away as far as possible. I was still taking her in when two more foreigners entered. Once again they were both female, but dressed in Western clothes this time. Finally, a statuesque blonde in jeans and a battered sheepskin jacket entered, completing the ensemble and compounding my confusion. On the one hand, it was difficult to resist the hypnotic rhythms of the drums, and, on the other, the tiny room seemed to produce foreign women by the minute. I had never experienced anything like it.

Much to my chagrin, there was no pause between the songs, thereby giving me no time to speak to Mustafa. I simply sat there rooted to my spot. By the third song, the first girl—whose name was Xaviera and who I later learned was French—and the blonde in jeans—who was Dutch—had both taken up drums, and I had to concede that they played as well as any of the men. The blonde, especially, thrust her guedra drum between her legs, and as her hands flew up and down, I noticed that they were red and callused from many years of playing. But she was oblivious to my gaze. As much as her neighbours, she'd lowered her head and was going at the drum as if in a frenzy. The very battlements seemed to throb.

At length, there was a pause in the music, and it allowed me to catch my brother's eye. We went outside, to the courtyard, where a thick mist was rolling in from the sea, and the air had taken on a brackish taste.

What's the matter, Hassan? Mustafa asked. They're bringing

out the kif in there, and we're going to miss out. It's the very best quality; Omar gets it directly from his Spanish contacts in Melilla.

I was barely able to speak.

I have no intention of either smoking kif, I said, nor going back inside. Have you lost your mind? Those women are stripping down to their T-shirts! I can see their bare shoulders, smell them sweating like swine. Have they no shame? Have you no shame? How could you bring me here?

Mustafa protested my accusations.

They are lost in the moment, Hassan, dwelling in the music. The last thing on their minds is their dress. Surely you, of all people, must know that kind of possession?

I know nothing of the kind, I retorted. Do you find me taking off my clothes when I tell my stories? I've never heard of anything so ridiculous!

Mustafa took a couple of steps back and measured me coolly with his eyes. My mortification seemed to have left him unmoved. We gazed at one another in silence until, at length, he spoke in a dangerously soft voice.

My poor provincial puritan, he said with a pitying smile. Wake up and smell the coffee.

I stared at him in bewilderment.

What is that supposed to mean? I asked.

It's an American saying. It means welcome to my world.

What world? I don't know what to say to you.

He held my gaze for a long moment, then suddenly seemed to lose patience.

Very well, have it your own way then, he said. You're proving yourself a narrow-minded misogynist incapable of understanding, let alone empathy. The music is what brings these women here, believe it or not; they are genuinely interested in drumming. But I will tell you what you want to hear. These women are not like the girls back home, that much must be obvious. They are here by choice, and they are—how do they themselves put it?—consenting adults. In other words, they know what they're doing. And I am not oblivious to their charms. For instance, the two Americans, Shania and Johanna, are sisters, and want to bed me; the French girl, Xaviera, wants to marry me; while the blonde from Amsterdam doesn't know what she wants. So which one do you fancy? Just tell me, and I'll set it up.

Repulsed, I lurched back and collided against the half-open door on which was pinned a colourful poster of some skinny black man with matted locks. In an attempt to regain my balance, I clutched at a corner of the poster and managed to rip it in half.

My god! Mustafa whispered as he gazed in horror at my handiwork. What have you done?

Why? I said savagely. Is this your new idol? Someone those hippies worship? Have you forgotten that you are Muslim?

You idiot! My religion has nothing to do with it. That's Bob Marley, the reggae king. Omar reveres him. Now he will have my hide!

As much as his sentiments, it was the crudity of his language that devastated me. I lost my head and replied in kind.

You called me an idiot! Have you no respect for the fact that I am, after all, your older brother? Where are your manners? Or have you forgotten them in that pigsty with your foreign whores?

Oh, screw you, Hassan! I am so sick of your ceaseless pontificating! If you can't accept the way I live, then why don't you just go back to where you came from?

We glared at each other with mutual loathing, though my own feelings were not unmixed with despair. I wanted to slap him across the face but managed not to, recognizing that it would simply make a bad situation worse. So we each paced around the circular courtyard until, with a shrug of his shoulders, Mustafa signalled that he was going back inside. I watched him leave without speaking. There was a bitter taste in my mouth. I lowered my eyes and walked away with a heavy heart, but not before my brother had remembered to dart back out and give me the key to his room.

PLUNGE

These were my thoughts during that ill-fated night on the Jemaa as I resumed my search for my brother. It was the first time in my life that I had cut short a storytelling session, but I felt I had no alternative. My continual distractedness had soon passed into an agitated state that so interfered with my concentration that, more than once, I found myself pausing because I simply could not remember what thread in the story to pick up, and why. Cursing my brother under my breath, I drew on all my reserves to remain calm and not get angry, for there is no catharsis to anger, only a self-defeating corrosiveness. And somehow I sensed that I would need all my wits about me that night.

Astara

On the square, things were far from calm. The rumours swirling around the two foreigners, especially those concerning the rare and dazzling beauty of the woman, had infused the air with an excitement uncommon even by the frenetic standards of the Jemaa. Of my brother, however, there was no sign, and as I made a quick circuit of the square, I began to feel more and more perturbed. It unsettled me, and I decided to seek out my friend the henna artist Dounia, who, along with her eight daughters, usually knows more than anyone else about the goings-on in the square.

Dounia was at her usual place, near the nut-roasting stalls at the northern end of the Jemaa, a location she preferred because it enabled her to work in the light of the massive braziers that lined the entrance to the adjacent potters' souk. We greeted each other, and she offered me some strong mint tea but gathered almost immediately from my troubled expression that something was amiss. When I explained that I was searching for my brother, one of her daughters immediately pointed me to the Qessabin Mosque where, she said, she had seen Mustafa enter about twenty minutes earlier.

My brother went into the mosque? I said, unable to believe my ears.

He ran there all the way from Mahi's ice-cream shop, she said excitedly. That was where I heard he'd had a run-in with a couple of foreigners.

How do you know that? I asked in wonder.

Because she applied henna on the woman's hand shortly afterwards, another of Dounia's daughters said with a laugh.

Yes, yes, I painted a fish on her left hand and an eye on her right to ward off evil spirits. You will recognize my marks. She was beautiful, and very kind. We talked while I worked, and she told me about what had happened at Labes. That brother of yours! He's mad.

Aren't my daughters wonderful? Dounia said with an indulgent laugh. Come to us for news of the world. We have eyes and ears everywhere.

I must go and find my brother now, I said, and got up to leave.

Give him my regards, Dounia called out after me. And tell him to get a hold of himself. There is a line between the infidels and our kind that must not be crossed. Besides, it's bad for business.

I acknowledged her advice with a wave of my hand.

The entrance to the mosque was a few paces from Dounia's stall, and I removed my footwear and went inside. The prospect of yet another argument with my pigheaded brother disconcerted me, especially in a place of worship, and even as I regretted the secular matter that had brought me here, I silently recited a prayer as I looked around and immediately felt calmer.

Alas, my brother was not in the mosque. Both disappointed and relieved, I slipped out and decided to rest for a moment and take stock of the situation. I sat down on a bench in the narrow alleyway behind the mosque. To my left, I could smell the meat cooking in the tanjia stalls; the glare from their acetylene lamps cast long shadows that fell just short of where I was. To the right, the alley was deserted and no longer suffused with the daytime banter of traders and artisans. I glanced in that direction and, as I did, I caught a fleeting glimpse of Mustafa moving towards the square. He seemed headed for the centre of the Jemaa, where a rwai ensemble from the Souss Valley had just commenced their performance around a bonfire. I heard the lively opening notes of their single-stringed fiddle, the rabab. The leader of the group, the raïs, was calling out for an audience in a high, piping, and surprisingly penetrating voice. I saw people swarming there like ants. The rabab began playing the instrumental prelude, the astara.

Amarg

By the time I reached the rwai, the raïs had begun singing the amarg, the poem that held the performance together, but I was no longer listening. I sought my brother, when my eyes fixed on the couple standing across from me with the reddish-yellow light of the bonfire illuminating their faces. I didn't need an introduction to know who they were. I couldn't take my gaze off the woman. That she was beautiful there could be no doubt. She was taller than I'd heard her described, with clear ivory skin and wavy, dark hair. There was a seriousness to her, an air of gravity, but also a vulnerability, a naïveté, that took me aback. It was that quality of ingenuousness, of the child latent in the woman, that left an indelible impression on me. She stood motionless, taking no notice of her surroundings but looking straight ahead, her entire attention focused on the musicians.

The circle of listeners began to move to the infectious rwai rhythms. In no time at all, I found myself next to her. She smiled at me and went back to watching the performers. One of the musicians invited her to sit on a low chair, but she declined. The lutes came on, followed by the drums.

During a lull in the song, she turned to me and asked in Arabic if I could tell her what they were singing about. I cannot follow their language, she said. It must be a Berber tongue.

It is, I replied. They are singing in Tashilhait, a Berber dialect. The song is about Isli and Tisli, the legendary young lovers who were prevented from being together and filled up two lakes with their tears. The lakes do exist, I added, on a plateau northeast of Imilchil, high up in the Atlas Mountains. Every year, there's a marriage fair there. It's famous. You must go sometime.

Oh, but I am already married, she said, and laughed. Thank you anyway. I will mention it to my husband.

May I ask you your name, madame?

It's Lucia, she said, but before she could say any more, the music interrupted her, the circle of onlookers began to move once again, and we were separated.

Soon afterwards, I found myself standing next to her husband. I studied him through the corners of my eyes. As if aware of my scrutiny, he glanced at me and nodded. He seemed a pleasant young man, dark-complexioned and relatively innocuous, and I tried hard to understand why he had affected my brother Mustafa the way he had. At that moment, he turned to gaze at his wife and his eyes lit up with a glow that startled me with their brilliance. It made his glasses seem like an affectation, as if by wearing them he sought to conceal a natural vivacity of spirit behind a mature, more sober façade.

Once again, there was a lull in the music, and I decided to take advantage of it to engage him in conversation. For one, I wanted to hear what his voice sounded like.

In my rudimentary English, I said: I hope you won't mind my asking, monsieur, but are you Muslim?

His response was noncommittal. Why do you ask? he said casually. Because of my beard?

Well, not entirely; as you may already have noticed, it is not the fashion in Morocco to wear beards, yet we are a Muslim nation.

I am not religious, he said shortly. I am a writer.

I laughed.

Indeed? So am I. I too make a living from telling stories.

That caught his attention. He turned to look at me directly. We held each other's gaze for a moment before he glanced away to where his wife was standing and gave an enigmatic smile.

Just then the music resumed, putting an end to our conversation.

Soon he stood across from me and that gave me time to study him further. Everything about him seemed to be in a low key. His clothes were simple, yet of impeccable taste, their very modesty enhancing their elegance. It led me to wonder if it was precisely that element of cool unobtrusiveness that made him impossible to define. At the same time, it became increasingly clear to me that he was oblivious to the danger in these surroundings.

The next time we were together, I reached over and grasped him by the arm. Speaking rapidly and urgently, but also lapsing into Arabic without realizing it, I said:

Monsieur, you shouldn't be here tonight and neither should your wife. You are serving as a magnet for the worst possible elements here. Please take her and leave this square before some mishap overtakes the two of you. That is the truth. I am frightened for you.

He freed his arm from my grasp and moved away with a shrug. It was then that I realized that I'd spoken in a language he couldn't understand. He walked over and stood next to his wife. I saw her look at him questioningly, and he tapped his forehead gently, twice.

What happened next was entirely predictable, but the rapidity of it took even me by surprise. A group of thuggish-looking men elbowed him aside and surrounded his wife. Before either one of them could react, an army of hands had reached forward to grasp at her. I glimpsed hands sliding across her breasts, cupping her hips, stroking her thighs. She froze, her eyes widening in shock and fear. Then she jerked away and stumbled towards her husband. It was a moment of shame. They staggered back from the crush.

SHAME

Can shame be erased? Can it be expunged? Or does the memory live with us for the rest of our lives?

I raised these questions in a conversation with my closest friend, Nabil. At the time of my story, Nabil was the headwaiter at the Argana, the famous restaurant which faces the square. He is a Berber from a village in the Tafilalt, in the Oued Ziz Valley, one of the most beautiful oases in the northern Sahara. What brought him to Marrakesh is a story in itself, and I will tell it later. But for now, in response to my questions, Nabil raised some of his own.

What is your first emotion upon encountering the Jemaa, Hassan? he asked. Isn't it excitement? An excitement of the senses? Come now, admit it. In other words, it appeals to your sensuality. But I will go even further and suggest that the Jemaa, especially at night, is all about unadulterated sensuality. It is the nature of the place. Why introduce shame into it?

I don't think it's as simple as you make it seem, I countered. It's more complicated.

Of course, it must seem more complicated to you, Nabil answered with a smile, but that's because you're a storyteller. You enhance reality with your own mythologies.

My own mythologies?

Yes, yes, mythologies. Have you ever asked yourself where your stories come from? They are nothing other than the result of your own preoccupations, obsessions, fantasies.

I will have to think about that, I said with a frown.

Take as much time as you need, he replied. Personally, I do not think the matter has a clear resolution, but I can well understand your fascination with the two foreigners, believe me. I myself have yet to come to terms with the full implications of my own meeting with them that evening.

THE RESTAURANT ARGANA

The moment they walked in, Nabil said, I knew something was wrong. We'd closed the restaurant about twenty minutes earlier, but it was still brightly lit inside and the doors weren't locked so there was no way they could have known we weren't open. Indeed, two young busboys were just then rolling an empty barrel of olive oil towards the doorway so that they had to step aside to let them pass.

I hurried over to them, sensing from their ashen faces that they needed a sanctuary. The man was very correct, even in that situation. He must have intuited that we were closed, for he offered to leave if that was the case, but I reassured him.

In that case, he said, speaking with urgency, may we have a table as far away from the square as possible?

I led them to a table at the back of the restaurant, where they wouldn't be seen. I chose a narrow space that would protect them from the Jemaa's boundlessness. As I drew back her chair, I noticed that her hands were shaking violently. I looked away so as not to embarrass her and busied myself in pouring water. She drank, but some of the water spilled onto the tablecloth. He apologized on her behalf, and I sensed that it would be a while before she was able to attend to such niceties herself. For the moment, she simply sat there silently, with a shadow over her face. It was clear that they needed time to themselves, and I excused myself.

I hurried back to the front door and looked out at the Jemaa. The air had filled with the smell of burning leaves. There was a huge bonfire in the middle of the square. The smoke resembled a tinctured pitchfork undulating in the breeze. It swayed like some malevolence come to life, snapping out a long tail and lashing at the assembled crowds.

Far to the west, beyond a reef of crimson clouds, a red stroke of lightning blazed soundlessly. It made the shadows of the souks bang against the stones of the square. Closer by, I heard a drunken laugh and spotted a man taking a leak in front of the Argana. I told him to get lost and he slapped his thighs and laughed again. Red clouds, red moon, red laughter. I marvelled at the Jemaa's thousand guises and bolted the doors to the restaurant.

When I returned to the couple's table, the man rose to his feet and expressed his gratitude for my consideration in letting them stay.

Thank you for accommodating us, he said. It's clear you had closed for the night.

I said: Here on the Jemaa we open when we like and close when we like. It isn't like London or Paris; there are no fixed hours. The Jemaa has its own rhythms and they change from day to day. Nothing is set in stone and everything is open to negotiation. Otherwise what pleasure would there be to being here? So: welcome to the Argana, and I hope we can make up for whatever it was that you experienced on the square.

My words seemed to provoke a reaction from his motionless companion. She tilted her head to one side and stared at me for a long time without saying anything. Her smoke-coloured eyes shocked me with their intensity. It made me uncomfortable and, unable to hold her gaze, I looked away.

When she finally spoke, her voice was pitched so low that I had to ask her to repeat herself.

I had expected more of Maghrebin chivalry, if not hospitality, she said.

That struck close to the bone, and I flushed fiercely.

There are people out there on the square who are hopelessly confused, madame. It causes them to act in shameful ways. I hope you will not see them as representative of our culture, which is very different.

She studied me closely. I could tell that she was making up her mind about whether or not to trust me. At length, she said:

What confuses them?

I mulled over an appropriate response, then decided to be blunt, if only to help her comprehend what had happened and thereby avoid a recurrence of the incident.

I said: What confuses them is your beauty. To them it is a temptation, but also terrifying.

Terrifying?

Yes, terrifying in its totality, its nakedness. Forgive me if I am too frank, but against the night you are aryana, as naked as the sun, and those who seek out the darkness will be attracted to you almost despite themselves.

Her face grew sad, then hard, with a bitter line to the mouth. A vertical furrow appeared between her brows.

That is elegantly put, she said, but it doesn't take away from what was done to me this evening. And it doesn't take away from the hundred pairs of eyes that were trained on us like guns, tracking our every move across the square.

She paused and, in a gentler voice, said:

Do you have anything more to add?

Nothing, madame, except to caution you against visiting the Jemaa this late at night. Come back in the daytime. There, in the middle of the sun-drenched square, you can experience all the deep memories of the place, its magical gestures, simple and at the same time majestic, immemorial. But not after dark, never after dark.

She was silent for a while. Then she looked at me with composure and straightened her back.

That is unfortunate, she said calmly, because I do intend to return there tonight. The music moves me, and I want to hear it in its natural surroundings. It's why we are here. There is no equivalent in the daytime. So there you have it. We are going back.

I lowered my eyes and turned away. I feared for her safety and, clearly, it showed on my face. I also wondered if she sensed how beautiful I thought she was. For the first time in my life, I cursed the twisted nature of the Jemaa, its Janus face.

Her husband shifted in his chair, staring past us in the direction of the square. I followed his gaze. Quick shadows crossed the windowpanes. The Jemaa was speckled with bonfires and torches.

There was absolute silence inside the restaurant. Outside, we could hear the sounds of the drums, along with the usual medley of cheers, clapping, catcalls.

Her husband stirred and looked away from the windows.

Speaking almost to himself, he said: Sometimes one is grateful when a new crisis occurs; it takes the attention off the previous one which may be preying unhealthily on the mind.

I couldn't tell if his words were addressed to me. I was about to ask, when he reached across the table and held his wife's hand. Slowly he stroked her long fingers, her palm, her wrist. This time quite clearly speaking to her, he said: When the big things in life seem out of control, then control over the smaller things assumes inordinate importance.

She looked calmly and steadily at him. Though she had her profile to me, I could see that her eyes and thick lashes were clouded with tears.

We must go back, I heard her say.

He drew her near him and continued to stroke her hand. She sat with her legs crossed, motionless, her head resting on his shoulder. They both gazed straight ahead of them at the darkness of the square. Their absorption was so complete that I had the sense they had forgotten my presence.

She snuggled closer to him.

How far is the desert from here? she asked.

Not far at all, my love. It's always present here, he said.

Some say it is fathomless, like the bottom of an ocean.

Desert sunrises and sunsets are the most beautiful in the world, or so I've heard, when the crimson light washes over the dunes, the white rock faces.

She gazed steadily at him.

It's certainly a temptation, isn't it?

He appeared to concur by inclining his head.

Perhaps over time one becomes part of the desert itself, he said, a mere shadow, without substance.

They continued to gaze out. He turned her wrist over and I glimpsed the angry weal of a scar across her veins.

At length, as if recalling that they were not alone, he glanced at me and smiled apologetically.

Thank you for caring about what becomes of us, he said. But don't worry, we are capable of taking care of ourselves. We'll be leaving in a moment.

I realized that I'd been dismissed. I bowed my head in acknowledgement and withdrew with sadness. My last sight of them was of their sitting at that table side by side, not as if they were two separate worlds but as if they were fused into a single entity, indivisible.

ΠABİL

I stared at Nabil incredulously.

So you're telling me that you allowed her to go back to the square, despite everything, and that even her husband didn't counsel her otherwise?

Yes, my dear storyteller, she did. Why do you find that so difficult to believe? It was her explicit desire, and, personally, I don't believe that either her husband or I could have changed her mind. She would have gone whether or not I advised against it. As for her husband, I think he simply recognized the inevitable and went along to avoid conflict.

Somehow I found that difficult to swallow and said as much.

Why do you find it shocking? Nabil asked. It is in the nature of women to desire what's forbidden.

No, I said stubbornly. That isn't right. I cannot agree with your assessment.

But of course you can't, because you are a hopeless romantic.

He glanced at me with a troubled look.

Which brings me to an entirely different question, he said. There was something about them—about him, especially—that reminded me of you. You share a particular quality.

What is it, do you think?

I have often asked myself that question, Hassan, but have yet to come up with a satisfactory answer. It could be as simple as your belonging to the same tribe: that of storytellers. Or it could be something else altogether, something much more complicated.

Much more complicated? How so, my friend?

I've often thought about it, he said pensively, and dismissed as outrageous the question that arose foremost in my mind.

What question?

I was hoping you wouldn't ask me that, Hassan.

I am.

Then you will see, as soon as I articulate it, why I termed it outrageous. And that would embarrass me as much as it would you.

It doesn't matter. Go on.

All right. Were you their accomplice that night, or their antagonist?

I laughed. You're right. That is outrageous.

I told you.

And, in any case, I added, I wouldn't tell you if I were either one of those things. I wouldn't betray them.

THE BLACKSMITH

It is perhaps time now to talk a little about my friend Nabil, who is closer to me than almost anyone else. So, with your leave, my dear listeners, I will do precisely that.

Somewhat unexpectedly, I heard murmurings of discontent from my circle of listeners and paused, surprised. A rough voice spoke up. It came from a man built like a blacksmith, burly and beetle-browed.

Enough of these asides! he said. We don't want to hear about your friend Nabil. We want to find out what happened to the foreign woman and her husband. Get on with the story.

Forgive me, I replied, trying hard to keep my voice under control, but my friend Nabil is here amongst you tonight, and since he was closer to finding out the truth than anyone else, I must acknowledge his provenance. It's the way we do things here.

What is the truth? the blacksmith demanded.

If only you will exercise some patience, I said with acerbity, then perhaps you'll be closer to it than you are now with your interruptions.

You are indulging in perfectly unnecessary digressions! he insisted.

I spread my arms in amazement.

Did you expect it to be any different? After all, I am a storyteller and a very traditional one at that. If you want quick entertainment, go to the nearest movie theatre and enjoy the show to your heart's content. Patience is not only your duty as a listener, it is your exercise of freedom in the face of the rush of time and the stream of necessities. To listen to a story without raising objections, without even the compulsion to understand but simply to be familiar, should always suffice. A story is a work of contemplation and you must accept responsibility for it inasmuch as your attention contributes to its vitality and its life.

A little more conciliatorily, I added:

If there were only answers to questions, there wouldn't be

anything to relate. So far as a storyteller offers only answers, he offers nothing that is real. His art has life only as long as the blood of mystery circulates. That is why the intelligence of the ideal listener observes, it discovers, but it does not seek revelation. The elements of a story are not absolutes in themselves, they are a way station, a means to an end.

What is that end? the blacksmith asked, still obdurate.

I studied his face and took my time formulating an answer. At length, I said, as politely as I could under the circumstances:

The freedom of the story to wander and escape.

That appeared to silence him, and I heard no more disaffected mutterings from my audience. I linked my fingers and waited for a moment; then I resumed speaking, calmly picking up the thread from where I had earlier left it off.

FANTASIA

Like me, I began, my friend Nabil is a traditionalist. This may have something to do with the fact that he is from one of the oldest families in the Oued Ziz Valley, where his grandfather once owned one of the finest date-palm oases in the Tafilalt.

To a certain extent, I went on, I model myself after Nabil. For one, I would like to live as he does now, though under less tragic circumstances. A few years ago, Nabil lost his eyesight while cleaning his grandfather's ancient rifle, and retired with his life's savings to Taouz, a village on the verge of the Sahara. There, at the edge of the Hamada du Guir, the stony wasteland notorious for its violent sandstorms, he lives in isolation with his French-born wife, Isabelle, whom he met in Marrakesh, and who has since taken the veil. I have not had the pleasure of meeting her—Nabil is understandably protective of her privacy—but I have heard that she is very beautiful and a solace to my friend in his blindness. It may explain why Nabil is content with his desert existence. Only once a year, during the cold season, does he deign to leave his dwelling to visit Marrakesh, coinciding his stay with my own sojourn in the Jemaa. Inevitably, these visits are scheduled around the night I relate the story of the disappearance of the two strangers, for, as much as me, Nabil remains fascinated by the enigma of what happened to them.

I paused and took Nabil by the arm affectionately.

How am I doing so far? I asked.

He merely smiled and shook his head, his natural modesty making him diffident at being the centre of attention.

I paused for a while longer, giving him the opportunity to demur, but when he remained silent, I resumed speaking about him.

Nabil's grandfather was a gentleman farmer by inheritance and a falconer by choice, I said. Nabil relates how, at any one time, the old man kept as many as thirty falcons under his roof, attending to their upkeep and training all by himself. This was in the days when the family's renowned date-palm holdings thrived under the generous bounty of nature, and little had to be done to look after them other than to attend to their annual harvest every October. Then, one year, without any warning, the dreaded Bayoud palm disease struck, and, in the course of the next twelve months, as many as two thousand of the magnificent trees perished. The next few years, the same story repeated itself, and Nabil's ageing grandfather, incapable of dealing with the extent of the blight, retreated into the depths of his ksar and the darkness of an incipient and gradually encroaching madness. As Nabil tells the story, it was a while before members of the household—conditioned by tradition to blind obedience to the patriarch—realized that the old man was no longer in control of his faculties, and even then, the temptation towards denial proved too overwhelming to resist. Nabil's father, the only son and heir, was away studying electrical engineering in Rabat, and the terrified women of the family did not dare question the old man's increasingly erratic ways. It was only when they heard the thirty gunshots early one morning and ventured out of their quarters to find the still-warm corpses of the octogenarian's beloved falcons, each one shot so cleanly through the head that the only evidence of violent death was the small drop or two of blood on the beaks, that they realized the full extent of the calamity that had befallen them. But by then, it was too late. The old man had already saddled his favourite horse, a jet-black Arabian crossbreed with flowing mane and tail, and ridden down to nearby Erfoud to take part in the moussem which crowns the three-day-long date festival there. At exactly noon, when the sun was at its zenith, he had ridden in formation with his fellow patriarchs at the fantasia, as he did every year, and, to the accompaniment of drumbeats and applause, at the very end of the performance, when the charging horsemen fired off their mokalhas—their prized, long-barrelled, silver-plated rifles—he'd keeled over off his horse and plummeted to the ground, dead.

It was in the course of cleaning this same accursed rifle that

Nabil lost his own eyesight, but his pride in his ancestry is such that the gun still graces the mantel of his humble pisé dwelling in the desert.

To return to the story, Nabil's thoroughly modern father refused to have anything to do with his tragic and problematic inheritance. Returning briefly to his father's house to dispose of the remaining date-palm tracts at a fraction of their worth, he had gone back to Rabat and busied himself in his career as a manager in an electrical concern owned by the government. In this capacity, he had been responsible for the successful laying of electric cables along the steep Tizi n'Test and Tizi n'Tichka Passes across the High Atlas Mountains. At the very height of his career, when he was tipped to go on to a ministerial position, he'd suddenly died at home at the age of forty from an accidental electrocution while building his son a toy railroad set.

In Nabil's telling, his father's precipitous return to Rabat and subsequent turning his back on his inheritance can be explained only by a refusal to deal with the traumatic circumstances of his grandfather's death. But that is pure speculation, as Nabil himself is the first to admit, and perhaps more part of his own attempt to come to terms with what happened than anything else. In the meantime, Nabil lives with the consequences of his blindness with a stoicism that is a matter of great admiration among all of us who know him, and we are glad to welcome him to Marrakesh during the one time of the year when he leaves his desert sanctuary and ventures into the outside world.

LABYRINTH

All through my narrative, since the early hours of the evening, Nabil had been listening to me with his face hidden beneath the shadow shaped by the hood of his jellaba. Now, at my invitation, he stepped forward with a diffident smile, though he still kept his head modestly bent under the triangle of the brown woven cloth so that I couldn't tell if he was hiding his emotion or underlining it in that way. But as I contemplated him, he stood up straight, his cheeks slightly flushed, his sightless eyes musing.

Thank you, my dear Hassan, he said in his distinct, mellifluous voice. I recognize some of that introduction and am flattered by the rest. What manners are to the prince, the imperative to idealize is to the friend, or perhaps, as in this case, the friend who is a prince in his loyalty, but also a storyteller.

He made his way slowly through the ring of onlookers and came and stood next to me, his cloak giving off the dusty aroma of the desert. I felt a rush of affection, but also of protectiveness as I surveyed his erect carriage. With the self-effacing manner which had become second nature to him since his accident, he spoke to me in an undertone.

Which way are we facing, Hassan?

You are looking at the souks, with the Koutoubia behind you, I answered.

The Koutoubia, he repeated after me, and smiled. Does its minaret still rise like a golden brushstroke through the air, with the three great balls of copper crowning its summit?

Indeed, my friend, it does.

He smiled again. Good, then we are facing the Argana, where I used to work. On its terrace, I once saw the shadow of a horse with a steel-clad rider.

Turning to my audience, he addressed them, a faint ironic expression on his lean face.

As Hassan has already informed you, I come to Marrakesh once a year and time my visits to overlap with the night he talks about the disappearance. I continue to be intrigued by its consequences and like to indulge myself by eavesdropping on Hassan's telling of it, which, remarkably, changes almost imperceptibly every time as he investigates new directions and explores novel alternatives. It is almost like a game we play, in which only he and I know the players involved and the stakes. What we are concerned with is the exploration of memory or, shall we say, more accurately, its approximation. We ask each other questions and, in so doing, challenge ourselves to imaginatively reconstruct what might have happened on that night of macabre interest to both of us. Call my own fascination the intellectual indulgence, if you will, of a blind man, but this storytelling is something I look forward to all year with great anticipation.

Is it merely an intellectual indulgence, Nabil? I interjected.

Well, yes, naturally, he said.

Then he paused and thought some more, before qualifying himself. No, he said, perhaps you're right, it isn't purely intellectual. I marvel that every time I myself listen to this story, I am moved anew. It speaks to me and serves as a reminder that my life is not yet over, and that, in itself, must be some kind of miracle.

The air was getting chilly, and he paused and adjusted his sheepskin cloak around his shoulders. His hood slid back from his head. The moon lit up his sightless eyes. As he stood there, with his head raised, I had the feeling that he could see the sky. It prompted me to move closer to him, link my arms with his, and stand shoulder to shoulder gazing up at the stars.

After a few minutes, he lowered his head and spoke to me in his soft baritone.

Why do you think those two came here, Hassan? Why did they come to the Maghreb, to Marrakesh, to the Jemaa? Were they seeking oblivion? There was certainly that element to them of wanting to forget. But to forget what exactly?

Perhaps the world they came from? I speculated. Modernity? The West? These are the things we will never know, I suppose, things to which there are no clear answers.

I wonder, he said, shaking his head slowly, but whether in agreement or disagreement I couldn't tell. He seemed content to limit himself to that cryptic response.

What else could it be? I persisted. The Westerners are losing confidence in their ability to shape their futures, and they've been trickling down here in their tens and dozens looking for solutions to the dead end in which they find themselves. We see it every day. Their world carries within itself its lack of soul like a disease. And they are unable to purge it because it is inherent in the law that governs them. They've replaced spiritual values with material dross, and the result is the reign of nothingness. Theirs is not a world of faith, nor is it a world of skepticism. It is a world of bad faith, of dogmas sustained in the absence of genuine convictions.

I hear what you are saying, Hassan, and I think there is some

truth to it, but I don't think that that was their particular crisis.
I think it was somewhat different.

What was it, then, in your opinion?

Turning in my direction and stroking his toothbrush moustache, he said: As much as you, I have thought long and hard
about this, and it is my conjecture that the answer, if there is
one, lies in the mystery of the effect the Jemaa had on them.
I am convinced that somehow, during their time spent in and
around the Jemaa, in the course of their many interactions, they
experienced a slow but genuine and profound enlightenment. It
took them a while to come to terms with it, but when they did, it
was life-transforming in its impact on them. I think I witnessed
some of it—albeit unknowingly at the time—when they were in
the Argana. What was it, you may ask? Put simply, I think it
was something along the lines of a liberation, a coming to terms
with the immeasurable disproportion between the reality of
their lives and the immensity of the universe. It lay in their real-
ization that there are no certitudes in life apart from the absolute
unimportance of what is known, compared to the greatness of
the unknown, which is nevertheless the only thing that matters.
In my opinion, this is the truth that is infinitely superior to any
factual truth about their lives.

What would you call this truth?

I would call it fate; others have called it destiny. It's the
moment of the rediscovery of the wisdom that life is governed
by everything that is unknown and that cannot be known.
Man is part of an infinitely fluid and intangible whole, and the
part can never comprehend or regulate the whole. The great
error is to search for truth in temporal events, because time is

both fleeting and irrecoverable. And the more you interrogate memory, which is nothing other than the search for certainty in time, the more you increase your dependence on chance. Do you understand now why I attach less importance than you to the specific equations of their individual lives than to the larger movement that carried them to the meeting with their fate?

I think I do, I replied, reassuring him with my concurrence. He appeared contented, but also tired.

By the way, Hassan, he said in a low voice, which way am I facing now? I've lost my bearings.

You are looking at the Koutoubia, I answered.

Excellent, he said, and smiled. Since the onset of my blindness, I've often browsed among the bookstalls that stand outside its walls.

I stared at him.

The manuscript market ceased to exist long before our lifetimes, Nabil, I pointed out.

Oh, I know, he replied serenely. It makes my browsing all the more worthwhile. You see, it is one of the peculiar advantages of my condition that I can live on the verge of the desert and still spend all my time here, in the environs of the Jemaa. After all, what else is this place but a vast library, where each person is like a book, if you will? I browse here to gather raw material for my thoughts, and when I return home I spend the rest of the year reading what I have collected.

Do you read me? I asked, intrigued.

He turned his perfectly white eyes in my direction.

All the time, he replied. I see the lamp of your body, I see many other lamps in the darkness. I see the presence of the dead manifesting themselves in any number of telling details. That is why, increasingly, I believe that it isn't the reality that you see but the other kind that matters.

Do you fear what you see?

Why should I be afraid? Fear is a moment of solitude wasted. Besides, fear arises from an inordinate apprehension of death, and that has long ago ceased to hold any terror for me.

I reflected on his words and, during that interval, I also ruminated upon a theme that had long been on my mind. Giving voice to it, I asked: Why do you isolate yourself in the desert, Nabil? What demons have exiled you there?

He gave me a shy smile.

Isn't it clear? There are no demons. Rather, I have finally found a place for myself.

And a companion as well?

He inclined his head in agreement. That too, he said.

Amydaz

At this juncture, with an air of some considerable embarrassment, the indefatigable blacksmith spoke up.

I still don't understand why they returned to the square that night. Were they tempting fate?

Nabil considered him with a languid and indifferent smile. Then he turned away from him and gazed in the direction of the Koutoubia.

Perhaps, he replied.

A shadow passed over his face.

A lengthy silence followed. Nabil continued gazing at the mosque. Finally, I asked him what he was thinking of.

I was thinking that the most important thing in life is a meaningful death; in the end, nothing else matters.

How so? I asked.

He thought about it for a moment.

Consider my grandfather, for instance, he replied. By all accounts, he lived a life that was meagre in its achievements, and yet, in my mind, in the manner of his death he more than redeemed himself.

Then he added, his voice heavy with sadness:

Perhaps that is why I was also reminded of my old home in the Oued Ziz Valley. I was thinking about watching the desert wind furrow the date-palm oases. I left my home when I was eight years old. It was a place of love and joy.

He kept on looking at the mosque.

What do you see there, my friend? I asked.

I see days of heat. I see beards of yellow grain in the shadow of the palms. The tallest trees stand more than thirty metres high. The region of the Tafilalt is immensely fertile. They call it the Mesopotamia of North Africa with good reason. It floats like an enchanted garden above the face of the desert.

I would like to go there with you one day, I said with a smile. I would like to see your old home and talk about your grandfather.

There is nothing left, Hassan. The roof of the house collapsed two years ago. The beams are rotting between the red pisé walls, which the wind devours day and night. The shutters of the triangular windows hang from broken hinges; the lintels dyed with indigo have turned to dust. There is a hole in the ceiling through which sand has entered. The fountain in the courtyard is filled with mud and dirt and choked with vines. It is a house fallen to decay. A dead house. And I am to blame. I ought to have devoted my life to rescuing my inheritance, but, instead, I emulated my father and fled the Tafilalt. I spent the better part far away, in Marrakesh, while the home of my ancestors collapsed into decay out of neglect.

No one is to blame, I said staunchly. You had your own life to live; you followed your own dreams.

Nabil bent forward and his face was lit up by the fire.

You are a good friend, he said, but even you cannot absolve me of the dead weight of the past. These are questions of fate and destiny. It is the way of the world. Meanwhile, this blindness is a blessing. I can be here, there, and everywhere at the same time.

He straightened up and stared off unseeingly into space.

My childhood was a gift. Now I look back and am grateful. Perhaps that is why I like to imagine visiting there. There are lots of details that I hadn't noticed before. I take early morning walks with the wind as my companion. We go down to the banks of the Oued Ziz that have always been maintained as meadows. In the wake of the sun the damp soil is steaming. We walk through the tall grass fields that surround the house. The orange groves are interspersed with pomegranates and figs. The mules flip their tails at swarms of black flies. A procession of ants climbs the long brown datura stems. Little drops of water dampen the red mud walls. We listen to the echoes made by the dawn fog.

He heaved a sigh. His eyes were blinking like those of a person staring into the sun.

In the evening, he went on, the shadows are silent and thick, and the burning day seeks repose on the verge of the river. The smell of water and wet earth lies heavy over the darkness. The air is cool and light. Stars fill the sky. The tallest palm trees are black strokes in the night.

He smiled, passing his tongue over his mouth as if to taste the damp air, but his lips, I noticed, were dry and chapped.

These are some of the things I hadn't observed before, he said. I like to dwell on the details. There is a great joy to be derived from the simplest things.

And all this from gazing at the mosque?

There is truth in prayer, and meaning in mysticism, he said. Or so the greatest poets, in the guise of Nature—river, mountain, ocean, and breeze—tell us.

I'm in agreement with you there, I replied.

Good, because I have often wondered if that is how you dream your stories, in the same way that I dream of stones along the trembling perimeter of the world.

I do, I replied.

I see. Isn't it beautiful then? It's just as it is, for pleasure.

He got down on his knees before the fire.

Have I told you of the eagle that crashed into my room when I was a child? It was a massive bird. Its wingspan exceeded the width of my grandfather's arms. It was chasing a pigeon that got away at the last moment. But the eagle lay without stirring on the floor of the room. Only its eyes moved. They reflected every colour in the world.

He extended his arms and held them out. Then he began moving them slowly. He became the eagle. We watched him stagger to his feet and stretch his talons. Calmly, deliberately, he flexed his wings, and then he launched into the air and sailed out of the window.

He held up his hand.

Listen! he said. The wind is speaking.

What is it saying, Nabil?

Softly, he cautioned, speak softly! The wind is making a hole in the sky, and through the hole the years are pouring backwards. Now the days are not pressed together but made up of distinct images like clouds, and across these the wind must traverse in order to become the sleek, sharp scimitar of time.

THE WITNESS OF POETRY

It was the midnight hour, when time stops in the Jemaa.

In the sixteenth-century storyteller Hassan el Mansour's wonderfully evocative chronicle *Plain Tales from the Jemaa*, he describes midnight on the square:

The shadows of trees lay like lances across the Jemaa. The air was scented with frost; a light breeze tracked down from the mountains. The sky was clear, the moon was bright. The clouds had peeled back to reveal millions of stars. The Hunter was roaming there, along with the Great Dog, the Twins, the Crab, and the Lion. The Milky Way filtered through their hearts, it warmed their skins and the grottos of their loins. Their blood pumped in time to the music of the Jemaa. The whole sky vibrated with the echoes of drums. We felt a throbbing vitality flowing down from the sky to the earth. The square began to swirl around us. It tilted and sloped up toward the stars. The roofs of the houses in the medina slid back. The Jemaa rose high above the black branches of the mountains. It passed Saturn, Jupiter, the outermost planets. Seven stars pinned it to its designated place in the sky. Then, abruptly, without warning, it collapsed into the space of a grain of sand.

CHRONICLE OF A DISAPPEARANCE

It's curious that you should bring up Hassan el Mansour, a voice observed meditatively, before revealing its possessor to be a thin, dark man with a wispy beard.

What's even more curious, he added after a pause, is that I should be present in this unlikely setting, on a stray visit to your city, when you should choose to make your allusion to his work.

I'm Farouk, he said. I'm a researcher in our nation's history attached to the National Library in Rabat, and I wonder if I'm the only one here who has also read El Mansour's *Chronicle of a Disappearance*, which was not, of course, part of the better-known *Plain Tales from the Jemaa*, but nevertheless should be of especial interest to this audience given that it concerns a case uncannily similar to the one being debated this evening, except that it took place nearly four hundred years ago, and the man involved in that instance was a Turkish nobleman, while the woman was a minor Italian princess from Salerno who eloped with her lover and sought refuge in the Moroccan court from both the wrath of her own relatives and the displeasure of the court of the Sublime Porte to which he was attached.

I only raise this, he added mildly, because I find the parallels between the two sets of disappearances to be rather remarkable.

What you probably do not know, I replied, and what you cannot possibly have surmised, is that El Mansour was an ancestor of mine. In fact, believing him to be related to us from my grandmother's side of the family, my father named me after him, but I'm not certain that the claim holds up. For one, his Berber antecedents are unknown. For another, there is apparently a contemporary biography in the Qarawiyin Library in Fès, which conclusively establishes that he was an Andalusian migrant born and brought up in Córdoba before he moved to the imperial court in Marrakesh. To settle the matter to my father's satisfaction, one of these days I must remember to ask my brother Ahmed if he can get permission from the authorities to examine the manuscript.

In any case, I continued, I do know about the chronicle that you refer to, and am, in fact, rather pleasantly surprised by your knowledge of it, since I'd believed that only a single copy existed in the archives of the Glaoui Pasha of Marrakesh, from where a friend of my father's got hold of the story, but that copy subsequently disappeared and was presumed to have been irretrievably lost.

It may have disappeared from the Glaoui Pasha's holdings, the scholar from the National Library replied with a smile, but it found its way to Rabat a few years ago and passed therein into the safekeeping of the collection where it presently reposes.

How did that chronicle end? someone called out. Was that pair of lovers found?

Alas no, the scholar replied, and neither, in the end, was El Mansour.

What do you mean? I asked, taken aback.

The librarian rose to his feet and stepped out of the crowd.

May I . . . ? he asked.

Yes, of course, I replied, as intrigued as anyone else in the circle.

It's like this, he said. From what I've been able to establish, El Mansour's *Chronicle of a Disappearance* was not only based on fact, but strayed uncomfortably close to the involvement of a member of the imperial court in the affair. As a result, Mansour became— shall we say—a dangerous man to have around. When the Sultan Abu Yussuf Ya'qub al-Mansur subsequently decided to despatch a force of four thousand men to raid the Songhai strongholds of Gao, Timbuktu, and Djenné on the far side of the Sahara, your ances- tor was willy-nilly attached to the invading force despite being possessed of no martial experience whatsoever. As is well known, the raids destroyed the Songhai empire, enriched the Moroccan treasury beyond measure, and led to the Sultan's assuming the title "the Golden One," but of the storyteller El Mansour nothing more is heard. It's assumed that he perished somewhere along the way in the unforgiving sands, although there is a single, intrigu- ing mention in a different source of his having been poisoned and his body buried in an unmarked grave. This source is not the official biography in the Qarawiyin Library, by the way, which I have seen, and which contains no information about his final years. His bones have never been found.

I had no idea! I exclaimed. Here's a story within a story!

Or rather, a story within a story within a story, a veritable cornucopia of fictions, so to speak, the scholar slyly remarked.

I couldn't follow his learned allusion, but was content to nod in agreement while still bemused by the turn the tale had taken.

It's extraordinary what one can stumble upon in the course of one's researches, he concluded with a smile.

And I think it's wonderful that you should remember these facts with such clarity, I said admiringly.

. It's an occupational hazard, he replied, and laughed, clearly pleased.

He turned to Nabil, who'd been listening to him attentively.

And what of the two foreigners who form the basis of our story? he asked. The last we left them, they were in the Argana, gazing arm in arm at the darkness of the square through the fogged-over windows of your restaurant.

BLACK ROSE

I wanted them to fly away, Nabil answered in a slightly dreamy voice, but, alas, it was not to be. I knew their time had come. They stood up and the husband put down some change next to the pitcher of water. I watched them leave their table and hesitate before they stepped out of the doors of the Argana.

Come, I heard him say as he took her hand. It is time.

She followed him out.

They advanced with great composure and gravity. She walked

slowly, her head leaning against his shoulder. He scanned the square with watchful eyes. Their shadows seemed to lengthen.

I want you to know, she said softly, that I will love you for the rest of my life as much as I love you now. I love you. I love you.

She put all her tenderness into her voice.

I have never been as happy as I am today, she said.

It's been like a dream, he agreed. I could be here with you every night without ever growing tired of it, my love.

He looked at her and breathed more quickly.

Free? he asked.

Yes.

The shadows began to detach from the darkness and approach them one by one.

AMMUSSU

At this point, I cleared my throat and stepped into the middle of the circle. With an eye to my audience, I placed myself before the fire. Raising my gaze over their heads, I said:

I sent my eyes scouring all over the square, and when I saw them emerging from the Argana, I plucked them and inserted them back into the circle of rwai musicians. They seemed surprised, and reassured, to find themselves there.

I paused and smiled in response to the sighs of relief from my listeners.

To make the story even better, I said, I will place them next to each other in the circle, with their hands tightly linked.

I was about to continue when a voice interrupted me:

But before they got there, Hassan, I presented her with a bouquet of roses. You forgot to mention that, or perhaps you were unaware. But it's important for the veracity of your story. After all, it must have been one of their final encounters in the Jemaa.

So saying, a slim man in a voluminous burnous stepped forward and pantomimed that long-ago meeting. It was Marouane, the juggler, who was famous in the Jemaa for having mastered the art of making a ball stand still in the air.

This is how it went, he said. She was walking there, and I was standing here. I stepped across their path and held out the roses.

He thrust back his hanbel and extended his hand in imitation of his gesture.

This bouquet is for you, I said to her in my schoolboy English. A token of your visit to our beautiful city, Marrakesh. The City of Roses.

I don't want it, she said, surprised.

I picked them for you, madame, from the Agdal Gardens. It is a garden that smells of the sun in the morning, and roses at night. Take them, please. They are a tribute to your beauty. As Muslims, we know that such beauty belongs in paradise.

Who are you? her husband asked warily, inserting himself between the two of us.

There is no cause for concern, I replied. My name is Marouane. I am a juggler who performs here. I've been watching the two of you since the early hours of the evening. Your wife's beauty moved me, so I went to the Agdal and picked this little bouquet. The language of flowers is universal. Take it, please. It's a trifle. It is nothing.

And everything, the man said, as he took the bouquet from my hand and gave it to his wife.

They're beautiful, she agreed, and smiled.

For your pleasure, I said.

You've no idea what this means to us, she added, pressing her face to the blossoms. Thank you very much. You have brought us happiness.

Your happiness is mine, I said.

You've altered our perception of the square, her husband said warmly, and for this as well we are grateful to you. We had an unpleasant experience earlier this evening. It left a bad taste in the mouth.

May I apologize on behalf of my compatriots? There are many sinful men here. They live inside cocoons, divided against themselves. It leads them to behave in ways that are depraved.

You give us hope, he said, and, to my great surprise, he took off his watch and gave it to me. That's for you, he said, in exchange for the gift of roses. You can unscrew the back and insert a picture of your beloved.

I handed the watch back to him in alarm.

No, no, monsieur! I cannot take your watch! It is too valuable! And all for a few modest roses!

But he insisted upon his gift, pressing it into my hand.

I have no more need for it, he said.

How is that possible? Do you no longer need to tell the time? He laughed.

Can you tell us what day is it? Is it yesterday, today, or tomorrow? You see—you don't know. And what does it matter?

Ah, so you are a philosopher. You remind me of my late father, who was a hajji, may heaven rest his soul.

She touched his arm.

We have to go now, she said, and smiled at me apologetically. Thank you again for the roses. I will treasure them.

Where are you bound, madame?

We are going to listen to the rwai musicians. We were there earlier. They're marvellous; they've so much life!

The rwais are like fire, I said, and there is nothing like a good song to warm the heart. Very well, if that is your wish, I will accompany you there. Then we will go our separate ways. Perhaps we will meet tomorrow? You must come and watch me perform.

Marouane hesitated and rubbed his chin thoughtfully. He stared at the fire. He put his hand to his heart and looked at us.

This is the point where things took a strange turn, my brothers, he observed. I escorted them to the circle surrounding the rwai. The ammussu—the choreographed overture—had just begun. We were separated instantly as they worked their way to the front of the circle. I cast a quick glance around, but there was no one there that I recognized, which was unusual. There was something perturbing about this gathering of strangers, and I couldn't put my finger on it. But the music was heating up; it was hypnotic, and it grabbed me by the ears. I decided to stay and listen for a while. I looked across to where my erstwhile companions were standing, but they were already absorbed in the performance. The young man kept his arms protectively around his wife and his gaze was wary. Smoke from the bonfire had ignited the air and it cast a golden-red patina on her face. She stood erect and light; she looked very young.

The theme of the ammussu was true love, which, by its very nature, is doomed to remain stillborn. The raïs was putting his

soul into the song, and the images he evoked were both melancholic and beautiful. He sang of a love that was radiant and
pure, as immense as the sun and as inconceivable in real life as
waterfalls in the desert. I listened as he mourned the fragility
of this most exalted of emotions, and the lyrics brought tears to
my eyes.

I glanced at the two foreigners and it was clear that she was
following the meaning of the song. Her face was flushed, her
expression had turned grave, and her lips involuntarily trembled. It was impossible not to identify with her distress and I felt
my heart going out to her. Suddenly the Jemaa seemed cold and
uninviting, and I shivered with the premonition that had arisen
in me earlier. I wanted to go up to them and advise him to take
her away from here, but I held back.

The song grew muted, the raïs expressing his yearning in bell-
like, crystalline notes. One of the musicians extended a chair
towards the girl, and she accepted, sitting down with crossed
legs and gazing disconsolately at the fire. Her husband kneeled
next to her, keeping his eyes fixed on her face. The raïs's voice
died down to a whisper. Just when the music was at its most sublime, with only the notes of a single lute sounding like a bell in
the silence, dark figures appeared at the edge of the circle. Their
voices—coarse, thick, loud—joined in with the song, instantly
altering the mood. They were hooded, their faces swathed in
black cloth, and I wondered where they had come from. There
was a heavy, malignant intentness to their movements, and I
think the musicians sensed the danger, because they paused and
looked irresolutely at them. Trying to preserve a demeanor of
calm, the raïs began to say something, when a mocking whistle from the back cut him off and I saw a couple of shadows

lunge at the girl. Her husband rose instantly to fend them off but someone tripped him from behind and sent him sprawling. The next moment, the unity of the circle had disintegrated into pandemonium. The musicians scrambled out of the way, intent on saving their instruments. I heard screams and shouts. The light from the bonfire flitted across faces. People began to run. I scrambled towards the girl but a hand descended on my shoulder. I attempted to resist, striking out with my arms, but a cuff on my head knocked me senseless.

When I came to, the ground was littered with ashes from the fire, which had gone out. A ring of police cars with flashing lights lit up the square, and there were uniformed policemen everywhere. Next to me, a man lay unconscious, his hands and arms bruised and scratched. I staggered to my feet and was instantly surrounded by officers asking questions. I glimpsed the husband leaning against an ambulance, his clothes in tatters. A medic was attending to him, but he was sobbing like a madman. I turned away in distress and answered the officers' questions the best I could. They took down my name and address when they were finished and let me go with the caution that they would be in touch with me again.

When I returned to the Jemaa the next morning, parts of the square had been cordoned off. Some of the stalls had opened for the day, but the overall mood was subdued and dark. I walked over to the place where the rwai had played and found a single rose lying on the ground. It had turned black, and some of the petals were charred. Wondering if it could be from my bouquet, I picked it up, but it smelled burnt and I tossed it away with a sense of despair.

Marouane paused for a moment, crouching before the fire. Then he turned away from it and looked at us one by one. His gaze was troubled and withdrawn.

That is the way I remember that accursed evening, my brothers and sisters, he said in a low voice. My heart broke at the sight of her husband, whom I have since seen many times over the years, as, I'm sure, have many of you, wandering the square like a lunatic, searching every face for traces of his beloved. They say that, bereft at his loss, he abandoned his home and livelihood and now lives somewhere in Marrakesh. They say he talks to himself and his face is all tics and grimaces. But I don't know that for certain. All I know is that I will never forget his face that night. May I never witness such grief again. It is enough to disturb a man's peace of mind for an entire lifetime.

That is the truth, he said.

ABERDAG

That is not the truth! It is a distortion of the truth!

A man stepped out of the ring of listeners. He was tall and thin, with high cheekbones and a bitter cast to his mouth. The lower part of his face was wrapped in a scarf that muffled his chin.

That is not the way I remember the events of that night, he announced. His voice had an acerbic tone as if he expected little of us.

Show us your face, my friend, I said. It isn't polite to conceal your features.

He unwrapped his scarf with an abrupt movement and I blanched in horror. His jaw was completely eaten away and disfigured. His eyes flashed contempt as he registered my reaction.

I used to be a guard in a penitentiary, he said. A prisoner threw acid.

He wrapped the scarf back around his face so that we could only see his eyes. They glittered, then seemed to darken. He surveyed us with a military bearing, his body held stiff and taut.

My name is Walid, he said. I am an ex-soldier and a bachelor. I live by myself in the Kasbah. I was in the circle watching the rwai that night. I went there for the music because I play the lotar myself now and then. It is an exacting instrument and a demanding art. I had no interest in the two strangers.

He looked at us fiercely as if daring us to contradict him. When no one uttered a word, he resumed speaking.

The rwai who played that night, he said, were Chleuh Berbers from a village near Taroudannt. They were a large group, with two rababs, two lotars, cymbals, and a battery of bendirs. The raïs was not the best I've heard, but he was energetic, and skilled in drawing crowds. His voice sowed the wind, while the music shaped images behind him. Images of rivers, meadows, star-shaped seeds, harrowed earth. The songs were joyful, and they brought back memories of good harvests. Every new song drew bigger crowds.

With his fingertip, the ex-soldier counted off the songs. Satisfied that he'd accounted for all of them, he held up his fingers and said:

They'd already performed four or five songs when the two foreigners appeared. They were rude from the beginning. They elbowed their way to the front of the circle and I found myself standing next to them. I did not care for the woman from the very first moment. There was a crazed look in her eyes. She turned to me and said something about the red moon. I do not like strange women speaking to me, so I did not reply. I found her very presence there, as a woman, at that time of the night, scandalous. I wasn't surprised when she began to draw stares.

In a while, she started moving to the music. I stepped back in distaste when I saw her undulating her hips. To my eyes, she lacked any sense of modesty. There was nothing demure or becoming in her movements. She was out-and-out provocative, a real hussy, like most Westerners. And that husband of hers was little more than a cipher, content to remain silent while she made a shameless spectacle of herself.

Watching her gyrate, it struck me how little these foreigners respect our culture. They import their mores and flaunt them before us, they exoticize us, to them we are the great unknown, a blank slate on which to impose their fantasies. And we encourage them, to our lasting shame.

When a woman thinks she can behave like that, what happens? Men's minds thicken. They begin to think primitive thoughts. They forget the words of the music and feel only the throbbing beats. Then even that turns into something else: a dull, burning pain. Their hearts sting, their faces turn black with heat and rage.

You can't blame the men for what happened next. A woman like that isn't worthy of respect. She was dancing like an animal in the dusty earth. She'd advanced into the middle of the circle by this time. Now she stopped a few times before some of the men as if challenging them. She was stoking their fire, taunting them to let themselves go.

But the men did not move. They were watching the red moon. There was a bitter smell to the air, like the odour of sap. The raïs was shrilling all around, but we scarcely heard his voice.

That was when she threw off her shoes and loosened her hair. We heard her bare feet scratching the ground. There are some animals that do that when they go to drink in the desert at night. It is a bestial, rutting sound, and it invites a swift response. With two quick movements, one of the men advanced and lifted her into the air. He was a basket weaver from Smara, and he was joined by someone else. They began to dance like bears while carrying her above their heads. Her husband raised his voice in protest, but the men ignored him and turned their backs. When he tried to free her from their grasp, a scuffle broke out, and I glimpsed something flash in the dark. Someone had struck him with a metal hook and stretched him out flat. He crawled away on his hands and knees. They hit him on the head, on the neck, on the shoulders and the arms. His wife began to scream and the men let go of her. She plunged to the ground. Then she fell silent and didn't utter a word. Her teeth were clenched, her mouth wet with saliva. I thought she was going to pass out.

Suddenly there was a sharp whistle. I saw silhouettes emerging from all sides of the square. The next thing we knew we were surrounded by dozens of policemen. They formed a cordon around us. Some of the men tried to escape, but they didn't make it. Everyone was running here and there, and then things calmed down. I didn't try to go anywhere myself; I was content to stand on the side and watch the fun. It was black work under a dark sky. Then the fog crept in, weighted with reddish shadows and cold, heavy air.

That's when we heard an unnerving cry. It cut through the stillness like some wild animal's scream. It was the woman, yelling in despair. What have you done with him? she shouted. You sons of bitches!

All around us there was silence when we heard that. The policemen fell back. No one knew what to say or how to react. We tried to make out where she was. The fog had wadded the Jemaa with thick grey tufts. The smell of fear was strong everywhere. The night had turned to lead.

They found her squatting on the ground with a bruise on her forehead. Her shirt was torn, her mouth striped with blood. One of the constables offered her a handkerchief but she flung it away.

They began searching for her husband, but he was nowhere to be found. No one knew where to look. They searched the square, the souks, the qaysarias. An impossible task. Time passed swiftly. The fog got in the way.

The last I saw her, she was lying on the ground, weeping. An officer was kneeling next to her, urging her to get up. From time to time, she would open her mouth wide as if to scream but nothing came out. After a while, she stopped crying and silently allowed herself to be led away. She reminded me of something, but it was a while before I realized what it was. It was a sheep being led to slaughter. She had the same look in her eyes, the same smell. I should have felt sorry for her, but I didn't. I felt nothing. Well, what did she expect?

The ex-soldier paused and stood back. He had spoken rapidly, and he paused to regain his breath. He lit a cigarette and

220 Joydeep Roy-Bhattacharya

stood silently for a while. On his ravaged, extraordinarily bitter face there appeared traces of fatigue. He gave me a long, hard look before he began speaking again.

I heard that for the first few years after her husband's disappearance she flew down to Marrakesh every winter to seek news of him. An acquaintance of mine once saw her on the square and said she appeared perfectly composed. She was wearing some typically inappropriate Western outfit and parading around. But then she stopped coming and, as far as I am aware, nothing has been heard of her since. I assume that she went back to wherever she'd come from.

Breaking with convention, I acknowledged his contribution in a manner that was barely polite. I gazed at him with distaste, and the malevolent line between his eyes grew even more marked as he said: That's the way it was, and it isn't my fault if you don't like it.

That isn't the way it was, I replied firmly, and you know it.

This made him so angry that he began to repeat his allegations, but I cut him off and the others in the circle supported me with their remarks. Seeing that the mood was clearly against him, he said with venom: I can see that you can't take the truth. His voice was even colder than his words.

There would be no point, I replied. No point at all in trying to reason with you or put you straight.

Is that so? he said, wearing that wrinkle between his eyes like a gash. You're on the side of the foreigners—so that's it then!

I am not going to be drawn into an argument with you. Cure yourself.

I will remember you. I won't forget this moment.

Is that a warning or a threat?

It's neither. I am not threatening you. I am speaking with disdain. As much as your brother Mustafa, you have sold your soul.

He drew aside his scarf and spat on the ground. Without waiting for a reply, he threw me a final, icy glance, bowed stiffly to the others, and made his way out of the circle with a contemptuous deliberateness. He'd advanced about a dozen steps when he stopped suddenly and shot me a glance over his shoulder. He found me staring intently at him and made a slight movement of recoil. I watched him dart into the shadows and then I couldn't see him anymore.

I felt a hand touch me gently on the shoulder. I started and turned to see who it was. Then I realized my fists were clenched.

TAMSSUST

A young man stood behind me. He was swaying unsteadily. His pupils were dilated, his breath reeked of kif. He wore a dirty brown jellaba with the hood drawn back; he was pale, with a freckled face, and his greyish-yellow eyes hinted at mixed blood.

La bes darik, he said, greeting me in Tashilhait. Hello.

La bes, I replied.

That entire account you just heard was a lie, he said slowly. I was there that night. It was a very bad experience, but it was nothing like that man said it was.

You have a better version? I said dryly.

It's a long story.

Let's hear it.

Well then . . . he said, and paused.

His eyes were heavy. He raised his hand before his face and peered through his fingers at the fire.

I controlled my impatience and asked him what the matter was.

Nothing, he replied.

Are you feeling ill?

No.

Then what is it?

Pointing to the middle of the square, he said:

God knows I am the last person who should be venturing an opinion on the truth. In fact, I'm not even sure I know what that means. But this much I can surmise. Perhaps only a single thread separates us from the truth, or perhaps an entire ream, but we will know for certain only when we look at the whole weave.

Who are you? I asked, without raising my voice.

My name is Rachid, he answered. I sell whirligigs on the square. You might have seen me around. I used to sell music cassettes next to the Café de France, but that didn't work out.

Whirligigs?

Yes, I make them myself out of thuya wood. I guarantee them for a lifetime. They are the best in the world.

I'll take your word for it.

You look at me as if I am mad, but I'm not. I'm perfectly sane. I've had a little kif, that's all. Just like I had that night, I will not deny it.

A little?

Yes, only a little, he said, drawing a deep breath. Without the

kif there'd be a buzzing in my head and I'd be able to say nothing at all. I'll be the first to admit that I am perhaps not the most
reliable of witnesses. But there were so many anomalies in the
previous two accounts that I feel compelled to speak.

What do you mean, anomalies?

Just that.

Were they lying, according to you?

I'm not saying that. But it was remarkable, all right, the things
they made up.

Then why don't you tell us about it once and for all?

Do you have a cigarette?

I don't smoke, I told him, but someone from the audience gave
him a Gitane. He lit it, and his face lit up. As he smoked, without
looking at anyone, the cigarette trembling in his hand, he began
to speak softly, with many pauses, and I knew better than to
interrupt.

She was wearing a bright red beret that night, he said. I
remember it because a week later I found it in a gutter in the
potters' souk and handed it over to the police.

He drew deeply on his cigarette.

Like everyone else, I didn't like the look of the red moon that
evening. When it faced the dying sun, it was as if there were two
wounds in the sky. Everywhere you turned, the sky was bleed-
ing. It was completely unnatural.

He drew on his cigarette again, nodding to himself a couple
times, his voice gaining in assurance with every passing moment.
His head tilted to one side, his eyes gazed past us as he spoke,
and his expression grew increasingly contemplative.

No, I didn't like the look of that moon one bit that evening, he
repeated. And I wasn't the only one. I recall someone shouting

from the middle of the square: The end of the world has come!
The end of the world has come! The words seemed to well up
in the air until they were fit to burst. It was some doddering
old Yehudi from the Mellah, half out of his mind. The police
whisked him away, but looking at that sky you were almost persuaded he was on to something.

Then the lights of the stalls came on. The Jemaa el Fna at
night. Everything in motion. Performing bears, music, acrobats, the Gnaoua's shiny brass instruments. The Place Foucauld
had filled up with long black shadows and glowing cigarettes.
Bicycles and motorcycles raced diagonally across the Avenue
Mohammed V. The windows of the Café de France and the Restaurant Argana were like bared teeth in the darkness.

Smiling at the recollection, he began to dance slowly around
the fire. Welcome to the circus, he sang. Where everything's an
illusion.

Withdrawing to one side, he turned and placed a hand on his
heart.

I'm a child of the sea, he said. I come from the west coast,
from Akhfenir, and, to my eyes, the Jemaa that night resembled
a storm-tossed ocean. Its lights and reflections imitated boats,
rocks, waves. The woodsmoke was spray from the surf.

I crouched behind one of the food stalls and snacked on a plate
of fish eyes. It was a gift from my friend Noureddine, who's from
the coast, just like I am. Six, eight, ten—such a wealth of eyes, so
very delectable, and, at the end, everything washed down with
strong, hot tea—it's enough to make a man feel reinvigorated.

Satiated, happy, I stretched out on a bench and—well, why
not admit it?—I carefully prepared a kif cigarette and shared it
with Noureddine. We lay side by side, smoking in pleasurable

silence, but then he wandered off somewhere and I was left with only the golden air as my companion.

The night sky was all shooting stars, black holes, and the occasional aeroplane flickering like a will-o'-the-wisp from a child's fairy tale. I heard the strains of a rwai orchestra playing from somewhere in the square and hummed along. I sucked on the lemon that had accompanied the fish eyes and fell to wondering whether I'd be lucky enough to win the lottery that year. My thoughts were scattered, but they were gay, like laughter. A lovely haze threaded through them, lighting them up in bright colours. Through that haze I heard someone say good evening to me in French and I replied in kind. It was a woman's voice, and I didn't think too much of it. Everyone knows everyone else in the Jemaa. Good morning, good evening, whatever you please, I replied.

Then I sat up.

An unbelievably beautiful woman stood next to my bench. I thought I was dreaming, and it took me a moment to perceive that she was a foreigner because she was dressed like a native, in a seroual, kaftan, and with a striped serdal headscarf. The light from the food stalls glinted off the wreath of coins on her forehead. I wanted to say something gallant and poetic but could come up with nothing at all. So I decided to keep it simple and merely say Bonjour! but found myself soundlessly opening my mouth and closing it, in perfect imitation of a fish. My hand holding the spliff trembled. I lowered my eyes. The moment passed.

What are you smoking? she said with a smile.

I told her, and she asked me if I would share.

She sat down next to me and we smoked together. She leaned back languidly and blew perfect rings in the air. I wanted to ask her where she was from, what had brought her to the Jemaa, how long she was going to be here, all kinds of questions; but, as it was, I was so overcome by shyness that I couldn't even stir up the courage to ask her her name. I simply sat there in a stupefied silence.

Looking back on it, I still can't comprehend what happened to me that night. I've thought about it many times. I'm not usually a demure person. We were sitting right next to each other, looking at the same stars, and yet she might as well have been on another planet. There's no explanation, no consolation. I really let myself down.

Finally, she stood up and thanked me for my company. More: she thanked me for my silence, for not bothering her with unnecessary questions.

To know when to be silent is the greatest gift of all, she said.

Making a pretense of understanding, I stammered and offered an inadequate reply. I managed to ask her for a sigri, my kif-thickened tongue wrapping around the word.

She looked at me in bafflement.

Sigri, I mumbled. Can you spare a sigri?

She continued to stare at me for a couple of minutes until comprehension finally dawned and she shook her head and smiled.

I'm afraid I don't smoke cigarettes, she said.

She wished me a good night and a good year to come.

Don't go just yet! I pleaded silently. I don't know anything about you. My name is Rachid. It's too soon to part.

I glanced past her to where a shooting star was aiming for the Koutoubia's minaret. It was very swift, very bright. When I looked down again, she had left.

Of course, it was only then that I recovered my voice. I felt something burst inside me, and the dammed-up words came pouring out in a flood. All right, I heard myself say, enough of this nonsense about silence my name is Rachid what's yours I sell whirligigs what do you do where are you from I have three sisters my father has ten sheep will you marry me can we talk about paradise I'll build you a house with a garden we will have many children what do you think of my moustache can I touch your heart we'll grow all the kif you want . . . and so on and on . . .

. . . and on.

And all the while, out there in the middle of the square, the rwai were lighting sparks with their songs. The air was heating up. I unbuttoned my shirt. I lay down, sat up, lay down, sat up again. The rwai sang, drummed, sang, grew silent, then sang again. At length, giving up on trying to still my heart, I decided to walk over and join the circle watching the rwai perform. I didn't really want to go, but you know what it's like. Your feet start moving of their own accord, and then it's all you can do to keep up. I left my bench and made for the musicians but they were further away than I'd surmised. I lost my way and found myself on the opposite side of the square. Faces came and went like banners in the wind. I passed a tightrope walker holding up an umbrella in the air. A man was juggling knives next to a boy selling painted terracotta fruit from a basket. A bare-chested giant with his hair painted yellow was holding up a massive tree trunk. His wife walked around with a wooden bowl taking a collection. As I ducked out of her way and neared the rwai, the crowds began to thicken and I picked up snatches of conversation.

. . . her beauty is like a red rose.

. . . the fire itself seemed to pale beside her.

. . . her eyes are dense and blue; in them you can see the ocean.

. . . I had to leave, I couldn't take it anymore; she left me breathless. I'll wager that a single kiss from her could teach you all you ever needed to know about love.

I didn't need to guess who they could be talking about. I quickened my pace and reached the rwai at a run.

The band had just launched into a tamssust, a lively song about love. The raïs was going at it as if life itself were at stake, and the onlookers were clapping along and egging him on. I looked around the circle, scanning the faces for a glimpse of her, and then I calmed down. She was sitting on a low chair next to the musicians. There was a slim, dark youth standing behind her with his hands on her shoulders. Her headscarf had slipped off and she had retied it like a bandanna around her neck. Instead of the scarf, she now wore a bright red beret. I stared at her companion and my heart sank. From the way his hands rested on her shoulders it was clear that she belonged to him. I gazed at them in despair and the raïs sang my thoughts:

Girl of fire
Girl of fire
Made for my arms
Made for my desires
I have waited for you
I have waited so long
Now all is lost
Now all is shattered

Rachid's voice died down to a whisper.

My friends, my brothers, those were some of the worst moments of my life. The black sky closed over my head. The air smelled of my despair. I cursed the kif that had robbed me of my voice. I wanted to quit that place that very instant and crawl into a hole somewhere. It's better to leave, I thought to myself, and then I thought, It's better not to leave. I convinced myself to remain for a few minutes longer in her presence.

I don't know how long I tarried there. It was like being paralysed. Such anguish cannot be put into words. I wondered if I should leave her one of my whirligigs as a souvenir. I even took one out of my bag, but then I dropped it on the ground. How I suffered, my brothers! I willed my courage not to desert me as I prepared to leave her forever.

He blushed awkwardly, nonplussed, it seemed, as much by the memory as by his continuing bashfulness and longing. There was a sense of resignation about him. He spoke slowly and without animation.

He said:

And then, imperceptibly, something changed, as if mirroring the state of my own heart. Everyone began to stare openly at the woman. The mood of the circle shifted. All our eyes undressed her. Even the music reflected it, the drums beginning to echo ominously. It might have had to do with the group of men who'd appeared from out of nowhere, their heads and faces shrouded. Or it might have been the outcome of the words with which the raïs ended his song:

Now you have hurt me
Now you have ruined me

What choice have you left me
But to stab you through the heart?

I turned irresolutely and began to edge my way out of the circle. My misery must have showed on my face because someone nudged me with his elbow and gave a mocking laugh. I was in no mood for jollity and attempted to squeeze past but found my path blocked.

Oho! I heard a voice call out. Here's another one slain by the houri.

Furious at his affront, I raised my hand and was about to push him out of the way when pandemonium broke out. I heard a sharp whistle cut through the music. Someone began to shout madly and there was a terrified scream. I attempted to turn around to find out what was going on but tripped and fell headlong. As I struck the ground, I felt legs trample me as they rushed past. I tried to rise to my feet but fell back again. A hazy darkness began to close in and I raised my arms to fend it off. I felt myself sliding into an abyss, cold and black. The last thing I saw was the fragment of a dress, and then I lost consciousness.

When I came to, I was lying in a clean white bed in a room next to a garden. It was in a hospital in the Hivernage district. I was there for a day before I was released. I learned that I had to report to the Jemaa police station the first thing the next morning.

At the police station, I was interrogated by two inspectors and a sergeant. They told me that both the foreigners had gone missing after the melee in the rwai. I answered their questions to the best of my ability, but they didn't seem terribly interested, and they let me go in less than an hour. I'd lost my bag of whirli-gigs and I filed a complaint, but was told that the chances of their being found were slim.

When I ventured out into the Jemaa it was in the dazzling sunlight and everything that had happened to me the past two days seemed like a hallucination. I returned to the place where I'd listened to the rwai and found a storyteller holding forth avidly on those two doomed lovers from the desert, Layla and Majnun. I listened to him for a while, but it all seemed unreal, and I left him with an acrid taste in my mouth. I decided to quit the square for the day and go home, and, on my way out, I picked up a rose that was lying on the ground but it sank a thorn into my thumb. Tears came to my eyes as I watched the blood oozing out. Even the flowers that morning had a sting.

Rachid stood for a moment looking into the shadows. There was scarcely a sound in our circle, save for the crackling of the fire. None of us moved.

Rachid fumbled in his pockets for something. He found it, took it out, and held it close to his face. It was a talisman, a fili-greed Hand of Fatima on a silver chain. He touched it to his lips before slipping it back into his pocket.

It still bothers me that I didn't get to find out her name, he said, because names are keys.

You mustn't have been present here when I revealed her name, I said. It was Lucia. It means light.

Light, he said, and gave a faint smile. How appropriate.

Without another word, he returned to his place in the circle and sank down on his knees. He sat still for a moment, and then he lay down and curled up on his side, his head cradled in his arms.

Cover him with a blanket, I advised. He has suffered.

Someone draped a hanbel over him.

Phoenix

The moon was gliding through the clouds in the west. The souks had gone black. The gardens behind the Koutoubia slumbered in the night. Beneath a flowering rosebush, an orange cat was licking his paws. Deep in the Mellah, in a dark room crisscrossed with silence, a one-eyed poet was putting the finishing touches to a song about sadness. The first line:

What is life, after all, but a passing fancy?

The moon, the cat, the poet, this circle of listeners—we all stand on the same page. Between the lip and the talisman, the throat and the voice, the heart and the hope, something is always trembling, something is always living and dying. Is it hope? Is it madness? Is it the sea?

It is love.

Look: there it goes, soundless, tremulous, a few timid glances, a fugitive gesture, a poem about kif, an evening's worth of delirium, and then, nothing.

It is love. It has five senses, seven sounds, nine skins, eleven illusions. It is soft. It is a flower that grows in the deepest oceans. It is a flickering candle, a sign in the snow, a beautiful country, desert ash. It is a call and a curse and a long-drawn-out incantation to be chanted in the evening. It is a photograph, a lament, a chronicle, a painting. It is in Pandora's box, in a sunlit park, in the Crow Tree. It is elation, confusion, loneliness, loss, dream.

It is love. It is that most beautiful of all birds.

KHETTARA

Reports of what had happened that night varied wildly. It wasn't even clear who had disappeared. Some newspapers reported the missing woman, others that the man was missing, some claimed that both had vanished. They said the inconsolable husband was badgering the police and driving them to distraction; they said the wife had taken to sleeping on the steps of the police station in despair over her husband's disappearance; they said that a number of foreign consulates had gotten involved in the attempt to find out what had happened to their missing citizens. Official accounts were equally contradictory. First, we heard that the couple had been tracked down to Banana Beach, a surfers' paradise near Taghazout, but the woman there turned out to be Dutch, her partner was of Syrian origin, and after a week of rigorous questioning, they were released. Other reports announced sightings in Tangier, in Chefchouan, in Paradise Valley, in Immouzer, and inside the Rialto cinema hall off the Avenue des FAR in Agadir. A number of foreigners were detained, mostly on the basis of their resemblance to the missing couple, though the case of the seventy-year-old Swedish architect and his teenage paramour was a little more controversial. Then, after the passage of a few days, news about the incident died down altogether. It was rumoured that the powerful Jemaa traders' guilds had lobbied to have the local authorities suppress the story because it was adversely affecting the morale of both vendors and tourists. Soon we ceased to hear anything and the incident seemed destined to become nothing more than one of the many legends of the Jemaa, albeit a particularly mysterious addition to its numerous myths. And yet, questions remained, questions that seemed to beg answers. There were as many theories as there were puzzling aspects to that evening. Why, for instance, did no one investigate the Mercedes that had pulled away from the square during the fracas, its tyres screaming? They said it belonged to an Arab sheikh. Who was he, where had he come from, what had happened to him? Or what about the mysterious group of men with shrouded faces? From all accounts, there was something indubitably menacing about them, something corrupt and compromised. Who were they, were they questioned by the police, and, if so, what was their story? Some said that they'd heard hints of very powerful people being implicated in the incident; others said that the powers-that-be were disputing the existence of the couple altogether. But what about records in the Foreign Ministry, the Passport Controller's office, the Bureau of Strangers, the army?

Many performers claimed they could feel a baleful energy emanating from the square following the events of that evening and it led some of them to decide to quit the Jemaa altogether and move to Meknès or Fès or Tangier. Some even went so far as to make the hazardous journey across the Straits of Gibraltar to Europe; a troupe of Tazeroualt acrobats from the Ameln Valley, near Tighmi, now work in a circus in Madrid.

As I found out later from a cousin employed in the Jemaa police station, for the first three weeks following the disappearance, it was a beehive of activity. The officers methodically divided the medina into a system of grids and proceeded to search every section. Nothing was spared, no place was deemed beyond suspicion, and everyone, Marrakchis and foreigners alike, had to endure the indignity of the search warrant. The police searched individual houses, they searched official buildings, they searched riads and hotels and brothels and palaces. They sent search teams into the qaysarias, the souks, the kasbah, the mellah, the tanneries. I was told they even searched the medersas, the hammams, and the ancient underground khettaras that had remained unused for centuries. But, in the end, despite their best efforts and despite the men and resources they'd put in, they could come up with nothing. It was as if the entire episode had been a figment of the collective imagination.

And then, at the end of the third week, on a bright and sunny morning, my brother Mustafa walked into the Jemaa police station and turned himself in.

THE AFICIONADO

This is what followed inside the station after the first few moments of incomprehension. The sergeants in attendance pounced on my brother and stripped him of his belongings. Every item was tagged and placed in the black plastic bag Mustafa had been carrying with him at the time. When I received the news of his arrest and rushed to the station, I was handed the bag without a word. Bewildered, I emptied it on my lap and found, among his things, a small inkwell such as scribes use, carved out of red softstone in the shape of a lion. I sat there, clutching that little lion, my mouth dry, my mind blank. I turned that lion over and over in my hand, thinking about how strange life is, when all is said and done. We think that it is all about memories, chronicles, situations, testimonies, comprehensions, and ostensible conclusions, and yet, at the end of it, we are left irredeemably ignorant. Ya Allah! I raged silently. Where is the meaning to anything? Is life nothing but illusions?

I gazed at the lion and felt my eyes fill with helpless tears.

The constable on duty looked at me curiously but also with sympathy. What's that? he said, pointing to the lion.

It's an inkwell, I replied.

More to distract myself while I waited to meet with Mustafa than for any other reason, I decided to tell the policeman the story of where the inkwell came from.

Wait a moment, he said, surprising me with a smile. First let me get you some mint tea to moisten your throat. Let it not be said that we are ignorant of basic notions of hospitality here.

The tea was piping hot and too sweet for my taste, but I thanked the constable for his consideration. He sat down across from me, crossing his legs and waiting expectantly, for my reputation as a storyteller was well known, and, as he told me later, he liked to think of himself as something of an aficionado.

SAHARA

When we were young, I began, our father took us on our first trip to the Sahara. We went to the Hamada du Drâa, the forbiddingly arid plateau that runs along the southernmost boundary of Morocco and forms its border with Algeria. Father had a friend there who was a storyteller. He lived in the village of M'Hamid al-Ghizlan, M'hamid of the Gazelles, near the 'Irq al-Yehudi, the Dune of the Jews, on the edge of the Hamada. The fraternity of storytellers is a small and tightly knit one, and my father's friend lent us his camels to make the journey to Chigaga, where the dunes are at their highest and most impressive in the area.

We were beside ourselves with excitement at the prospect of finally encountering the desert. I have heard it described as akin to the emotion felt by a prince when he inherits his kingdom. As Father says, the Sahara is like a golden snake that swims through our blood.

I can still remember the seemingly endless banquet which Tayeb, my father's friend, set out for us on the evening of our departure. In the open courtyard of his house, beneath the starry sky, a huge fire of juniper logs provided the perfect accompaniment, as it were, to course after course of delectable lamb and chicken kebabs, quail stew, couscous made of the lightest semolina, pigeon pie, goat cheese, pastilla, dates, figs, and the local delicacy of spiced watermelon sherbet. As my brother Ahmed, who has a keen eye for such things, remarked under his breath, for a storyteller Tayeb seemed to have done very well for himself. Unfortunately for Ahmed, Father overheard the comment. Equally under his breath, he leaned over to his middle son and told him to keep his mouth shut if he wanted to enjoy the privilege of accompanying us. Ahmed bit back his retort, for the desert beckoned like a seductive vision from beyond the perimeters of the courtyard. Sated with food, we stretched out on our backs on the daybeds provided for the purpose, and listened to the breeze murmuring through the date palms. The auburn light wrapped around us and made the evening mellow.

We travelled at night to avoid the heat.

Father walked in front, leading the camels, while the three of us took turns riding them. On the way, we passed Tayeb's neighbour's house which was in darkness. The entire family was in mourning on account of the youngest son's new bride who had run away after giving birth to a stillborn child. She was a native of the Tafilalt, accustomed to its fertile green valleys, and it was rumoured that she'd been finding it difficult to take to the desert's barren vastness. I wanted to know more, but Father told me it was none of my business.

My brothers had other, less morbid thoughts on their minds. Both of them were fascinated by the plumes of dust sent up by the camel's hooves as they traversed the sand. Mustafa compared them to white-winged moths; Ahmed said they reminded him of the feathery white down with which the thrushes lined their nests in our backyard. Then Mustafa compared them to the foam which stretches along a beach when the waves fall back, while Ahmed said they were more like the foam when Mother cooked rice in a pot. They fell to bickering about whose analogies were more accurate, with Mustafa accusing his brother of being hopelessly banal; meanwhile, our tongues bumped against our teeth as our camels plodded along, making us all feel more than a little light-headed.

We reached Chigaga in the middle of the night and set up our tents in the shadow of a sand mountain. Branches of moonlight lit up the sand. It was a white world, the earth a lighter colour than anything we had encountered before. The dunes shouldered their way through the endlessly undulating landscape, as smooth and majestic as an eagle's flight. The air was crystalline in its clarity, but when the wind ruffled the sand the dust that rose was like smoke across the face of the night.

Once the tents had been erected, Father gave me permission to go on a short walk. I rounded the nearest dune and followed its slope to the bottom where it came to rest in a narrow gully sheltered from the wind. Miniature cascades of sand grains accompanied my passage with a whispering sound. The air was sweet and still. I knelt down and pressed my palms to the ground, listening through my fingertips to the desert's voice. It was an ancient voice, more resolute than the mountains, and stronger than the ocean. That took me aback, for I hadn't expected such power, and I realized that I would have to revise my picture of the order of the natural world. It reminded me of something that Father had said before we'd set off on our journey: Until you have seen the Sahara, you have seen nothing.

I strolled along the bottom of the dune, following its contours until I could see its roots emerging from a plate of solid rock. On impulse, I stretched out on my stomach, caressing the roots with my hands, feeling them communicate to me in a peculiarly intimate language, as vast and remote as the desert night. It was a language I understood instantly, and it was humbling. Lost in wonder, I began to draw lines in the sand, tracing them so that they echoed the wavelike sounds I was hearing in my mind. There was a light breeze blowing, and it sent up little spirals of dust that followed in my tracks, randomly scooping up sand and interrupting my smooth furrows with miniature ridges and craters. Oblivious to its portent, I watched it for a while as one would a friend. It worked its way through the sand the way a net sifts through water and soon it had erased all my songlines. Slightly irked, I wondered whether I should carry on with my communing, when, from the top of the dune, I heard someone call out:

Hassan!

It was Mustafa. His voice carried in the stillness.

The wind has shifted, he cried out. Father says to come back!

By the time his voice had died down, he was already at my side. He laid his hand on my shoulder and stood there, panting.

How ridiculous! I thought. We've only just reached here. There's so sign of danger. I'm not yet ready to go back.

Mustafa noticed my hesitation because he pointed to the east.

It's coming from that direction and bearing down on us rapidly. Just listen!

He cupped his ear with his hand and stood motionless.

From the horizon there arose an eerily high-pitched sound. It made the hairs on the back of my neck prick up. The entire sky seemed to fill with its menace. There was a sharp sulphurous smell in the air.

The desert's on the move, Mustafa said. There's no time to lose.

I don't know how I could have been so oblivious, I muttered, annoyed at myself, but even more so at my eight-year-old brother's gumption in ordering me around.

Take my hand, he directed.

What are you talking about? I snapped. I can find my way back on my own! Come on.

He eyed me uncertainly.

What's the matter? I asked.

Why are you facing that way?

Because it's the way I came from!

No it isn't, Hassan. The camp is in the opposite direction.

The wind was beginning to pick up now, and we could see it cantering with big white hooves across the sand.

Well then? Mustafa said urgently. Shall we go?

It's this way, I said. Let's go.

It's the other way, Mustafa insisted. You're turned around.

I marched straight back the way I had come, but no sooner had I taken a few steps than I felt the sand begin to swirl around my legs. The slope of the dune began to ripple as if alive.

Look at the horizon if you don't believe me! Mustafa shouted.

There was no horizon. It was terrifying. Instead of a clean white line etched against the night I could see nothing but a billowing brown haze. A stinging wind slapped my face, making my eyes run.

Mustafa ran up to me, his eyes wide with apprehension.

Listen to me, won't you? he yelled. I know the way!

There's no time! I yelled back, reaching out and clamping down on his arm. We have to get out of this gully and reach that boulder above us. Do you see it? It's about ten paces to our right.

Hitching up our jellabas, we scrambled up towards the boulder. The surface of the desert was beginning to peel off like snakeskin. It crested into an immense wave and sped in our direction. The first sharp grains of sand began to buffet us just as we reached the rock. The dust in the air made it impossible to breathe.

Get down behind the rock! I screamed. Cover your face and hold on with all your strength!

We rammed the hoods of our jellabas over our heads. I whipped off my cloak and wound it around us as tightly as I could. I heard a rustle like hail and then, with a deafening hiss, the sandstorm rushed down the dune and began breaking all around us. Its velocity was astonishing. It whipped through the air and over the ground and seemed to come at us from all sides at once. I clutched on to my brother and gripped him around the waist. We wedged our heads between our knees and pressed hard against the rock. The sand surged through our clothes and into the crevices between our bodies. I felt thousands of needles scrape the skin off my back. My eyes began to smart and stream. Mustafa was gasping and coughing by my side. A long-drawn muffled roar filled my ears. I began to choke and felt my brother's body sag against me. His hands slipped from my waist. Just when I thought it was all over for us, the storm died down. The sand stopped tearing at my clothes. The air suddenly seemed to grow lighter. I reached out tentatively into the darkness and felt nothing strike my arm.

We'd survived the full fury of the Sahara.

We had to dig ourselves out of the sand which had buried us to our waists. I tottered to my feet and flung back the hood of my jellaba. A thick cloud of dust enveloped my face. I spit sand from my mouth. Mustafa was retching at my feet, and I pulled him up. His face was caked and he looked as if he was wearing a white mask. He cracked his mouth open and his lacerated lips welled with blood. I patted him gently, too shaken to speak.

Mother! he said softly in a sobbing voice.

Around us the landscape had altered completely. The dunes were no longer where they used to be. It was as if we were in a different place altogether. We looked around slowly and realized that neither one of us had any idea which way we needed to go to return to the camp. The sky was still cloaked with dust and we couldn't even orient ourselves by the stars. I began to think of the countless unfortunates who'd perished in the Sahara and felt a clammy terror. Then I thought of Father and Ahmed, who were perhaps dead, and I sank to my knees and buried my head in my arms. Waves of despair combined with uncertainty and a crushing sense of helplessness, but, more than anything else, the feeling that eclipsed all the others was that of guilt. To this day I am convinced that I myself caused the sandstorm by inadvertently overstepping the bounds of nature by communing as I had with the spirit of the desert. There must have been more to those songlines than I could ever have fathomed.

Naturally, at the time, I kept these thoughts to myself and refrained from sharing them with my brother who, given his tender years, could hardly have been expected to understand.

As if reading my mind, he broke the silence.

Hassan, he said in a small voice.

What?

I think we're lost.

I thanked him silently for stating the obvious.

Let me think for a moment, won't you? I said crossly.

I had a handful of almonds in the pocket of my jellaba and I fished them out and gave them to him to munch. I drew his attention to the fact that the wind could no longer be heard.

We were lucky that that was a minor storm, I said, speaking with a self-assurance that belied my utter ignorance of the facts. If that had been a major storm, I went on, we'd have been buried way down deep under the sand. So count your blessings and thank your stars.

Which one?

What do you mean, which one?

Which star should I thank? he said miserably. You told me to thank my stars but I don't know which ones are mine. In any case, I can't even see a single one through this haze.

I placed a reassuring arm around his shoulder.

Then you'll just have to wait until the dust settles down, I advised. In the meantime, stop chattering. I need to decide what to do next.

All of a sudden he shivered as if he'd been taken by a chill.

How quiet it is! he whispered. I'm scared, Hassan.

There's no need to be scared, I answered. Let's climb to the top of the dune. This might be a big desert, but between the two of us we'll find our way out of it.

All right, he agreed, obviously glad to be able to engage in any form of activity. I'm with you. We won't get lost.

We reached the crest of the dune, and the night opened out in all its stillness. Dust was suspended everywhere, and the air smelt acrid and sharp, like scorched plaster. In the distance, we could hear a whisper where the storm was still raging. But where we were, it was mercifully silent. As Mustafa later remarked, the desert was soundless, but the silence was profound.

I don't like it here, he said.

Don't worry, we're not staying. We're moving on.

I'm exhausted, Hassan.

I know, but we need to travel now, by night. By day the sun will finish us off.

Not if we start early enough, before the sun comes up.

Don't argue with me! I know what I'm doing.

I studied the horizon and made up my mind about which direction we should walk. I told Mustafa and was relieved when he didn't demur. We set off at an even pace, proceeding fairly quickly. Although there'd been no rain, the sand had congealed in clumps. I wondered if the sheer force of the wind could have done that.

At a certain point Mustafa said: You don't have to pretend.

Pretend about what? I asked without slowing down.

That you know where we're going.

I stopped and glared at him, nettled.

Do you really think I'd spend the night traipsing around just to entertain myself?

He gave a loud sigh.

That's your pride speaking, he replied. Be reasonable, Hassan. We need to rest. We can't walk around forever. I think we should wait until the sun comes up. Or, at least, until the sky clears and we can see the stars.

In spite of myself, I had to concede that he was right. I admitted as much to him with irritation, embarrassment, and a distinct sense of relief. He looked at me with sympathy.

Don't worry about it, he said brightly. I knew all along that you were lost. We'll get out of here tomorrow. It's as you said, between the two of us, we'll come up with something. But for now, can we just get some sleep?

I wanted to ask him how he could think of sleep at a time like this, but I kept my peace. Instead, I looked around and suggested a spot on the leeward side of the dune that we were on.

We made a small depression in the sand and sank down in it. The wind tiptoed around us, and it was freezing. It brought home to me the reality of our situation. Now that we'd borne the brunt of a sandstorm, we would have to contend with a new and equally malignant enemy, the chill of a desert night. It made me wonder if it wouldn't have been better for us to just keep walking—at least we'd have stayed warm. As I weighed our prospects, my teeth began to chatter.

I glanced up at the sky and saw that it was clearing. I could already make out the first constellations directly above us. Finally we had the map we needed! I turned to Mustafa to point that out to him, but he didn't stir. He was fast asleep. Deciding not to wake him, I wrapped my cloak around us. Immediately I felt the warmth of his body embrace me like a blanket. What a unique introduction to the desert, I thought, but even as I did, exhaustion overtook me and I fell asleep.

That night I dreamt of being swathed in long white sheets. The dream seemed both exotic and familiar, and I've often wondered at its meaning since. Were the sheets meant to represent the desert chill? Or were they meant to stand in for a funeral shroud, as my father later suggested, a sign of how close I'd come to dying? But there was neither fear in the dream nor any perception of threat. Rather, a feeling of the most languid luxury I'd never known. It was like something out of the *Book of the Thousand and One Nights*. Whatever the truth—if there is ever such a thing as a single truth in dreams—I look back on it now with no more sense of enlightenment than when I experienced it.

The fluting kuit-al kuit-al call of a desert bird woke us up. We couldn't see it, but the call was persistent and filled with life. Mustafa, who loves birds, said that it came from a crowned sandgrouse. He returned the call, and, to my surprise and delight, the bird called back.

We rubbed the sleep from our eyes and rose to a pink dawn. All around us, the night was dissipating, its shadowy walls drawing back. As we watched, the paling moon slipped down and the last stars dissolved.

In the grey light we were able to see more clearly the damage done to us by the sandstorm. Both of us were covered with bruises and abrasions, and Mustafa said that I had a nasty cut on my right cheek. I pointed out that we had survived and that was the most important thing.

Yes, of course, he said with laughter in his voice. What a story we'll have to share with everyone!

Well, there you are then, I said gently. It's the attitude that counts. With the right attitude we can conquer the world.

I felt a lump in my throat as I contemplated the day ahead of us and estimated our chances of survival. My greatest fear was to be caught in the open in the full glare of the sun, but I kept my apprehensions to myself. I merely nodded to my brother and we directed our footsteps towards the red glow on the horizon. The caramel dunes reminded me strangely of waves of the ocean.

After we'd walked for a while, Mustafa said:

Did you know that my friend Salah's father was lost in the desert?

No, I replied curtly, I had no idea.

It wasn't around here, but more to the east, near Merzouga. It was during the Paris-Dakar rally. He was an auto mechanic and he'd gone there to help out one of the teams. I don't know the details, but it was in the papers. They searched for him for days but eventually gave up. Still and all, Salah's mother got a certificate from the rally's organizers as proof of his participation.

I gave him a withering glance.

Do you have any more stories to tell about people lost in the desert? I waited for his response, but my irony was lost on him. He thought for a moment and admitted that that was the only one.

Well, I'm glad, I replied.

You didn't like it? he asked, genuinely surprised.

Perhaps I would have liked it more had he been found, I answered.

He pulled a face. Oh well, he admitted, there is that, of course. I guess I see your point.

He was about to carry on when he stopped abruptly in mid-stride.

Look, he said softly, there's someone up ahead of us.

Where?

Right there, can't you see? By that arrow-shaped rock.

The desert's playing tricks on him, I thought, and scanned the area he'd indicated. I could make out the rock, but, as far as I could tell, there was nothing else there.

Mustafa had already begun to run in that direction. His heels kicked up little puffs of dust. I followed behind him and heard him call out: Hello there! Can you help us, please? We're lost.

He slowed down just as he neared the rock and I was able to catch up with him. He turned to me and his face was pale, his eyes narrow with caution. All of a sudden he moved off noiselessly to one side. From his expression I could tell that something was wrong.

Hassan, he said quietly, come here quick.

All right, I said, and began to advance reluctantly.

A putrid smell crept down to me and I noticed the buzzing swarms of flies. Even the air seemed heavier in the shadow of the rock. Mustafa sensed my uneasiness and raised his hand.

What is it? I whispered, and he pointed.

Someone was sitting very still on the other side of the rock.

It was a slender young woman clad in a gold-embroidered crimson dress. Motionless and emptied of life, she sat there with her frail frame leaning back against the rock. Her face was desiccated and black, her bleached eyes stared straight at the sun. In that pristine gaze was a profound and complete acceptance of her fate.

Mustafa, I whispered, I think we've found the runaway wife.

To my horror, he stepped forward and touched her face.

Come away! I said, shaken.

How long has she been dead, do you think?

I don't know. Come away!

Hold on, won't you!

He tugged gently at the silver ornaments in her hair.

So much thought must have gone into wearing these, he said, and I was startled by the tenderness in his voice.

With quick eyes he scanned her face.

This is so sad, he said in hushed tones. What do you think happened to her?

I have no idea.

Do you think she died of heartbreak?

It could be.

I would never want something like this to happen to us.

He reached down to touch her hand. At first I thought he was after the white butterfly that flitted away just as he brushed her fingers. But he ignored it and, instead, prised something loose from her grasp. It looked like a contoured red stone but turned out to be an inkwell in the shape of a lion. Staring at it, my brother said, in a peculiarly sombre voice: I love you, Hassan. If you are ever in trouble, I will give my life to save yours.

We'll save each other's lives, I said, correcting him.

Yes, but I will save yours first.

Thank you, I said, moved by his insistence. I'll keep that in mind.

To my surprise, he kissed the lion and slipped it into his pocket, which I found inexcusable.

What are you doing? I said indignantly. It belongs to her!

She's dead.

Put it back and don't argue! We're not thieves.

It's mine now, he said, his jaw setting in a familiarly stubborn line. Finders keepers, he added. It's the way of the world.

I wasn't going to debate the ways of the world with him. If he wanted the inkwell that badly, he could have it. All I desired now was to find my father and Ahmed before the sun became too strong.

Fine, I said shortly. If it matters that much to you, go ahead and steal from a corpse. I'm glad you're not superstitious.

It speaks to me. It's going to be my good-luck charm.

Much good it did her, I scoffed. Come on now. Let's go.

My legs felt unsteady as we set out once more. Our feet sank into the sand with every step we took but we soldiered on, orienting ourselves by the sun. Although it was still far from its full strength, it blazed down on us with fury. It hurt to look up at the sky. Our shadows began to melt. Even the banks of clouds on the horizon were almost too white. Gradually, inexorably, our eyes began to crust and our throats grew parched. The sand burned our feet. There was no shade for miles. When Mustafa complained that he was beginning to see multiple suns, I feared the worst. I reached out and grabbed him by the hand and pulled him along. Just as the heat was getting the better of me, I heard our names being called:

Hassan! Mustafa!

We raised our faces and cocked our heads. With wide eyes we traced the calls to their source. There, on top of a dune some considerable distance ahead of us, stood Father and Ahmed, each waving a bright red blanket. Against all odds, we had found them. Mustafa broke into a jig with a shrill whoop of joy. As for me, I simply closed my eyes and sank down to my knees in relief.

THE STONE LION

My audience of one stirred when I'd finished.

The Sahara is indeed not to be trifled with, he said gravely. I am not a Berber, but I can understand its hold on your people.

He paused and gazed up at the ceiling where a fly was perched.

That dream you had was strange, he pronounced somewhat unexpectedly. Do you dream a lot?

I do sometimes.

I don't. If I did, I'd be a storyteller like you. Instead, I'm stuck in this pen with all sorts of criminals.

He became morose.

It all comes down to money. I've a large family to feed. With six children, you have no idea how much of a struggle it can be.

He stared at the ceiling again where the fly seemed to have taken his fancy.

Well, that was indeed an interesting story, he said at length. He drew my attention to the fact that during the time he'd been listening to me he had reduced the walnut twig that he had been chewing to shreds. That had never happened before, he confided as he cleared his throat and spit the fragments into a metal bucket.

Did you report finding the missing bride? he asked.

Yes, we did, but they couldn't find her.

Another unexplained disappearance?

I suppose.

Some wild animal or other must have carried her off, he suggested.

It could be.

What a terrible end to a life. And at that age, what's more.

Suddenly he broke off and peered around him in puzzlement.

I say, where did all this sand come from? I could have sworn the sweeper cleaned this place a couple of hours ago. That's strange.

He scraped the floor with the toe of his shoe and asked, a bit awkwardly, if he could see the inkwell.

So that's it? he said, eyeing it warily. I guess it didn't bring your brother any luck either. You should have insisted that he leave it behind. If I were you, I'd get rid of it, and fast.

Where is my brother? I asked.

He glanced at his watch and started. Looking at me apologetically, he excused himself in order to go and find out what was keeping Mustafa.

I'll bring him to you myself, he said. I won't be long.

As good as his word, he returned with Mustafa moments later.

I stared at my brother in dismay. It was wrenching to see him in prison clothes and shackles. His face was lined and careworn, there was a large purple bruise on his forehead, and he seemed to have aged at least twenty years overnight. All the same, there was a peculiar tranquillity to him. He sat down on the stool they had provided and gazed at me calmly through the intervening grille. I stared back at him, finding it impossible to come to terms with his drastically changed circumstances.

Oh, Mustafa, Mustafa! I burst out in despair. What have you done?

Hello, Hassan, he said. S'bah l'khir. Good morning.

He spoke softly and without any visible emotion. There was a sense of remoteness about him, and I attributed it to his situation. Indicating his bruise, I asked: Did they beat you?

He shrugged.

It's the way they do things here.

I glared at the constable and gestured pointedly at my brother's face. He flushed and avoided my eye from that moment on.

Mustafa kept gazing at me calmly. Then he noticed me holding his plastic bag.

I see they gave you my things, he said. I'm glad.

254 Joydeep Roy-Bhattacharya

I held up the stone lion: Where did you get this?

I'll tell you in a moment, he said, glancing meaningfully in the direction of the constable.

Until today I have refrained from telling you how heavily your theft weighed on me at the time, I said. Now I can't help thinking it's brought us bad luck.

He shook his head.

My congenitally superstitious brother. When will you ever learn? He made a casual gesture, passing his hand through his hair.

This isn't very important, he said, but while we're on the subject of things, please give my collection of music cassettes, especially the ones by Khaled, Cheb Mami, and DJ Da Cool, to my friend Omar in Essaouira. You know where you can find him. You visited his drum shop with me a few years ago.

Yes, of course, I answered, wondering why, of all things, we should be talking about some godforsaken music cassettes.

He must have intuited my thoughts because he gave me a wan smile, as if to say, Forgive me, I know they mean nothing to you, but they are of great value in my world.

What do you intend to do now? I asked, feeling rather foolish even as I voiced the question.

His answer left me speechless.

In a perfectly composed voice, he said: I intend to spend the rest of my life in solitude and repose. After a lifetime of indulgence, I hope to find peace in confinement. In keeping with the tenets of our faith, in which the space of the mosque is a foretaste of paradise, I plan to transform my cell into a sanctuary for prayer. I don't expect it to be too difficult. After all, there is no religion as elegant in its simplicity as Islam.

I stared at him, finding it difficult to believe what I'd just heard. Finally, I managed to speak up.

You have found religion?

My voice must have betrayed me because he smiled.

Why do you find that so hard to comprehend?

I don't know. It's just very sudden, that's all.

You'll come to terms with it, Hassan, just as I have. Give it a little time.

I thought your entire aspiration in life was to be an urban sophisticate.

That changed from the moment I set eyes on her.

I looked at him for a very long time, wondering how best to respond. It wasn't any use. I gave up and could only tell him that his actions were beyond my comprehension.

Why incomprehensible? he asked.

So disappointment in love has led you here?

I don't know if I would put it that way. I feel fulfilled and at peace with myself. Only true love justifies sacrifice, and I've sacrificed myself to the greatest love of all: that which is certain to remain unrequited. You see, I love her with all my heart, and when you love someone that much, you are prepared to give her up.

But she was never yours to begin with! I protested.

That's beside the point, he replied, and his voice was so matter-of-fact that I began to fear for his sanity. With a slight smile, he continued: Each one of us journeys in solitude to love, in solitude to faith and to death, but sometimes a beautiful moment can serve as the anteroom to paradise. I glimpsed eternity in the time that I spent with her. How can anything else compare to those moments of pure feeling? All I want now is to hold on to them.

So you plan to turn your back to the world? I asked, trying my best to stay calm.

I intend to take it one day at a time, he answered. I'm not going to think about the future; I'm not going to think about the past. Only the present matters, and my present will be lived in the realm of the spirit, where there is nothing but peace and quiet.

I could no longer control my impatience.

All right, I'm glad you've found your peace, I said. But what about the rest of us? What am I going to tell our parents, for instance, or Ahmed and his wife? Shall I tell them that you have gone from being a sybarite to a mystic overnight? And this in prison for a crime you didn't commit? Does that make sense to you? Please tell me because it certainly doesn't make any sense to me.

I don't know what to tell you, Hassan. I don't have the answers to your questions. They are your questions, not mine. All I know is that I have reached a very different place in my life. It may be difficult to comprehend from the perspective of the world you live in, but please understand that I have left that world behind.

I felt a rush of despair when faced with this perfectly inscrutable stranger who was my brother. I felt myself searching for words that wouldn't come. How could blood be so alien to blood?

Mustafa, I said, my world is falling to pieces.

Something must have touched him in my voice, because he moved close to the bars of the grille and pressed his face against them. His eyes looked even more mysterious to me, compassionate and filled with pensiveness.

Tell me how I can help you, he said, and I will try my best.

Look, I said, I don't believe for a moment that you had anything to do with the events on the square. At least tell me what you told the police. What's your story? What did you tell them to have yourself put behind bars?

Don't worry, Hassan, he said with a smile. You can rest your mind. I'm as good a storyteller as anyone in our family.

But why did you do it? You know that you are innocent!

Do you remember what I told you in the desert after the sandstorm? About giving up my life to save yours?

Yes, yes, of course I do. But what does that have to do with anything?

And do you remember how you used to tell me: All great creative acts are gestures of defiance? Well, here it is. Here's my gesture on your behalf. Listen to my story and tell me what you think.

SAND

Wait a minute, I said, and turned to my erstwhile friend, the police constable, who was sitting in a corner of the room and keeping a watchful eye on us. I asked him how much time I had for my meeting with my brother.

Half an hour or thereabouts, he answered.

In that case, will you excuse us?

He looked at me stolidly. I am not allowed, he replied.

I walked over to him and handed him a large bill I'd brought

explicitly for the purpose. Neither one of us spoke as he pock-
eted the money. To my surprise, however, he continued to sit
there, and I realized that other, stronger measures were called
for. I reflected for a moment while he stared at me impassively.
Then I took a step back and directed his attention to the sand
littering the floor.

That sand you noticed earlier, I said quietly—it's from the
Sahara.

He stared at me as if I'd lost my mind.

Get out of here! he scoffed.

I leaned forward and looked him straight in the eye.

I'm quite serious, I said. It seeped into the room while I was
telling you my story. Tell me how else it could have entered
here.

He was about to contest me again when I raised my hand.

By the way, I said casually, will you check your pockets,
please?

He looked at me uncertainly, then plunged his hands into the
pockets of his trousers. Rifling through them like a man possessed, he brought out fistfuls of sand.

Eyeing me with a measure of astonishment not unmixed with
fear, he whispered: How is this possible?

I have the power, I replied. Now leave us, please.

I had the sense that he was glad to leave the room after that.
When I turned to my brother, I saw him gazing at me with
amusement.

Nice work, he said, and smiled. Where did you learn that
trick?

From my friend Akram, the magician, I replied. It's nothing.

Mustafa looked at me intently.

I'm sorry to have put you through this, he remarked. I see you're not smiling. Well, I'm grateful that you're here.

The things I have to do for you, I said dryly. In any case, what do you have to tell me?

He tipped his head back and half closed his eyes.

What he said next took my breath away.

What do I have to tell you? Simply this. I saw her again that night following the rwai.

He paused for effect. I knew that he was watching me closely.

Really? I said. Why should I believe you?

Do you have an alternative?

MUSTAFA'S STORY

When I didn't reply, my brother leaned forward and began to speak very quietly, almost in a whisper, as if worried that, although the constable had left the room, he was still listening. As he spoke, I could hear the sounds of the traffic passing by outside, or pedestrians conversing noisily. At those times, I had to lean forward to hear him better and it occurred to me that the two of us must have made quite a sight, with our faces pressed together through the bars of the grille.

To begin with, Mustafa said, I need you to understand that, in every sense, that was the evening of the best day of my life. I hope to feast on its memories for the rest of my days, and I assure you that I am not exaggerating. Of course, it didn't start out that

way. First, there was the unfortunate encounter with the two of
them in the ice-cream parlour, following which I searched for
her all over the square until the free-for-all at the rwai attracted
my attention and I ran into them again. Since you were there as
well, I'm not going to go into any details about the melee save to
tell you that even I found it terrifying. I spotted her immediately
and, of course, I was desperately happy; then the reality of the
situation struck home and I waded into the brawl with my fists
swinging. I saw it as the perfect opportunity to prove myself by
saving her from those thugs who were obviously intent on mal-
ice. One of them, a particularly nasty customer with a shaven
head, was in the midst of slinging a burlap sack over her when
I tapped him on the chin and he went down with a whistling
sound that carried above the din. As I struggled to free her from
the folds of the sack, she appeared to recognize me.

My husband! she gasped. Please save him!

What can I tell you, Hassan? Words cannot describe my feelings. I went warm inside and then cold. She couldn't have hurt
me more had she slapped me. So that bearded youth was her
husband! Although I threw my head back proudly, I was devastated. Of course, I wanted her for myself and my first impulse
was to abandon him, but my better instincts prevailed and I
rushed with her to where he was struggling with his assailants.

Come with me! I shouted in English, pulling at his arm. I'm
a friend!

Save my wife! he shouted back without looking at me. I can
hold them off for a little while longer, but save her, please!

She's safe! I yelled, managing to drag him away at the same
time that I grabbed her arm. She gave me a grateful look as I
propelled them forward.

To the souks! I panted. Quick!

They glanced at each other as if unsure of whether or not to trust me. I drew their attention to the shadowy group of figures who were detaching themselves from the fracas and heading purposefully in our direction.

It's up to you, I said, but make up your minds fast, for heaven's sake! These men mean business!

I'm terribly frightened, she whispered, and as I felt the weight of her fear, I was overcome once again by my love for her.

Trying to preserve a façade of calm, I swung round to her husband. What about it? I said.

He glanced over his shoulder with constricted lips.

Let's go! he said, and we broke into a mad dash.

Behind us, I heard the sound of our pursuers giving chase.

We ran like the wind. Someone yelled at us, but we didn't slow down. I don't think I've ever run so fast in my life. We hurtled past the shuttered food and juice stalls, the Café de France, the Qessabin Mosque, and then straight into the rabbit warren of alleys that lead into the souks.

At this point, with a slightly apologetic gesture, Mustafa paused and asked me if I remembered the game Father would have us play as children when we accompanied him to the Jemaa. The one, he said, where he'd have us imagine that we were disembodied eyes roaming the square. Well, I can tell you I've never been more grateful than I was that night for that exercise in familiarizing myself with the Jemaa and its surroundings. I knew exactly where to go, and how to find my way there in the darkness.

It was to the shop of my friend the shoemaker Karim. I knew that behind his shop he had a secret showroom where he sold shoes copied from the latest designs in Milan and Paris. I knew where he kept the keys—concealed beneath a loose brick—and that is where we found ourselves in a matter of minutes. I shut the door behind us and we stood panting in the darkness, listening to the sounds of the chase echoing through the galleries, now near, now distant.

What do they want from us? she whispered in a frightened voice.

They want you, I said bluntly, and I sensed her husband drawing close to her even as he signalled his agreement.

He's right, he said. It's clear enough.

He took her face in his hands and I heard them kiss.

He turned to me. What do we do now? he asked. Should we stay here for a while? When is it going to be safe to return to our hotel? Or, should I rephrase that?—Is it going to be safe in our hotel?

Frankly, I don't know, I replied. You've attracted the attention of some very dangerous people. Certainly people with plenty of determination, and, above all, money. Thugs of the sort that aren't shy of attempting an abduction in a place as public as the Jemaa don't come cheaply. There's too much organization involved, and they seemed to be working to a definite plan. So I think it would be best to wait here for a while. As for your returning to your hotel, I would advise holding off at least until dawn. Hopefully, they will have stopped looking for you by then. In the meantime, while you catch your breath, I'll bring back a couple of jellabas you can wear to disguise yourselves.

In the darkness, I sensed both of them staring at me, and then he said: Why the disguises?

Because you can't afford to risk losing your wife. News travels fast in the medina, and the men who were after her won't take their setback lying down.

I sensed her reaching out to clutch his hand, and her fingers brushed against my sleeve. Her proximity made my heart race. I leaned my forehead against the door and tried not to let my feelings show. With all my heart I wished that her whole pliant body would bend involuntarily towards me. She must have sensed my struggle because she edged away from me, retreating into the part of the room where it was darkest. I heard her exhale softly and sink down to her feet.

Naturally, her husband rushed over and they kissed again, noisily, in the manner of Westerners.

It was cold in the room. I felt the chill in my heart. I turned away and willed myself not to look at them. I felt no pain, only a glimpse of what was forbidden to me. My god, I reflected, how mysterious life is, how utterly incomprehensible! She was my immortal beloved and I should have been able to claim her as mine, but it was not to be. I could have been like her husband, or, even better, I could have been her husband, but fate had decreed it differently. Here I was in the same room with her, and she was sucking tongues with someone else. It all seemed so absurd and pointless.

What was worse, after all of that running around, my knee was beginning to throb from the old injury from when I'd thrown myself off the cliff. Leaning against the door, I flexed the knee and came to terms with the inevitable: I would have to give up my hopes of winning her. It was a sombre thought, and I glanced at them and suddenly felt my solitude anew. It was as if I were invisible. It made me want to quit the place at once and leave them to their own devices. And yet I told myself that I had shouldered the responsibility for their safety and my honour demanded that I conduct myself accordingly.

Even as I was lost in these thoughts, I heard her murmur tenderly to him. Sensing that they needed time to themselves, I detached myself from my station by the door and resolved to give them some privacy.

I'm going to leave you now and fetch the jellabas, I said. I won't be gone long. When I come back, you can decide what to do next.

Her husband walked over and pressed my hand fervently. We haven't even thanked you, he said.

Don't thank me yet, I replied. You're not out of danger. Inshallah, this night will be over soon and you will make it out of here in peace. Until then, let us hope for the best.

Inshallah, he said, and I heard her echo her thanks from the back of the room. I raised my hand in a gesture of solidarity, cracked the door open, and looked around to make sure the coast was clear. Then I slipped out and locked the door behind me. Little did I know as I ran down the pitch-black alley that that was the last time I would see them.

Inscriptions

Mustafa paused, and I held my breath; a dark flame seemed to singe my brother's eyes. His face contracted as in a spasm and he drew himself up. Running his hand over his forehead, he stood up abruptly and took a few agitated steps along the nar-

row space between his chair and the wall behind him. His eyes
roamed over the low-ceilinged room, settling on nothing. After
a few minutes of this restless appraisal, he halted and turned
to look at me with a disconcerting intensity. His dark eyes glittered. I thought he was going to return to his seat, but he merely
murmured:

What can I tell you about what happened after that, Hassan? There's very little to tell, really. I came back in a while
with the jellabas, as I'd said I would, but when I found the
door to the room ajar I knew at once that something was
amiss. I plunged into the room prepared to do battle but there
was no one there. A dense weave of shadows met my eyes;
everything was perfectly still. I even switched on the light to
make sure that I wasn't imagining things. But no, they were
gone, and I had no idea what might have happened to them —
save one thing.

With his eyes still fixed on me, he walked back to his seat.

I looked inquiringly at him.

And what was that? I asked, even as I experienced a renewed
feeling of discomfiture; it struck me that a subtle change had
come over not only my brother's expression but his entire bearing toward me.

Bending his head a little, and with his eyes more on the bars
that lay between us than on me, Mustafa replied in a tone that
seemed altogether removed from our surroundings:

It was a small inkwell in the shape of a lion, carved out of
soft stone and painted red. Someone must have dropped it by
accident in the alley just outside Karim's shop, and I recognized
it immediately, as well I should. Why, I would have recognized
it in the dark. You see, I'd found it in the Sahara a long time

ago, when I was a boy. I'd taken it from a dead woman, and it had been in my possession all these years until I'd given it to my beloved older brother, Hassan, on the occasion of his thirtieth birthday. He is a storyteller who loves to write with pen and ink in his sheepskin journal and I thought he'd have more use for it than me.

The mood in the room had undergone a sea change while my brother had been speaking. Now he looked at me awkwardly, even shyly, though his eyes were pained, his face long and sad.

I'd had your name inscribed on the bottom, if you recall. So there could be no mistaking it, Hassan. It was none other than the one I had given you.

He broke off and directed his gaze almost apologetically at the inkwell in my hand.

Mousharabiyya

My dear friends, I would have burst into outraged laughter had the accusation been levelled by anyone other than my own brother. As it was, I stared at him in amazement. We were of the same flesh and blood; I could look at the world through his eyes, and yet I couldn't look through his heart and fathom his reasoning.

He mistook my silence and attempted to jog my memory.

You do remember when I gave it to you, don't you? It was in the evening, at home, in the garden. We were all standing around. Ahmed had just played the flute for you; Father had recited a poem.

Even though I didn't dare trust my voice, I felt compelled to reply. Mustafa, it was less than two years ago, I said. I'd hardly have forgotten.

Well then?

I had to smile, the ridiculousness of it all saddening me.

Have you gone mad? I asked him.

He stared at me. Of course not, he retorted, colouring fiercely.

Then you are delirious, perhaps?

Absolutely not.

Then how can you assume that I had something to do with the disappearance?

He began to bluster, but I cut him off.

And so one seeks the truth in the small, palpable objects as a remedy to the great impalpable that is life, I observed.

He seemed taken aback by my words.

You don't believe me? You think I'm making it all up?

Oh no, I do believe you, I said. Don't forget that I'm a story-teller. That is how I make my living. For me, whatever is imagined must, by definition, aspire to fidelity. And yet . . .

I paused and chose my next words carefully.

Let me put it this way. As Father likes to say, it takes more than just a healthy imagination to make an adept storyteller.

I did not imagine it. It is the truth.

It is not the truth. It cannot be. A vital element is missing.

There was a pause.

He appeared put out. Then he ran his tongue over his lips.

I don't understand what you're getting at. What would make my story more believable, according to you? What is missing?

The element of proof.

What do you mean?

Simply this. I'd gone there looking for you that night. I searched for you in all your usual haunts in the medina, determined to dissuade you from the course you had chosen.

You went to Karim's shop?

Yes, I did, and to Dounia and her daughters, and the Qessabin Mosque where they'd seen you enter, and many other places besides. Obviously the inkwell must have fallen out of my pocket when I was standing in front of the shuttered shop, where I'd hoped that Karim would be working late, and you'd be with him, and we'd be able to talk some sense into you together.

He gazed at me in disbelief. You cut short your storytelling session in the Jemaa?

And dismissed my audience. For the first time in my life.

I had no idea, Hassan!

No, of course you didn't. You were too caught up in your own madness.

I extended the inkwell towards him.

We share the same mother's heart, Mustafa. If there is any doubt in your mind about my complicity in the affair, then I will personally reveal your suspicions to the police.

My brother stared at the inkwell and then at me in supreme confusion—his face a compendium of many feelings, both complementary and conflicting—before sitting back with a dazed expression.

So you see, I said, it made for a nice story, though one too slight for my taste. It could have done with—how shall I put it?—more gravity, but also more suspense. To consider only one instance, that fight in the Jemaa was vicious, as I remember it, and I don't think you did justice to it. Also, you rushed through the best parts, which is usually an error that most amateurs make when it comes to judging pace. A less breathless tone would have made it seem more seasoned, less glib, and certainly not so much like a B-grade movie. All the same, it was a valiant first effort. Or was it a first effort?

Realizing abruptly that I hadn't the faintest idea, I jerked forward and fixed him with my eyes. Mustafa, I said with sudden alacrity, is that what you told the police?

Of course not, he said, flushing. A hint of irony, so fleeting that only my watchful eyes could have noticed it, played on the corners of his lips. He met my earnest gaze and said: There's a time for secrets and a time for confessions. I told you that you could set your mind at ease.

Yes, I said wryly. You've told me a lot of things.

He flushed again and contemplated me with an air of contrition.

I care about you, Hassan, he said. Immensely. I always have. Never forget that.

Thank you, I replied. All the same, it won't change my opinion that you are an idiot and also quite mad. And totally reckless, to the bargain.

He frowned but did not utter a word. His face still bore traces of his astonishment arising from my refutation of his claim concerning the inkwell, and it was clear that he now preferred discretion to valour.

Exercising restraint, I joined my fingertips and regarded him with immense forbearance.

You do realize, don't you, I said, that there was no need for you to have acted as you did? You've behaved like a complete fool.

He hung his head without a word.

Well? I prompted.

He sat back and closed his eyes. On his handsome, weary, and bruised face there now appeared traces of helplessness. To my surprise, he seemed close to tears.

I realized at once that I'd been too harsh and attempted a more conciliatory tone of voice. Mustafa, I said, I am sorry about what I just called you, and I apologize as well for coming down hard on your story, but at least where the latter is concerned I have my standards, and they are high.

I'm well aware of that, he said, and, opening his eyes, he brought his face close to mine. A sense of shame seemed to be oppressing him, checking his rising tears. He looked at me for a long time before turning away and casting his glance around the room with a look that was oddly ambivalent.

May I have another chance? he asked. His voice was hoarse.

My heart felt heavy as I gazed at my brother.

The room smelled of our sweat, both his and mine.

I turned away from him and said: Only if you tell me what really happened that evening. As your brother, I deserve no less.

Somewhere on the floor above us a tin cup clattered loudly. Neither Mustafa nor I reacted to it. Instead, we continued to stare at each other, not daring to take our eyes off one another's faces for even an instant. Finally, he stirred. His tired face seemed to have grown even more exhausted.

All right, I will tell you what happened, he answered.

Thank you, I said. It's only fair, you'll agree.

I could see him composing himself. Turning a little red in the face, he coughed, twice, paused to catch his breath, and then, in a ragged, spent voice, told me the story of his love for a complete stranger and the sacrifice he'd made for her.

PERFUME

I'll begin at the point where I returned to Karim's shop with the jellabas, Mustafa said. When I entered the room, I found, to my great surprise, that she was alone. Seeing her again, I immediately felt better and asked her where her husband was. Instead of answering, she blurted out a question of her own.

Oh, she gasped, why did you have to come back so soon?

I stared at her uncomprehendingly, trying to make sense of her distress. Perhaps it was because she was apprehensive of being alone in a dark room with a stranger? All the same, I was reassured by the fact that she didn't seem angry with me for having returned, and I hastened to allay her fears.

It's all right, I said gently, don't worry. You're safe with me. Where is your husband?

There was a prolonged silence, and then she said:

He has gone.

Gone? But how did he let himself out? I thought I'd locked the door.

He found a way, she said. Her voice sounded tense; she seemed on edge.

I stared at her in astonishment, hesitated, and was silent. I didn't know what to say; it simply didn't make sense. Where could he have gone at this time of night? And how could he have left her by herself? The more I reflected upon it, the more I felt bewildered, until suddenly a very different train of thought encroached upon my mind. I hardly needed to explain it to myself, but I wondered if her husband had abandoned her. It seemed bizarre, but her words had seemed to hint at a more permanent departure than a merely temporary absence. Perhaps they had had an altercation and he had walked out on her? Stranger things have been known to happen. If that were so, then the field was clear for me; I could claim her for myself. He had gone away—and she could go with me! She could be mine! We would never need to be apart again.

While these thoughts were racing through my mind, she'd been standing in statuelike repose in the shadows. Now she stirred and broke the silence. Speaking in low, rushed tones, she said:

Why are you staring at me like that?

Try as I might, I couldn't reply. I'd hardly heard what she had said, and, in any case, I seemed to have lost my voice. I wished I could see her face, but it didn't really matter because I had committed it to memory. I knew exactly where the mole on her right cheek was, the barely visible scar above her right eye, the dimple on her chin. I felt myself tracing her arms, shaping her elbows, encircling her wrists. Gazing at her shadowy form, I felt parched, like some desert creature whose thirst only she could satisfy. My heart began to pound, a tremor shook my body, I . . .

Excuse me, she said, intruding into my thoughts again. You're making me uncomfortable, standing there staring at me like that.

I started and came back to reality. I realized that her husband might return soon and I had to make the most of the time that I had with her. I surely wouldn't get an opportunity like this again, and I knew that I'd never be at peace with myself if I held back now from telling her about my feelings. I decided to reveal the truth. I saw no point in hiding it.

I'm in love with you, I said boldly.

I sensed her looking at me and hesitating. She took a step back and thanked me, but her tone lacked assurance.

You're very kind, she said, but you forget that I'm married and terribly in love with my husband, who will be back any moment.

It doesn't matter, I said resolutely. My love for you will alter the way you feel. Love begets love, longing begets longing, and the same can be said of desire. You can learn to love me.

But I already love someone else! My husband is my world. He means everything to me.

I bit back a retort and pressed on.

That may be so, I said, but nothing in the entire universe means what you mean to me. It's been that way from the very moment I set eyes on you. In all that you say and do you are the woman of my dreams. I look at you and know that you are where I want to be. I want to write songs to your eyes. I want to swim in your heart; you are my ocean and my prayer and the fount of my seed.

Listen! I added breathlessly, forestalling her response. Have you ever swum with dolphins?

By her long silence I could tell she was taken aback.

At length, she ventured: Dolphins? No.

What about swordfish? I persisted.

No, she said again, and I could sense her wondering if I'd gone quite mad.

Then I will take you to a place off the isle of Mogador where you can see them jump right out of the water as you swim.

Oh? And why would they do that?

To please you, I said. As a tribute to your beauty.

In the darkness, I sensed a smile hovering on her lips.

Liar, she said.

I don't lie about these things. I live in Essaouira, by the sea. I worship the sea gods. The ocean is my garden.

Don't you think you're mixing the sacred and the profane?

Her voice no longer sounded apprehensive but amused, and once more there came upon me that strange sense of buoyancy, of boundless confidence, and a proud awareness of my own feelings.

I love you, I said again. I've never said that to anyone.

You're very direct, she replied a bit crossly, but I could tell that she was pleased. It was clear that she was listening to me, and her air of calm consideration encouraged me.

Yes, I am direct, I confessed. That's because I am young, like you. We work quickly, like fire.

Fire burns. I had a room burn down around me once. It was terrifying.

You're not frightened of me, I hope?

No.

Good, I'm glad, because I am speaking from my heart.

She did not answer.

You are my prayer! I added fervently. If only you could see yourself through my eyes. Your heart is my universe; your soul fulfills my needs.

But you don't know anything about me, she pointed out.

On the contrary, I not only know you, I've been waiting for you all my life.

I sensed her shaking her head.

You're glib, she said.

I'm sincere.

Then you are deceiving yourself.

That is not what my heart is telling me. You are my salvation, my redemption, my promise.

You speak of redemption, she said, suddenly sombre, but I can tell you from experience that for every redemption there is a price to be paid.

I will pay it. Without regret.

Do you understand what you are asking for?

I am asking for your heart in exchange for mine. Listen to me, we'll live by the ocean. I'll be the sand that surrounds you, grain and beach. You'll be the air I breathe.

Stop speaking to me like this! she said. I haven't given you permission.

And I haven't asked for it, I said gaily, because my love for you has made me giddy and swept away all the usual proprieties, which I find tedious, in any case.

You're like a greedy child who hasn't learned self-control.

I'm like the ocean burnished by your sunset.

You're incorrigible!

I am, and I readily admit it, as long as you acknowledge being my guiding light, my golden thread, the compass of my world.

Are you a poet? she asked, and I sensed a return of her smile.

No, I replied, but you inspire me.

I think you should take up writing poetry.

That is my father's province, I replied, and my brother's. I'm a humble artisan. I make lanterns out of camel hide and sheep-skin. Sometimes, I paint. But that's the extent of my artistic endeavors.

Then you are a painter with words.

You are too gracious, but I'll accept your compliment. Let me assure you that I am also capable of backing up my words with actions.

Oh, I'm sure you are, she said hurriedly. I have no doubt about it.

Then bless my feelings for you with reciprocity.

You know very well that I can't.

Why not, for God's sake?

For all the reasons that I've already explained to you, she said patiently.

You are heartless, cruel—and I've never felt as helpless as I do now! Can't you sense my despair?

I'm sorry, she said in a small voice, but I'm not responsible for your illusions.

Illusions! What you call my illusions are now the sum and substance of my reality.

Then I can't help you, she said gently.

Kiss me, please. Just once, out of pity.

No, I can't. I don't want to hurt you but you must understand that I won't compromise my loyalty to my marriage.

I hung my head.

Then at least breathe with me for a moment if you won't grant me anything else.

There was a silence. Then, with a catch in her voice, she asked:

Breathe with you? What do you mean?

I want to feel the rivers of your breath resound in my soul, I said with fervor. I want to carry that feeling with me for the rest of my life.

She was light on her feet. She came over and kissed me on the cheek. I could see her eyes shining in the darkness. My own emotions left me dazed and a full minute must have passed before I grasped what she was telling me.

I will always be with you, she said. But you must leave now.

The firmness in her voice took my breath away.

I don't even know your name, I protested.

Names aren't important. Now go, please.

I stared at her, my confidence deserting me.

Couldn't we talk about this? I asked, suddenly deflated.

She swung away from me with a quick, lithe movement.

If you truly love me, she said in a low voice, then you will do as I request. I can't force you to leave, but I'm counting on your feelings for me. Don't ask me for explanations. Please.

Don't worry, I murmured. I'll go.

Thank you, she said.

I crossed the room helplessly. As I approached the door, a feeling of impotence, of sheer despair, surged in me, followed by a sense of rebellion. I checked my steps and turned around. Trying to control my vexation, I said:

Why do you insist on my leaving you? I love you, and with love comes responsibility. I accept the fact of your marriage. I will come to terms with your being in love with another man. I give you my word that I will not contest it. So why must you force me to go away prematurely? Every moment that I spend with you now will sustain me for the rest of my days. Let me

wait here until your husband returns, at least, and as soon as he
does, I will take my leave.

No, she said with a peculiar obstinacy, you can't stay here.
Please don't argue.

The words had come in a rush; she obviously wanted me gone.
This wasn't going the way I would have liked, and I continued to
hesitate. Her disapproval, even her impatience, far from checking me, simply goaded me on.

It isn't safe to leave you by yourself, I observed.

Must you argue? This is embarrassing. I trusted in your
goodwill and you are reneging on it.

I tried to keep the hurt out of my voice.

You talk about goodwill? Well, that goes both ways, doesn't
it? I rescue you from the square. I bring you to a safe place. I
leave to get you clothes that you can wear. But when I come
back, your husband has disappeared without explanation and
you can't wait to see me go. Tell me, is that goodwill? May I also
remind you that this is my friend's shop? His name is Karim.
You are here by my good graces.

There was a long silence as we stood facing each other. I
knew that she had ceased to smile, but her lips were still parted,
for I could see the white gleam of her teeth. The smell of her
perfume drifted towards me, and it took me some effort to exercise restraint. I contented myself with gazing steadily at her face
and, exhausted by my tirade, held my peace.

She'd been standing stiffly erect, but now she bowed her
head. Speaking haltingly but clearly, in a subdued and softer
tone of voice, she said: We're both very grateful to you for
what you have done for us. A friend couldn't have done more.
You've been wonderful, and I'm moved by your concern for my

safety. It means a lot to me. I know that my intransigence concerning your departure must be difficult to accept. But please understand that, if that is so, it's because it's the way things are. Beyond that very inadequate explanation, I simply cannot tell you more and can do no better than to ask for your forbearance.

Much as I wanted to respond in kind, I held myself back.

You're right, I said coldly. I don't understand. If you are worried about getting out of here, I know the souks like the back of my hand. I can help you find your way out in an instant.

We are already being helped.

Oh? By whom?

A man.

A man? That tells me nothing. Is he a friend? Does he live here? Is he from here?

I can't tell you that.

I drew myself up. A whole series of contradictory feelings swept over me. We'd spoken in undertones, leaning a little towards each other, and I'd had a closer view than I'd had the entire evening of the pale beauty of her face, made vulnerable by fatigue. I felt bewildered and overtired myself, at the mercy of every impulse.

I hesitated. The more you speak, the less I understand, I said.

Perhaps that is why I have held back from telling you more, she said. She didn't say anything else, and I did not press her further.

I was turning to go when all of a sudden she said:

Tell me about the dolphins again.

Ah, I said, halting in mid-stride, they will not leap anymore.

Why?

Because they will know my sadness.

You asked me my name. It is Lucia.

I am Mustafa, I said.

She extended her hand and I grasped it.

You've touched me with your nearness to the sea gods, Mustafa, she said. The last time I was blessed by them was in Mexico, in a place called Baja California. It's very far from here. It was a time of immense joy for me, great peace; I met my lover there. One night we were sleeping out in the open, on the beach, beneath a starry sky. You must know what that's like. The air was damp and salty, the surf white and black in the darkness. I thought: This is the most wonderful night of my life. I fell asleep to the music of the ocean, but I woke in the middle of the night to a very different sound. It was high-pitched and barely audible above the roar of the waves. I sat up, my curiosity aroused, and was astonished to see a pod of dolphins swimming by the beach, alarmingly close to land. I watched them for as long as they were there, and when they returned, one by one, to the depths, I bid them farewell.

They were fishing, I said. They were corralling the fish in the shallow waters and chasing them down. You were lucky to have seen them.

Yes, it was beautiful. I thought you would understand.

I do understand. Thank you for sharing it with me.

Even though she probably couldn't see me, I pressed my hand to my heart.

She was silent for a moment.

There are things that you will understand, she said, and things that you won't. If I've held back from telling you the truth about my situation, it may be because you will find it implausible.

You must not think too highly of me if you can say that.

And you won't think less of me if I tell you?

No, I said.

I don't know . . .

Try, I prompted, scarcely daring to breathe.

She did not reply, but I sensed that she was gathering her courage to speak. She took a few steps around the room while I stood quite still, following her every movement, all my attention centred on her, my breath coming rapidly but fully.

She turned and stood before me. Her step was firm and determined, as if she had accepted the consequences of her decision. Speaking with a composure that aroused my admiration, she said:

The man I am with is not my husband. My real husband—whom I had the misfortune of marrying when I was too young to know better—is a powerful man of great wealth. My marriage to him died the night it was consummated. I cannot tell you more; it's too difficult and sad. Besides, there isn't time. Perhaps the only good that came out of it was to make me realize that there is nothing more precious than life and that it is so terribly short.

She paused, her shoulders stiffening a little and betraying the tension in her body, while my own posture conveyed nothing but the most sincere affection, my attitude both concerned and protective. She stared into the shadows, her silence taut with a sense of constraint, almost of shame. Then she shuddered, her shoulders sagging, and the ordeals she must have had to endure made my heart go out to her. Lowering her voice until I could hardly hear her, she fell to telling me the rest of her story.

Yes, life is precious, she said, and strange. Years later, when I met my beloved and had my faith in the world restored, I sought to leave my husband, but he wouldn't hear of it. He said it would compromise his position in society and insisted that I do as I was told. He encircled me with custodians, with lawyers, and guardians; he refused to listen to my pleadings, he refused to let me go. Every day brought new humiliations, new degradations. Finally, after all our attempts to reason with him had failed, my lover and I saw no way out but to escape. It wasn't a decision that we took easily, but the alternative was a slow stifling to death. But my husband is a stubborn, angry man; he pursues us everywhere.

So those men on the square . . . ?

They could have been his minions, though I am not certain. He's made it clear that he'll stop at nothing to get me back, and I fear for my beloved's safety. We've had several narrow escapes, and every time we've gotten away he's managed to track us down.

Is that why you've needed to pretend that your companion is your husband? To throw your pursuers off your tracks?

Only partly, yes. He is my husband in spirit.

But not in fact, I said, feeling the need to stress the distinction.

No, she conceded, but we've been through too much together for me to think of him in any other way. We are partners for life.

A pause followed, during which time she took a step back.

Realizing that I might have upset her, I said, very simply, that I understood—and also that I would hardly consider myself a stickler for convention—and it seemed to reassure her.

With a renewed note of confidence in her voice, she said:

Last year, after my lover had survived yet another mysterious accident, we confided our troubles to a friend. He's a writer, a very clever, ingenious man, and also kindhearted. He came up with a solution to our quandary. It entailed our coming to Morocco, where neither of us had been before. It also entailed taking someone else—a friend of his—into our confidence. At first, the whole thing seemed far-fetched, but we had nothing to lose, so we agreed to chance it. And now we're nearly there, she said with a confidence I ought to have found touching, except that I could only confess to the most complete confusion.

I'm afraid I'm not following you, I said, trying to keep my voice level while not revealing how utterly bewildered I felt. Forgive me if this question offends, I went on, but are you faking a disappearance? Was the attack on the square staged?

She appeared genuinely distressed.

Oh, please, no more questions!

Her reaction told me all that I wanted to know.

But what if you're found out? I asked.

It's a risk, but one that we're prepared to take.

What is the plan? Where do you go from here?

Hopefully to a place where we can never be found.

I could not meet her gaze. I tried to smile in agreement, but my lips stayed tense. Every minute she was growing more and more of a stranger to me. I suddenly felt hurt, though she'd said nothing to provoke that response in me. And although I already knew what her answer would be even before I assayed the question, I offered, nonetheless, to help.

She responded with alarm.

No, no! she said. Please listen to me and try to understand. It's all been arranged.

Oh, very well, I answered, resigned to being relegated to the periphery.

But what do you think of it all? she asked. From the renewed note of affection to her voice, I could tell that her confession had made her feel lighter.

Do you know me better now? she said.

Yes, I do, I lied. And what about me?

I do not know you at all, but that is how it should be.

I was still so preoccupied with her story that I did not think of querying her further.

She looked at me with gleaming eyes.

I'm glad that you understand. And I hope you also understand that if I have not asked you for anything, it's because I haven't needed it.

I understand that as well, but only in part, I said.

She surprised me with her next action. She took off the scarf that she'd been wearing and gave it to me. The cloth was warm.

Find a woman for yourself, she said. She will gain by being with you.

I have found her, I said sadly.

I would like to believe that the affection you have offered me is akin to brotherly tenderness, she said.

That is hardly the same thing, I replied, and you know it.

She withdrew her hand from my arm. Go in peace, she said. And remember me as you do the ocean.

Think well of me, I replied in parting. I will be wherever you like it best.

DREAMS AND DELUSIONS

Mustafa paused and regarded me with despondent eyes.

What else can I tell you, Hassan? My last sight was of her standing there in the middle of the darkened room, her white muslin dress clinging to the folds of her body, her head bare now that she'd given me her scarf.

I didn't know what to say to my brother. In telling me the story of his love, he had revealed an unexpectedly chivalrous side to him that I hadn't known existed. What was more, swayed by the extent of his distress, I was now only too ready to believe what he'd told me, and I murmured some vague remark that hardly did justice to my changed feelings. Never had I been more in sympathy with him.

Oblivious to my thoughts, he continued in a resigned tone:

You can probably surmise what happened next. Difficult as it was, I walked out of the door with the silent promise to her to respect her sentiments and not go back, regardless of my own feelings. Barely conscious of where I was going—all I registered was the dim glimmer of moonlight seeping through the over-head trellises—I wandered about the souks in a daze, trying to hold on to my resolve. But my concern for her well-being was paramount and I began to fret, all sorts of questions plaguing me and robbing me of my peace of mind. Was her lover able to find his way back to her through the maze of galleries, a difficult enough undertaking in broad daylight, let alone in the middle of the night? And would they be able to make it out of there without

losing their way and betraying their presence to those searching for them? Unable to ignore my presentiments—which were
growing stronger by the minute—I began to fear the worst. I
felt the need to respond, to move, to do something. And so it
was with a vast sense of relief, not undiluted with guilt, that I
found myself reversing my steps. I justified my breach of promise by telling myself that her safety warranted it. I began to run,
and, as I did, I felt the surrounding galleries tilt towards me and
embrace me with approbation. It was a heady, charged feeling,
made all the more intense by the freedom of my emotions. I felt
invincible; I could have taken on an army just then. I ached to
be of fuller use to her and for her to be the mirror of my actions.

Exhilarated, I rushed back to Karim's shop and burst into the
back room, prepared to fall at her feet, only to find it deserted.
An image of her swam fleetingly before my eyes, held still for a
moment, then shattered into a million pieces. She was no longer
there, and, with her departure, the precariously poised edifice of
my hopes came crashing down.

Oh, Hassan, he said, it was more than I could stand! The room
was empty, like a void; not even a whiff of her perfume was left. I
broke down and wept as I had never before in my life.

I felt a chill just listening to Mustafa. I could see the darkened
room, the shadowy corners. I envisaged him standing there, his
face streaming with tears, his gaze defeated. It was a harrowing
vision.

A brother's anguish, I thought, yes, that is what I'm feeling.

Mustafa said: It was all an idle dream, unrealizable, prema-
ture, grotesque, but at the time, it hurt so much. It hurt to be
there when she was gone. I sat on the floor trying to go over my
memories of her but my mind was in shock. It was as if my heart

had been broken twice over, once when I found out that she was spoken for and then when I had to experience losing her all over again, this time with no possibility of reversal.

He rested his forehead against the bars.

It was hell, Hassan, pure hell! I felt as if life had ended for me. I was in a state of collapse.

What did you do next? I asked.

With his forehead still resting against the grille, Mustafa said:

I sat there in the room, distraught. I've no idea how long I remained there. Then the darkness got to me and, for the first time that night, I groped around and switched on the light. It took me a moment to adjust to the brightness, and as soon as I did, I held up the stone lion and reached my hasty conclusion about your part in the episode. Once again, I beg your forgiveness, Hassan. It simply did not cross my overweary—and, I admit it—jealous mind that I was rushing to judgement.

I don't want you to think any more about it, I said firmly. It was a misunderstanding based on the facts at hand, and I've accepted your apology. That is all there is to it.

I glanced at the clock on the wall.

I don't know how much more time we have, I said, but I wouldn't want to leave without hearing the entire story. It would take a more astute listener than I am to piece together the path you have travelled between that dark room and your present residence and I certainly cannot do it without your help.

My irony was intentional and intended to be humorous, but Mustafa didn't smile. It was clear that he took my remark to heart, for his mouth drew down at the prospect of having to continue to recall his disappointment in love.

I felt for him, but my curiosity—that fatal weakness of every storyteller—triumphed over my discretion. When he remained silent, however, his face tense with emotion, I apprehended that perhaps he was forcing himself to come to terms with my selfishness.

I understand, he said quietly, intuiting my thoughts. Your storyteller's inquisitiveness—if one can call it that—is indeed all-consuming. To think that even here you can't manage to let go of it, to leave it behind!

His eyes dwelt on my face.

Well, I brought it upon myself, didn't I, with my bragging about being on a par with Father and you. I have only myself to blame.

He paused and turned away and his face grew sombre.

OCEAN

Hassan, he said in a low and earnest voice, what does it mean to be the ocean? I am haunted by what she said to me when we parted.

I thought about it for a while before venturing an answer.

I think it means to be in the one thing and in all things at the same time. I have heard it described in mystical terms as being the energy that flows through everything.

So to identify with the ocean—to be the ocean, as she described it—would mean a merging with that energy?

Certainly a merging, but more; it would imply being that

energy, its oceanic tranquillity and calmness, as well as its depth and gravity. In that sense, it is probably synonymous with what we understand as truth.

Can one become the ocean?

One can certainly try.

He contemplated my answer, and then he said: It makes me wish I had some of that energy that night because by the time dawn glimmered on the horizon, I felt all done in.

He massaged his eyebrows with the tips of his fingers and smiled at me grimly. Don't worry, he said, I'll reconstruct that morning for you, though the onset of the new day did not bring light for me but a long winter's darkness instead.

The ocean was silent?

Completely.

I'm sorry, I said, and bowed my head.

What for? It's the way things are, isn't it? We sink, we swim, the ocean's indifferent. As for misery, there's no remedy for it. Or so I discovered when I left the room and wandered aimlessly around the souks, still hoping to turn a corner and find her there. But it wasn't to be. There was no miracle, and she didn't appear. At dawn, I admitted defeat and trudged like a beaten creature into the square. It hurt to be alive. I felt all alone. It hurt to be in the world with a broken heart. I don't really remember what followed.

He winced, and I caught on his face, like an echo from the past, a glimpse of the utter exhaustion with which he must have endured the darkest moments of his life. It induced in me a sudden nausea, as if I myself had lived through the experience.

Do you remember getting lashed by the sandstorm in the desert? he asked. That was nothing compared to the way I now felt.

Once back in Essaouira, I went about trying to resume my former life but everything seemed aimless. I could no longer sleep, I
had no desire to work, I lost interest in my friends. I tried reading
books—on wisdom, on love, on immanence—but soon gave it up;
unlike you, I was never a reader. Even the walks on the beach
that had always sustained me no longer sufficed. It was like an
apprenticeship in solitude, and, depending on your definition of
success, I either failed miserably or surpassed the highest expec-
tations. And all the while, I had endless conversations with her in
my head. I imagined that we were together, and it kept me going.
I went over every moment I'd spent with her, every word, every
nuance of gesture and expression. It filled my waking hours, lent
substance to my dreams. I visualized her always next to me, the
corners of her lips poised in a smile. The imagination is a powerful thing.

You took it too far, Mustafa, I observed.

He made an evasive gesture as if to imply that that was no
concern of mine. But he also fell silent, lost in thought, and I
took the opportunity to ask him a question. I tried to pose it
tactfully, but it still came out sounding indiscreet.

I asked: Can love be so separated from reality?

He looked at me obliquely, and I could tell that I had hurt
him. My poor brother, captive to such a magnificent and hopeless obsession! How much he had in him of the valour and also
of the blindness of those who are consumed by love and sacrifice
themselves to it. I felt for him, and yet, more and more, I felt
myself distancing from him. His passion was too extreme for
my comfort—perhaps I am a little conservative when it comes to
these things—and under different circumstances it might have

been riveting, or even diverting, but for the fact that he was in prison as a result of it.

At length, conscious of my awaiting his answer, he shrugged his shoulders.

Perhaps I could answer you, he said, if I understood your meaning more clearly. As it is, all that I can tell you is that love is hardly the most logical thing in the world.

I refrained from looking at him. Speaking a bit brusquely, I said: I'm not going to argue with you about logic, Mustafa—even I'm not that obtuse. But I do believe that love must have some grounding in reality. It isn't some abstract idea to be gleaned from books. It's no wonder that the ones you tried reading had nothing to say to you. Love is touch, sound, taste, smell, sight—everything that makes the world what it is. Of course it may be based on an ideal, but it cannot survive solely on ideals. It needs something more tangible to sustain itself. Consider your own analogy of the ocean, for instance. You can be inspired by the ocean, you can admire it, but you cannot swim in a photograph of it, however pretty it may be. For that, you must have the real thing.

That's a tremendously biased analogy, Hassan! he protested. We're obviously not going to agree about this.

That may be, but it's hardly the most important thing, I replied. I couldn't care less about whether or not our ideas about love coincide, but you have to let go of her, Mustafa. You have to let go of her or you will find no peace.

Ah, but that's where you're wrong, Hassan! he exclaimed.

In his voice was a rare excitement. He leaned through the bars and seized my hands. I was astonished by the suddenness of his transformation.

I cannot let go of her, he said animatedly, nor is there any need to. She is already in me. The ocean isn't something outside the self. It is the self. It gives it dimension, lends it meaning. Believe me, I know this for a fact. I've come through the most difficult phase of my life and what's kept me going has been my love for her. But here's the thing: I didn't actually do anything. One day I woke up and I was someone else. It's as simple as that. I cannot come up with a better explanation for it.

His cheerful, boyish laugh rang across the room.

It happened this way, he said. I was lying in bed early one morning when I heard the muezzin's call from the mosque nearby, and the next thing I knew, I felt myself falling up. It's the only way I can describe it. I was swept up in the cascade of that voice. It opened up my senses, and I became the ocean. I was so grateful; I felt such peace. I felt unconquerable. I went singing to work. On the way, the morning papers caught my eye. They were going on and on about the disappearance. I looked up and saw the seagulls flying. I said a silent prayer and made up my mind. It was clear to me what I had to do next.

He straightened up, stuck out his chin, and said:

I would eliminate any risk of the discovery of their plan by declaring them dead. I would claim that I had abducted and killed both of them. That would stop her husband in his tracks once and for all and permit them to get on with their lives—as they deserved to. And, having resolved this, in loving peace and harmony, I put it into effect. I freely confess to having lived out this dream.

I became the ocean, he said again, smiling.

Lion Ash

Having made his announcement, Mustafa sat quite still, tranquil and sanguine. I was reminded of the days of our youth when he would stand before the mirror, his chin up, his arms clasped behind his back, his attitude emblematic of his innate rebelliousness—for, in his decision to turn himself in, I intuited a very large degree of rebellion against reality.

For some time neither of us spoke. Then I said quietly:

Is any woman worth this degree of sacrifice, Mustafa?

He too spoke quietly: I can answer that only if you can tell me why she and I were fated to meet.

I turned away from him and contemplated the floor. I couldn't think of an adequate response. After all, I reflected, who was I to venture an opinion on destiny? Abandoning the high ground of abstractions, I decided to turn to more immediate realities. Trying to keep the despair out of my voice, I said:

I beg you, will you please tell this story to the police?

Of course not! Are you mad? I would never compromise her!

From his mounting colour I could see that I had deeply offended him. For some minutes we remained thus, facing each other, not exchanging a word. He'd lost his unbending pose; his head had sunk between his shoulders, and he gazed at me sullenly. At last I drew in my legs and passed my hand over my forehead. Very slowly, choosing my words hesitantly and carefully, I asked: So there is a third version of what happened that evening?

He gave a contemptuous, half-uttered laugh.

Yes, there is. But don't worry. It's one that doesn't involve you or her or anyone else. Only me.

The singing tone had gone out of his voice.

I realized then that the only way I could make my brother see reason would be to go against the grain of my own sentiments and cast doubt on the veracity of what she had told him. I decided to risk all in a direct question.

Did you believe her story? I asked.

Mustafa flinched as if I'd slapped him. In that instinctive reaction, I read all that I needed to know about the possibility of convincing him differently. I gave up even before he replied disdainfully: Are you questioning her credibility?

Well, there is the matter of plausibility, don't you think?

What plausibility? he retorted, his manner implying that he was at a loss to see any connection between my question and all that had gone before it.

I hesitated, then added: The standards of plausibility by which any rational person must judge the truth or untruth of whatever it is that he is being asked to believe.

There was a short silence. Then his voice rang out stridently.

I love her, I love her, and I don't want to hear anything else! When you love someone like I do, you worship them. You worship every part of them. You don't disbelieve them. You don't question their veracity. That is beside the point. It doesn't interest me.

I could not repress an outburst of annoyance.

That in itself is a problem, isn't it?

His eyebrows arched into scornful crescents.

I always knew that you were a cynic, Hassan, but I suppose I didn't know the extent of it. Find fault in me, if you will, but leave her out of it. She doesn't live by your rules. She isn't part of your world. One has to believe in something, and I've chosen to believe in love.

Cynic, romantic, these are words, Mustafa, but here is the sad truth, and it is not—to our great, and shared, misfortune—a fiction. You are in prison, for a crime you did not commit but have admitted to committing. Believe me, even I couldn't have thought up a story more improbable or compelling. Where the two foreigners are concerned, if they are safe, wherever they are, I wish them well. But as for you and me, there is only one reality, and that is the life before us—and it is bleak.

Mustafa said nothing; he simply cast an aloof glance at me. In the flawless oval of his face there was such a sense of superiority that I could no longer look at him. I gazed down dejectedly, fixing my eyes on my slippers. They were yellow leather babouches, creased and scuffed at the heels. Although I had acquired them in Marrakesh, something about them reminded me of our village in the mountains. That life now seemed so distant, so much a part of what was unrecoverable that I felt a consuming sadness.

My brother deferred to my silent mood. Without looking at each other, without speaking, we sat across the partition that divided us, each lost in his own thoughts. Our meeting seemed to have floundered on the formidable reef of his love, and I didn't know how to salvage it. As more time passed, I sank into dejection, while noticing that exactly the obverse seemed the case with him. Increasingly, something of the tranquillity with which he had first entered the room appeared to manifest itself once more in him. It made me wonder if the sanctuary of his love was akin to the solace provided by religion. And yet, I reflected, what was it worth to gain a kingdom if it meant losing your life?

When at last I spoke, my question was an echo of my thoughts.

How do you pray at a time like this?

For a change, he didn't appear displeased by my question.

His response was calm, unshaken.

I call to the god who believes in me. I ask for his help in tearing away the veils that cloak the world. It's like swimming for a distant shore when you know that the ocean around you is vast and deep and there's a good chance you won't make it.

There was a sound behind me and I turned around.

The police constable was standing at the door. He entered the room and pointed to the clock on the wall. I rose from my chair, almost relieved at his intervention. I felt drained and lacked the strength to prolong the meeting. Faced with my own helplessness, something like a terminal exhaustion overcame me. My heart hurt; my chest felt tight. I glanced apologetically at Mustafa, but he had risen as well. He leaned forward suddenly and in a different tone, tenderly solicitous, murmured: Hassan!

I wish I could share your faith, I said wearily.

MENARA

Before leaving the police station, I sought out the officer in charge of the case and asked him what, in his opinion, would be the likely sentence against my brother.

He's going to be in prison for life, he said indifferently.

He is innocent, I said. Whatever he's told you is a fabrication. He made it all up.

His response surprised me.

I know, he said. I've broken enough murderers in my life to know that he isn't one of them. I've interrogated him, and he couldn't give me any details. Not a single thing. But he's admitted to the crime and we'll have to hold him unless something else turns up. Frankly, I think he's gone crazy. This foreign woman has turned his head.

He's in love with her, I said.

He leaned back on his chair and contemplated me for a long time without speaking. His eyes narrowed until he seemed to be peering into me. Just as I was beginning to feel distinctly uneasy, he said: Aren't we all, just a little?

He stared at me, hesitated, and turned away.

I left the constabulary profoundly confused and despondent. On my way down the steps, I realized that I was still clutching the little stone lion. I wondered what I should do with it. I had no desire to be reminded of my brother's folly. After mulling over the matter for a couple of days, I went down to the Menara garden and flung it into the deep pool adjoining the central pavilion. As the waters closed over it, I uttered in silence the words that I hoped would lessen the burden on my conscience. I thought that if anyone was going to save me from my memories, it could only be me. I walked along the edge of the pool, preoccupied. Its face was dappled by a gentle breeze. It reflected the blue sky, the serried banks of clouds. For an instant I had the impression that I was alone in the world. I couldn't hear the din from the street or see the crowds of tourists milling around the pavilion built for imperious sultans on romantic trysts. I paused for a moment and gazed at the balustered balcony from which, it was said, every morning one of the sultans would toss the concubine with whom he had spent the night into the water. Suddenly, something strange happened to me. Maybe it was the astonishingly blue sky or the orange-and-jasmine-perfumed air or the chorus of birds that sang in anticipation of spring. Or maybe it was my coming to terms with the fact that Mustafa was an adult and had made his decision for reasons that only he could fully understand. After all, in the end, it was his life to live, even if it didn't make sense to me. Whatever it was, I resolved to go on with my life, as difficult as that might be. I returned home much calmer than I had left it.

THE FABLE

Following Mustafa's imprisonment, I avoided the Jemaa for a while, finding it too crowded with unpleasant associations. In fact, for a few days, I abandoned Marrakesh altogether and sought refuge in my parents' home in the mountains. At the same time, I could not stay away from the city for any great length of time given that I felt obliged to visit my brother in his prison cell, and that necessitated my return sooner than later. But even after I came back to the city, it wasn't easy for me to face up to the possibility that Mustafa would be behind bars for life. I was afraid for him, and my fear combined with despair to render almost unbearable the prospect of our meetings.

In the beginning, I tried to talk sense to him. I obsessed for days on end about the right way to make him see reason and even enlisted Ahmed's help for the purpose. But we soon discovered that rational explanations were useless with a man bent on making reality conform to a dream. With the passage of time, Ahmed gave up on what he called a ridiculous endeavor, while I realized that with his uniquely irrational decision Mustafa had at least ceased to suffer inwardly. Pain, like remorse, subsides over time, but my brother's love seemed to grow and take on a miraculous intensity that transcended everything. Still possessed by his memory of Lucia, he not only was incapable of talking about anything else, he could not even feign an interest in the rest of the world. In his determination to believe, he lived as if he had already made her his own. He laughed as he spoke and made me blush when he described her with impassioned words. It was obvious he had observed her closely in the little time he'd spent with her in order to appreciate her all the more. A smile, an intonation, a mere gesture, everything lent substance to the completely sincere but elegiac picture he drew of his beloved.

And so it was that, by and by, through him I came to know

more about this perfect stranger, or, at least, that version of her he had made his own. In my presence he would recall that image, embroider it, adding all the qualities he'd ever imagined in his ideal woman, and become increasingly animated when my close and silent attentiveness appeared to encourage him.

One day he leaned forward through the bars and rested his hands on my shoulders. It comforts me to confide in you, Hassan, he said. I hear myself recalling her to you and it makes her more real for me.

I'm glad, I said.

She fills my world, my Lucia . . .

He said her name with such tenderness, his voice so choked with the intensity of his emotions, that I turned my eyes to the ground out of respect.

Ah, Hassan, he went on, if I could only tell you what she's like! Every day that I spend with her memory is like falling in love all over again. It's like a daily revelation. It makes everything else incidental. How could I ask for more from life?

He was silent for a moment and then he said with a smile: That's why I've come to believe that it is better to imagine than to possess.

Why do you say that? I asked.

Because possession destroys the dream. The dream itself is the truth, and she has given me the dreams of a poet.

He paused again, his eyes sparkling with passion. Then, in a low voice, he said: Make my story into a fable, Hassan, as only you can.

I seized the opportunity to urge him to tell me, once and for all, the truth about what had really happened that night in the souk.

I have already told you the truth, he replied in surprise. You are my brother and you practice a mantic art. Why would I lie to you?

I ignored his response, insisting on the unadulterated truth.

Make one up, then, if you choose not to believe me, he said with equanimity. You have all the necessary information.

Is that a response or an evasion? I countered, sounding more irascible than I'd intended.

It is neither, he answered.

So what you are proposing on my behalf is a series of variations based on lies?

Truth lies, Hassan. It is always masked by words. As a storyteller, you ought to know that more than anyone else.

My stories do not lie, I said doggedly. That is not in our tradition, nor in the legacy Father passed on to me, as it was bequeathed to him by his forefathers.

Mustafa threw up his hands.

You take my meaning too literally, he protested. There's no point in my seeking your understanding in this matter. All we do is go round in circles.

He sounded deeply hurt, and I felt too disappointed in his continuing refusal to tell me the truth to consider his request. In the end, sitting across from each other, we remained lost in our own thoughts.

At length—more, I suspect, to break the uncomfortable silence than for any other reason—he asked me to describe the square as I had found it on my way to visit him.

Regretting my earlier recalcitrance, I engaged all my powers of description. I had the sensation of composing, of painting images from deep within myself. A sense of relief overcame me at being able to thus render service to my unfortunate brother. I felt repose as I narrated, and satisfaction.

Knowing his affinity for Essaouira, I began by comparing the shimmering lights of the Jemaa at night to the sea. This brought up the memory of sitting with him on the seawall during my visit to Essaouria and the sudden gust of wind that blew up from across the promontory. We had needed both our hands to hold on to the single umbrella we'd brought and even then we'd been soaked by the spray from the sea.

I told Mustafa that I'd been reminded of that marine wind by the light breeze that had been blowing across the Jemaa as I'd made my way to the prison. In the radiance of the afternoon I had enjoyed the brisk walk. Casting my mind back, I went on to describe the winter sky, the play of clouds and sunlight, the Jemaa's quicksilver shifts of mood, its iridescent crowds and colours. The bright light had made the square resemble a snowy plain such as is found in the foothills of mountains and it had made me homesick for the highlands. Everywhere there was a sheen as though a spray of water had just passed over. But in the depths of the souks, it was, as always, as black as night.

I went on in this manner for a while, adding all kinds of details to my descriptions so that my brother would know exactly what I had seen, such as the motionless cloud above the Koutoubia minaret that seemed to encapsulate all the colours of the universe, or the trail of kilims hanging in midair on a clothesline in the alleyway behind the police station, or the mellow winter sun that stood directly above the Jemaa as if on a pedestal.

That was wonderful, Hassan, Mustafa said with a dreamy glint in his eyes when I'd finished. Thank you for indulging me.

He gazed at me at length, as if seeing me for the first time, and I saw the gratitude in his look. I knew that he had forgiven me for my earlier obtuseness, and I experienced such intense compassion that tears came to my eyes. The thought that I could transport him out of his cell with a few simple words moved me so deeply that my breath caught at my throat. I felt unable to speak when he asked:

Do you remember how hot it used to be when we came down with Father during the summer? Sometimes it was so hot I saw double. There was so much heat. So much light.

He seemed to forget everything as he watched the dying rays of the sun through the window set high in the wall. I joined him in contemplation and had a sensation I hadn't experienced in years: of seeing life through new eyes. In that half-light, the dingy room transformed into a space of tranquillity. Everything seemed boundless. In the immensity of that moment, my brother's love was all that existed in the world, and it was all that mattered. I sat there in silence, refraining from interrupting the idyll, watching the sky turn from light to dark and wondering at the swiftness of the alteration. Only the horizon, with its thick mantle of clouds, remained bright and luminous. Then even that darkened, and an indigo aureole spread across the firmament.

Before leaving, I asked Mustafa if he needed anything from the outside world.

Nothing, he answered gently. Thank you, Hassan. You give me enough. You help me recall my beloved and engrave her memories ever deeper into my being. It's the finest, most considerate gift anyone could ask for.

Truth and Beauty

İn the years that followed his incarceration, I realized that even though I could not free my brother from prison, his act could help me learn about life. The essence of my lesson lay in a deceptively simple insight: that beauty is truth's companion and, in much the same fashion, it provides the purest form of sustenance. Beauty must be contemplated as a mystery, accessible only by lightning strokes of intuition rather than any form of rational comprehension—because beauty of the first rank holds all the exceptionality of a miracle. That is why the experience of falling in love is akin to mystic conversion. It is a single and abrupt event—a falling upward, as my brother described it—and what results is the only thing that matters in the end: the meeting of a man and his soul. In true love, the soul envelops the body. It creates a world which can exist nowhere but within. From that aspect, my brother's determined withdrawal from the world made perfect sense. In the solitude of his love, he was completely fulfilled. The more his imagination transcended fact, the more otherworldly it became, the more his sense of autonomy, and, hence, his dignity, was prolonged. To know that the unfathomable exists and that it manifests itself in beauty—this wisdom forms the core of genuine belief. The rest is nothing but the irresolvable disharmony between the individual and the world.

THE DESERT OF LOVE

A voice now spoke up from the edge of the circle of listeners, a low voice, arising as if from out of the depths of a ruminative silence.

Have no opportunities ever arisen to save your brother?

I felt no surprise at having to address this query. I tried to make out who the questioner was, but it was quite dark in that part of the circle and I couldn't bring myself to leave the warmth of the fire and walk over.

Of course there have been opportunities, I said, but none of them, save one, came anywhere near to achieving his freedom.

I waited for a response, or perhaps another query, but when there was none forthcoming, I decided to go ahead and tell the story. I narrowed my eyes in search of the right words to convey what I wanted to say, but my instinct warned me that it should remain largely hidden.

It happened like this, I said.

South of the mountains, past the border with Algeria, there is a wadi known to the locals as the place where camels go to die. Past this grim, skeleton-strewn landmark, the black stone deserts give way to the immense sandy expanse that is the first intimation of the Sahara proper, and it is here that a certain brand of foreigners—mostly from the West—bid farewell to their lives and set off into the desert. There is nothing left in their world for them. They are glad to leave it all behind. They walk into the desert and keep on walking until they collapse, usually from extreme thirst and heatstroke. A trail of litter marks their way. It's as if they can't wait to shed their skins. The first things to go are the wallets and the laminated bank cards, then the paper money and coins, followed by the identity papers and tags. They hold on to the photographs of their loved ones right up until the final stages, and then, in most cases, even these are surrendered. The desert has a way of claiming everything, and death is mercifully quick in the end. The sand washes over them, undresses them, bleaches their bones. If they are found before their flesh has decomposed, inevitably they have smiles on their faces. They have entered paradise, and it shows in whatever is left of their mortal traces. The local Sahrawis call this stretch the Desert of Love; they say that compassion marks this territory of the eternal embrace.

It was here, in this trackless, utterly desolate region, that an itinerant camel trader stumbled upon a tattered and faded Indian passport a few years ago. He brought it to the Wednesday souk in Smara, hoping to sell it for a few dirhams, I heard about it from my friend, Nabil, and we managed to procure the passport and turn it over to the Marrakesh police in an attempt to prove my brother's innocence. But our endeavor proved unfortunate. Rather than interpret the evidence as proof that Mustafa had nothing to do with the disappearance, the police contended that it pointed precisely to his guilt, and my brother remains in his prison cell to this day.

A MAN OF RELIGION

This is all very interesting and highly romantic, a soft, suave voice suddenly spoke up, but it is hardly a salutary conclusion to a man's life.

After a brief pause, the same voice added in a deeper, more sombre timbre: A Muslim life.

I glanced with curiosity in that direction and recognized the bearded cleric who'd interrogated me at the very onset of the evening. He held my gaze and smiled as he continued speaking.

I sought you out, he said, because I'd heard of your reputation as a clever and innovative storyteller. I was looking forward to an evening of entertainment and digression from the cares of the world. As you know, I arrived early so as not to miss a word. I was willing to keep an open mind, but I should have known from the moment you began that you would not deliver what you promised.

He paused meaningfully and scanned my face.

The art of storytelling, he resumed, is a subtle one, at least as it is practiced among our people, and anyone who decides to devote an entire evening to a woman—and a foreigner at that— has already strayed very far from the ideal. I listened to you with a growing disbelief that soon turned to anger. Your story was not only not salubrious, it was a thoroughly misbegotten endeavor. There was nothing in it to emulate, no universal values or aspirations, nothing—nothing at all—worth salvaging. If there was any truth in it, it lay in its level of degradation, truly one of a kind.

I'd been listening attentively, but now I interrupted him.

Isn't love a universal value? I asked. Isn't true love an aspiration that applies to everyone without exception?

This "love" of which you are so enamoured can be directed only towards the divine, he replied. It is not manifested in the story of a man who dedicates himself to nurturing his own torment.

Is there nothing divine in beauty?

Not if you elevate mere human attributes as you've identified them in a particular individual and ascribe to them divine status. I too was present the day the two outsiders visited the Jemaa, and I found nothing in them that merited the sort of attention you've devoted to their story.

That may be so, I said swiftly, but surely, as a man, you must have been moved at some point in your life to admire a beautiful woman?

That is hardly the most important thing!

Let's not talk in generalities then, I suggested, and consider, instead, the particulars of my story. Why don't you tell us, for instance, what the two strangers looked like?

He smiled at the transparency of my manoeuvre, and his reply was appropriately terse. They were graceless, he said, like all Westerners.

She possessed no grace whatsoever, in your eyes?

He gave an amused laugh.

I can hardly contend that I admired her. Rather, she aroused pity. Certainly she might have possessed an animal magnetism, but that's all it was, at the level of beasts. Unlike you, he added pointedly, bare flesh does not excite my imagination, and her dress that day was hardly modest.

I haven't heard it being described as immodest, either, I
pointed out.

It doesn't matter, he said smoothly, as if to infer the contrary.
As your anecdotes have shown, she can scarcely be lauded for
being pure and delicate in her thoughts and actions.

He went on to ridicule all the weaknesses he perceived in
women from the West. He spoke with absolute assurance, his
face constricted with distaste and contempt, his voice increasingly strident.

I have lived in London, that modern Gomorrha, he said. I
know these creatures. They're no better than qahba, whores.
They lack all sense of the diffidence and dignity befitting their
station in life.

I wondered if he was being parodic, given the extreme nature
of his sentiments, but then I heard the strain in his voice and
realized that he was dead serious. The absurdity of this tirade
was heightened by the irony of a conservative cleric speaking in
intimate detail on the topic of fallen women.

As for you, he continued, turning his attention to me, you
are the perpetuator of a hodgepodge of dreams and inflamed
imaginings. Why have you devoted an entire evening to nurturing an illusion? This woman may have been sweet and
beautiful in your eyes, but she was corrupt by any standards.
She was an immoral slut who abandoned her lawfully wedded
husband, who was well within his rights to pursue her. Let
her soul rot in hell! In turning her into a myth, you are per-
petuating your brother's fallacy—your unbelievably misguided
brother, who, having fabricated a self-destructive fiction, has
learned to love his suffering, finding satisfaction in abasement.
It's all too obvious that the two of you enjoy speculating in

titillations. The fascination that binds you is avid and disturbing. You have willingly embarked together on the same sick adventure.

He repeated this last sentence, the words sounding constricted, the tone more strident. His fury seemed excessive, his breathing coming faster and faster, and the only explanation I could fathom for the extent of his hostility was that my brother's story must have touched some nerve in him.

As much as anyone else, I said coolly, my brother wants to live, to enjoy life. Under impossible circumstances he has succeeded in infusing his love with a heroic idealism and he is worthy of admiration for it, not condemnation.

What rubbish! he retorted. Does any woman exist such as you've described this one? My word! How she has ensnared you! If she had existed in reality as you've made her out to be, she couldn't have made you more entirely her captives. In the absence of spirituality you have filled your empty lives with the basest carnal desires.

Not carnal, I replied calmly, but idealism incarnate. If my brother has learned anything from his experience, it is to worship beauty. What is wrong with that? The art of remembering grace is a healing one.

Worship? he said in a soft, dangerous voice. I would advise you not to blaspheme within sight of a mosque. Take some time to sort out your thoughts.

Turning his back to me and addressing my audience with an irrepressible intensity, he said: You have all fallen under a kind of spell, a collective psychosis. You think you are giving voice to memories but all you are doing is embellishing falsehoods. You are flattered to listen to each other, admiring, as you do, the heights of your great passion. Your stories express gratitude and wonder when you should be feeling embarrassment. You were used, and yet you have constructed a legend out of your hazy recollections. Nor are your motives pure. You are driven by pride and the desire to possess. Children of Muslims, you are idolizing infidels! The West has branded you with its influence and you don't even realize it!

A heavy silence followed his diatribe. I stared at him, nonplussed by his virulence. In my mind I could only contrast the turmoil this man of religion had brought into my circle with Mustafa's calm sanguinity in the face of adversity.

Realizing that my comparison would only infuriate my interrogator, I asked him quietly where his bile came from.

He bared his teeth, his throat tight with anger.

Now you insult me? It's a wonder I don't strike you just as I would that depraved woman!

You advocate violence?

Certainly. It can be useful to bring people to their senses.

I must respectfully disagree. Our religion does not support your sentiments.

Are you the man of religion or am I?

You may be a man of religion but you are driven by rancour.

Do you blame me? In Muslim lands a war is raging, putting our people to the sword and to flight.

What does that have to do with my brother's story? I protested. Mustafa is filled with love, and a love such as his knows no boundaries of race and creed. It simply is and must be accepted as such.

Perhaps recognizing that he was on shaky ground, my interrogator beat a hasty retreat. I'm not going to argue semantics with you! he snapped. This isn't a theoretical question but a cry for common decency.

Love isn't a matter of theory. That may be why you and I perceive the world with such different eyes.

I should say we do! You've been corrupted by dreams. Your eyes are blinded by lust.

At that point, I decided I'd had enough. I walked up to him and placed a hand on his shoulder. In an amicable tone, I said: Leave. Now.

He stared at me. I haven't finished, he replied.

It doesn't matter, I said firmly, because I have, and this is why. As a cleric you have the power to make life better, to make people happier, but instead, I discern in you a malignance, a hatred that stems from the frustration you must feel when faced with your helplessness concerning the state of our world. No matter. Your bitterness has nothing to do with the affair that has brought the rest of us here. You are an interloper, and as such, you have no place in our gathering.

He took a step back and raised his fist in a manner that ended all pretense of reasonableness. His reply, when he spoke again, was icy.

You consider an insult to our moral codes a trifle? Very well. I will say only this to you. I am not alone. There are others who think as I do. You can behave however you like, but we will deal with you as we see fit.

He spoke so coldly that the seriousness of his intention could not be doubted.

I bowed my head with extreme courtesy.

CASA VOYAGEURS

The fire in the centre of our circle had died down and, in the prolonged silence that followed the cleric's departure, I added some kindling to it. It gave me time to collect my thoughts.

I stirred the roots of the fire and tufts of flame sprouted like stems. A blue column of smoke rose to the sky. The moon had slid right across its meridian, leaving behind the chalk mark of its trajectory.

The night is marvellously bright, isn't it? a man said tentatively.

Still preoccupied by my altercation with the cleric, I didn't answer or search for the speaker—I didn't recognize the voice—but simply nodded in agreement.

He spoke again, and this time I turned to see who it was. He was a small man with thick, greying hair. He asked for permission to speak.

I have something to add to your story that might be of interest, he said.

I drank some water flavoured with mint leaves and signalled my assent, whereupon he got up, clearing his throat awkwardly and patting down his hair, his bashfulness evident in his every gesture.

I've never spoken in public, he said, so I hope you will forgive my incoherence. My name is Hamed. I'm a licensed porter at the Casa Voyageurs railway station in Casablanca, but I'm originally from the village of Aïn Leuh, south of Azrou, in the Middle Atlas Mountains. I went to Casablanca when I was

eighteen, looking for work, and I've been a porter at the Voyageurs ever since.

I cleared my throat and looked at him impatiently.

After a brief pause, he raised his head and went on in a rush:
So there I was in a bus on my way from Casablanca and I ran
into these three strangers . . .

Dissatisfied, he paused and looked at me a bit helplessly.

Can I tell it again? he asked.

Go ahead, I replied.

He shuffled forward a couple of steps as if committing himself
irreversibly to the endeavor. Then he resumed speaking, his voice
gaining in confidence as my smiles and nods encouraged him.

I would like to tell you of a particular episode in my life, he
said, that I think has some bearing on your story. It concerns
my journey from Casablanca to my village in the mountains
around the time of the disappearance that you've been talking
about. My mother had fallen ill and, as the eldest son, I had
my responsibilities. There were four of us on the bus bound
for Aïn Leuh—myself and three strangers who kept their faces
shrouded throughout the ride, which was six hours long, with
a change in Meknès. Only one of the men spoke to me, in flu-
ent Darija. He had a sonorous voice, a lot like yours, but the
woman and the other man were altogether silent. But even the
one who spoke was reticent and, beyond answering my query
about their final destination—somewhere in the mountains—he
said, without giving any details—they kept to themselves. It
was only when they got off at Aïn Leuh that I overheard the
woman saying something for the first time, and, from the manner in which she spoke Arabic, I realized that she, at least, was
a foreigner. I could see only her eyes but even so, their beauty

gave me the chills. They were large, golden green, lined with kohl, and they ensnared my imagination and made me want to know more. I found myself offering my brother's services as a guide if they were willing to wait while I fetched him from his house, but they declined and went on their way. It was very odd: I have seldom encountered a group of people as uncommunicative. All the same, I would probably have forgotten about them except that a few days later, in the course of a conversation with my friend Talal, I learned that the three strangers had hired him as a guide for part of the way. It appeared that the man was from far away, from Iran or India, while she was half French, half American. He appeared very protective of her, and every few minutes they would come together as if bound by an invisible thread. It was quite intriguing, Talal said, and it made him notice them more.

As for me, Hamed said after a pause, I confess freely that I admired the youth as much as I did his slender female companion. There was a virile strength and a selflessness in his devotion to her that I found extremely moving.

He stopped abruptly, seeming overwhelmed. Gazing at his feet, he said: I thought I'd share this with you. Perhaps the people I encountered had no connection with the ones who disappeared that evening, but one can never tell. Thank you for listening.

He turned to look at me and found that I was already staring pensively at him. He lit a cigarette and I noticed that his hands were shaking. For an instant the match flame illumined his features. He seemed ill at ease, but I didn't turn away. After a longish pause, I could think of nothing better than to ask him what had brought him to Marrakesh.

My daughter lives here, he said, instantly brightening up. She is studying to be a Mourchidat, a woman preacher. We are the first Muslim country in the world to promote this initiative, and, Inshallah, she will be in the first batch of graduates. Everyone in our family is proud of her. As for my being here tonight, that is purely accidental. I was passing by, and I didn't think I'd be listening to your story, but that's life, isn't it? How strange that I should have had something of my own to contribute! The element of chance. It's how things happen sometimes.

He glanced at me, for vindication perhaps, but I remained aloof, a faint ironic smile on my face. After a brief hesitation, he lowered his eyes, his own expression one of inviolable verity. I gazed at him for a moment longer until, feeling the need to retrieve my story, I turned away from him and addressed my audience.

I said: I would like to tell you about a dream.

THE VALLEY OF FLOWERS

When he was alive, I began, my father's oldest friend, Mordechai, a blind piano player in the Mellah, was fond of relating a dream he had the night the two foreigners disappeared. In the dream he visited a remote valley deep in the Atlas Mountains. Snow-clad peaks rose all around it. The slopes were covered with cedar forests. Interspersed between the forests and the meadows, vibrant carpets of flowers shimmered in the radiant light. The air smelled of juniper and cedar wood and pine resin. A holm oak's shadow embraced a broken well. Green gloves of lichen weighted down the roots of the tallest trees.

There was only one house in the valley, a partly ruined, crenellated kasbah, with walls of dark red pisè and four stone towers
in the corners. In a room adjacent to one of the towers, a closet
door creaked and opened by itself one morning. In the back of
the closet, which was deep, Mordechai glimpsed glimmering
braids of butterflies. He was taken aback and stayed there for
a while transfixed by the sight. Then he stepped aside and the
entire room filled up to the brim with butterflies: green fritil-
laries, marbled whites, sulphur cleopatras, large tortoiseshells.
Mordechai threw open all the doors and windows and the butterflies poured out in great ascending streams. They painted the
valley with their colours, with their names, anecdotes, memories. All day long they fluttered uphill and downhill, papering
the stones and the flowers, the springs and the marshes. After
sundown, they took to the highest branches; at dawn, in a single
movement, they rose towards the sun and that was the last time
Mordechai saw them. In the cedar forests and meadows they left
behind dense black shadows, groves of silence, white columns
of air stretching without limit towards the golden sands on
the other side of the mountains. On especially clear days, their
reflections spread across the entire curve of the horizon. Mordechai saw all of this with his blind eyes as he stood surrounded
by invisible shadows, black lines, milky clouds, red walls of
pisé. On the terrace he glimpsed a man and a woman locked in
a silent embrace. He continued to stand there, engrossed. Not
feeling as if he was intruding, he soon had the impression that
he was a part of them. Later, he heard their footsteps growing
distant on the gravel.

The night before his death, Mordechai dreamt that he returned
to the valley. When he woke from his sleep, we hardly recog-

nized him. He was like a younger version of himself, charming, robustly handsome, courteous. He seemed filled with a strange wisdom somehow, and humanity, compassion. He gestured towards the old cupboard that stood next to his bed. Inside, it was stuffed with hundreds of paperback novels, but that wasn't what drew our attention. Between two fat books on the top shelf was a bright red woollen blanket embroidered with an abstract geometric pattern representing butterflies. In the knotted folds of the blanket we found glistening pomegranate seeds and petals of blue germander and jasmine. One of us also found a fragment of a butterfly wing still quivering.

THE VALLEY OF BIRDS

A few years after Mordechai's death, my brother Mustafa inherited his dream, or, at least, part of it. He dreamt that he visited the partially ruined kasbah in the navel of that remote valley in the mountains. Once there, he found that one of the wings of the house, along with the accompanying tower, had been carefully restored since Mordechai's visit. Mustafa said that he hesitated outside the house for a while, but then he decided to enter because the doors were wide open. There seemed to be no one around, but all the signs pointed to a home lovingly maintained. The ceilings were reinforced with broad beams of cedar, the walls were tadelakt, the floors tamped down with limewash and clay. In the middle of a large room lay a grey Berber rug in the shape of a cloud. In another stood a beautiful marque-

try writing desk of dark wood with stacks of leather-clad journals containing neatly handwritten notations. Mustafa opened
one of the journals at random and read: "Ce qui importe c'est la
vérité." There were a few books on the floor next to the desk, but
they were all in languages he couldn't read. Above the bed in the
adjoining room was a charcoal sketch of a scarf-shrouded face
with large, kohl-lined eyes that Mustafa swore followed him
wherever he went. In the high-ceilinged room adjacent to the
rooftop terrace he peered into the closet but found no signs of
butterflies, only a pile of red woollen blankets. He took one with
him as evidence of his visit; it was embroidered with a geometric
pattern resembling butterflies. On the whitewashed door of the
terrace were embedded rows of nails from which hung shawls,
scarves, masks, and cloaks, both hooded and unhooded. The
ceiling of the largest room in the kasbah was covered with a trel-
lis of painted shadows. It contained a spinning loom shrouded
by a gauzy white coverlet. The shroud accentuated Mustafa's
own feelings of solitude and displacement.

Empty houses have a strange quality about them, their life
altogether apart from when their owners are present. To be in
them is like inhabiting a familiar space at night when one is used
to seeing it only by the light of day. Once Mustafa had explored
all the rooms in the kasbah, he wandered barefoot into the sunlit
garden. There were signs of a woman's touch everywhere: in the
rows of carefully planted herbs, in the star-shaped flower beds,
the pink-pebbled fountains, and the embroidered silk cushions
on the painted wooden benches. Bird feeders made from old
bottles hung from the branches of orange and lemon trees. A
zellij-tiled pool scattered with red and white rose petals soothed
Mustafa's eyes and evoked in his mind the image of paradise.

As he lingered by the pool, he unexpectedly glimpsed two eyes staring back at him from its depths. They were totally lucid, their gaze calm and without any signs of fear or discontent. In the space between the eyes, lines of rhymed quatrains scrolled across the water but a gentle breeze dissolved them before Mustafa could decipher what they meant.

Since that dream, my brother says, he's had no choice but to see the world with those eyes when he sleeps—and he is content.

Tabbayt

The fire at the centre of our storytelling circle had died down again and, this time around, I made no attempt to revive it. Instead, I cast my gaze past my listeners and took in the night. The mist had lifted and the starry sky shone with the moon's blue light. The houses encircling the Jemaa lay in deep shadow, their outlines as distinct as if drawn with a pencil. The paved surface of the square mirrored the stars, each stone glistening with hoar frost. The stars seemed everywhere: in the sky, on the ground, hanging from the branches of trees, deep inside the sanctuaries of the mosques, even embedded in the eyes of my patient, faithful listeners. I gazed at those stars and my heart stood still. Moved by their radiance, I stood up, gathered my robes around me, and addressed my band of listeners in low, fervent tones.

What is a star? I asked. What is inspiration? What is passion? What is longing? I look down from the stars and feel the spirits of my ancestors among you. Their eyes shine like black seeds, their faces like dim mirrors reflecting the ages. They are timeless, fathomless; the ghosts of their shadows mingle with your shadows. Each of them has a crow on his shoulder, each carries a black staff, and the rows of staffs stretch towards the horizon like serried stalks of wheat. In this ocean that is their universe, you know me as Hassan, the storyteller of the Jemaa, the keeper of its chronicles. I know you as my brothers and sisters. We are of one religion, one culture; we share the same heritage, and it is beautiful. Like entering a new world, you join me every night, enabling me to reclaim what is ours by right and must stand revealed as our common inheritance. In the vicinity of our circle, the hours of the night slow down, its measures ring at a different pace. But the hour is now late, and the time has come to end this night of storytelling.

Tomorrow is another day. Tomorrow will bring another round of stories. Tomorrow I will say, as I did today: Welcome to my world, I hope it will envelop you in smoke. Tomorrow, once again, for the space of a few hours, we will be companions in this journey that is life. My best stories are supple and have weathered the test of time, and a story is only as supple as the links that hold it together. I have four or five such stories in my repertory that have come down in my family for hundreds of years. They are seasoned by the centuries and guaranteed to satisfy, perhaps unlike the one I shared with you tonight, which was of more recent vintage. That one I must confess to feeling driven to relate once a year to air out the dark corners of my mind, even though the airing is somehow never adequate. But tomorrow will be different. Tomorrow I will strive to tell you a story so unreal, so far-fetched, that even those of you who are among the most credulous may find it difficult to swallow. But who knows? Who can tell about these things? Human gullibility is infinite and the desire to believe unfathomable.

With that message of farewell, I embraced a few of my listeners and raised my hand to my heart to the rest. As they trickled away across the square, I counted my earnings for the day, gathered up my belongings, and took Nabil's arm, for he had been waiting patiently for me right up until the end. He asked if we could stretch our legs around the Jemaa for a moment before I walked him back to his room in the Mouassine, and I readily agreed.

The Jemaa was relaxed in the silence; the souks and the qaysariyas breathed deeply in repose. We strolled along the perimeter of the square, which was deserted at that hour of the night except for Tahar, the trapeze artist, and a couple of tightrope walkers practicing their routines for the next day. I mentioned them to Nabil and he smiled and said: How many people realize the kind of preparation that goes into the acts they see every day on the square?

After I lost my sight, he went on, I would imagine you during the hour before you began your storytelling sessions. Perhaps you'd sit in some corner going over the story you intended to tell, filling in some forgotten detail or other at the very last moment. You'd take off your slippers, feel the dust between your toes, watch the sun turn your skin golden. And all the while, you'd be lost in thought: creating, connecting, concluding. And then . . . Nabil paused, slowing down until he came to a standstill. Then what would happen, Hassan? Perhaps a space would suddenly open up beside you and you'd travel back in time one hundred, two hundred, or even five hundred years. And right there in front of you would be someone trying to sell you a camel or a story or the beaten-bronze sword his ancestor had used when he was a general in an army long dead, the sword he must now dispose of, alas, to pay for his daughter's dowry. And you'd bargain with him, wouldn't you? Your Berber blood would rise to the challenge and you'd forget your circle of listeners patiently waiting for you to make your appearance, myself most humbly among them.

Pausing again, he shot me a sly glance, and we both laughed. I clasped his shoulder affectionately.

You ought to be a storyteller yourself, I said. Perhaps I should have you substitute for me sometimes. It would be a pity to let such a fine imagination go to waste.

Oh, but it isn't merely my imagination, he replied, it's the magic of the Jemaa. For as much as the Jemaa el Fna is history—your history, my history, our people's history—it is also the eye that sees history happen. It records its impressions in the leaves that lie scattered across its broad expanse, the leaves that we glimpse blowing here and there in the wake of the occasional breeze. Some of the leaves find a final resting place on the eaves and terraces of mosques and palaces; others are swept away, washed away, forgotten. But a few attract the watchful attention of my friend, the storyteller of the Jemaa, Hassan, and he picks them up and takes them home and binds them into chronicles which he then proceeds to narrate to his audience in the square. And so the circle is completed.

At the last word I made a quick gesture with my hand.

That describes all my other stories, but as for the one I related tonight, the circle will never be completed.

Nabil turned his face in my direction and I had the curious feeling that he could see right through me.

When are you going to stop telling Mustafa's story?

When I can make peace with my conscience.

Is it a matter of art or conscience? he asked softly, with only the faintest trace of irony.

We are speaking about my own brother, I replied, bristling. I won't deny that his story remains unbearably eloquent and fuels my art, but my main purpose is to tell the truth.

With a melancholic smile Nabil turned away from me, murmuring in a breath: Of course. Of course, I know all about that.

But I don't know, Nabil, I added. I'm worn out. There are times when I ask myself why I need to keep returning to this story that has no conceivable end.

He had let me go a little ahead. Now he took my arm and, limping a bit, gently remarked: Perhaps it's as you said earlier, in the repeated tellings you impart meaning to what must strike anyone other than your brother as utterly meaningless. Yours is a work of love—fraternal love—always to be resumed anew.

I reflected on his words, and even as I did, I felt my shoulders sag, as if the true extent of my weariness had just manifested itself—yes, manifested itself in the dead weight of thoughts that could not be spoken aloud but that I always felt dragging after me.

I wonder if that's all that there is to it, I said, and sighed. Maybe you were closer to the truth when you suggested otherwise. Certainly I am driven by my love for my brother, but I am also moved by something else. In my breath I form my work. Fraternal love, on the other hand, is usually unworthy of its name.

But even that kind of work can be clairvoyant, wouldn't you agree? Ideas are like seeds, full of the promise of germination but with no energy of their own. They need people like you to plant them in men's minds and grow them into stories, to release

them into the wind. It is work for the intelligence and the heart.
Not many can combine those two qualities.

I drew my cloak about me, my head bowed to the chill. I felt
a need for solitude. After a moment's pause, I said:

You flatter me.

I speak the truth. Tell me: What moves you the most?

The longing to transform, to change, perhaps even to elevate.
The essence of my storytelling is nothing less than that longing
brought to bear on the banal and the everyday. I'm haunted by
the mystery that lies at the heart of life, Nabil. That mystery
inspires my creativity and I take great care to preserve it.

Nabil had turned his face towards where the tightrope walkers were throwing themselves into the air with shrill yelps. His
attentive gaze seemed to be interrogating the air. Then his sightless eyes settled on me and his face lit up.

When I listen to you speak, he said, I think about the story
you related tonight. Parts of it made me sad while there were
other parts that made me smile. But what was most important
was that you let your listeners imagine that they were innocent,
which was a pleasant fiction. You can do that because your art
supersedes morality. It is an act of will, and you carry it off
superbly. It's what makes you a storyteller. You create your own
mythologies. You can make anything come true, Hassan. You
can make anything seem real.

He hesitated before adding in an undertone:

And you have.

His tone was detached, as though he were making a general
observation, without a trace of circumspection or condemnation
or regret.

I turned to him and regarded him for a moment before asking:
Do you blame me?

He shook his head gravely.

I am your friend, he said with dignity. Your secret is safe
with me.

He stretched out his hand and grasped mine tightly in a sign
of loyalty.

DREAM

We left the Jemaa for the shelter of the souks, and as we
did, unbeknownst to us, a man and a woman appeared on the
periphery of the square. They walked slowly past the gleaming white calèches parked in rows for the night. The man was
slender, bearded, the woman had long dark hair that came down
to her waist. Emerging from the shadows, they hesitated on the
verge of entering the Jemaa, as if unsure of their own intent.
But the man suddenly extended his arms towards his companion and she hastened to him with a smile. He drew her to him
and they clung together for a moment, her arms around his neck,
her knees slightly bent. He kissed her on the forehead. She gave
a languid laugh, unconscious of anything but their closeness.
They entered the Jemaa arm in arm, and she led him to the middle of the square where the embers from a storyteller's fire still
glowed dully on the pavement. They gazed down at the embers,
their eyes reflecting the dying sparks. With a shy, almost girl-

ish movement, she brushed his cheek in the lightest of caresses, while he reached for her hand and slowly stroked her long fingers, her palm, her wrist. Neither of them noticed the shadowy form watching intently from the darkness of a window bay. Everywhere around them was silence.

Acknowledgments

First and foremost, *The Storyteller of Marrakesh* owes everything to Nicole Aragi, who, among many happy synchronicities, shares my love of Marrakesh and all things Moroccan.

My indefatigable editor, Alane Salierno Mason, is beyond compare; no words would suffice to adequately acknowledge her contribution.

Grateful thanks to Denise Scarfi who gives so much, so often.

Thanks to Louise Brockett, Ingsu Liu, Jeannie Luciano, Winfrida Mbewe, Amy Robbins, Bill Rusin, Nomi Victor, Chris Welch, Devon Zahn, Nancy Palmquist, Don Rifkin, Tara Powers, and all at W. W. Norton.

I owe a great debt to those who inspired me to persevere:

JoAnne Akalaitis, Atish Bagchi, Thomas Bartscherer, Valeria Berchicci, Karl Heinz Bittel, Ronald Briggs, Lana Cable, Marisa Caramella, Sebastienne Charrier, Stephanie and Christopher Cherdel, Elizabeth Frank, Jim Hanks, Chris Hedges, Maryline Herron, Liz van Hoose, Pierre Joris, Gerald Jung, Benjamin La Farge, Rachel Lambusson, Torgil and Jennica Lenning, Mathilde Levitte, Alexandra Ludwig, Gail and Robert C. Ludwig, Eshragh Motahar, Lily Oei, Patricia and Donald Pitcher, Julie Pulerwitz, Joan Retallack, Robert de Saint Phalle, Françoise Songe, Marielle Songe, Benjamin Stevens, Claudia Strobel, Françoise Ostriker van Willem, Maurizio Zollo.

Finally, this book was inspired by Stefanie Herron.

Glossary

ABERDAG Dance; a musical movement of a RWAI performance.

AL QARAWIYIN Vies with Al-Azhar in Cairo for the title of the world's oldest university. It was founded in 857 by the daughter of a wealthy refugee from the city of Qarawiyin in Tunisia.

ALHAMDULLILAH All praise is due to Allah; praise to God.

ALMORAVIDS The first great Berber dynasty of Morocco (1062–1147) founded by Youssef ben Tachfine (1061–1107); the Almoravids originated from a tribe of Sanhaja Berbers in present-day Mauritania.

AMANAR The guide; the constellation Orion.

EL AMARA "The red," indicating Marrakesh (also AL-HAMRA, "red-walled city" or "red city").

AMARG The sung piece, the heart of a RWAI performance.

AMMUSSU The choreographed overture of a RWAI performance.

AMYDAZ Poet; the leader of a group of IMDYAZN.

ANDALUS From the Andalusian region of southern Spain.

ARIB Ruhhal tribe of the Western Sahara.

ARYANA Naked; Moroccans often refer to an unveiled woman as "naked."

ASTARA An instrumental prelude to a RWAI performance, played on the RABAB, giving the basic notes of the melodies that follow.

B'STILLA Pigeon pie from Fés.

BAB City gate.

BABOUCHES Leather slippers, usually yellow.

BAJADOZ The battle of Bajadoz (1086) in which the ALMORAVIDS, tribesmen from the High Atlas Mountains, crossed into Spain and defeated the Christian army under Alfonso VI, King of Castile and León.

BARAKALAUFIK Thank you, please.

BENDIR Frame drum.

BERBER Native African inhabitants of Morocco who form the majority of the present population.

BESSALAMA Goodbye.

BISMILLAH IR-RAHMAN IR-RAHIM In the name of God, most Gracious, most Compassionate.

BOUBOUS Voluminous, floating embroidered robes originating from Senegal and other black African countries.

BURNOUS Voluminous woollen cloak worn by both men and women.

CASA VOYAGEURS The main railway station in Casablanca.

CHABAB Adolescent, unmarried youth.

COUSCOUS A staple made from semolina, wheat flour, and water.

DARBUKA / DOUMBEC Metal or clay goblet-shaped drum.

DARIJA Arabic dialect of Morocco, which bears little resemblance to classical Arabic.

DEFF A double-sided tambourine.

DELLAHS Watermelons.

DERB Street.

DESS Flooring made of pounded lime mixed with clay.

DIRHAM Unit of Moroccan currency.

EL MAGHREB AL AQSA "The land of the far west"; "place of sunset."

ERG Expanse of sand or a ridge of dunes.

FANTASIAS Display of horsemanship at the larger festivals or moussems.

FASSI Native of Fés.

FEKKAS Sweet aniseed biscuits.

FIL-BADIA In the desert.

FIRWAL Veil.

FNAA End of the world.

FOUNDOUK Inn and storehouse; caravanserai.

FOUQIYA / JABADOUR Long men's garment secured at the front.

FOUTA Traditional scarlet-and-white-striped garment typically worn by the women of the Rif mountains.

F'QIH A Muslim religious authority, an expert on FIQH, or religious scholarship. By extension, a F'QIH is also a teacher of any kind, regardless of subject taught, or level of instruction.

FUSHA Classical Arabic.

GANDOURA Short, loose, sleeveless garment.

GHAITAH A type of oboe.

GIMBRI / GUENBRI A long-necked folk lute.

GLISSA Cushion.

GNAOUA Religious brotherhood of itinerant musicians of West African origin (from the same root as Guinea).

GUEDRA A large drum resting on the ground.

HABIBI My dear.

HABRA Steak.

HADITH Collections of sayings and stories attributed to the Prophet Mohammed; six major collections of hadiths were eventually compiled.

HAJJI A person who has made the pilgrimage to Mecca.

HAMMADA Stony, arid plateau in the Sahara.

HAMMAM Turkish bath.

HANBEL Carpet or blanket worn by Berbers.

HAND OF FATIMA Representation of the hand of the Prophet Mohammed's daughter, Fatima Zahra, said to be a sign of good luck.

HARATIN Formerly of the slave class.

HARISA A condiment made from pureed hot red peppers.

HEGUIN Of the two lines of camels in the Sahara, the Heguin is the larger, and is prized as the unmatched transport truck of the desert; the other is the smaller, MEHARI, known for its speed.

HELBA Sweetmeat.

HOURI The extraordinarily beautiful women who exist only in Jannat (paradise) in the afterlife. Their beauty is said to be beyond parallel.

ILM Knowledge.

IMAZIGHEN Noble or freeborn, as the Berbers consider themselves.

IMDYAZN Itinerant professional musicians of the Atlas Mountains.

IMOHAR Tuareg nobleman.

INADEN Tuareg craftsmen, smiths, also storytellers and transmitters of oral traditions.

INSHALLAH God willing.

JAMUR Roof spike made of enamelled baked clay or metal carrying up to five balls of diminishing size and often crowned by the Moroccan national emblem, a star inside a crescent moon.

JBEL Mountain.

JEBANA A long-necked vessel to serve coffee.

JEHUDI Jew.

JELLABA Wide-sleeved garment worn by both men and women.

JEMAA Mosque; or village assembly of the heads of families in Berber tribes; or a place of assembly; or Friday, the main day of worship.

JEMBE Goblet-shaped, skin-covered drum held between the thighs and meant to be played with bare hands.

JINN Evil spirit.

KAFTAN Long women's garment secured at the front and decorated with passementerie and embroidery.

KARKABATS Double castanets used by the GNAOUA musicians.

KASBAH Fortified house with crenellated towers; citadel.

KEFTA Spiced meatballs.

KEL TUAREG tribe; TUAREG society is divided into kels.

KHAMSIN An oppressively hot south or southeast wind occurring in North Africa and lasting for fifty days in spring (from the Arabic *kamsin*, or fifty).

KHETTARA Underground irrigation channels.

KIF Marijuana.

KILIM A woven rug.

KSAR Fortified village surrounded by solid walls set with towers (from classical Arabic, QASR, or palace).

LA BES DARIK Hello.

LEVECHE A warm wind originating in the Sahara and moving towards Spain; also called the Sirocco in other parts of the Mediterranean.

LOTAR Lute.

MA'ALEM A master craftsman.

MABROUK Congratulations.

MAGHREB "Land of the setting sun." From GHARB (west), it is the Arabic name for the westernmost part of the Arab world comprising Tunisia, Algeria, and Morocco.

MAGHREBIN A dweller of the MAGHREB.

MAKHZEN Festival tent.

MANIYYA Fate as allocated death.

MAQTU'A Old and poor.

MARABOUT A holy man, and his place of burial.

MARRAKESH "Open door to the desert."

MARRAKCHI Native of Marrakesh.

MAURI Western Berber tribes, inhabiting Mauritania.

MECHOUAR Assembly place, court of judgement, parade ground.

MECHOUI Roast lamb.

MEDERSA Quranic school with resident students.

MEDINA Traditional Arab city enclosed by ramparts.

MEHARI TUAREG camels.

MELLAH Jewish quarter of a MEDINA.

MENARA A public garden in Marrakesh with a central pool and pavilion.

MERGUEZ Spicy lamb sausage.

MINBAR The pulpit from which the imam leads the Friday mid-day prayers.

MOGADOR Island off the bay at Essaouira.

MOKALHA Long-barrelled, intricately worked silver-plated rifles from the sixteenth and seventeenth centuries, prized by Berber tribesmen and used on ceremonial occasions such as FANTASIAS.

MOURCHIDAT A woman preacher educated by the state to teach and interpret the Qur'an, though not to lead prayers.

MOUSHARABIYYA Wooden latticework panel used as a screen in front of balconies or in the windows of houses and mosques.

MOUSSEM Pilgrimage festival.

NAI Flute.

NAKOUS A small cymbal played with two rods.

NASIB Remembrance of the beloved; the first movement of the pre-Islamic ode or QASIDA.

NASRANI Nazarene (Christian); more generally, foreigner.

NISHAN Honest.

OUD Lute.

OUED Wadi; dried-out river channel.

PALMERIAE Famous palm grove in Marrakesh.

PASTILLA Pigeon pie, also known as B'STILLA.

PERI A fairy; a beautiful or graceful being.

PISÉ Building material made of sun-baked earth, grit, and, occasionally, straw.

PISTE Trail, path, track.

QAHBA Whore.

QA'ID Chief of a defined territory; district administrator.

QALB Heart.

QAYSARIA Covered galleries in the souks.

RABAB A single-string fiddle.

RAI A pop music form originally from the Algerian port of Oran, expressing an opinion, outlook, or point of view on topical issues.

RAIS Leader of a RWAI ensemble.

RAWI Storyteller.

REGUIBAT "Heroes of the desert"; legendary raiders of the Western Sahara.

RIAD Patio garden; also the house built around such a garden.

RIF The great crescent-shaped mountain barrier straddling northern Morocco.

RIHLA SA'IDA Bon voyage.

RUAGH Hebrew for wind, breath, spirit, soul.

RUHHAL Nomadic inhabitants of the Sahara over the eleven-hundred-mile range from Timbuktu to Morocco (from the classical Arabic RUHHALA, to wander from place to place).

RWAI Groups of professional Chleuh Berber musicians from the Souss Valley; a RWAI performance usually comprises movements entitled ASTARA, AMARG, AMMUSSU, TAMSUSST, ABERDAG, and TABBAYT.

SAADI The first Arab dynasty in Morocco (1554–1669) since the Idrissids, the Saadians marked the end of Berber rule. Their most impressive ruler was Ahmed "El Mansour" (the

Victorious) who defeated the Portuguese army under King Sebastião in the Battle of Three Kings (1578).

SAFAVID Shi'a dynasty (1501–1722) originating in Ardabil in the Azerbaijani region of Iran, the Safavids established the greatest empire in Persia since the Islamic conquest of the region.

SAHEL From *sahil* (border, shore, coast of the Sahara Desert), primarily a belt of savannah, running from the Atlantic Ocean to the Horn of Africa, it forms the boundary zone between the Sahara in the north and the more fertile region to the south.

SAHRAOUI Inhabitant of the Western Sahara territory.

SAHRIJ Cistern; water basin in the courtyard of a house.

SEER FHALEK Go away.

SERDAL Brightly coloured scarf decorated with coins, worn by Berber women.

SEROUAL / SERWAL Loose, calf-length trousers fastened at the waist and knees and worn under the JELLABA.

SFINGE Doughnut.

SHEIKH Leader of a religious brotherhood; chief of a tribe.

SHIRAZ, TABRIZ, HERAT Cities of the former Persian empire, and the schools of painting originating in these cities.

SHRÁB Mirage.

SHUKRAAN Thank you.

SIDI Lord.

SIMOOM A hot, dry, dust-laden breeze blowing at intervals in the desert

SOUK Market, or market quarter.

SQALA Ramparts; fort.

SSALAMU 'LEKUM Peace be upon you.

SUFI　A Muslim ascetic and mystic.

SUPRATOURS　Express tour buses run by the national train company.

TABBAYT　The finale of a RWAI performance.

TABIA　Mud building material such as PISÉ.

TADELAKT　Polished plaster surface made of powdered limestone and impermeable to water.

TAFILALT　Region of date-palm oases in southeastern Morocco, beginning in Erfoud, its principal town and gateway.

TAJINE　A stew of meat and vegetables cooked slowly over a charcoal brazier in an earthenware dish with a conical lid, also called a tajine.

TAMASHEK　The language shared by the TUAREGS and the Berbers.

TAM-TAM　Bongos.

TAMSSUST　A lively song; part of a RWAI performance.

TANJIA　Meat cooked very slowly in an earthenware pot.

TAR AND TAARIJA　Types of tambourines.

TASHILHAIT　The Berber dialect spoken in the mountains of southern Morocco.

TASSILI　Tassili n'Ajjer, "plateau of the rivers" (TAMASHEK), a massif in the Sahara in southeast Algeria.

THUYA　A variety of wood used by the craftsmen of Essaouira.

TIZI　Mountain pass.

TOURIQ　Botanical ornamentation used in architecture, derived from the Arabo-Andalusian tradition and composed of interlacing floral, foliage, and palmette patterns.

TREQ SALAMA　Bon voyage.

TUAREG　Nomadic Berber tribesmen from the Western Sahara.

WADI Riverbed that is dry or partially dry except during the rainy season; river; river valley; see OUED.

ZAHRA Venus.

ZELLIJ Geometrical mosaic tilework, typically arranged in colourful patterns.

ZEPHYR A soft gentle breeze, originating from Zephyros, the ancient Greek name for the west wind.

ZOUAQ Painting on wood.